BEFORE HE VANISHED

DEBRA WEBB

MYSTERIOUS ABDUCTION

RITA HERRON

MILLS & BOON

First Published in Great Britain 2020
by Mills & Boon, an imprint of HarperCollins*Publishers*
1 London Bridge Street, London, SE1 9GF

Before He Vanished © 2020 Debra Webb
Mysterious Abduction © 2020 Rita B. Herron

ISBN: 978-0-263-28021-0

0320

MIX
Paper from
responsible sources
FSC™ C007454

This book is produced from independently certified FSC™ paper to ensure responsible forest management.

For more information visit: www.harpercollins.co.uk/green

Printed and bound in Spain
by CPI, Barcelona

BEFORE HE VANISHED

DEBRA WEBB

This book is dedicated to the many, many children who go missing every day and the determined folks who work so hard to find them.

Chapter One

NOW

Friday, March 6
Winchester, Tennessee

Halle Lane listened as her fellow newspaper reporter droned on and on about the upcoming community events in Winchester that he planned to cover, which was basically everything on the calendar for the next month.

She couldn't really complain. Halle was new. Hardly ninety days on the job, but she knew Winchester every bit as well as Mr. Roger Hawkins. She couldn't bring herself to call him Rog. The man was seventy if he was a day and he'd covered the social events of Winchester for about fifty of those years.

How could she—a fading-star investigative journalist from Nashville—expect to get first dibs on anything in Winchester? Hawkins had the social events, including obituaries. Her boss and the owner of the newspaper, Audrey Anderson-Tanner, generally took care of the big stories. The only potential for a break in the monotony of covering barroom brawls and petty break-ins was the fact that Audrey was pregnant. At nearly thirty-eight, she was expecting her first child.

Halle had wanted to jump for joy when she heard the news last month. She was, of course, very happy for Audrey and her husband, Sheriff Colt Tanner, but mostly she was thrilled at the idea that she might actually get her hands on a real story sometime this decade.

So far that had not happened. Audrey had covered the big federal trial of Harrison Armone last month. His son's widow, the sole witness against him, had been hiding out in Winchester for months. Surprisingly for such a small town, Winchester had more than its share of big news happenings. This time last year a body had been discovered in the basement of this very newspaper building. Halle's gaze shifted to the head of the conference table, where her boss listened with seemingly rapt interest as Hawkins went on and on.

It seemed Winchester also had more than its share of family secrets, as well. A man posing as a Mennonite had turned out to be a former member of a Chicago mob. Not a month later, Sasha Lenoir-Holloway had uncovered the truth about the deaths of her parents. Cece Winters had come home from prison a few months back and blown open the truth about her family and the cult-like extremists living in a remote area of Franklin County.

Nashville had nothing on Winchester, it seemed.

"This all sounds good, Rog," Audrey said, her voice pulling Halle back to the here and now.

The boss's gaze shifted to her and Halle realized her mistake. She had been silently bemoaning all the stories she'd missed and now it was her turn to share with those gathered what she was working on for this week's Sunday edition.

"Halle, what do you have planned?" Audrey asked.

For five endless seconds she racked her brain for something, anything to say.

Then her gaze landed on the date written in black across the white board.

March 6.

Memories whispered through her mind. Voices and images from her childhood flooded her senses. Blond hair, blue eyes...

"The lost boy," Halle said in a rush. The words had her heart pounding.

Of course. Why hadn't she thought of that last month or the month before?

Audrey frowned for a moment, then made an "aha" face. "Excellent idea. We've just passed what? Twenty-four years?"

"Twenty-five," Halle confirmed. "Andy Clark was my neighbor. We played together all the time as kids."

Brian Peterson, the editor of the *Winchester Gazette*, chimed in next. "What makes you think Nancy Clark will allow an interview? She hasn't in all these years."

Audrey made a frustrated face. "That is true. You tried to interview her for both the ten-year and the twenty-year anniversaries, didn't you?"

Brian nodded. "I did. She refused to talk about it. Since her husband passed away year before last, she's practically a shut-in. She stopped attending church. Has whatever she needs delivered." He shrugged, shifted his attention to Halle. "Good luck with that one."

Halle's anticipation deflated. Hawkins looked at her as if she were something to be pitied.

"Still," Audrey said, "if you could get the story, it would be huge. Maybe since you and the boy, Andy, played together as children before he vanished, she might just talk to you."

Halle's hopes lifted once more. "I'm certain she will."

The conference room started to buzz with excitement. Titles were tossed about. Potential placement on the front page above the fold.

All Halle had to do was make it happen.

HALLE CRUISED ALONG the street on the east side of the courthouse, braking at a crosswalk for a mother pushing a stroller. That little ache that pricked each time she saw a baby did so now. Passing thirty had flipped some switch that had her yearning for a child of her own.

Now that she was back home, her chances of finding a partner, much less having a child, had dropped to something less than zero.

Winchester was a very small town compared to Nashville. With a population of around ten thousand, if you counted Decherd in the mix, it truly was the sort of place where everyone knew everyone else.

There were times when this could be a very good thing. Like when Andy Clark went missing twenty-five years ago. Halle had been just a little kid, but she remembered well how citizens from all over this county as well as those surrounding it had rushed to help look for Andy. Headlines about "the lost boy" scrolled across every newspaper in the state. His face was all over the news. Detectives and FBI agents were in and out of the Clark home for months.

But Andy had vanished without a trace.

Halle turned onto South High Street. The Clark home was on the corner of South High and Sixth Avenue. The historic Victorian was among the town's oldest homes. A meticulously manicured lawn and sprawling front porch greeted visitors. She pulled to the curb in front of the house and shut off the engine. The ancient maple on the Sixth Avenue side of the lawn had been Andy's and her favorite climbing tree.

Next door was Halle's childhood home. Her parents, Judith and Howard, had been thrilled when she'd announced last Christmas that she would be moving back to Winchester. They had, of course, insisted that she move back into her old room. As much as she appreciated the offer and adored her parents, that was not happening. Eventually the two had talked her into taking the apartment over the detached garage where her Aunt Daisy, the old maid everyone always whispered about, had once lived, God rest her soul.

Considering she would have her own parking spot and a separate entrance, Halle decided it wasn't such a bad idea. She would have her privacy and her parents would have their only daughter—only child, actually—living at home again.

A win-win for all involved. As long as she didn't dwell on the fact that she had turned thirty-two at the end of last month and that her one and only marriage had ended in divorce two years ago or that her ex-husband had since remarried and had a child—no matter that he had said they were too young for children when she had wanted one.

Not.

Maybe the garage apartment was fitting consider-

ing her mother's peers all now whispered about her un-
married status. *Bless her heart, she's like poor Daisy.*

Halle heaved a weary sigh.

The divorce had turned her world upside down,
shaken her as nothing ever had. She'd lost her footing, and the upheaval had shown in her work. Just as
she'd begun to pull her professional self together again,
she'd been let go. Cutbacks, they had said. But she'd
known the truth. Her work had sucked for two years.

It was a flat-out miracle they had allowed her to
keep working as long as they had.

Luckily for Halle, Audrey was open to second
chances. She had understood how one's life could go
completely awry. Though the *Winchester Gazette* was
only a small biweekly newspaper, it was a reasonable
starting place to rebuild Halle's career.

She climbed out of the car, draped her leather bag
over her shoulder and closed the door. The midmorn-
ing air was crisp but Halle much preferred it to what
would come between June and September. The melting heat and suffocating humidity. The not-so-pleasant
part of Southern living.

Stepping up onto the porch, she heard the swing
chains squeak as the breeze nudged this wooden main-
stay of every Southern porch gently back and forth. On
the other end of the sprawling outdoor space stood a
metal glider, still sporting its original green paint, offering a restful place to sit and watch the street. But
Mrs. Clark never sat on her porch anymore. Halle's
mother had said the lady rarely stepped out the door,
just as Brian had also mentioned. But Mrs. Clark did
come to the door as long as she could identify the per-

son knocking or ringing her bell. Whether she opened the door was another story.

Halle hadn't attempted to visit her in years. She was relatively certain she hadn't seen the woman since her husband's funeral two years ago. The one thing Halle never had to worry about was being recognized. With her fiery mass of unruly red curls, the impossible-to-camouflage freckles and the mossy green eyes, folks rarely forgot her face. The other kids in school had been ruthless with the ginger-and-carrottop jokes but Andy had always defended her…at least until he was gone.

God, she had missed her best friend. Even at seven, losing your best friend was incredibly traumatic.

Halle stepped to the door and lifted her fist and knocked.

"What do you want?"

The voice behind the closed door was a little rusty, as if it wasn't used often, but it was reasonably strong.

"Mrs. Clark, you might not remember me—"

"Of course I remember you. What do you want?"

It was a starting place.

"Ma'am, may I come inside and speak with you?" She bit her bottom lip and searched for a good reason. "It's a little chilly here on the porch." Not exactly true, but not entirely a lie.

A latch clicked. Anticipation caught her breath. Another click and the knob turned. The door drew inward a couple of feet. Nancy Clark stood in the shadows beyond the reach of daylight. Her hair looked as unruly as Halle's and it was as white as cotton. She was shorter than Halle remembered.

"Come in."

The door drew inward a little more and Halle

crossed the threshold. Her heart was really pumping now. She reminded herself that just because she was inside didn't mean she would manage an interview.

One step at a time, Hal.

The elderly lady closed the door and locked it. So maybe she anticipated Halle staying awhile. Another good sign.

"I was having tea in the kitchen," that rusty voice said.

When she turned and headed deeper into the gloom of the house, Halle followed. She knew this house as well as she knew her own. Until she was seven years old it had been her second home. More of those childhood memories whispered through her, even ones her mother had told her about before Halle was old enough to retain the images herself.

Her mother had laughed and recounted to her the many times she'd had tea with Nancy while the babies toddled around the kitchen floor. The Clarks had not always lived in Winchester, Halle's mother had told her. They had bought the house when their little boy was two years old, just before Easter. Judith Lane had been thrilled to have a neighbor with a child around the same age as her own. Halle had been twenty months old. Even the fathers, Howard and Andrew, had become fast friends.

It was perfect for five years.

Then Andy disappeared.

The shriek of the kettle yanked Halle's attention back to the present.

"You want cream?"

"That would be nice." She forced a smile into place

as she stood in the kitchen watching Mrs. Clark fix the tea.

Nancy prepared their tea in classic bone china patterned with clusters of pink flowers ringing the cups. She placed the cups in their saucers and then onto a tray. She added the matching cream pitcher and sugar bowl.

Halle held her breath as the elderly woman with her tiny birdlike arms carried the tray to the dining table. To be back in this home, after so many years, to be talking with this woman who'd occupied a special place in her heart because of her relationship to Andy was enough to make Halle feel lightheaded.

"Get the cookies," Nancy called over her shoulder.

Halle turned back to the counter and picked up the small plate, then followed the same path the lady had taken. They sat, added sugar to their tea and then tested the taste and heat level. Mrs. Clark offered the plate of cookies and Halle took a small one and nibbled.

Rather than rush the conversation, she reacquainted herself with the paintings and photographs on the wall. Beyond the wide doorway, she could see the stunning painting over the fireplace in the main parlor. Andy had been five at the time. His hair had been so blond, his eyes so blue. Such a sweet and handsome boy. She hadn't a clue about what handsome even was or any of that stuff back then; she had only known that she loved him like another part of her family…of herself. They had been inseparable.

"Twenty-five years."

Halle's attention swung to the woman who sat at the other end of the table. She looked so frail, so small. The many wrinkles on her face spoke of more than age.

They spoke of immense pain, harrowing devastation. Worrying for twenty-five long years if her child was alive. If he had been tortured and murdered.

If she would ever see him again.

"Yes, ma'am," Halle agreed.

Nancy Clark set her tea cup down and placed her palms flat on the table. "You want to write an article about him, don't you?"

Halle dared to nod, her heart pounding. This was the moment of truth. Would she be able to persuade Mrs. Clark to open up to her, to give her the answers she needed as much for the story as for her own peace of mind? "It would mean a great deal to me."

"If you've done your homework, you're aware I've never given an interview. Nor did my Andrew."

"I am and I understand why."

Her head angled ever so slightly as she stared down the table at Halle. "Really? What is it you think you understand?"

Halle nodded. "How can you adequately articulate that kind of loss? That sort of pain? You loved him more than anything in this world and someone took him from you. How could you possibly find the right words?"

Mrs. Clark's gaze fell first, then her head bowed.

Halle held her breath. Whether the lady believed her or agreed with her, Halle did understand. She had loved Andy, too, and she had missed him so very badly.

Deep down she still did. A part of her was missing. There was a hole that no one else could possibly fill. The bond between them had been strong.

When Mrs. Clark lifted her head once more, she stared directly at Halle for so long she feared she had said the wrong thing. She was making a decision, Halle knew, but what would it be?

"Very well," she said slowly but firmly. "I will tell you the story and *you* can find the right words. It's time."

Halle's lips spread into a smile and she nodded. "I would love to."

Silence filled the room for a long minute.

"I was almost forty before the good Lord blessed me with a child."

Halle reached into her bag for her notepad and a pen. "Do you mind if I take notes?"

A glint of bravado flashed in Nancy's gray eyes. "I'd mind if you didn't."

A nervous laugh bubbled up in Halle's throat, and she relaxed. She placed her notepad on the table and flipped to a clean page, then readied her pen.

"Andrew and I were so happy when Andy came into our lives," Nancy said, her voice soft, her gaze lost to some faraway time and place. "We wanted to raise our boy somewhere safe, with good schools. We did a great deal of research before selecting Winchester." She sighed. "It was perfect when we found this house right next door to a couple who had a child almost the same age." She stared at Halle for a moment. "Andy adored you."

"I adored him."

Distance filled her gaze once more. "We were happier than we'd ever believed it was possible to be."

"What do you remember about that day, Mrs. Clark?"

It wasn't necessary for Halle to be more specific. The other woman understood what she meant.

"March 1. Wednesday. I walked to school with you and Andy that day. It was chilly, like today." Her lips—lips that hung in a perpetual frown—lifted slightly with a faint smile. "He was wearing that worn-out orange hoodie. He loved that thing but it was so old and shabby. I feared the other children would make fun of him."

"I remember that hoodie. I begged my mother to get me one just like it but, you know my parents, they're hardcore Alabama football fans. No orange allowed. And don't worry, no one ever made fun of Andy. All the other kids liked him."

Mrs. Clark dabbed at her eyes with her napkin. "Thank you for saying so."

"My dad picked me up early that afternoon," Halle said. "He'd had to take Mother to the hospital."

Nancy nodded. "I remember."

What Halle's mother had thought was a lingering cold turned out to be pneumonia. She'd almost waited too long before admitting that she needed to see a doctor. They'd hospitalized her immediately. Halle had stayed with her Aunt Daisy for a solid week in that garage apartment where she lived now.

But that day, March 1 twenty-five years ago, the police had arrived before supper. Within twenty-four hours reporters from all over the state were camped out on the street.

Andy Clark had vanished.

"I was late," Nancy confessed, pain twisting her face. "Andrew was at work in Tullahoma and I had a flat tire. With your parents at the hospital, there was nothing to do but call someone to repair my tire. By the time I was backing out of the driveway, school had been out for only fifteen minutes but that was fifteen minutes too long."

"According to the police report," Halle said, "witnesses stated that Andy waited about ten minutes and then started to walk home."

She nodded. "There were witnesses who saw him less than a block from home."

Whoever took him had snatched him only a few hundred yards from his own front door.

"There was never a ransom demand," Halle said. "No contact at all from the kidnapper."

"Nothing." A heavy breath shook the woman's frail shoulders. "It was as if he disappeared into thin air."

"You and your husband hired private investigators." Halle's parents had said as much.

"The police and our community searched for weeks. But there was nothing. Not the hoodie. Not his backpack. Nothing. No other witnesses ever came forward."

These were all details Halle already knew. But perhaps there would be others she didn't. Something that no one knew. There was one thing she would very much like to know. She hoped the question wouldn't put Mrs. Clark off.

"I would like to ask you one question before we go any further."

The lady held her gaze, a surprising courage in her expression. "I'm listening."

"What made you decide to grant an interview now? To me?"

The courage vanished and that dark hollowness was back.

Halle immediately regretted having asked the question. When she was about to open her mouth to apologize, Mrs. Clark spoke.

"I'm dying. I have perhaps two or three months. It's time the world knew the whole story. If anyone tells it, it should be you."

A chill rushed over Halle's skin. "I will do all within my power to tell the story the way you want it told."

"I'm counting on you, Halle. I want the *whole* story told the right way."

Halle nodded slowly, though she wasn't entirely clear what the older woman meant by the *whole* story. But she fully intended to find out.

Whatever had happened to Andy, the world needed to know.

Halle needed to know.

THEN

Wednesday, March 1
Twenty-five years ago...

HALLE HATED HER pink jacket.

Pink was for scaredy-cat girls. She was a girl but she was no scaredy-cat.

She was a brave, strong kid like Andy.

She wanted an orange hoodie like the one he wore.

"Wear this jacket today," her mom said with a big sigh, "and I will get you an orange one."

Halle made a face. She might only be seven but she wasn't sure if her mommy was telling her the truth or if she was just too tired to argue.

"Promise?"

Judith smiled and offered her little finger. "Pinkie promise."

Halle curled her pinkie around her mommy's. "Okay."

"Come along," Mommy urged. "Andy and his mom are waiting."

At the door her mommy gave her a kiss and waved as Halle skipped out to the sidewalk where Andy and his mom stood.

He had on that orange hoodie and Halle hoped her mommy was really going to get her one.

"Hey," Halle said.

Andy tipped his head back the tiniest bit. "Hey."

He had the bluest eyes of any kid in school. Halle wondered how it was possible to have eyes that blue. Bluer than the sky even.

"How are you this morning, Halle?" Mrs. Clark asked.

"I'm good but my mommy's still a little sick." Halle didn't like when her mommy or daddy was sick. It made her tummy ache.

"I'm sure she'll be better soon," Mrs. Clark assured her. "That pink jacket looks awfully pretty with your red hair."

Halle grimaced. "Thank you but I don't like it very much." She gazed longingly at Andy's orange hoodie.

He took her hand. "Come on. We're gonna be late."

Halle smiled. He was the best friend ever. They were going to be friends forever and ever.

They walked along, swinging their clasped hands

and singing that silly song they'd made up during winter break.

We're gonna sail on a ship...
We're gonna fly on a plane...
We're gonna take that train...
We're taking a trip...

But Andy wasn't supposed to go without her.

Chapter Two

NOW

Wednesday, March 11
Napa, California

"This one is addressed to you personally."

Liam glanced up from the monthly reports he'd been poring over. "What was that?"

His assistant peered over her reading glasses. "Please tell me that's a dating site you're focused on, because if it's work, I'm going to be very upset. This is supposed to be a day off for you. You've been working seven days a week for months now. You need a life, Liam Hart! And I need at least one afternoon to try organizing this…clutter." She surveyed the stacks and piles of binders and folders around his office. "You need someone to do your filing."

Liam closed his laptop before she dared to come around behind him and peek at his screen. "I like my filing system," he pointed out. "You know as well as I do that a little extra time in the fields goes with the territory after a particularly wet season. All that rain calls for extra attention. We both know there's always plenty to do in preparation for—"

She gave him a look that stopped him midsentence. Shelly Montrose had kicked aside the idea of retiring at sixty-five, over two years ago. She had worked for this vineyard for most of her life, first as a picker when she was a child, right after the operation was started by the Josephson family. Then as his father's and now his personal assistant for the past twenty odd years. She was in charge and no one was going to tell her differently.

Certainly not Liam. She knew as much about running this place as he did. Probably more.

"Claire said," he offered in his most amenable tone, since the last thing in the world he wanted to do was upset his favorite lady, "there were reports I needed to see, so I only came by for a couple of hours and then I'm off. I promise."

Claire was his younger sister. At only twenty-five she'd already finished college and had proven herself as a master winemaker. She would say that their continued success since their father's passing was as much Liam's hard work as her own, but that wasn't entirely true. Yes, he was out there in the fields working alongside his crew through the process of winemaking, from tending the plants to bottling. But it was Claire who had the creative vision in developing unique blends and tastes that had put them on the map over the past two years. Their father would be proud.

"Claire." Shelly huffed a breath. "That girl is as bad as you are. She's never going to find a husband if she doesn't stay out of this vineyard! Your daddy took time to raise the two of you and the vineyard didn't go to pot. Your mother is traveling all over Europe and she has repeatedly invited the two of you to join her. Now would be the perfect time for a nice vacation."

"You're right, Shelly." Liam stood and gave her his best smile. "I'm heading out for lunch with a friend right now. The monthly reports be damned."

Her eyes rounded. "A female friend?"

"Yes, ma'am." He reached for his cap and tugged it on. "She's a pretty, blue-eyed girl."

Shelly rolled her eyes and extended the envelope toward him. "Your sister doesn't count."

Liam accepted the letter, tucked it into the hip pocket of his jeans and started around his desk. "I won't tell her you said that."

He left the office and walked through the winery. He loved this place. The rustic beams overhead, the decades-old barrels used for aging. The cobblestone floor. This was his life. Deep down he wouldn't mind having someone to share it with, but that hadn't happened so far. Maybe it was his fault for being so focused on work. But he loved his job. He couldn't imagine not doing exactly what he did every day.

Outside, the stunning valley view never ceased to make him pause to take it all in. The trees and the pond, all of it gave him a feeling of home. He'd lived right here on this former chicken farm for as far back as he could remember. His father bought the place from the previous owners who had lost interest in trying to jump-start the business after several years of hard times. Over the decades his father had renovated the place into one of sheer beauty and productivity. The vineyards were gorgeous. But they had never been able to compete with the top winemakers when it came to the wines they created.

Liam's father had been good, damned good, but not nearly as good as Claire. She was one of a kind. A rare vintner with a special touch.

He climbed into his truck and slid behind the steering wheel. The crinkling of the envelope in his back pocket reminded him that he had mail. He started the truck and reached for the envelope.

As Shelly had said, it wasn't addressed to the Hart Family Vineyards, but to him. Liam Hart.

No return address on the front or on the back. He frowned, lifted the flap enough to slide his thumb beneath it and to tear it open. Inside was a newspaper, or, at least, part of one. The front page, to be precise. He unfolded the single page and first noted the name of the paper, *Winchester Gazette*, Winchester, Tennessee. Then he scanned the bold headline at the top of the page.

The Lost Boy—25 Years Later.

His frown deepened. Why would anyone send him a newspaper clipping from Winchester, Tennessee? He checked the postmark. Yep, definitely from Winchester.

To his knowledge he didn't know anyone in the area. He searched his memory. There was, if he recalled correctly, a winery near Winchester. Though not one he'd ever visited. Rather than beat his head against a brick wall trying to remember, he started to read.

Seven-year-old Andy Clark disappeared on March 1, twenty-five years ago. To date there have been no remains found. No further witnesses came forward with reports of having seen the child. He left school, walking, and was nearly home when he vanished, never to be heard from again.

The article went on about the boy and his devastated family and the endless search.

Liam's gut tightened. He avoided stories like this. Every time he heard about a missing child on the news, he felt sick. A natural reaction, he supposed. Who wouldn't get sick at the idea? What kind of person stole a child?

He started to fold the paper and toss it aside, but his gaze landed on the series of photos included with the article.

The beating in his chest lost a step, then suddenly burst into hyper speed.

The photos of the little boy were…

Him.

Not just the chubby-cheeked image of any child, but his particular features, his smile, his eyes, his… attitude.

"No way," he muttered, his face pinched as he stared at the images.

Okay, this was bizarre. Shaking his head at his foolishness, he backed out of the parking slot and drove across the property, past the pond and the visitors' deck, to the private residence. Both he and his sister lived in the house. She had the wing that had once been the guest suite while he slept in the room he'd had for as long as he could remember. Suited him just fine. Though he had stored away the sports trophies and award certificates from school. His space was more of a bachelor pad.

A bachelor who still lived in the house where he'd grown up.

"Nothing wrong with that," he said to his reflection in the rearview mirror.

The newspaper clipping clasped tightly, he climbed out of the truck and walked to the house. He entered the key code and opened the door.

His heart still raced as he strode across the entry hall and toward the family room. His mother had all the family photo albums lined up on shelves. She loved nothing more than showing off her kids. She was actually Liam's stepmother; his biological mom had died when he was a baby. But Penelope Hart had treated him as much like her own as she had Claire—whom she'd given birth to.

If Penelope were here she would get a kick out of the photos in the newspaper article. He managed a smile at the thought but still…this felt weird. Particularly since someone on the other side of the country had mailed it to him. As far as he knew, he had no friends, relatives or even acquaintances in the area.

This was obviously someone's idea of a joke.

He spread the newspaper's front page on the coffee table, then strode to the bookcases built along the wall adjacent to the fireplace. Penelope had carefully dated each album. Finding the one for the proper time frame was easy. He carried the album to the coffee table and sat down on the edge of the couch.

His breath caught in his throat. The resemblance between him and the missing boy was uncanny. Completely bizarre. He removed two photos from the album and placed them next to the images in the newspaper.

"Holy…" Looking at the photos side by side triggered a strong emotion he couldn't label, which sank deep into his bones.

There had to be an explanation. Maybe he'd been a twin and his parents hadn't known. The missing child could have been his twin brother. His father had told him that he and his mother had been homeless when he was born. Living in the hills and woods of northern California like a couple of disenfranchised hippies. Who knew what sort of prenatal care she received?

It was possible that there had been two babies.

He moved his head side to side. Even as shaken as he was at the moment, he recognized he was reaching with that scenario.

Leaving the disturbing newspaper where it lay, he walked out of the family room and along the corridor until he came to the office that had been his father's—the office that was his now. He hit the switch, turning on the lights. The closet had been turned into a built-in safe. Using the dial, he quickly went through the combination steps, lifted the lever and opened it. He located the file with birth certificates and withdrew his. His fingers roamed over the state seal as he considered the information printed on the document. Nothing unusual or unexpected there. Closing the safe, he moved to one of the many file cabinets and looked through the folders until he found the one with his name. Inside was his school vaccination record. His academic reports.

He flipped through page after page.

It was all there. From kindergarten through senior year and then his acceptance papers for the University of California.

What was he doing?

He closed the filing drawer and walked out, turning off the lights as he went. Whoever sent the paper to him had accomplished his mission. The joke was on Liam.

As he left the house, he grabbed the newspaper

and the photos of him as a kid. He had to show this to Claire.

His sister was a hell of a mystery buff. Maybe someone would get a laugh out of this.

Angele Restaurant

"I THOUGHT I'd been stood up," Claire chided as he pulled out a chair at her table.

"Sorry, there was something I had to do." He reached for his water glass and considered ordering a shot of bourbon. Sweat had beaded on his forehead during the drive here.

It was ridiculous. Heart palpitations and sweating? He was a little freaked out. He had to get a grip.

Maybe Shelly was right. He had been working too hard. He needed a break.

"I've already ordered for the both of us. Roasted chicken salad." She placed one hand atop the other on the table and studied him. "What's wrong? You look—" she shrugged "—strangely unsettled."

His sister had Penelope's eyes. Blue but a light blue, almost gray. Her hair was a darker blond than his, as well, more brown than blond. But the high cheekbones and the Roman nose, she'd gotten both those from their father, just as Liam had.

He pulled the folded newspaper and the two photos from the family album out of his hip pocket and placed them on the table. "Someone mailed this newspaper page to me. No name or return address. Just the front page of this small-town newspaper." He tapped the now wrinkled page.

While Claire read, Liam surveyed the restaurant.

He'd been here a hundred times at least. The rustic French decor was not unlike their home, which Penelope and his father had turned into a classic yet rustic French château. It was warm and relaxing, much like this restaurant. And the food here was the best in Napa. He had yet to order a single dish that was anything less than incredible.

Claire placed the newspaper on the table, folded so that the photos of the boy—Andy Clark—were prominent. Then she laid the two photos of Liam next to them.

"Holy moly," she whispered. "This is...this is totally cray cray."

Crazy. Definitely.

"There was no name on the envelope?" she asked though he'd already told her as much.

He shook his head. "No name. No address. But the envelope is postmarked Winchester, Tennessee."

She stared at the paper again. "Have you ever been to this place?"

"Never."

"Well." She refolded the paper and tucked the loose photos inside the fold before passing the tidy bundle to him. "Someone thinks you have."

He made a sound he'd intended as a laugh, but it came out more like a choking noise. "What does that mean?"

"It means that whoever sent you this newspaper clipping believes you are this boy."

This notion had been festering in the back of his brain since he opened the damned envelope but he had refused to allow it to fully reach the surface.

"That's insane." He shook his head. "How would this person even know who I am or where I live?"

"I don't know." Claire's brow lined the way it did when she was stumped by some issue with a new blend she'd created.

"Hey," he argued, "come on. We grew up together. You know this is impossible as well as ridiculous."

She stared at him, unblinking, unflinching. "You were almost eight when I was born. We grew up together after that point." She glanced at the bundled paper lying next to his water glass.

"Now you're just being a—"

"No," she countered, "think about it. This could be real, Liam. Go back to the house and look at the family photo albums again. Try to find any of yourself—at least any in which you can see your face—between being a little baby and seven or eight years old."

"What?" Now he got it. She had done this. As a prank. Yes, that had to be it. She wanted him to work for the payoff, sending him on a wild-goose chase. "You did this because of what I did on your birthday." He shook his head, felt a sudden rush of relief. "I told you I was sorry. You didn't have to go to this extreme."

When she'd turned twenty-five, he'd put one of those happy birthday ads in the *Napa Valley Register* announcing that Claire was actually thirty. She had not thought it was funny. She had warned that she would get even with him.

He laughed. Laughed long and hard, almost lost his breath as waves of giddy relief washed over him.

When he'd finished, the people at several tables were staring at them.

"You finished?" she demanded, one eyebrow hiked up.

He held up his hands. "You got me, sis. I have to tell you, I was freaking out."

"I didn't do this, Liam." Her tone was flat and serious.

That chill he'd been fighting since he'd opened that damned envelope seeped into his bones anew.

"Okay." He suddenly wished he hadn't told her. Maybe she didn't have some fake newspaper printed and mailed to him from Winchester, Tennessee, but she was sure taking advantage of the opportunity.

"I even asked Mom once."

Enough. And yet, he couldn't not take the bait. "Asked her what?"

"Why there were no pictures of you during kindergarten or when you were three or four. There are hundreds of me, but there's this big gap in your documented history. I thought it was strange."

"I can honestly say I've never noticed." Why the hell didn't the food arrive? Anything to change the subject. Now he didn't want to talk about it.

"Of course you haven't. That's a girl thing. The women maintain the family photos and store keepsakes. Most guys don't even notice."

"What did she say?" He really wanted this discussion to end. He should have taken the day off like Shelly said.

"She said the photos and stuff for that time period were lost in a fire."

"There you go." He shrugged, felt some measure of relief once more. "That explains it."

"No, that doesn't explain anything. Because I asked Joe about the fire and he had no idea what I was talking about."

"Joe Brown?" Liam held up his hands. "Claire, Joe died when you were thirteen."

Joe had been the vineyard manager when Liam was growing up. In truth he'd been like an uncle to both him and Claire.

"I asked about the photos when I was twelve. Remember that school project I had to do using family photos? It was that ancestry thing."

He shrugged again, his frustration building far too rapidly. "Not really."

"I'm telling you that I asked Mother and she made up a story about a fire in the family room. When I mentioned the fire to Joe, he said there was never a fire in the house. Never, Liam."

"I'm not talking about this anymore." He didn't know what he'd expected Claire to say when he'd shown her the clipping and photos, but once he'd latched on to the prank theory, he'd realized how much he wanted that to be true. Not this...this other possibility.

Thankfully, the food arrived, saving him from having to argue further with Claire. He should have known better than to tell her about this.

When the waiter had moved on, Liam dug in. He hadn't realized until that moment that he was starving. Hopefully, Claire would take his cue and eat instead of pursuing this ridiculous idea.

Unfortunately, the silence didn't last long.

"We should call Mom."

"For the love of God, Claire." He put his fork down and braced his palms on the table. "I don't want to talk about this anymore. The whole notion is ludicrous. I shouldn't have shown you the article."

She reached across the table and snatched up the

newspaper, opened it enough to find whatever she was looking for. She tapped the byline beneath the headline. "You need to call this Halle Lane. Maybe she sent the newspaper to you."

When he didn't respond, she went further. "Maybe you should do better than call," she said. "Maybe go to Winchester. Check this out in person."

He looked at her as if she'd suggested he go to the moon. He now regretted even reading the article, let alone sharing it with her.

"I think you should." She gave him a nod. "Maybe the visit will trigger a memory of living there."

He rolled his eyes. "The only thing I remember about being seven is a bicycle accident that gave me a broken arm and a concussion."

It was the worst memory of his childhood.

But it was real, and his father had been right there with him through the whole thing.

THEN

Twenty-five years ago...

"I'm scared and my head hurts bad. My arm, too."

His father's arms tightened around him, pulling him closer to his chest—close enough that he could feel his heart pounding. His father was scared, too.

"You're going to be fine, son. The doctor says you have a mild concussion. I promise you'll be better in a few days."

He closed his eyes tighter and tried to remember why he was so scared. He remembered the headlights coming at him. He remembered falling. For a moment he'd thought he was dead.

Then his father had been there telling him he was okay. Calling an ambulance.

He remembered drifting in and out. He wanted to stay awake but it was so hard. He couldn't keep his eyes open and going to sleep made the pain go away.

His father wouldn't let him sleep. He'd wake him up each time he drifted off.

"Stay with me now."

Lights pulsed in the darkness. Made his head hurt worse. He wanted to go home. He was cold. So cold. His head hurt so bad. And his arm. He couldn't move it without the pain making him cry harder.

Two men in uniforms suddenly hovered over him in his memory or the dream he was having. It was hard to tell which. They kept telling him he would be okay. They were taking him to the hospital. He would get to ride in the ambulance.

But he didn't want to go to the hospital.

He wanted to go home.

Why couldn't he just go home?

He felt his body being moved. Lifted onto a stretcher and then they rolled him to the ambulance.

His father climbed in with him, sat close to him, kept telling him he would be fine.

He only wanted to close his eyes and pretend this didn't happen. He didn't want to be in an ambulance. He didn't want his head and arm to hurt so bad.

He wanted to go home.

The ambulance was moving now and he suddenly felt the urge to throw up. He struggled to hold it back. Didn't want to throw up in front of these strangers.

He felt weird. Like he was here, except not.

He just wanted to go home.

Tears slid down his face. He felt them slip into his ears. His head and arm hurt too much to bother trying to wipe them away.

He felt hands on his face, wiping away his tears. His father leaned close, his lips to his forehead. "Shhh, don't cry, sweet Liam. Everything will be fine. *You* will be fine."

He realized then why he was so afraid.

Who was Liam?

Chapter Three

Thursday, March 12
Winchester, Tennessee

Halle had beamed all week. Today was no exception. Lunch with Audrey, her boss, had proven she had every right to be excited. The entire staff at the paper was immensely proud of her, even Rog.

Her story on the lost boy had been picked up through wire services in some of the largest markets in the country. Reporters had flocked to Winchester. One of the biggest network morning shows had asked to interview her.

She had done it. She'd made her comeback as a journalist.

A grin slid across her face. And her old friend Andy Clark had helped her. This was the story she had needed to get her career back on track. It had been right under her nose all along.

She'd spent the afternoon walking on clouds but now it was time to get to work. Reality had slammed into her at about four. It was five thirty now. Most of the staff had gone home. Only Tanya, the receptionist downstairs in the lobby, and Brian, the editor, were still in the main office. Halle was fairly certain Brian never went home. He probably had a cot in the basement. As for Tanya, Halle was equally certain she had a thing for Brian and hung around just to be near him.

Audrey wanted Halle to focus solely on this case. They'd been swamped with tips since the story ran, everything from alien abduction suggestions to complicated tales of crime rings. Audrey wanted her to find the rest of the story. What really happened to Andy Clark? Mrs. Clark had said she would be happy to talk to Halle more.

If the police and the FBI hadn't been able to figure it out, how in the world was she supposed to do it?

She wanted to, certainly. She would have her choice of any assignment in the country if she managed to dig up that whole story.

But the idea was a little off the charts.

Halle moistened her lips, ordered her heart to slow its damned galloping.

Maybe she could do this. Audrey had given her full access to any necessary resources. She'd even offered to introduce her to Luther Holcomb, the chief of police at the time of Andy's disappearance. Holcomb was a bit of a hermit nowadays but Audrey's husband, Sheriff Colt Tanner, knew the man personally.

Before she did anything else, she needed to see Mrs. Clark again. The older woman had gotten a headache and had to lie down the last time they spoke about Andy. On Sunday afternoon, she had gone to her house again and taken her two copies of the newspaper. She'd reiterated then that perhaps they could make the articles a series. Get deeper into the story of before and after Andy. Mrs. Clark had actually sounded excited about the possibility.

What Audrey had asked Halle to do was different. Her vision was about finding the whole story, to do what the police and detectives hadn't been able to do—discover what really happened to Andy. Mrs. Clark had said she wanted the entire tale told. Maybe she should start by asking where would Andy be now if he was alive? Where did he go that day and who took him? What parent wouldn't want to know what really happened to their child?

It was worth a shot. She cringed as she thought of resurrecting Mrs. Clark's pain. Reporters weren't supposed to have soft hearts. Being ruthless and relentless was more than a little important to get to the truth.

Still, this was different. This was Andy and Andy's mother.

Mrs. Clark had okayed pursuing the story so far. If Halle had misunderstood the woman's intent, she would have to back off. She didn't really want to go down this path without her blessing. It felt wrong.

She wouldn't use Andy or his mother just to advance her career. If she continued with the story it would be because she wanted the truth as much as Mrs. Clark did. She stared at the stack of messages on her desk. Networks and newspapers from across the country wanted to talk to her.

She could do this even if Mrs. Clark changed her mind after all the notoriety—as long as she was careful not to cause pain for the woman. Of course she would never do such a thing. Mrs. Clark and her husband had been victims of the worst kind of crime. They didn't deserve to be hurt any further. Halle couldn't be the reason for that.

She wouldn't be.

Her cell rang and she checked the screen. *Mom.*

"Hey, Mom." She almost added that yes, she would be home for dinner since that was likely the reason for the call.

"Hey, sweetie. Just wanted to warn you that the reporters have already started to camp on the sidewalk."

The crew had been here in the parking lot all day every day this week. They had figured out her schedule, particularly when she headed home. So far, a deputy had escorted Halle to her car each evening. But she hadn't called for an escort today. The reporters had figured out her MO. Now they waited for her at home.

She couldn't hold it against them. She would do and had done the same thing.

"Do you and Dad want to meet me for dinner somewhere?"

"No, that's not necessary. I've already started dinner. Your favorite, lasagna. I just wanted to be sure you would be here and to warn you about the vultures out front."

Halle laughed. "I'm one of those vultures, Mom."

The whisper of her chuckle reached across the line. "I'm sure you're always thoughtful and considerate when going after a story."

"Of course," Halle fibbed as she remembered times when she'd had to be aggressive to get to a reluctant source. "You and Dad raised me that way."

"So you'll be here? Maybe you can park on the street behind us and sneak in again so they won't bother you. Or I could have Daddy sit on the porch with his shotgun."

The idea made Halle smile in spite of herself. "No, Mom, that's not necessary. I'll be fine. I'll be home around six or so."

"All right, sweetie. Love you."

"Love you, too."

Halle ended the call and stared at her cell for a moment. Her parents had raised her to be kind. Though she had always been relentless going after the story, she did try to be considerate—most of the time.

She pulled open her middle drawer and picked up the photo she'd brought to the office as inspiration while she wrote the article on the lost boy. It was a picture of her with Andy the fall before he went missing. They were at the school Halloween carnival. She had been dressed as a fairy with wings and all. He'd been Batman, complete with the cape and mask. Their faces were jammed cheek to cheek for the shot. She couldn't recall which mother snapped the pic, hers or his.

There were so many fun times like this one. She'd spent the first year after he was lost in a state of depression. Her parents had tried every way to cheer her up but nothing had worked. Finally, she had moved on to some degree. By the time she was ten she had stopped being so sad but she still missed him.

But she had always wondered what if. What if he hadn't disappeared? What if they had grown up together? Would they still be friends? Would it have turned into more? They had pretended to get married once. A smile tugged at her lips. She and her parents had attended the wedding of the daughter of a friend of her mother's. Halle had been so enthralled by the decorated church and the wedding dress she had rushed home afterward and told Andy they had to get married.

He'd shrugged and said okay. He'd always been up for whatever made her happy.

Funny, maybe that was why she'd never found the right guy. Maybe the right guy had disappeared twenty-five years ago.

"I'm sorry, Halle."

She looked up as Tanya burst into the room.

"I tried to tell him we were closed. I was locking up when he bullied his way through the door."

A tall man stood in the corridor beyond Tanya. She watched his nervous movements through the open door. He was looking side to side as if he feared security would be showing up any second.

"He says he needs to speak with you about the article."

She sighed. "Is he a reporter?"

"No. He said he has some information, though. And some questions."

They'd had a lot of emails with "clues" since the article ran, nearly all of them crazy, some asking if there was reward money, many mentioning children who looked like the photos of Andy, as if he would still be seven years old. She wasn't up to talking to one of those tipsters face-to-face.

Tanya went on, "He says he has some pictures."

A shiver ran up Halle's spine. Maybe she'd talk to this one, just this one, and get him out of the way so Tanya could go home.

"It's all right, Tanya." Halle stood. "I'll talk to him."

Tanya nodded and turned to go. The man stepped out of her way and she hurried off down the corridor.

That was the moment Halle got her first full glimpse of the unexpected visitor as he stepped into her office doorway.

Tall, blond. Very good-looking.

His gaze collided with hers.

Blue eyes. The bluest she had ever seen.

Her heart stumbled. Tension rifled through her, and her face flushed, her muscles clenched.

"How…" She cleared her throat of the strange emotion lodged there. "How can I help you?"

He held out a wrinkled page from a newspaper. "Are you Halle Lane?"

She nodded, still grappling for composure. Who was this man? "Yes."

He stepped fully into her office, still holding out the newspaper as if it were a weapon or something otherwise lethal. The thought chilled her. Why had she said she'd see him? "Did you write this article?"

She extended her arm across her desk. He shoved the newspaper close enough for her to take it from him without touching his fingers or his hand. It was the front page of Sunday's paper, the one with her article on Andy's disappearance.

"Yes. I did."

His jaw tightened. "Did you mail that to me?" he snapped.

She blinked. "What? No. I don't even know your name, sir. How could I mail anything to you?"

He had no discernible accent. His skin was tanned. He wore jeans and a tee. The tee sported the logo from a Napa Valley vineyard. Surely he hadn't come all the way from California to talk to her. If he had…

The curiosity she'd experienced earlier morphed

into fear. Maybe this was a mistake. She suddenly wished Tanya had called 911 and wondered if she could surreptitiously dial it on her cell.

Something was very, very wrong.

Rather than respond to her question, he stood there, staring at her as if he'd suddenly lost his ability to speak. Frankly, he looked shell-shocked. Halle wasn't sure whether she should call for medical assistance or the police.

"Are you okay?" she asked, then decided calming him was the best course of action. "Why don't we begin again?" she suggested "Please, have a seat. I'm sure we can sort this out."

Somehow he found his way into the chair in front of her desk without taking his eyes off her face.

Halle settled into her chair. "You know who I am. May I ask your name?"

"Liam." He swallowed hard. "Liam Hart."

Summoning a polite smile, she gave him a nod. "Mr. Hart, why don't you tell me what happened? You mentioned someone mailed my article to you?"

His head moved up and down, slowly. "Yesterday. It was addressed to me at my office in…in California."

"You came all the way from California to ask me about the article?" She tried not to allow the tension to slip into her voice again.

He looked away. "I'm not some stalker or crazy person." His gaze met hers once more. "I came because…"

Rather than finish his sentence he reached into the pocket of his tee and withdrew something, tossed the items on her desk. Photographs. She grabbed them, her pulse racing toward some unseen finish line for reasons still unknown to her.

"I came because of the photos that accompanied your article."

Halle stared at the two photos. *Andy.* "Where did you get these?" she practically whispered.

For a moment he only continued to stare at her.

Who was this man? How did he have these photos of Andy? Why were his eyes so blue?

The idea that he might be… No, no, it wasn't possible.

Was it?

"Those photos came from a family album," he finally said. "My family album."

She left the photos on her desk and clasped her hands together to conceal their shaking. "Do you…" She moistened her lips, tried to swallow, but it wasn't happening. "Do you know the boy in these photos?"

The question was foolish. The photos had been in his family's album. Of course he knew who the boy was.

"Me."

The single syllable quaked through her. Not possible. "I'm not sure I understand." She held up one of the photos. "I know this boy. His name is Andrew— Andy Clark. He went missing twenty-five years ago."

Mr. Hart shook his head. "Those photos are me. That house you see in the background is my home. In California."

Halle stared at the photo with the house. It certainly wasn't a house in her neighborhood. Definitely not Andy's house.

"The dog in the other one," he said, "that's Sparky. The dog my father got me for my birthday."

Halle's head was spinning. This was incomprehensible. She struggled for rational thought, for what to do next. "Mr. Hart, I can't explain why you look exactly like Andy." She simultaneously shook her head and shrugged awkwardly. "I honestly don't know what to say. I can see why you were shaken by the article and the photos. If the photos you brought with you are of you—" she tapped the newspaper "—and I know these are of Andy…" She looked him in the eyes. "Let me pursue this. With you. We could both work on it. In ways that law enforcement can't."

The reporter in her wouldn't allow the opportunity to pass without trying to get to the truth.

LIAM STARED at the woman. He'd been doing that practically from the moment he laid eyes on her. She seemed so familiar to him. Like someone he'd gone to school with or met at a party. Somehow he knew this Halle Lane. From the wild mane of red hair to the freckles and those too familiar green eyes.

"I came here to ask you," he said, his chest heavy with some emotion he couldn't define, "about this Andy—the boy who went missing. I tried to google for information but what I found was vague at best. There was no explanation of what happened to him."

"I can tell you anything you want to know," she assured him. "Andy and I were neighbors and best friends. But, to my knowledge, no one knows what happened to him. The police, the FBI, even private investigators were never able to solve the case."

Best friends. Neighbors. Liam drew in a big breath. "All right." He glanced around her office. "My flight got into Nashville and I drove straight here. I don't have a hotel yet, but maybe we should have dinner. Talk. I'll find a place to stay later."

He felt like a total idiot. Talk? Dinner? But then, he was here. He'd come a long way to get some answers. He might as well get those answers straight from the horse's mouth, so to speak.

"There's a couple of options for lodging," she said. "As you say, we can worry about that later. I don't know about you but I'm starving. My parents are expecting me for dinner. Why don't you join us?"

He blinked, startled at the invitation. "Sure. If you think your parents won't mind."

She laughed. "I can guarantee you they won't mind. And a dinner out might draw attention you don't want or need."

He grabbed his photos from her desk and tucked them back into his pocket. "I can follow you."

"Actually—" she picked up her shoulder bag "—it would be better if we rode together. We'll have to park on another street and sneak into my backyard. Reporters are camping out in front of my house."

He wasn't so sure that being without his own transportation was a good idea.

"Don't worry," she offered, "I'll bring you back for your car."

Too tired to argue and too curious to miss out on the opportunity, he said, "Fine."

Fine might be an overstatement but he would ride it out.

The dreams that had haunted him last night wouldn't fade. As a boy, he hadn't been able to remember his name at the ER when he'd broken his arm. The doctor had assured his father that it was probably the concussion causing the confusion and it would likely clear up in a couple of days. And it had.

Maybe the newspaper article wouldn't have gotten to him if it hadn't been for that one disturbing memory in that hospital…and Claire's insistence that there were no pictures of him.

He was here. He intended to find out what his true past was.

SHE PARKED ON a short, shady street that wasn't so different from some of the streets back home. Liam surveyed the neat yards and the quaint old houses. He reached into the back seat and got his jacket. He'd almost left it in his rental. The temperature had dropped dramatically after sunset. Something else that reminded him of home.

"This way," she said in a stage whisper.

He followed her between two houses and across the backyard of the one on the right. No exterior lights came on, no dogs barked. The moon and the glow from the windows provided just enough illumination for their trek across the property. A clothesline and a swing set were the only items they encountered.

"Mrs. Jolly is the neighbor who lives behind us," Halle said in a low voice. "I warned her on Monday that I might have to use her backyard to avoid the reporters."

Liam glanced at the back of the small house. He spotted an older woman peering from one of the windows. The light behind her highlighting her presence.

"Here we go."

His guide stopped at a white picket fence and

opened the gate. Once they were through, she closed it behind them.

"Home sweet home."

She marched to the back porch and climbed the steps, chattering the whole time about how good her mother's lasagna was and how excited she would be to have a guest for dinner.

The overhead light came on and the door opened as they crossed the porch. An older version of the woman he'd followed through the darkness stood in the doorway. Her red hair was shot through with gray and pulled back in a long braid.

"I was beginning to think you weren't coming."

"I was held up at the office. Mom, this is Liam Hart. He's joining us for dinner. Liam—" she glanced at him "—this is my mom, Judith."

"I hope that's okay, ma'am," he said when the mother stared openmouthed at him.

"Yes, of course." She blinked once, twice. "Come in."

As they entered the house, Judith called out, "Howard! Halle's home and she brought a guest."

The kitchen smelled of garlic and fresh baked bread. Liam watched as the two women chatted excitedly— as if he was some celebrity or something. A tall, gray-haired man entered the room.

He hesitated, assessed Liam, then thrust out his right hand. "I'm Howard, the father."

"Liam," he said as he shook the man's hand. "Liam Hart."

"Let's eat before it gets cold," Judith announced.

They gathered around the table that stood on one end of the massive kitchen. The whole back of the house appeared to be a kitchen. It was nice. Homey.

Looked well loved. That was one of the things he liked most about his family home. It was a real home. Used and loved and…his. His home. Whatever happened here twenty-five years ago had nothing to do with him. Whoever mailed that newspaper to him had made a mistake.

"So, Liam," Howard said as the various dishes made the rounds of those seated at the table, "tell us about you."

"I'm from Napa. My sister and I run the Hart Family Winery. It's been in my family for more than two decades."

"Oh, my," Judith said. "Would you prefer wine rather than the sweet iced tea?"

"No, ma'am. The tea is fine."

"Sweetheart," Howard announced, "I do believe you've outdone yourself. The lasagna is splendid."

Liam ignored his salad and took a bite of the lasagna. Halle's father was right. It was exceptional. He smiled at Judith. "Really outstanding."

She beamed at him. Something deep inside him shifted. He looked from Judith to Howard and then to Halle. These people shouldn't feel so damned familiar to him.

This was all wrong.

THEN

Monday, October 31
Twenty-five years, five months ago…

HALLE DIDN'T WANT to be a fairy. She wanted to be Robin. Andy was Batman and she wanted to be Robin.

They were best friends after all. Just like Batman and Robin.

Their moms walked behind them, not allowing them to get too far ahead. Even though they knew everyone on this street and all the other streets around them, their moms always worried.

"I like your costume," Andy said.

Halle smiled at him. "Like yours, too. I wanted to be Robin."

They walked on, heading for the next house.

When they turned up the sidewalk, Andy leaned close and whispered, "You are Robin. You're just in disguise. Sometimes superheroes do that."

A big old grin spread across her face. "Yeah. I am Robin. In disguise."

They rushed to the front door and rang the bell. It was her turn, so she was the one to press the lit button.

When the door opened they shouted, "Trick or treat!"

Mr. Olson made a surprised face. "My goodness, I had no idea Batman was in the neighborhood. Who's your friend, Batman?" Mr. Olson winked at Halle.

"It's my friend Robin—in disguise."

"Well, this really is a special visit." He held out the bowl. "Robin, you and Batman take all the treats you want."

Giggling, they grabbed a handful of candy each and dropped it into their pumpkin-head pails.

"Thank you!" they recited simultaneously before dashing away.

"Be careful out there, Batman and Robin," Mr. Olson called after them.

The mothers waited on the sidewalk by the street. Halle and Andy hurried past and headed for the next house.

"Thanks for letting me be Robin even in this fairy suit," Halle said as they skipped up the sidewalk to the next house.

"You'll always be my Robin," Andy promised.

"Forever and ever," Halle said on a laugh.

By the time their moms made them go home, they had a ton of candy each. They were never going to run out of candy.

When they reached their end of South High, they parted ways, waving and laughing. It was a good night.

Halle couldn't wait to go to sleep. Tomorrow was a school day. She and Andy were going to trade sandwiches at lunch. On Tuesdays they always did. Halle loved his mom's pastrami sandwiches and he loved her mom's peanut butter and jelly ones.

Maybe she'd sneak some of her Halloween candy in her lunch box to share with Andy.

She couldn't wait until morning.

Chapter Four

NOW

"Dinner was great," Liam said. "Inviting a stranger into your home was very kind of you."

Judith blinked a couple of times. "Oh…of course. Friends of Halle are always welcome."

Liam managed a single nod. But he wasn't a friend. Whatever these people thought, he was a stranger. He had never lived here. He didn't know them or the boy, Andy, who was lost all those years ago. They just happened to resemble each other as children. It happened. No big deal. The question was how had anyone from Winchester found him? Connected him to this old tragedy?

Some reporter—maybe even Halle Lane herself—had likely gone to a great deal of trouble to locate someone who fit the profile of this Andy Clark. Made for great headlines, didn't it?

"I should get a place to stay for the night," he said, suddenly finding himself completely out of place, out of sorts. "I have a flight back home tomorrow."

Just saying the words made him feel more relaxed. He needed to get back home. To feel grounded.

"So soon?" Halle asked.

"I—I hadn't planned on staying long. Just long enough to…" To what? Now his decision to come all this way seemed silly. What had he hoped to find here? Had he thought he'd be able to tell who sent him the article in a glance, a chance remark? It was a fool's errand, and he was beginning to feel very foolish and uncomfortable.

"Before you go," Halle said quickly, "you can look at my research."

He had flown across the country on a whim because of this mystery. Of course he wanted to see her research. Maybe it would provide a clue to who had sent him the article. "Yes. I'd like that."

"Great." A smile perked up the corners of her mouth. She had those really nice lips. Full and…

What the hell was he doing?

"Let us know if you need anything while you're here, Liam," Howard offered. "Winchester is a nice town. Lots of friendly people."

"Thank you." Despite their comments, he felt uneasy. Friendly people didn't send articles about a lost child to him with no explanation. Someone in Winchester had done that.

As he wondered again about the sender, Halle stood, placed their plates in the sink and announced she would take him to see her research before it got too late. He rose, too, and helped clear the rest of the table with her.

"Mom, Dad, good night," Halle said when they were finished.

"Thank you for dinner," Liam added. He smiled for

the parents once more, grabbed his jacket and followed Halle out onto the porch. The breeze held a bite. He pulled on his jacket as they descended the steps. "We going back to your office?"

"We're going to my place." She pointed to the detached garage at the end of the long driveway. "I have an apartment over the garage. It's more an office and a place to sleep. I can't even remember the last time I actually watched the television and I've never cooked a meal there."

"Why didn't you stay in Nashville?" He already knew a little about her after he'd done some research on her during the flight today. She'd had a rising career there until things started to go downhill a couple of years ago. She'd been married. No kids.

The internet was full of information about Halle Lane. Not so much about Andy Clark. Most of the information about Liam was related to the winery. There weren't even that many photos of him to be found.

"I made a mistake," she admitted as she started up the stairs on the side of the garage. "I allowed my personal life to invade my professional life. It was a mistake that I paid dearly for."

He mulled over her answer as she paused on the landing to unlock the door. "Sometimes it's difficult to keep things separate."

Running a family-owned and-operated vineyard and winery, he knew from experience that it was next to impossible to keep his personal life from his professional life. They were basically one and the same.

She walked through the door, waited for him to enter, then closed the door. "Sorry about the mess."

She gestured to the large open space. "This is the real Halle. Disorganized and perpetually on the run."

An L-shaped sofa sat in the middle of the room. A square coffee table nestled in the vee. Like the coffee table, the sofa was littered with piles of folders and notebooks. On the other side of the sofa was a bay window with a built-in seat. Probably looked out over the backyard. A few feet away was an expanse of cabinetry and small appliances that represented the kitchen. A narrow island was covered with notes and photos. One of the two stools fronting it held yet another stack of folders.

Beyond the kitchen area was a king-size bed—unmade. Its hotel-style white linens lay twisted and crumpled. A door stood on either side of the bed. He figured one was a closet and the other was the bathroom.

"It's larger than I expected," he said. If she ever visited his office she would feel right at home. Shelly was constantly threatening to bring in a bulldozer to clear it out.

She tossed her shoulder bag on the sofa, walked to the loaded stool and began to move the stack of files. "It used to be just storage. But when I was a little girl, my father turned it into an apartment for his younger sister, Daisy." She smiled as she plopped the stack into the window seat. "Daisy was a romance writer. She never told anyone. Only the family knew. She liked having her little secret. No matter that her Lola Renae books were quite popular, she kept her career quiet. Everyone thought she was just the old maid who lived over the Lanes' garage."

"Interesting. My mother loves romance novels." Penelope kept a stack of Harlequins on her bedside table.

"She's probably read a Lola Renae or two."

"I'll have to ask her. She's in Paris right now. Since my dad died, she hasn't spent a lot of time at home. She says she's giving my sister—Claire—and me our space, but I think it's more about not being able to bear the memories now that Dad isn't there."

"Sounds like they had an amazing love story of their own."

He nodded. "They did. Dad said he was totally lost after my biological mom died. She died before I was two. Dad didn't meet Penelope, the only mom I've ever known, until I was five. They had Claire when I was seven."

Liam had no idea why he'd just told her all those personal things—things that had no bearing on what they had to discuss. Flustered, he slumped onto the stool she'd cleared. She slid onto the other one.

"This is a copy of the case file from the local authorities. Getting a copy from the FBI was not going to happen. Chief of Police Brannigan was kind enough to provide everything he had."

Liam opened the file. Right on top was a photo of the boy, Andy Clark. Again, something in him shuddered. The image shook him. How could the two of them look so much alike?

"That's his school picture from that year. Second grade." A smile tugged at her lips even as her gaze grew distant. "Everyone in the class loved him. The teachers loved him. He was such a sweet kid."

Liam swallowed hard. "He was walking home from school?" Liam had garnered that much from the internet.

"Yes. Usually, we walked together but my dad

picked me up that day. Mother was really sick. She'd had to be hospitalized. He picked me up to go see her and then took me home. By then the police were swarming all over our street."

The image of official vehicles parked this way and that on the street flashed through his mind. Dogs barking echoed in his brain.

A shiver coursed through him. "How long did the search go on?"

"For weeks, but each day after the first week, fewer and fewer showed up to participate in the search parties. They checked pools and ponds in the area. Empty houses and buildings. That first week the dogs were involved. Several different police departments from surrounding counties brought their dogs and members of their communities to help in the search. It was a massive undertaking." She exhaled a big breath. "By the first of April, hope had diminished, the same as the search parties."

"You mentioned private investigators." He could imagine that any family with the means would have hired a PI to try to find their missing child.

"The Clarks hired several. No one ever found anything useful."

"Sounds like the kidnapping was a professional job." He couldn't see amateurs getting that lucky.

"Possibly. Or someone who had done this before. A predator."

His gut clenched at the idea. "Sometimes these kids come back, right?"

"Of the hundreds of thousands of children reported missing each year, about ninety-nine percent come back alive. A lot of work is being done to ensure children are found and returned home quickly. But some, like Andy, aren't so lucky."

"So kids like Andy are in the minority."

"That's right. Still, even one percent is too many. One child is too many. My family and I watched the devastation take a toll on the Clarks. Their life was never the same. When they lost Andy, they lost everything that mattered to them, because with him gone, nothing else was relevant."

"Understandable."

He felt her looking at him. She had questions. He still had questions of his own. The trouble was, neither of them had the right answers.

"Tell me about you, Liam Hart. Besides where you're from and what you do for a living. Tell me about your childhood, your life. Accidents? Surgeries? Illnesses?"

"You want my social security number, too?" The surprise on her face made him smile. "Just kidding."

She put a hand to her throat. "Sorry. I know I can be a little pushy sometimes."

"Sometimes," he agreed. "To answer your many questions, other than the one time I had to be taken to the ER as a kid, I've never been hospitalized. Never been sick really. I guess I was lucky that way. My childhood was uneventful beyond the fact that my sister and I roamed the vineyards. Our parents were always worried we'd hurt ourselves. I thought I had to take Claire everywhere with me. Dad said sometimes he thought I was terrified of losing her." Liam shrugged. "Maybe I was. I didn't like it when she was out of my sight."

Saying those words now seemed wrong somehow. Why would he have been afraid? He'd never lost anyone except his mother and he'd been a toddler at the time, so he had no memory of the event.

"We were inseparable," he went on. "Sparky was our constant companion all through childhood. I was away in college when he went to doggie heaven as Claire bravely informed me by phone."

Halle hadn't stopped smiling since he'd started talking. "I didn't realize how lonely being an only child could be until Andy was gone. We were like you and Claire. We did everything together." She laughed. "We even got married once."

Images of a little red-haired girl and blond-haired boy exchanging childish vows sifted through his mind. "What brought this on at such an early age?"

"My family and I attended a wedding. I wanted a dress just like the one the bride wore. The whole ceremony enthralled me. As soon as I got back home I informed Andy that we had to have a wedding. He was always happy to accommodate me. I dug my mother's wedding dress out of the keepsake trunk in her room." Halle shook her head. "I think I almost gave her a heart attack. At least I didn't damage it."

Silence lapsed between them. He might have only met this woman a few hours ago, but he knew what she was feeling. He knew what she wanted, and he couldn't give it to her. It hurt him to think of hurting her.

"I'm not the long-lost kid you're looking for, Halle. Today is my first trip to Winchester. I can see how badly you want this story to somehow have a happy ending but I can't be that happy ending for you. I'm just a guy from California who received a strange piece of mail about a missing kid." A strange piece of mail that had him hopping on a plane.

"Can I tell you something else?"

He heaved a big breath. "Sure, why not?"

"Andy had a dog named Sparky, too. He went missing just a couple of weeks before Andy. There were people who worried that Andy had gone off looking for Sparky and couldn't find his way back home. Of course that wasn't true." She shrugged. She'd been holding this back since the moment he showed her that photo of his dog. "Your Sparky looks exactly like Andy's Sparky. Tell me that isn't a hell of a coincidence."

He held up his hands. "You didn't mention a dog before I did." Had she deliberately withheld that information or conjured it up to keep him interested?

"We hadn't gotten that far. The subject hadn't come up. But there are photos I can show you."

"This is too much." He shook his head.

"There's one way we can potentially rule you out."

His gaze narrowed. "I'm happy to leave a DNA sample, but I can't hang around to wait for results."

"I wasn't thinking about DNA, but I will gladly take a sample to the lab. Thanks for offering."

He'd walked right into that one. "What did you have in mind?"

"Andy had a birthmark."

Liam digested the statement. "If that's the case, then you can rule me out now because I don't have any birthmarks."

This news should have made him feel relieved. Strangely it did not.

"You might not be aware you have one," she countered. "And there's always the possibility that it has faded. You—Andy still had it when he was seven. Usually this particular type of birthmark is gone by the age of one. If it stays, it's usually there for good."

He held his hands up as if in surrender. "So where was this hidden birthmark?" Now he was just irritated. He had really allowed this thing to go too far. He should have left after their meeting in her office.

What the hell was he doing here?

She scooted off her stool and went around to his right side. "It was in the hairline just behind his right ear."

Her hands reached toward him and he froze.

"I'm sorry," she shook her head. "May I look? I'll have to touch you to do that."

He nodded, suddenly unsure of his voice.

Her fingers felt cool against his skin as she swiped the tips through his hair. The new thread of tension roiling through him annoyed him further. Of course he wouldn't be aware of a birthmark in a place like that. If he did have one, maybe she had seen it and was making the whole thing up. This could be her way of launching her story into the stratosphere. He didn't know this woman. She could be—

The sound of her breath catching derailed his next thought. Her fingers fell away from him.

Liam turned to look at her. "What?"

Eyes wide, lips parted, she pressed her fingers to her mouth and stepped back.

Fury, hot and unreasonable, erupted inside him. "Show me," he demanded.

Without a word she walked to the door on the left side of her bed, turned on a light and left the door open for him to follow.

He stepped into the bathroom as if he were crossing

into enemy territory. She pulled a mirror from a shelf above the toilet and passed it to him.

The maneuver was awkward and it took a minute, but he finally got his head, arms and the mirror positioned just right so he could see what had freaked her out.

The pinkish mark was shaped like upside down lips.

"It's called an angel's kiss," she said, her voice whisper thin. "This is the exact same shape, color and placement as the one Andy had."

He wasn't doing this. It was ridiculous. A sham, a trick to help her further her career. Why had he been so stupid, coming here?

He carefully placed the mirror on the counter and turned to face her. "I have to go now."

He squeezed past her and stormed across the room. His hand was on the doorknob, ready to turn, when her voice stopped him.

"Let me get my keys."

Damn it. He closed his eyes, wanted to kick himself. He'd left his rental at her office.

He waited while she gathered her bag and her keys. She led the way down the metal staircase attached to the side of the garage. He stayed behind her, not wanting to engage in conversation. All he wanted was out of here. They reached her car on the next street and they both got in without speaking. His plan to avoid any further discussion worked until she pulled away from the curb and he was a captive audience.

"I don't know how you can continue to pretend there isn't a strong possibility that you're Andy Clark," she said firmly.

"My name is Liam Hart." He stared into the night.

"I can't force you to believe what I'm telling you." She sighed. "But I knew it was you as soon as you walked into my office."

"Stop."

She said no more, and he was grateful she left it at that. They drove in silence across the quiet town. The businesses on the square were closed for the night. Traffic was near nonexistent. When she turned into the parking lot behind the newspaper building, he relaxed just a little.

"Give me your cell number," she said simply. "Here." She gave him her phone to enter his number. When he didn't respond, she said, quietly, "Please. In case I get more information."

After a pause, he did as she asked. Then placed the device on the console between them.

"There's a hotel near the Kroger on Dinah Shore Boulevard. There's an inn but it's farther out of the downtown area." She braked to a stop, slid the gearshift into Park.

"I'll find it." He reached for the door handle.

"Whatever you or I believe, Liam," she said, waylaying him, "someone sent that article to you. Someone knows something about you and your past. Maybe something you don't even know, the way you didn't know about the birthmark. You can't just walk away from this."

"Yes, I can. Coming here was a mistake." He opened the door.

"Andy's mother is sick. She needs to know," she said. "Are you going to just walk away and pretend it doesn't matter one way or the other?"

He looked at her then. "Yes."

He climbed out of her car and strode to his. This wild-goose chase was over.

GETTING A ROOM was quick and easy.

He threw his bag onto the bed and collapsed next to it. He closed his eyes and struggled to banish all the voices and images from his head. None of this was real. It couldn't be real. This must be a mistake. Someone's twisted idea of a joke.

His cell vibrated and he tugged it from his pocket. If it was Halle…

Claire.

"Hey."

"Why haven't you called me? I've been going crazy with worry. What did you find out? Did that reporter send you the article?"

He rubbed his head with his free hand. God, he needed a drink. "I was having dinner with the reporter and her family, and no, she didn't send me the article. That part is still a mystery."

The dead air space told him that his mystery-loving sister was not satisfied.

"I should have come with you. I'm better at this sort of thing than you."

"Claire—"

"I've been through all the family papers. All the photo albums. I'm telling you there are no photos of you between when you were a baby and seven years old. Something is wrong with this, Liam. You have a right to know what that is."

"What if I don't want to know?" There was no way he was telling her about the birthmark. Lots of kids had birthmarks. So what if he had the same kind in the same place as this Andy Clark? That didn't mean anything.

"You're in denial. I should call Mom. She has to know what really happened. If this is some ridiculous joke someone is playing on you, she'll know. If it's not, she'll know."

"Do you actually think she would tell you if she and Dad stole a seven-year-old kid? Come on now, Claire. That's a little far-fetched even for you."

"Is it? It wouldn't be the first secret they kept from us."

This was unfortunately true. They'd kept the news about his dad's illness a secret until he was hardly able to get out of the bed.

Liam recalled another incident that Claire wouldn't remember. When Liam was twelve he'd made friends with the son of one of the summer workers. The kid and his father suddenly disappeared—didn't show up for work, rental house was empty—and Liam's father had said they'd had to leave because of a family emergency. Later, Liam had overheard some of the workers whispering about how the boy had been a kidnap victim. The parents had divorced and the father had disappeared with him to prevent the mother from getting sole custody. When Liam demanded the truth from his father, he'd explained that he was concerned Liam would be traumatized by the news.

He'd been traumatized all right. It was the first time his father had lied to him.

Or was it?

"I'll be back tomorrow," Liam said. He didn't want to talk about this anymore.

"See you then but I'm still phoning Mom," his sister warned.

Liam ended the call and fell back on the bed. He needed rest, oblivion. He had hardly dozed since receiving that article.

A good night's sleep would give him a new perspective.

THEN

"ALL I HAVE to do is say I do?"

This was kind of weird but if it made Halle happy, he was cool with it. She was his best friend.

"Yes. I'll ask a question and you say 'I do.' Then you ask me a question and I say 'I do.'"

Her wild hair was like a lion's mane framing her face. It made him smile. Sometimes when they were watching TV he would try his best to count her freckles. He always lost count. Kind of like when they tried counting stars.

"Okay." He smiled. "Ask me and I'll say it."

Halle straightened her dress. It was really her mother's dress. It was all white and had lots of lace. He'd never seen Mrs. Lane wear it before. No matter that it was way too big, Halle looked pretty.

"Give me a minute to remember," she said, making a face like she was concentrating real hard.

"Oh yeah. Do you take this woman—" she pointed to her chest "—that's me, to be your lif'ful wedded wife?"

He frowned. "What's lif'ful?"

She shook her head, her hair flying with the move. "I dunno. Just say I do."

He nodded. "I do."

She grinned. "Now you ask me."

"Do you take this woman—" he began.

"Not woman, silly," she chided. "Man! You're the man."

"Oh yeah. Do you take this man to be your lif'ful wedded wife?"

She rolled her eyes and groaned. "Husband, not wife!"

He laughed so hard he couldn't breathe.

Her face told him he was not funny.

"Okay, okay. Do you take this man to be your lif'ful wedded husband?"

Her grin was back. "I do!"

He stood there a moment. "Now what?"

"Ah…oh yeah. Now I 'nounce you husband and wife."

"Does that mean we're married now?"

She frowned. "Wait. There's one more part. You gotta kiss the bride."

He glanced around, confused. "What's a bride?"

"Me, silly!"

"Oh." He frowned. "Like on the lips?"

She nodded.

He shrugged. "That's kind of gross, but okay."

She closed her eyes, her lips puckered and lifted toward him.

This was the silliest thing…

He wiped his mouth, puckered his lips and leaned forward. He kissed her the way his mom always kissed him. Just a quick touch of lips.

She opened her eyes and smiled. "Now we're married forever and ever."

Chapter Five

NOW

Nancy Clark drew the covers back and sat down on the bed. She was tired tonight. More tired than usual.

She looked around the room. She'd pulled all those boxes down from the top shelf of the closet, which was probably why she was so tired. A woman her age had no business climbing up and down from a chair.

But she'd needed to look. To hold those precious keepsakes just once more.

Halle had promised to come back any time she wanted to start part two of her story—Andy's story, really. Nancy had decided to call her tomorrow. She would show her the things in the boxes and she would tell her the rest of the story. All of it, not leaving a single part out.

It was time.

She'd seen him on the back porch of the Lane home. She'd been sitting in the dark on her own back porch, watching. Her patience had paid off. She'd gotten to see him three times. Going into the Lane home, going out to Halle's apartment over the garage and then again as he'd left for the night.

He was so handsome. He had grown into a fine man. Andrew would be proud.

Goodness, how she missed him. After two years one would expect that she'd gotten used to being alone, but that was not the case. She missed her husband. Wept for him every night. As hard as she tried to maintain her composure, she would lie down at night, and just as she drifted off, the memories would fill her head. He had loved her so much. Been so good to her even after that horrible day.

Andrew had been a fine husband. A very good father.

It had hurt the two of them to go on after that day, but it had been the right thing to do. They had both recognized how important it was to press forward. Looking back would only add to their pain.

She sighed and fluffed her pillow, then turned off the lamp on the bedside table. She always slept with the door open and the bathroom light on. The glow filtering into the hallway cut the darkness without being right in her face. At her age, she didn't want to go stumbling around in the dark.

Tomorrow she would call Halle and maybe she would get to see him up close. Touch him even. Wouldn't that be nice? Then she would have Judith take her to the cemetery so she could tell Andrew all about it.

Their boy was home.

A shadow suddenly blocked the light.

Nancy's head jerked up. She couldn't see the face but someone was standing in her doorway. She yelped and grabbed for the lamp on the bedside table. One tug of the chain and it came on.

Then she recognized him, even after so many years. "What're you doing here?"

"We had a deal, Nancy. You and I and Andrew. Andrew kept his end of the deal, took it to the grave with him, but it appears you have not."

He moved a step closer to the bed and she wished the telephone extension was on her side of the bed, but it was not. It was on Andrew's side. She had never moved it.

"I... I don't know what you're talking about."

"Yes, you do. The one rule was that you were never to speak of it again. Never. To no one. Not even each other."

But they had. She and Andrew had spoken about it many times, inside with the doors and windows closed and the lights turned out.

"I haven't told anyone. You read the article. You know what I told the reporter. Nothing important."

He glanced around her room, spotted the baby blanket. "Oh, Nancy. Dear Nancy. You brought him back here and now there will be questions. A new investigation, perhaps. This won't do. It won't do at all."

Courage rose inside her. "We made a mistake. All of us. What you did to that...that woman was on you. We didn't ask you to do that."

He moved closer still.

Nancy pulled the bedcovers to her chest as if the well-washed cotton could somehow protect her.

"But I did and now we have a problem."

Fear crept up her spine. "It's your problem, not mine."

He nodded. "You're correct and now I'm going to fix it."

Chapter Six

NOW

Friday, March 13

Halle grabbed her shoulder bag, tucked her phone inside and started for the door. She'd hardly slept last night. She'd wanted to call him or go to the hotel and shake him, make him listen.

He was being unreasonable. This was all strange and unsettling but there was no point in denying what was obvious. Liam Hart was Andy Clark.

Her cell rang and she tugged it from her bag as she reached the door. *Mom* flashed on the screen. Frowning, she accepted the call. "Hey, Mom, what's up?"

"I know you're probably getting ready to leave for work."

"Leaving now," Halle confirmed. Her mother's voice sounded strange. "Is everything okay?"

"The police and an ambulance are next door. Your father has gone over to find out what's happened."

Was Mrs. Clark ill? Why hadn't she called for help? Halle and her parents had urged her over the years to call if she ever needed anything. "I'm heading there now."

Halle ended the call and shoved the phone back into her bag. She hurried out the door, almost forgot to lock it and double-timed it down the stairs. Poor Mrs. Clark, all alone and unable to protect or help herself. As she reached the front yard, another vehicle was turning into the drive next door.

The bold lettering on the side of the van stopped her cold.

CORONER.

"Oh, God." Ice gushed through her veins.

Her feet were suddenly moving again. She bounded across Mrs. Clark's yard, up the steps and onto the porch. Halle was through the open front door before the officer who was supposed to be guarding the scene noticed her. He was at the far end of the porch, vomiting.

The coppery odor of blood filled her lungs the instant she hit the hallway beyond the living room.

Low voices echoed from the kitchen. Halle changed directions and went into the kitchen instead of down the hall to the bedrooms. Eileen Brewster sat at the table, her face in her hands. Eileen cleaned house for Mrs. Clark once a week. Always on Fridays. A lump swelled in Halle's throat.

The man talking to Eileen looked up. Chief of Police William Brannigan—Billy, everyone called him.

"What's going on, Chief?" Her voice sounded oddly small. She suddenly wondered where her father was.

"Halle," he said with a nod. "Your daddy is out on the back porch. Maybe you should go out there and talk to him for a minute while Ms. Brewster and I finish up."

Halle nodded and moved quickly through the room. Brannigan's voice softened once more as he spoke gently to Eileen.

Howard Lane stood at the railing, looking out over the Clarks' backyard as well as their own. She and Andy used to stand on their porches at night and send each other flashlight signals. When Halle neared her father she saw the dampness on his cheeks. Oh no. Oh no.

"What happened, Daddy?"

He looked up, pulled Halle into his arms. "Someone came into the house last night and killed Nancy."

Halle drew back. "Oh my God. Who would do such a thing? Was it a robbery?"

Her father shook his head. "We don't know yet. The house wasn't ransacked. But boxes had been taken out of her closet and sat around the floor in her bedroom."

"Eileen found her?" Poor Eileen. Halle could only imagine the horror.

Howard nodded. "After several knocks on the door with no answer, she figured Nancy was away from the house for some reason, so she unlocked the door and let herself in. She said whoever killed her had taken a knife and cut her throat right there in her own bed."

Halle blinked fast, imagining the horror of it. She couldn't conceive anyone hurting Mrs. Clark. She had never done anything to hurt anyone. She was a beloved fixture in their community. The poor woman who lost her only child.

"This is crazy." Her next thought was that now Nancy would never know that Andy was still alive. No matter whether Liam wanted to believe or not, Halle was certain. He was the lost boy.

The back door opened and Chief Brannigan came outside. "Howard, can you take Eileen home? She's in no condition to drive."

"Sure. Sure." Howard scrubbed at his face. "Your mother's going to be devastated."

Halle agreed. Though Nancy and Judith hadn't been as close since Andy vanished, they were still good friends.

When her father was gone, Chief Brannigan turned to Halle. "I read your article."

Halle managed a nod. "Audrey told me." Her boss had said that the chief and the sheriff had read the article with interest.

"I told Audrey I was happy to let Luther Holcomb know you wanted to talk to him whenever you're ready."

"I would appreciate that, Chief. Mrs. Clark was excited about the possibility of finally finding the rest of the story."

"She had pulled out a bunch of boxes from her closet. Did she do that for you?"

Halle shook her head. "We talked, looked at photo albums but nothing more. When I came by on Sunday, she wanted to show me something in Andy's room. A photo of the two of us that had been his favorite. I passed her room on the way to Andy's and there were no boxes then. Just the bed and a dresser, a couple of nightstands."

The officer who'd been vomiting came around the corner of the house. "Burt's taking the body now, Chief."

"Good. Thanks, Sails." Brannigan turned to Halle. "I need to speak with Burt for a moment and then I'll be right back. Before I go, can you tell me if this visitor from California—this Liam Hart—is still in Winchester?"

"I'm not sure. He has a flight back home leaving from Nashville today, but he didn't say what time. He may still be at the hotel."

"If he's still here, see if you can get him to my office."

Halle stared after the chief as he strode back inside. Why would the chief of police want to talk to Liam? Who'd mentioned him to Brannigan—her father?

Certainly he had nothing to do with Mrs. Clark's death...

Halle drew out her phone and made the call. It went to voice mail. She hung up and called again. He could be at breakfast or in the shower. This time she left a message. "Liam, this is Halle. Something's happened." She decided not to tell him about the murder. "Chief of Police Brannigan would like to meet with you in his office at City Hall. If you haven't left yet, please come. I'll be there, too." She hesitated. Instead of goodbye, she said, "See you there."

By the time Halle put her phone away, the chief was back at the door. "You mind coming inside again?"

Rather than answer, she followed him inside. He paused in the middle of the kitchen, his trademark hat on the table.

"Audrey told me this Liam fellow showed up with a copy of your article that someone apparently sent him anonymously."

At least that explained how he knew about Liam's arrival.

Before she could say anything, he said, "Ro and I

had dinner with Audrey and Colt last night. She wanted to bring me up to speed."

Tanya, Halle decided. She hadn't spoken to Audrey about Liam until this morning. Tanya must have told her after he barged into the office last evening. Since Audrey hadn't known the rest until this morning, Brannigan had obviously called her after coming here.

"Did you speak to her again this morning?" Halle asked to confirm her conclusion.

"I did. After I saw what had been done to Mrs. Clark, I called Audrey to find out if she knew anything more about his visit."

This was wrong, wrong, wrong. "Chief, you're not thinking that he had anything to do with this?"

He held her gaze for a moment before saying, "I'm only thinking that he might have felt compelled to visit her. Which could explain all those boxes pulled down from the top shelf in her closet. If he visited her and she was still alive, I need to know if she mentioned anyone else who planned to come by or if he saw a vehicle parked on the street."

Reasonable, Halle decided. "I got his voice mail when I called just now. If he hasn't left yet, I'm assuming he'll show up at your office."

"When you were in Nashville, I'm sure you were at homicide scenes from time to time."

She nodded. "Lots of times."

"I'd like you to see something."

Adrenaline lit in her veins, whether fueled by anticipation or dread, she couldn't say. "All right."

As they moved through the house, she saw the crime scene technician. He and Eileen must have parked on the street because she hadn't noticed their cars in the driveway. Then again, she had been focused on getting into the house. Perhaps she simply hadn't been looking.

The odor of blood was stronger as they neared Mrs. Clark's bedroom. Andy's room was at the end of the hall. The family bathroom was on the left, along with another bedroom that Nancy had used for a sewing room.

The bed linens were covered in blood. More blood was spattered on the carpet. Halle kept the idea that this was Mrs. Clark's blood pushed aside. She focused on the details of the room. Gold drapes pulled tightly closed. Bedside table on each side of the bed. Lamps with beige shades adorned with gold fringe sat on the tables. A dresser stood on the wall next to the closet door. Beyond the bed on the far side of the room near the windows were boxes stacked on the floor. Three medium-sized boxes, the kind used for moving. The tape had been cut and the lids pulled open.

"Try not to step in the blood."

Halle followed him, careful of the crimson stains on the beige carpet.

The first thing she noticed about the boxes was a baby blanket lying on the top of whatever was inside one. The blanket was blue with a monogramed A in a lighter blue. Andy's baby blanket.

Brannigan pulled a pair of latex gloves from his jacket pocket and handed them to her. "Have a look at that box, the one closest to the bed, if you would."

Halle tugged on the gloves and moved closer to the boxes. The first box, the one with the baby blanket, appeared to be filled with stuffed animals and other toys. The next one had neatly folded clothes. Boy clothes. Andy's clothes. The ones he wore before he vanished.

The third box held another, smaller box. Halle reached inside the smaller box. Photographs. She shuffled through the loose photos. Most were of Andy. Others included Nancy and Andrew. And sure enough, there were photos with Sparky, too. She lifted the smaller box from the larger one and set it atop one of the others. Beneath that smaller box was yet another box; this one was really small and nestled amid more clothes.

She reached for the much smaller box and opened it. It was more like a gift box made for a scarf or perfume set. Inside were more photos.

Her heart stumbled.

There were photos of Andy. But not seven-year-old or younger Andy. These were Andy when he was older. Like ten and twelve. Fifteen…twenty. Halle's mouth went bone-dry. The fully grown Andy… *Liam.*

No question. He wore another tee that sported the logo of the Hart family winery.

How was this possible? "Why would she have these?"

Brannigan's voice dragged her attention from the disturbing contents of the box.

"I don't know." A realization suddenly expanded through her mind, stealing her breath. Could Mrs. Clark have been the one to mail him the article?

If she knew where Andy was, why didn't she do something? Why didn't she tell Halle during the interview?

"We need to speak to Liam Hart," Brannigan said.

Halle shook her head. "But he insists he's never been here before."

Not possible. She understood this without a single

doubt. He was Andy. He had to be. There simply was no other alternative. He either truly didn't know or he was hiding the truth for some reason. Perhaps protecting someone he had grown to love in his new life.

"He may not have been here," Brannigan offered, "but Mrs. Clark has either been to see him or had someone watching him."

This made no sense whatsoever.

She stared at the blood on the bed. What in the world had Mrs. Clark not told her?

LIAM PICKED UP his bag, took one last look around the room and headed for the door. He'd made it across the parking lot and into his rental car before curiosity got the better of him and he listened to Halle's voice mail.

He'd been in the shower when she called. He'd told himself it didn't matter what she had to say, but somehow it did. He wasn't sure how just yet, but there was this feeling—this annoying little voice—that wouldn't turn loose. It nagged at him like an errant weed choking at one of his grape vines, a weed that just wouldn't be thwarted.

He set the phone to speaker and hit Play. Her voice sounded strained, uncertain, worried. Nothing like the confident reporter he'd met.

The chief of police wanted to meet with him.

What? Why would Liam meet with anyone here, much less the chief of police? Did the people in this town want to solve this cold case so badly that they were grasping at straws? Surely that urgency didn't extend to the chief of police.

The little nagging voice that would not be silenced nudged him.

He blew out a big breath. The last thing he wanted was for trouble from Winchester to follow him back to California. Claire would be upset and Penelope would be hurt that he'd even come here like this. He had plenty of time before his 3 p.m. flight. He might as well get this meeting or whatever the hell it was over with.

Last night he'd managed to get himself lost finding his way to the boulevard. Seemed ridiculous in a town this small but it had happened, even with GPS. In view of Halle's call this morning, that turned out to be a good thing. He had passed City Hall while driving around and around the town square until he made the proper turn. Winchester's town square was somewhat like a big city roundabout but not as easily maneuvered—at least not for a stranger.

He turned left out of the parking lot, heading for downtown Winchester. He'd barely slept at all. He'd dreamed of a little girl with crazy red curls in a wedding dress. Her smile and those sparkling green eyes had mesmerized him. Or had it been Andy Clark in the dream? The kid looked so damned much like him it was difficult to say one way or another.

He shook off the frustrating notion. Being in this place, spending time with the reporter, it had all somehow managed to put strange ideas in his head. Why was that? Why was he susceptible to these bizarre feelings? He couldn't remember a time in his life that he ever doubted who he was or from where he'd come.

Why now? Was this some sort of early midlife crisis?

A delayed reflex to his father's death?

Or maybe he was just losing it. Stress could do

that, right? Shelly had a valid point. He'd been work-ing seven days a week for months. Maybe he did need a real vacation.

As soon as he got back home, he and Claire were going to have a long talk about the future and putting themselves first from time to time.

He parked at City Hall and climbed out of the rental. Two slots away he spotted Halle's car. She was here already. Good. At least he would know someone in the room.

Wait, did he really know her?

For all he knew, this could be all her fault. The ruth-less journalist who wanted to get the story regardless of the price to others. But that wasn't her way. He'd read a good deal about her. Yeah, it was stuff on the internet, but he hadn't read anything to suggest she was that sort of heartless reporter. She certainly could have saved her career had she chosen to lie and throw her sources under the bus during those last two big as-signments. Instead, she had refused and her career had crashed and burned. If anything, someone else had set out to screw her over.

But she'd let it go. Came home and started over.

Maybe she was a nice person.

He entered the lobby and came immediately face-to-face with a security checkpoint. A cold, hard real-ity of today's world.

"Keys, phone and anything else in your pockets goes in the tray," the uniformed officer told him as he ap-proached. "Belt, too, if you're wearing one."

"No belt," Liam assured him. Keys, phone, a couple of quarters went into the tray.

"Very good, sir. Just step through the metal detector and you're all done."

Liam walked through without setting off any buzzers. He collected his stuff and asked, "Where can I find the chief's office?"

The officer gave him directions and Liam started that way. The City Hall was a piece of vintage architecture from the early part of the last century. The soft soles of his sneakers were soundless on the marble floor. He pushed through the double doors sporting the Winchester Police Department logo and walked to the receptionist's desk.

"Mr. Hart?"

Apparently they were waiting for him. "Yes."

"This way, sir."

She escorted him to a conference room. Two men and Halle sat around the table. All, including Halle, stood as he entered the room. The receptionist turned to him and asked if he needed anything to drink. Water? Coffee?

"No, thanks." His full attention was on the three already in the room.

"Liam," Halle said, "this is Chief of Police William Brannigan." She gestured to the man on her left, then to the one on her right. "And this is Detective Clarence Lincoln. Gentlemen, this is Liam Hart of Napa, California."

Both men shook his hand. Brannigan gestured to an empty chair. "Have a seat, Mr. Hart, and we'll go over the reason I asked you to stop by."

It was nine already. As long as he was out of here by noon he had no problem listening to whatever the two men had to say.

When they'd all settled, Brannigan placed a photo on the table. The woman pictured was older, maybe seventy or so.

"Have you ever met this woman?"

Liam shook his head. "I haven't, no."

From the same folder he'd pulled the first photo, he pulled a second, placed it on top of the first. "What about this woman?"

His gaze rested on the woman's face. She looked to be forty or so. Blond hair, gray eyes. His gut tightened. She looked vaguely familiar. But he couldn't say he'd ever met her before.

"Sorry." He turned his hands up. "I don't know her, either."

Halle looked from Liam to Brannigan.

"What's this about?" He suddenly felt edgy, his nerves raw. His patience thinning.

"This woman—" Brannigan tapped the second photo "—is the same as the first. Nancy Clark, Andy Clark's mother."

Liam blinked, unsure of what to say or do at first. Then he shook his head. "I don't mean to be rude, but why are you showing these photos to me? Whatever Miss Lane has suggested, I am not Andy Clark."

Brannigan nodded once. "That may be so," he said. "But you arrived in Winchester yesterday afternoon. Spent some time with Miss Lane and her family. Then you went to the hotel. Is that right?"

What the hell? "Of course it's right." He looked to Halle. "She drove me to my car at the newspaper. I drove from there to the hotel. I stayed all night. Left the hotel and drove here." He avoided looking at Halle, focused on Brannigan instead. He asked again, "What is this about?"

"Nancy Clark lived next door to Halle and her family."

The fact that he used the past tense put Liam on alert.

"Around midnight last night she was murdered."

Liam couldn't speak. He thought of several things to say. *I hate to hear this but I didn't know her. My condolences to the family.* None of those words would rise from his tongue. His throat seemed to be closing and his stomach churned. He remembered Halle's words from last night, about Mrs. Clark being ill, and didn't he want to see her.

"Whoever broke into her house was knowledgeable in breaking and entering without leaving any evidence behind. The perpetrator walked into her bedroom and cut her throat, leaving her alone to bleed out and die."

Sweat formed on Liam's skin. "Robbery?" he managed to ask, his voice sounding unnatural. His mouth and throat were dry.

Brannigan shook his head. "Nothing was taken."

"We believe," the detective on the other side of the table spoke for the first time, "her murder was related to the article that brought you here."

Liam scrubbed a hand over his mouth. He felt sick. Really sick. "Where is your—" he stood, his chair rolling back, bumping into another "—bathroom?"

"To the left," Brannigan said. "Fourth door on the right."

Liam rushed out of the room. His body shook so hard it was difficult to walk straight. He shoved through the door marked Men and went to the sink.

He braced his hands on the cold porcelain and stared at his reflection. His gut roiled mercilessly. Turning on the faucet, he splashed cold water on his face.

Didn't help.

Bile burned in his throat.

He hurried to the nearest stall and vomited the hot sourness from his gut.

Hands braced on his knees, he took a minute to stop gagging, no matter that there was nothing in his stomach beyond the coffee and bitterness that had already spewed out of him.

"What the hell?" he muttered.

He flushed the toilet and went back to the sink to wash his face again. He cupped a hand and caught water to rinse his mouth, then used a paper towel to wipe the newly formed sweat from his face.

"Pull it together, man," he said to his reflection. None of this had anything to do with him. He was just overtired, stressed, and he'd let all that speculation Halle tossed at him get under his skin.

Deep breath and he was ready to get this done so he could get out of here.

Back in the conference room, the three waited. If they'd talked about him while he was gone, they didn't let on now.

"How about a bottle of water?" Lincoln asked. Rather than wait for an answer, he reached across the table and sat one in front of Liam as if he comprehended exactly what had transpired in the men's room.

Liam didn't trust himself to drink a drop for fear it would spew out of him again.

"Just so we're clear," Brannigan said. "We're not accusing you of anything, Mr. Hart. We've already spoken to management at your hotel. You checked in at ten and didn't leave your room until, as you stated, you came here this morning."

This was ludicrous. "Are you saying I was a suspect?"

"Yes," Lincoln answered for him. "The article goes viral. Stranger comes to town. The missing child's mother—his only living parent—is murdered. We wouldn't be very good at our jobs if we hadn't suspected you."

Liam nodded. Made some sort of bizarre sense, he supposed. "Is there something else you wanted to talk about? If not, I'd like to be on my way."

"You're free to leave whenever you wish, Mr. Hart." Brannigan shrugged. "I have no legal grounds to hold you here."

Liam readied to stand. He wanted out of here. The sooner the better.

"But," Brannigan continued, halting his rise from the table, "we believe you're the key. It would mean a great deal to me personally if you would stay a few days and help us figure out what happened."

Liam shook his head. "How can I possibly help you?"

His heart was pounding again, sweat beading to the point of sliding down his skin. Maybe he had food poisoning. No offense to Halle's mom but something was wrong with him and he hadn't eaten since having dinner with the Lanes.

"I honestly don't know," Brannigan admitted. "Maybe you can't. But Detective Lincoln and I believe someone thinks you can. The story on Andy appeared in the paper. You're sent a copy of it from an anonymous source. You come to town. Mrs. Clark is murdered. We think there's a connection between all this."

How the hell could he just walk away from that? He couldn't.

Chapter Seven

NOW

Halle didn't really have an appetite. Lunch was more or less a way to pass the time until the evidence tech was finished at Mrs. Clark's house. Chief Brannigan had given her permission to look through the house, as well as the boxes in the bedroom, for any useful information. Halle's mother, Judith, was the executor of Mrs. Clark's will and since the poor lady had no other family, it would be up to Halle's family to pack up her home.

Unless they proved that Liam was Andy. Then the property would go to him. Substantiating his true identity would change everything. If only Mrs. Clark had lived to meet him.

Halle's gaze landed on the man across the table from her in the small café near the center of town. She'd suggested he join her after the tense meeting with the police chief. Still dazed, he'd agreed, but she suspected only because he simply didn't know what else to do.

He was still in denial. No matter that the woman's death—a woman he insisted he had never met—had shaken him to the core. He'd gone pale when the chief told him the news. He'd rushed to the men's room. Somewhere deep inside him, memories obviously had stirred. Possibly he hadn't understood his reaction or perhaps refused to accept it for what it was, but it meant something far more than he wanted to see just now.

The tiny fragments of evidence were slowly coming together.

"Thanks for agreeing to have lunch with me," she said when he continued to stare at the menu. It wasn't that extensive or that interesting. His continued perusal was about avoiding eye contact and conversation.

Understandable, in view of the fact that he'd been considered and then ruled out as a homicide suspect. The news was enough to unsettle even the strongest guy. Watching this sort of thing on television or in a movie was vastly different from experiencing it in real life.

"I'm sorry you had to go through that in the chief's office."

He looked at her then. "I've only had one speeding ticket in my life. Nothing else. I've damned sure never been suspected of murder." His head moved side to side as his gaze dropped back to the menu.

She sighed, set her menu aside. She ate here all the time; it wasn't like she didn't know what she preferred to order—even if she wasn't hungry.

"The burritos are the best in town," she said, deciding to press on. "I rarely eat tacos but the ones here are really good."

He placed his menu atop hers. "Sounds like the best way to go."

Spotting their shift away from the menus, the waitress appeared. "Ready to order?"

Liam waited for Halle to go first. She imagined he wasn't hungry, either. But eating would pass the time, would occupy their hands and mouths. "Veggie burrito," Halle announced. "No extra sauce, please. Water to drink."

He requested the same except he wanted the extra sauce. The waitress picked up their menus and hurried away to turn in their order.

"It wasn't personal," she offered, though she felt confident her reasoning was skewed. "Like Detective Lincoln said, it was just a routine ruling out of possibilities. Standard procedure. Ms. Brewster had a key to her house. My mother does, as well. I'm sure they both had to be ruled out, too."

Okay, he seriously doubted the cleaning lady or Halle's mother were ever considered suspects, but he accepted her attempt to make him feel better.

He made a scoffing sound. "Don't even go there. We both know this was different."

Fair enough. "I suppose you're right."

The waitress arrived with glasses of ice water. Liam thanked her.

As soon as she was gone, he said, "What was that? I don't think I heard you."

Halle rolled her eyes. "You're right."

He executed a nod of acknowledgement. "I feel better now."

She couldn't help herself; she laughed.

"What now, besides lunch, I mean?" he inquired.

"I'm hoping that by the time we're done with lunch, we can go inside the Clark home and have a look at personal papers and photos." She hadn't told him about the photos she'd found of him after he was abducted. This was something he needed to see with his own eyes. She sensed he needed to absorb these truths slowly, through his own observations.

Or maybe she just didn't want to be the one to tell him.

Coward.

"I heard you discussing the possibility with the police chief, but I wasn't sure his agreement included me."

"I assumed it did," she fudged. If he was Andy Clark, he should have access to what was rightfully his. "If you don't mind, we'll go with my assessment."

"You're the boss." He shrugged. "For now."

Halle laughed. "You always let me be the boss."

The words were hardly out of her mouth when she realized her mistake. "I'm sorry. It was just a random voiced thought."

He held her gaze but he didn't bother to argue or to refute her words.

"Andy always went with whatever I wanted to do," she explained, then she smiled. "Not because I was always right or had the best ideas. I think he just wanted to indulge me. Even as a child he was a consummate gentleman. Mom used to laugh and say a good husband always did what his wife asked him to do." Halle made a face. "She never let me forget I sneaked her wedding dress out of that trunk."

A smile cracked Liam's serious expression. "I guess you recognized what you wanted even then."

"We were kids. I had a vivid imagination with little or no impulse control. What can I say?"

To Halle's relief the food arrived and keeping the conversation going was no longer necessary.

REPORTERS WERE HELD back at the end of the block. For now, no one except residents was allowed on the stretch of South High where Halle lived and Mrs. Clark had died. She wasn't sure how long this would go on, but Chief Brannigan had said she could go into the house and look around now. Looking was the extent of her access. She wasn't to remove anything from the house. Detective Lincoln would be on hand to bag anything found that appeared connected in any way to Mrs. Clark's murder.

The chief had passed along that Mrs. Clark's body would be ready for pickup from the coroner's office sometime next week. Halle's mother had already called DuPont Funeral Home to take care of the final arrangements. DuPont's had taken care of Mr. Clark. Of course his wife would want the same. As it turned out, Mrs. Clark already had prearrangements with DuPont's. Judith was grateful not to have to make all the selections.

Halle had given Liam one of her father's ball caps that she kept in her car to wear, in an effort to avoid the prying eyes and cameras of the reporters. She parked in Mrs. Clark's drive. Halle's mother was already there with Detective Lincoln.

When Halle shut off her car she turned to Liam. "You ready?"

"Sure." He reached for the door.

"Just remember," Halle offered, "sometimes we don't understand what makes the people we care about do the things they do."

He held her gaze, his filled with a resignation that

made her regret what he would see inside. But there was no undoing what had been done. She only wished Mrs. Clark were still here to explain.

"If you're trying to tell me something, it's not really coming through."

When she didn't explain further, he got out of the car. She did the same. He waited for her at the porch, always the gentleman.

By the time she reached the porch the door opened and her mother stood there, her face pale, her eyes bright with emotion. Halle went to her and hugged her. The Clarks had lived next door for as long as she could remember. It was like losing a part of the family. It was difficult enough when Mr. Clark passed, but now there was no one left. That era of their lives was over.

Except, she decided as she pulled away from her mother, for the man behind her. And he didn't want to be here. This was not his life. At least not one that he remembered.

For the first time in twenty-five years, Halle fully comprehended that Andy was lost forever. All this time she had told herself that he was somewhere living a good life. All grown up and probably married.

But she had been wrong. Even if she could prove that Liam was Andy, Andy was still gone. The boy she had known, the best friend she'd had, was gone forever. A new sadness settled inside her.

"Let's get started," Judith offered. She smiled at Liam. "It's nice to see you again, despite the circumstances."

He managed a smile and a single nod.

Inside, Detective Lincoln waited. He passed around

gloves. "We've already finished the evidence gathering but it's best if we wear gloves anyway."

Latex snapped into place on hands, the sound somber in the quiet house.

"Ms. Brewster confirmed that nothing was missing," Lincoln explained. "She's been cleaning house for Mrs. Clark for twenty years. If anything was taken, it was something hidden that she had never seen before."

Judith nodded. "I walked through the house and I didn't see anything so much as out of place."

"Except those boxes," Halle pointed out.

"Right," Judith agreed. "Even those were permanent fixtures in Nancy's closet. I helped her get one down once when she wanted a box of photos from hers and Andrew's early life. That one is still in the closet."

They progressed to the hall, like a funeral party moving toward the cemetery. Halle paused at Mrs. Clark's bedroom door. "Maybe we should start in Andy's room. Have a look around before we dig into those boxes."

Judith looked surprised at the idea.

Lincoln nodded. "Wherever you believe is the best place to start."

Halle walked to the end of the hall. She wanted Liam in this room before he had a look at those pictures. She doubted he would actually be in a reasonable emotional state once he saw those photographs.

Andy's room was just as it had been the day he went missing. Superhero posters on the wall. Framed photographs of him and his family, him and Halle, stood on the dresser, another on his desk. That photo included Sparky. The reading book he'd forgotten to take to school that day was on his desk. Halle had been so jealous of Andy's desk. She had wanted one just like his. She smiled. She'd always wanted to be just like Andy. She'd loved him dearly—as dearly as any seven-year-old could.

Liam touched the school banner thumbtacked to the wall. He wandered around the room, almost restless. Halle found herself watching him rather than inventorying the items in the room. He walked to the closet. Had a look inside at the toys piled into the corner. The sneakers on the floor. The clothes hanging on the old-fashioned rod that extended across the long, narrow space. Old houses weren't known for large closets. He closed the door and moved to the dresser. Opened one drawer, then the next, studied the contents of each without touching anything or commenting.

He stopped at the desk last. This time his fingers slid across the cover of the book, along the blotter pad covered in doodles. He picked up the one framed photo standing there. A picture of Halle and Andy the Christmas before he disappeared. They were grinning, crocheted caps on their heads, Sparky photobombing. They had been so happy. They'd both gotten bicycles for Christmas. All sorts of adventures had been planned for spring and summer.

Liam abruptly turned around as if he'd realized everyone was staring at him, and it was true. Judith looked away. His gaze met Halle's and she didn't hold back the "I told you so" from her eyes.

"Everything in here appears to be in order," Halle announced.

Her movements a little unsteady, Judith turned and led the way back into the hall. The dozen steps required to reach Mrs. Clark's room had Halle's tension twisting tighter and tighter. She wasn't sure how to prepare for this. Part of her wanted to warn Liam, but the other part—the reporter's instincts—wanted to see his initial, unbiased reaction.

The bloody bed linens were gone. Likely taken as evidence. The mattress was covered with a clean spread and the blood on the floor had vanished, likely Ms. Brewster's doing. She walked to the first box, the one with all the stuffed animals. "We should probably go through each box. Just to make sure there's nothing hidden under things like all these stuffed animals."

She dropped to her knees next to the box. Judith did the same.

Liam joined them, his expression showing how grudgingly he did so. "Why don't we just cut them all open to make sure nothing's hidden inside?"

Halle stared at him. "Is that what you want to do?"

"Are you still playing shrink?" he demanded, his tone bordering on angry. "That's why you insisted on going through the kid's room first, right? You hoped to evoke some life-altering or revealing reaction?"

Judith looked from Liam to Halle. "Why don't we get started?"

"Good idea," Halle mumbled. She didn't want to argue with him. The way he said the words made her feel mean and selfish. She didn't want to be either of those things. She wanted to do this the right way.

One by one they removed the stuffed animals and toys until they reached the bottom of the box. There were no hidden messages or unexpected items. Just Andy's toys.

Liam hardly looked at any of the items he touched. Rather, he just moved them from the box to the floor.

"I guess we can put them back," Halle suggested.

"You think?"

Her gaze connected with his, noted the anger simmering there. She had evoked a reaction from him, all right. Hard as she imagined he tried, his raw emotions wouldn't be contained. She suspected he realized as much, which was why he was angry and immediately looked away after snapping the remark.

Rather than respond, she and her mother began putting the toys and stuffed animals back. Liam hung his head and joined the effort.

The next box was mostly clothes. Again, the process was tedious. Remove, unfold, refold. Then the clothes all went back in. Again they found nothing of interest or that shouldn't be exactly where it was.

Next was the box with the smaller boxes of photos. They moved slowly through those. Liam paid closer attention now. He studied the boy in the photos. Seemed to analyze the parents shown in each.

"I remember this day," Judith said as she picked up the next photo. "We'd gone to the beach down in Mobile. What a good time we had."

Halle smiled as she moved through the other photos from that trip. "Andy and I buried each other in the sand."

Their attention lingered on the photos for a moment before they placed them back in the box. With that box finished, Halle reached for the one that would change everything. She removed the lid and picked up a photo. Liam did the same. Judith only stared at the ones readily visible on top of the small pile of photos.

"What the hell?" Liam muttered.

Halle looked from a photo to him. "This is you."

He didn't respond. She was right.

"Did she have someone watching me?" He shook his head. "This gets crazier by the minute."

Halle turned to Detective Lincoln. "It appears Mrs. Clark did know Liam. I'm guessing she had someone watching him, sending her pictures."

"If that's correct, then it's possible Mrs. Clark is the one who sent him the article," Lincoln suggested.

Halle looked to her mom. "I agree. Nancy never said anything to you about thinking the person in these photos was Andy?"

"She never showed them to me. You know after that first year, she refused to talk about him." Judith shook her head. "This is astounding. I had no idea." She gestured to the photos. "Someone had to be taking these photos for her. Nancy rarely left home once she gave up on finding Andy. You remember," she said to Halle, "we'd bring their Christmas gifts to them. Birthday cakes. It was as if this house became their tomb long before either one actually died."

Her mother was right. "This is something a private investigator would do," Halle said to the detective.

"It is," he agreed. "Do you know who she used?"

Halle looked to her mother. Judith shrugged. "I know they went to see more than one but I never knew their names."

"Maybe it's time to talk to Mr. Holcomb," Halle said. "He agreed to see me."

"I'll call the chief," Lincoln said.

"LUTHER HOLCOMB IS one of those folks who like living off the grid," Halle explained as she navigated her father's truck along the narrow road that snaked through the backwoods.

Liam was fairly certain this—he surveyed the thick woods around them—was about as off the grid as you could get and still be in the county.

"The chief says he lives off the land and almost never comes into town."

"Let's just hope he doesn't have an issue with strangers," Liam said, working overtime at being amenable. He was still rattled by those photographs.

"The chief called him. He's expecting us."

This news did nothing to make Liam feel more comfortable. In fact, he was fairly certain he'd never been more uncomfortable.

How the hell had Nancy Clark gotten those pictures of him? Most were taken at his home in California or somewhere on the vineyard. There was one from his high school graduation and then another from his college graduation. His father and sister had been right there with him in those photos. Penelope hadn't been in any but that was probably because she'd always been the one doing the taking.

He'd struggled to maintain his composure as they sifted through photo after photo. His emotions had almost gotten the better of him. Being rude or snippy had never been his way and yet he'd been both today in that poor dead woman's house.

But this was his life they were tinkering with. Causing him to question all that he thought he knew. As much as he had missed his father since his death, he had never wished he were here more than today. He needed him to explain how this was possible. Needed him to make some sort of logic or sense out of all this confusing information.

There was no logic and certainly, no sense to be found.

He was Liam Hart. He was not Andy Clark. Those flashes of familiarity he'd felt in the boy's room and in that house were nothing more than the power of suggestion.

Halle had him doubting himself. She, her mother and even the chief of police had planted these ridiculous seeds of uncertainty. He needed to go home and hug Claire and Penelope. To anchor himself.

He glanced at the woman behind the wheel. But all he'd wanted to do while they were in that house was hug *her*. Hold on to her while he rode out this hurricane of emotions.

But he was terrified that she would pull him under. She wanted him to be Andy. There were moments when weakness got the better of him and he wanted to be Andy for her…for the woman who'd collected pictures of him throughout his life…the one who'd possibly sent him that newspaper clipping, maybe in hopes he would come home to her. But he wasn't that person.

"Here we go." Halle shoved the gearshift into Park and shut off the ignition.

Liam stared at the rustic cabin as they climbed out. An older model pickup sat next to it. The door opened and a man walked out onto the porch. His hair was mostly gray, but it was long, pulled back into a ponytail. He carried a shotgun braced on one shoulder.

"Miss Lane," the former chief of police said, "I haven't seen you since you were a little girl."

"Chief Holcomb." She walked straight up to him and gave him a hug. "You look as if you're in your element."

"I am that," he agreed. "Got the peace and quiet I was looking for. No more cops and robbers for me."

Halle smiled. "Chief, this is Liam Hart. He's here helping me with my investigation into Andy's case."

Luther eyed Liam for a long moment. "When I first saw him climb out of your daddy's truck I thought you'd found Andy." He cocked his head and studied Liam openly. "You look just like him, Mr. Hart."

"That's what they tell me," Liam said. He figured that was a fair and reasonably safe statement.

"I have a couple of questions for you, Chief, if you have a few minutes."

He nodded. "'Course. Come on in." He turned and started back to the door. "It ain't much but it's mine and can't nobody tell me what to do or expect anything from me."

There was something to be said for that, Liam supposed.

Inside, he and Halle sat on a well-worn sofa while Luther settled into a recliner that looked about as old as he was.

"I'd offer you some of my latest batch of shine but I got a feeling y'all ain't the type."

"Thank you," Halle said, "but I'll pass."

Liam held up a hand. "I'm with the lady."

Luther propped his shotgun against the wall next to his chair. "Fire away, Miss Lane."

"You should call me Halle, Chief."

"Well, then you need to call me Luther. I haven't been the chief in a long time."

"Luther," she acknowledged. "I read the case file

from when Andy vanished. I'm convinced by what I read that you did all that was possible to find him. My father still sings your praises."

"Outside the boy's momma and daddy," Luther said, "there is no one who wanted to find him more than I did. But it didn't happen. This was no random abduction. Whoever took him had been watching for a long time, waiting for just the right opportunity. That's why we couldn't find him. The kidnapper had paid attention to every detail. Nothing was left to chance."

Liam thought of the detailed work his father did. When he'd died, Liam had been certain he would never be able to keep the books and operate the winery as meticulously as his father. He certainly would never be as organized as him.

But that didn't mean anything. His father had been a good man—a great man. He would never have stolen a child under any circumstances. No way. The idea was utterly ludicrous.

For a few minutes, they talked about what was already known, the time and place of the abduction, the way the police chief had investigated it, how interest had waned after a short time and he'd still kept the case open, hoping for a break.

"Mr. and Mrs. Clark hired a private investigator," Halle said. "Do you recall his name or the names if there was more than one?"

"They did talk to Doc Boone. I don't know what came of the visit. The Clarks never mentioned it again." Luther scratched at his chin. "The trouble is Doc Boone died a few years back. But his daughter, Jessie, took over the business. She probably has his files. She's a year or two younger than you, Halle, so I don't know how much she'll recall from the case. Don't hurt to ask, either way."

"It does not," Halle said. She stood. "Thank you so much for helping us out, Luther."

Liam stood, as well.

"Happy to." The former chief pushed to his feet.

"If you recall anything that might be useful, please let me know. Chief Brannigan gave you my number, I believe."

"He did, and I assure you I will."

Liam and the other man regarded each other a moment but neither said anything.

When they were in the truck once more, Liam asked, "We going to see this Jessie Boone now?"

"We are."

Liam had changed his flight for one on Monday. He wasn't sure staying that long was a good idea but it was done now. Might as well make the most of his time here. Prove to these people that he had nothing to hide. And prove to himself that he had always been Liam Hart.

THE BOONE AGENCY was off the square by one street. Luckily for them the office was open and Jessie Boone was willing to talk.

"Daddy always said that was the worst case of his career," Jessie said.

She was an attractive lady. Blond hair done up in one of those big hairdos. Her clothes were skintight. She had that sort of brassy, sexy vibe down to a science, and while Liam admired her style, she wasn't his type.

"It was a tragedy," Halle agreed.

"I'm happy to pull the case file and show you my

daddy's notes," she offered, "but I can tell you now there's nothing there. Luther called and asked me to help y'all out if I could, so I had a look to refresh my memory. Daddy wasn't one to take people's money. He only worked on the case a few days and when he didn't pick up a trail he told the Clarks he wasn't the man they needed."

"Do you recall or did your father perhaps annotate who they went to next?"

"He sure did." Jessie nodded. "Daddy recommended they go to Buster Dean over in Tullahoma. He had a bigger operation than Daddy's. Back then he had about four fellas working for him. I don't know about now. But he's the man you need to talk to."

Halle thanked the lady and they left the same way they had arrived.

Empty-handed.

Chapter Eight

NOW

Tullahoma

Before driving to Tullahoma, Halle exchanged her dad's truck for her car. She was more comfortable in her vehicle and had only used her father's for the rough ride to Holcomb's place. Once parked at their destination, she and Liam climbed out and walked around the corner to the PI's business address.

Buster Dean's office was situated on West Lincoln Street next to London's Bar and Grill on the corner at North Wall Street. Halle had never had any reason to visit the PI's office, but she had eaten at London's numerous times.

Dean's office was closed. No surprise. It was well after normal business hours. Still, it was disappointing.

"I guess we can try finding his home address and see if he's there," she suggested and pulled out her phone to go to an address search website. No luck. A PI would know how to keep his personal info private.

"Nothing," she said to Liam. She nodded toward the

restaurant. "Maybe someone next door will know him well enough to have his home address." She started toward London's. The trouble was, that person might not be willing to give out the info.

Only one way to find out.

London's was already packed. It was Friday night, after all. The vintage venue was chock-full of charm with its wood floors and exposed brick walls. A waitress, young, brunette and dressed like a model, approached and asked how many in their party for seating purposes. She glanced at Halle but her gaze settled on Liam and stayed there.

"Actually," Halle said drawing the other woman's attention from Liam, "I'm trying to locate Mr. Dean. His office is already closed and it's urgent that I see him. Do you think your manager might know his cell phone number or his home address? I'm a reporter and we're doing a story on his legendary history in the world of private investigations."

The woman blinked once, twice. "I'll ask her."

She turned and disappeared into the dimly lit sea of tables.

"Did you learn to improvise like that in reporter school?"

Halle met his wary gaze. "I learned that long before, but I've honed the skill over the years."

His eyes narrowed, telegraphing his suspicion and impatience.

"Don't worry, I would never improvise with the important stuff. Everything I've told you and shown you is the truth to the best of my knowledge."

He looked skeptical still, but he said nothing.

The waitress returned with another woman, this one

older and far more harried-looking. She wore black slacks with a white boyfriend-style shirt, the collar turned up. Her dangly silver earrings bounced against the white cotton. "I'm Kelly Kessler, the manager tonight," she said. "How can I help you?"

Halle restated her improvised mission, infusing as much excitement into her tone as possible. She even added, "I understand London's is one of his favorite hangouts."

The woman grinned. "For more than forty years now."

"Great," Halle enthused. "That's the kind of detail that will be perfect for my piece." She frowned then. "Unfortunately, I didn't make it down from Nashville in time to catch him in the office. It was supposed to be a surprise that he'd been chosen for the feature. Now I'm not sure I'll be able to find him and I have to submit the story early on Sunday morning."

"Oh, well, we can't have Buster missing out on this chance." She removed a card from her bosom and the pen from behind her ear and started to scribble. "I'll give you his cell number and his home address. This card has my number on it, so if you have any trouble, call me and I'll track him down."

She offered the card to Halle. "Thank you. I will absolutely call you for some more shout-out lines." She looked around. "This is a great place."

Beaming, the woman nodded. "Happy to help."

Halle thanked her and returned to the car. When they'd climbed in, she called the cell number and the call promptly went to voice mail. "Motlow Road it is," she announced, starting the car. She would not be defeated just yet.

Highway 55 led out of Tullahoma proper and it only took a few minutes to reach Motlow Road. Tullahoma was a nice town. Home to Motlow College and boasting its share of historic sites, golfing, boating and even a few tourist attractions like the George A. Dickel & Company Whiskey Distillery.

"Have you heard of this PI?" Liam wanted to know.

"I've heard the name over the years, generally related to some court case. Dean has been around the block a number of times. My father could probably tell us more about him. He falls into the category of men who people don't fully trust but they go to him when they need the kind of help only he can provide. But I've been gone for a while, so his reputation might be different now."

"Do you plan to stay? In the area?"

She glanced at him; he was watching her. Had been. She'd felt his gaze on her. "I don't know yet. Maybe. My parents are getting older and I'm all they've got." She shrugged. "I've always thought about writing a novel. My job here would allow plenty of time for that."

"Like your Aunt Daisy?"

Halle smiled. Surprised that he remembered. "Sort of, but I think I'd prefer true crime."

"What?" he asked. "You don't believe in romance? One failed marriage and you're ready to throw in the towel?"

Now, there was a tough question—two actually. "I do believe in romance. I look at my parents and I can't not believe in romance. It's basic. In our genetic makeup. But my writing interests run more to the kind of reporting I've done in recent years. Homicides. Missing persons. That sort of thing."

"So this is just another story for you."

She slowed for the turn onto Motlow Road. "No." She glanced at him again. "Not at all. This is about finding the truth. This is about a part of *my* life."

He didn't say more. Good thing. Halle needed to focus on the house numbers that were listed on the mailboxes. The houses were set too far back from the road for the numbers to be visible on the home's front door.

Buster Dean lived in a midcentury modern sort of farmhouse with all the typical architectural lines of the era but with board and batten siding and a metal roof. There was a barn and fencing for horses and, from the looks of the property, a good number of acres.

Halle hoped there were no dogs that might bite strangers.

She got out of the car. Liam did the same. Silence crowded in around them. No barking dog, thankfully. No sound of work being done somewhere on the property. Just the peace and quiet of country living. No one was around. Not what Halle had hoped for.

They crossed the yard uneventfully. A half dozen or so hard knocks on the front door and the silence still echoed in the air. No sound inside, either; at least none she could hear.

"Maybe he's out with friends," Liam commented. "Or on a case."

"Apparently. I'll try his cell again later." She surveyed the yard. "For now, it's back to Winchester, I guess."

More of that silence followed them out of the driveway and back to Winchester. Twenty minutes of no words, just the occasional sigh, mostly from her, and a little traffic noise as they maneuvered through evening commuters. She was glad there were no reporters holding vigil outside her house or the Clarks'.

When they had pulled into her drive, he said, "Maybe I should get my rental car out of the Clarks' driveway."

"No rush. It's probably a good thing that it's there. People will think someone is home."

He didn't argue. Instead he followed her up to her apartment.

"Several of the restaurants in town deliver. What's your preference? American? Chinese? More Mexican?"

"You pick," he said.

"Chinese it is, then."

Halle left her bag on the sofa and made the call. When she tossed her cell onto the coffee table, she said, "Forty minutes."

He looked around as if uncertain what to do next.

"Have a seat and we'll hash out what we learned today."

"Did we learn something?" He dropped onto the sofa.

She joined him, with an entire cushion between them. "We learned—" she picked up her cell and opened the photos app "—that Nancy Clark believed you to be her missing son." She passed him the phone with the photos she had snapped during their search of the boxes in Nancy's bedroom.

He swiped through the photos of him from various times in his life, his expression unreadable. "I don't know why she had someone watching me," he finally said. "I am not Andy." He passed the phone back to Halle.

Her shoulders slumped. "How can you still dismiss the idea? These photos are you. They were taken by a woman whose son looked exactly like you in his childhood photos. One coincidence I could buy, but two? As a child, you could have been Andy's twin. You had a dog—an identical dog—named Sparky. Come on. She probably sent you that newspaper because somehow she knew who you were."

"You can't be certain she sent it," he argued.

"You know she did. It's the only reasonable explanation."

"There is nothing reasonable about this, Halle." His jaw had gone rigid, blue eyes icy with tension. "Don't you think I would remember if I was abducted when I was seven years old? It doesn't make any sense. What are you going to suggest next? That my father did some sort of brainwashing technique?"

"I've done my research, Liam," she said calmly. She wasn't some rookie or a fool. "Most memories up to the age of seven are forgotten. The few that linger beyond that age are hardly ever reflective of reality. They've been reshaped into something that fits whatever your life is at that point. So the answer is no. Particularly with a little coaching, you likely wouldn't remember your childhood here if you were removed from it for the rest of your life."

"Come on. You're saying I was taken and suddenly I stopped being Andy Clark and started being Liam Hart? Give me a break."

"Of course I'm not saying that. It would take time and work. But you have mentioned plenty of memories of when you were eight. By then you were settled in, fully convinced home was where you were."

He shook his head. "I can't buy it."

"Will you believe DNA? You did say you'd willingly leave a sample for the test."

"Sure. Why not? The sooner I can put this behind me, the better."

Halle wished she could save him the wasted effort of pretending. He was Andy Clark. There was no other option.

"I'll call Chief Brannigan and see if he can set it up. That way it's official."

"Great." The sarcasm that accompanied the word made her flinch.

He was tired, frustrated and no doubt confused. Halle gave him grace for those reasons when what she wanted to do was shake him.

LIAM WAS READY TO RUN outside and down the stairs to yell at the top of his lungs. *My name is Liam Hart. I am not Andy Clark.*

Except…there were some things that needed to be cleared up. Like why that poor murdered lady had someone taking pictures of him for her. And why Sparky used to be Andy Clark's dog. Or at least a dog that looked exactly like Sparky.

Jesus Christ, he felt like he was in an episode of *The Twilight Zone*. He kept waiting for someone to wake him up from this crazy dream.

His gaze lit on Halle as she answered the door. Was the food here already? He blinked and watched as she paid the delivery guy. He should have done that, but he couldn't bring himself to speak up or to even move. He was stuck in this in-between place that felt completely wrong but somehow strangely right.

Some part of him felt a connection to this clever reporter. Maybe it was just plain old desire, considering he had been too busy for a social life—much less a sex life—for a few months now. Maybe it was nothing more than basic nature.

Except it felt like more. In the past twenty-four hours his instincts had drawn him closer and closer to her. He felt like he'd known her his whole life. He refused to tell her as much. Hell, she was already fully convinced that he was this Andy Clark.

But he couldn't be. If he was that would mean his entire life since age seven was a lie. He would not allow her or anyone else to take that from him. He loved his father. Missed him so much. He loved Penelope and Claire. He would not permit anyone to tell him that they weren't really his family.

He couldn't.

His cell vibrated in his pocket. He pulled it from his jacket. *Claire.* He walked to the kitchen area, his back to Halle and the delivery guy and answered. "Hey. Everything okay?"

He had sent his sister a text message today and told her he'd decided to stay a few more days but there hadn't been time to call and discuss his reasons. Now, he supposed, was as good a time as any.

"So why are you not coming home before Monday?"

She sounded curious but he heard no alarm in her voice. Good. "The woman who sent me the article was murdered last night."

"Oh my God, are you kidding?"

"Afraid not. The chief of police wants me to stay a couple days. He thinks she was murdered because I showed up."

"Are you a suspect?"

The alarm was loud and clear now. "No. No. I am not a suspect." He opted not to mention that he'd been cleared of suspicion.

Halle had placed the food on the counter and was looking at him as if she feared there was more bad news.

He turned the phone away and said, "It's Claire, my sister."

Halle nodded.

"Are you with *her*?" Claire asked.

Gone was the alarm and in its place was something like defensiveness or a protectiveness. Was his little sister worried about the big bad reporter? Liam had to smile.

"She's standing right in front of me," he said. "Would you like to speak to her?"

"No! Why would I want to speak to her?"

As his sister ranted on, he whispered to Halle. "She's a little shy."

Halle smiled and he relaxed. Her smile did that to him more often than not. Another of those strange connections between them.

"I called Mom."

Liam stilled. "Why did you do that? She's in Paris on vacation. This will just upset her and she doesn't need that in her life." His frustration spiked again. He had no interest in hurting or worrying Penelope. Not until he knew more, and the path was clearer.

"Because we need answers. She's the only one who might have some. Especially since you said that woman was murdered. Oh my God. This is just awful."

"What did you say to her?" Just how big a deal this

was going to turn into with Penelope was what Liam needed to know.

The scents of ginger and sesame and garlic were prodding his appetite. He'd been certain he wasn't hungry until those sweet and spicy smells invaded his olfactory senses.

"I told her about the newspaper article and that you were in Winchester looking into it."

He knew his sister. She'd just given him the condensed version. "And what did she say?"

"Not a lot really. She did a lot of listening and about the time she started to respond, the connection went haywire. All staticky and breaking up. She promised she would call me back but she hasn't yet."

He could only imagine what his stepmother was thinking. She had been a great mom to him, still was. From her perspective she might think he was casting her off in search of a new mother.

"I wish you hadn't done that, Claire." He pressed his forehead to the nearest cabinet door and closed his eyes. "I didn't want her upset by this."

"She didn't sound upset."

He dropped his head back and stared at the ceiling. "You just said the connection was broken and staticky. How do you know she wasn't upset?"

"Because what I did hear sounded brisk and commanding. Her usual tone."

"Okay—" he shook his head "—so she wasn't upset. She's angry. That's so much better." Why did little sisters—even after they were adults—have to be such a pain in the butt?

"Trust me, Liam, she is not upset or angry. She's just considering. You know, processing the information."

"Fine. Fine. Fine." He would hear from Penelope by tomorrow. He was certain of it. Maybe that was good, though. He could explain why he felt compelled to do this.

"When are you coming home? I mean, really."

He loved that her voice told him that she missed him, was worried about him. "Monday."

"Good. Don't delay your flight again. It sounds as if all this trip has done is create more questions than provide answers. I'm sorry I urged you to go."

"You have my word that I will not delay unless I have no other choice."

He frowned at his own words. He almost sounded as if he expected to have to postpone leaving again.

Ridiculous.

"Okay, if I hear from Mom, I'll let you know."

"Don't worry, Claire Bear, everything is under control."

"I always know when you're lying," she warned.

"Good night, Claire."

"Love you!"

"Love you, too." He ended the call and took a deep breath. He liked his life. Which was why he didn't like thinking of it not being real.

His gaze shifted to the woman opening Chinese takeout boxes. But some part of him wanted her in it. How screwed up was that? He barely knew her.

She turned to him as if he'd said the words out loud. "You call your sister Claire Bear?"

He smiled at the memory of his little sister as a baby. "She growled when she was a baby. I started calling her a bear and it stuck."

Halle's eyes were bright as if she were about to cry.

Had he said something wrong? Reminded her of some memory that made her sad? Oh wait, just looking at him made her sad because he looked exactly like her long-lost childhood friend. How could he forget?

"That's what I called Andy. Andy Bear. Because he was like a life-size, cuddly teddy bear."

Liam pressed his hand to his gut and went for a subject change. "Man, I'm hungry."

She blinked and turned away. "Well, let's eat, then. When we're done, we have a lot of talking to do. Details to go over."

He nodded. "Yes, ma'am. You're the boss."

She looked at him and he realized his mistake.

Andy always let her be the boss.

THEN

August 1
Twenty-six years, eight months ago...

"I CAN'T BELIEVE school starts in two weeks." Halle wasn't ready for second grade. She really, really wasn't. Her mom had bought her all those new clothes and shoes and still she was really freaked out about second grade.

"It's no big deal," Andy assured her. "It'll be just like first grade except we already know how to read. We'll learn lots of new stuff. Harder math and junk like that. It'll be easy as pie, as my dad says."

Halle groaned and rolled to her side to look at her best friend in the whole world. "I don't know about that harder math stuff. I'm not so good at it. Remember in first grade how I had a bumpy start. Ms. Gardner said so."

He stopped counting stars in the sky and turned his face to hers. "I'll help you. Just like in first grade. Don't worry."

She smiled. He was right. He had helped her past that bumpy start. "'Kay."

She relaxed onto her back and stared up at the dark sky and tried to find where she'd left off counting. Not possible. Ugh. They were lying on a quilt in her backyard. It was nearly bedtime. Would be bedtime already if school had started. But their moms let them stay up a little later in the summer to do fun stuff after dark. Like catching lightning bugs and counting stars.

"What if we're not in the same room together," Halle dared to whisper. She had crossed her fingers every night as she went to sleep, hoping and praying that she and Andy would be in the same room again this year.

"My mom said we will be in the same room," Andy assured her. "She spoke to the principal or something." He rolled his head to the side and grinned at her. "She said your mom did, too."

Halle made a pretend mad face. "She didn't tell me. All this time she's been saying, we'll see. We'll see." She said her mom's words in a silly-stern voice.

Andy laughed. "Even if we weren't in the same room we would still be best friends. Right?"

"Right." She turned back to the stars and silently repeated the words she'd said every night all summer:

Star light, star bright,

The first star I see tonight;

I wish I may, I wish I might,
Have the wish I wish tonight.
I wish to always be with Andy.

Chapter Nine

NOW

Saturday, March 14

Liam was surprised that he didn't hear from Penelope. Maybe she was too angry or hurt at his actions to call. He didn't blame her. She had gone above and beyond to treat him as much like her own child as she did Claire. He didn't want her to see this as some sort of betrayal to her or to his father.

He sat in his rental car across the street from the Lane and Clark homes.

Halle had asked him to be here by nine. It was eight forty-five now. He'd arrived a few minutes early just to think.

Two news vans still loitered on the street but the chief of police had warned them not to park in front of the Clark or Lane homes. A police cruiser went past every couple of hours. Liam had seen it go through five or so minutes after he had arrived.

Most of last night had been spent tossing and turning. His dreams had thrown him back and forth be-

tween this life—the one Halle had told him about—and
the one he'd always believed to be his.

He studied the house where Andy Clark had lived.
He imagined the boy playing in the yard, chasing after
his dog named Sparky. Climbing that big oak. Liam
shook his head. How was this possible? Instincts he
wanted to deny hummed, warning that there was more
to this than he wanted to see. Halle Lane felt as familiar to him as anyone he had known his whole life and
yet they had only met the day before yesterday.

Before he could stop himself he was climbing out of
the rental car. He strode across the street to the Clark
home. Yellow crime scene tape flapped in the breeze,
slapping against the front porch railing. He walked all
the way around to the back porch and sat down on the
steps. He stared out over the lawn, then closed his eyes.
In his mind he could see the basketball hoop that used
to be attached to the side of the garage. He opened his
eyes. It wasn't there but he somehow knew it once was.

He shook his head at the foolishness of playing this
game with himself. Yet, he closed his eyes again and
looked backward. Back to a different time. He saw
his dog Sparky, his tongue hanging out as he bounded
around, wanting to play chase or ball. A memory of
Sparky digging ferociously in one of the flower beds
had his eyes opening again.

He walked back to the flower bed he'd seen in the
memory, real or imagined, beneath the dogwood tree
and considered it for a time. He needed a shovel.

Before second thoughts could stop him, he strode
to the picket fence that separated the yards, hopped
over it and kept walking until he reached the Lanes'

garage. Halle exited her door and looked down at him from the landing.

"I was about to come looking for you."

He frowned. "Is it nine already?"

"Ten after." She started down the stairs, her bag slung over her shoulder, one of those thermal cups likely filled with water or coffee in her hand.

He ignored the idea that he'd been daydreaming in that backyard for nearly half an hour. "I need a shovel." He said this before his brain could catch up with his emotions.

He shouldn't be doing this…shouldn't encourage her delusions.

Except that he was the one having delusions now.

"Okay." She descended the final step. "My dad has all sorts of garden tools in there." She gestured to the walk-through door that led into the garage at the bottom of the stairs.

He went inside, turned on a light and located a small shovel. He didn't want to damage the flowers, so small would work best.

Shovel in hand, he turned off the light, pulled the door shut and walked back to the fence, hung a leg over and then the other one. At the dogwood tree, he walked around it once, then selected a spot and started to dig. Halle moved up beside him and watched while he nudged around between the roots. This was a really old, really big—for a dogwood—tree.

He found nothing. He moved over a foot or so, spread apart the daffodils sprouting from the soil and mulch and started to dig once more.

"Can I ask what you're looking for?"

"I don't know." The tip of the shovel hit something hard.

He scraped back more of the dirt with the shovel, careful not to damage whatever he was about to unearth. Something metal and shiny glinted as he scratched against it.

"It's the time capsule!" Halle crouched down. "Andy never told me where he buried it. He was supposed to, but then…"

"He didn't come back."

Liam stared at the metal object. It was shaped like a thermos, silver or stainless steel, something along those lines.

He squatted next to Halle as she pulled the time capsule from the ground. She swiped the dirt from it and gave the top a twist.

She grunted. "I can't budge it."

She offered it to Liam and he stared at it for a long while before taking it into his hands. The canister felt cold against his palms. He gripped the length of it with his left and grasped the top with his right. It took a couple of tries but the lid twisted open.

He couldn't look inside. His heart was pounding and a cold sweat had formed on his skin. He gave the thermos-like object back to Halle.

She placed the lid on the ground at her feet and used two fingers to reach inside. The first item she withdrew was a photo. Andy and Halle with their bicycles, his was blue, hers was red.

She laughed. "I wanted a big bicycle so badly. I warned my mother that when she bought me one it better not be pink. Pink was for sissies."

Liam stared at the photo and in his mind it seemed

to come to life, like those live photos he took with his cell. This was what he saw: he could hear Halle laughing. Watched his big grin as he burst into laughter, too.

"What were you laughing about?"

She stared at him—he didn't need to look, he felt her eyes on him. Then he realized what he'd done.

"We," she said pointedly, "were laughing at the idea that since we had big kid bikes we could see the world."

He passed the photo back to her. His gut clenched hard and more sweat oozed onto his skin.

She reached into the capsule again and this time she pulled out a folded page and something else fell out with it. He picked up the dried four-leaf clover that had fallen to the cold ground. Instantly images of the two of them on their hands and knees, combing through the grass, whispered through his mind. He blinked them away. This—all of this—was putting ideas in his head. The memory couldn't be his. It was hers...and Andy's.

She held the piece of paper and tears slid down her cheeks.

He closed his eyes and banished the feelings that surged. *Not real. Not me. Not possible.*

"Dear Halle, we're probably old now," she recited. "But whatever we are and wherever we are, we'll still be friends. Your best friend, Andy. PS: my mom helped me spell all the words right."

She swiped her eyes and tucked the letter and the photo back into the tube. Liam dropped the four-leaf clover inside.

"We should—" she cleared her throat "—straighten this up and head out to Tullahoma. That PI called me back. He said we could come by his house. Let me go wash my hands."

Liam grabbed the shovel and pushed the dirt into the now empty hole as Halle went back to her apartment, taking the time capsule with her. By the time he'd stowed the shovel back into the garage and washed up at the sink there, she'd descended the stairs. Hands empty and clean.

She nodded and led the way to her car. They climbed in and she put the car in Reverse and started to roll down the drive. Her mom waved from the kitchen window. Halle waved back and Liam did, as well. Mrs. Lane's face was suddenly replaced by the young face of Nancy Clark. She waved and smiled and his heart thumped.

Liam closed his eyes, shook his head to clear the image.

"Did you have breakfast?"

"Yeah." When she had backed onto the street he dared to open his eyes again. "You?"

"Are you kidding? My mother insists I come to her kitchen and have breakfast with her and Dad every morning. Then I hurry back to my place and brush away the smell of bacon and grits and seriously strong coffee."

No matter that his brain felt bruised from all the bouncing back and forth from the past to the present, he laughed. "That sounds way better than my extra dry muffin and fake OJ."

"You should have breakfast with us tomorrow," she suggested. "Mom and Dad would love it. Plus, if you're leaving on Monday it will be an opportunity to say goodbye."

"I am leaving on Monday." That pounding started

in his chest again. He took a deeper breath and ordered himself to calm.

"How did you know about the time capsule?"

For about three seconds he considered not answering. He'd had enough questions. The answers were even worse than the questions. He didn't want to do this.

"I didn't know. I just felt the need to dig around those flowers. It was…"

He didn't know what it was.

When she didn't respond he added, "I remembered Sparky digging at those same kinds of flowers. Maybe that's why I did. We have flowers like that back home."

"You had a memory of being in that yard."

Damn it. "The power of suggestion is a formidable force. That's why when there are multiple witnesses to a crime, the first thing the police do is separate them. If one witness hears the other's story, there's a good chance the second witness will mold his or her story to that of the first witness."

"True," she agreed. "But I didn't mention anything about a time capsule. I'd forgotten."

"You mentioned the dog." The words came out harsher than he'd intended. He pressed his head against the seat. He didn't want to think right now. He felt confused and rattled and in way over his head.

"I did mention the dog." She sighed. "I'm not trying to convince you, Liam. I'm really not. It's best if the evidence convinces you. I think that's happening and the evidence is prompting memories. Not me."

But she was wrong. So wrong. It was her. Her crazy red hair. Those green eyes. All those cute little freckles she didn't even bother to try and hide. It was the sound of her voice. The tinkling of her laughter.

It was everything about her.

THE DRIVE TO Tullahoma was as somber as a wake. Halle wished there was something she could say that would make him feel better but there were no words. This was real and he had to get right with it.

Understanding his reluctance was easy. He had a childhood and parents who loved him. He had a sister, a home. Memories. He didn't want those things to suddenly be wrong, and to suggest that one or both of his parents in California had somehow been involved in his abduction was the only way to make sense of the truth she'd thrust in front of him.

This truth was unpalatable. It called into question who and what he had thought he was. She wished there was a way to do this differently. To make the transition easier or smoother.

But there wasn't an easy slide into this reality.

There was only what they were doing right now.

Halle made the turn off Motlow Road into Mr. Dean's driveway. She rolled all the way to the end, which was quite a distance. He'd told her to come around back since he would be spending the day readying his garden for planting.

She and Liam exited simultaneously and she led the way around back. A German shepherd sat at the garden gate. His ears perked up, eyes keen on the visitors. Halle stalled. Liam did the same.

"Jinx won't bother you, come on in."

The voice came from beyond the weathered wood fence. Liam suddenly stepped in front of her and started forward. He walked past the dog with Halle on his heels. As his master had said, Jinx only watched them pass.

Buster Dean was a large man. At least six-four and 250 pounds. Even at his age, late sixties, Halle surmised, he looked ready to lead the defensive linemen for a pro football team. He was muscular and had the bearing of a man half his age. The only concession to his age was his gray hair.

He propped his garden hoe against the fence and dusted his hands off. "How can I help you folks?"

Halle thrust out her hand. "Mr. Dean, I'm Halle Lane. We spoke on the phone. And this is Liam Hart, my friend."

He shook her hand and then reached for Liam's, gave it a quick shake.

"You mentioned having questions about that lost boy. The one who went missing all those years ago." He glanced at Liam as he said the last.

"Yes, sir. Andy Clark."

"Well—" he scratched his head "—I'm not sure how I can be of any help, but fire away and we'll see what hits a target."

"Mr. Boone in Winchester recommended the Clarks to you when they were looking for a private investigator to help find Andy." Halle held her breath. Couldn't help it. She needed this man to know something that would point them in a helpful direction.

"That's right," he agreed. "Mr. and Mrs. Clark came to me about a month or so after their boy went missing. They were desperate to find him, like any parent would be."

"Were you able to find anything, Mr. Dean?"

He cocked his head and looked at her. "I read the piece you did in the *Gazette*, young lady. If this is for some sort of feature in a Nashville paper, I'd like to know now, seeing as you don't live or work there anymore."

Inwardly, she groaned. She'd been caught. The man was a PI. Of course he did his research. His friend from London's had called him. "I'm hoping this will be a feature. Maybe even a book one day."

She felt Liam's gaze on her.

"The truth is," she said quickly, "it doesn't matter whether it's another article or a book, I—we want to know what happened to Andy Clark. He was my friend, my best friend."

Dean heaved a big breath. "I found nothing. It's the only case in my entire career that left me stumped. The trail was as cold as ice. Whoever took that boy was careful. Meticulous. There wasn't a single mistake. A lot of painstakingly thorough planning went into that abduction."

"Did the Clarks give up at that point?" This was not what she had wanted to hear.

"I don't think so. The two didn't strike me as the type to give up. They wanted to find their boy. Mr. Clark mentioned a lawyer up in Nashville they'd spoken to about adoption. Evidently they'd had problems having a child of their own and were thinking about adoption at some earlier point in their lives. Suddenly she was having a baby and that was that. But she said this lawyer had a PI and they wondered if I knew anything about him. I figured they were willing to pay top dollar on another man, but I really didn't see anyone turning up anything new."

"Do you remember his name or perhaps you made a

note of him in your file on the Clarks?" Halle needed to know in case the Clarks had contacted him.

"I don't know who the PI was, but the lawyer was David Burke. He's the one with those billboards all over the place and the annoying commercials."

Halle knew the one. The jingle that played with every commercial was one of those things that stuck in your head. "Thank you, Mr. Dean." She pulled a card from her bag and handed it to him. "I hope you'll call me if you think of anything else that might help us in our search for the truth."

He looked over her card and nodded. "Be happy to. Y'all be careful out there, now. Some of the folks in my profession don't like to discuss their clients or their cases. They can take offense at anyone showing curiosity. Caution should be your watchword."

Halle thanked him again, then she and Liam walked back to her car. She'd hoped seeing the man in person would stir some memories or unearth more info than a phone call, but they still had little to go on.

When she had settled behind the wheel and he was in the passenger seat, she asked, "You up for a trip to Nashville?"

"Sure." He looked at her as she turned around and headed away from the PI's house. "If you would like, I can drive. I feel kind of useless being chauffeured around."

"Actually—" she flashed him a smile, thankful that the tension he'd felt since finding that time capsule seemed to be diminishing "—that would be great. I'll stop at a gas station before we hit Interstate 24 and you can take over."

"Sounds good."

"THIS IS IT," Halle announced as Liam slowed for a turn into the driveway of the Jackson Boulevard home. To her surprise the security gates were wide open.

The driveway rolled through the manicured trees and circled in front of the house, which was a grand three-story Southern antebellum mansion. Liam parked in front of the house on the cobblestone parking pad.

"This is where the rich people in Nashville live?" Liam asked as he surveyed the massive house and endless landscaping.

"Belle Meade. One of the neighborhoods where the rich live richly." She grinned. "Let's see if Mr. Burke is taking visitors."

They emerged from her sedan that looked completely out of place sitting so close to this multimillion-dollar home. On the way here, since Liam had driven and wasn't in the mood to talk, she had spent the time doing a little research on Burke.

He'd been married three times, had children with two of the wives. His children were grown and living all over the world according to Google. His last wife had divorced him, citing irreconcilable differences. Halle stared up at the towering mansion. Why would a single man want to live like this? The house had to be twenty thousand square feet.

But then David Burke was incredibly rich. At sixty-seven he had spent the first thirty years of his career taking all sorts of cases and pushing to win bigger settlements. At some point during the latter part of those first thirty years he'd found his formula apparently. He was suddenly one of the richest men in the southeast and was on every who's who list in the state. He still took the high-profile cases, but now people respected those silly commercials and repetitive billboards. After all, Burke was practically a celebrity.

Halle pressed the button for the doorbell. Traditional chimes echoed through the entry hall and good God, what an entry hall! She could see it through the windows on either side of the door. Marble floors and a sweeping, open-style staircase that rose up to the third floor, pristine white banisters overlooking the entry below. Select pieces of no-doubt priceless art hung on the walls. A chair and a bench were placed just so. And in the middle of it all was a beautiful fountain much like one you would see in a lavish mall. She wondered if the bottom would be littered with coins.

As they watched, the man himself strode to the door. Burke looked exactly like the photographs on the internet. Medium height, medium build. Dark hair that was fringed with gray. Ordinary. If you passed him on the street you would never know he lived in a house such as this unless you recognized the designer label that stated loudly and clearly that his suit cost a small fortune all on its own.

He opened the door, looked surprised. Apparently he'd been expecting someone else. "Who are you?" he asked, looking from one to the other. Then he held up a hand. "Please. I don't go to church and I have no interest in learning about your beliefs." He reached into his right trouser pocket. "If it's a donation you're looking for—"

"Mr. Burke," Halle interrupted, "my name is Halle Lane and this is Liam Hart. We're here to discuss the Clark case with you."

His gaze lingered on Liam. Halle wasn't sure if he

thought he recognized him or if he was simply interested more in Liam than Halle.

"Clark case?" He shifted his attention to Halle. "Are you referring to the boy who disappeared all those years ago? I saw something in the paper recently about that case."

Halle decided not to point out to him that it was her story he'd seen. Every newspaper in Nashville had picked it up.

"Yes, that's the one. I'm a friend of the family and Mrs. Clark recently passed away. In settling her estate and going through some of her papers, there was a reference to you. I thought perhaps you could shed some light on what sort of help you provided the Clark family." She'd come up with that cover on the way here, as well. It wasn't entirely untruthful. Her mother would be settling the Clark estate and they had been going through her papers.

"Yes. I recall now. Why don't you come inside out of the chill?"

It was a little crisp this morning. "Thank you."

Halle followed him inside and Liam stayed close behind her. Burke led them across the foyer that extended from the front of the house to the back, and to the right into a large great room or family room. There were two huge televisions hanging on the walls and a sofa large enough for a party of twenty. The sofa was a sectional, like hers, only leather and about five times larger. The view out the floor-to-ceiling windows was of more lush landscape and an enormous pool.

"Can I offer you a drink?" Burke held out his hands. "Water, coffee, something stronger? Scotch? A martini?"

"No, thank you," Halle declined.

Liam shook his head, declining also.

"In that case, let's get to the point. As we say in my line of work, time is money—even on Saturday. I have a client coming, which is who I thought you were." He gestured to the sofa. "Please, sit."

Halle lowered to the edge of the sofa. Liam sat beside her while Burke took a seat across the coffee table from the two of them.

"The Clarks came to me when they still lived in Nashville. I don't know, maybe thirty-three or thirty-four years ago."

"They wanted to adopt," Halle suggested. Mr. Dean had mentioned as much.

"Yes. You may or may not be aware but at the time older couples had a strike against them when it came to adoption. There were questions like potential health issues that might come into play during the adopted child's early years. The Clarks had run into a bit of that sort of thing and decided to try for a private adoption. Their finances were more than adequate to consider going that route, so they came to me. I had already forged quite a reputation. My name had become nearly synonymous with private adoptions."

"But they didn't go through with an adoption," Halle said, recalling the rest of what Mr. Dean had said.

"That's correct. Mrs. Clark learned she was pregnant and they decided not to pursue the adoption."

"When did they come to you next?" Liam asked, speaking for the first time.

Halle was startled that he had but she was glad. He was part of this; he should speak up.

"Maybe two months after their little boy went missing." Burke made a sad face. "It was such a tragedy. The rip-your-guts out kind of devastation."

"Were they planning to try adopting again?" Liam asked.

"No, no. They wanted my help with finding him. The police were coming up empty-handed and they thought I might be able to help. I have quite a team of investigators at my disposal. They had met the investigator who checked out all the birth parents for the adoptions I handled. I suppose they were impressed by his work and thought he might be able to help them find their son."

"Was he able to help them?" Halle asked.

"No, sadly not," Burke said. "I think that news was like a stake through the heart for the already desolate couple." He shook his head. "I wish I could have done more."

"We'd like to speak to this investigator," Liam said.

Halle was impressed. He was learning the tricks of her trade. "Being able to speak to him would be immensely useful," she tacked on.

"Unfortunately, he no longer works for me. In fact, we lost touch about seven or eight years ago. He opened his own shop. I think the emotions involved with the adoption process started to get to him."

"If you could give us his name, we'll pay him a visit and see if he can help us," Halle prodded. "I can't tell you how important this is, even now, twenty-five years later."

Burke's brow furrowed for a moment, then he raised his eyebrows. "Well, of course." He smiled kindly, ever the showman. "I can even tell you where his office is unless he's moved recently."

"Thank you, that would be very helpful." Halle pulled out her cell and readied to enter the information into her notes.

"Frank Austen with an *e*. His office is—or was—on Nolensville Pike." He provided the street number. Didn't have his new cell number. It had apparently changed since he worked for Burke.

"Thank you, Mr. Burke." Halle stood. "We really appreciate your help."

"Certainly." He smiled that megawatt smile he used in his commercials and on his billboards.

He walked to the front door with them. Once they were across the threshold Halle hesitated. "You wouldn't happen to have his home address? Since it's Saturday we might not be able to catch him at the office."

"I can tell you where he once lived, but I have no idea if he's still there."

"That's a starting place," Halle urged.

Burke provided the street address and Halle thanked him again.

When they reached the car, Liam said, "Why don't you drive? You know your way around downtown Nashville."

"Sure."

When they were driving away, Liam spoke again. "He watched us leave before going back into the house."

"He probably doesn't have people show up unannounced at his private residence very often."

"I got a bad vibe from that guy."

Halle glanced at him before pulling onto the road

that would take them back into Nashville proper. "I noticed he was checking you out when we first arrived."

"No, not that kind of vibe. The kind that tells me he's not a nice guy."

This was more true than he knew. Halle had found considerably more in her research than all the success stories about Burke. There were rumors he was in trouble with the IRS and he'd been sanctioned by the court on more than one occasion.

But if the name he'd given them could help find what they needed, Halle would be grateful.

Chapter Ten

NOW

Frank Austen's office was closed and he wasn't at home. No surprise there, Liam decided. He wasn't sure what they could expect on a Saturday. They had gotten lucky with the lawyer, Burke. If he hadn't been expecting a client, he probably wouldn't have been home and they would never have made it past his gate.

Liam would have expected a celebrity—a notorious one might be a better term according to all that Halle had told him—to have private security on site at his home. Maybe he'd given them the day off in deference to his expected appointment. Or maybe his security staff had been monitoring the meeting and would have appeared if needed.

Sometimes it was all about the appearance. He had a feeling David Burke liked to come off as relaxed and in control at all times. But no one was that good. Everyone made mistakes, kept secrets.

Even his parents, apparently.

He wanted to believe none of this was possible but

every minute of each day he was with Halle, he understood it was more than just possible.

This was real.

But Liam wasn't ready to fully accept that conclusion unconditionally. Not yet anyway. Some tiny part of him still held out a desperate hope that his life was really what he believed it to be and not something else… something sinister and filled with secrets and lies and betrayals.

"I'm taking you to lunch at my all-time favorite place," Halle announced. She shot him a questioning look. "If that's okay with you?"

He shrugged. "Sure. There's not much I won't eat."

She flashed him a smile. "Good. I like a guy who isn't afraid to be adventurous."

Just when he'd thought nothing could make him smile. "Good to know."

They shared a look and warmth spread through him. He knew that gaze: it was as familiar as his own reflection.

He decided to relax and enjoy the urban landscape as she drove. It seemed every time he opened his mouth he said more than he intended or the wrong thing. Or she looked at him a certain way and he suddenly felt that bond that couldn't possibly be real.

Traffic was a bear but Halle knew her way around. If she saw a bottleneck ahead, she changed their route. She was a bold driver. Nothing he hadn't expected. Her personality was bold.

When she parked in front of a seriously low-rent-looking diner, he was a little surprised and a whole lot skeptical. The place wasn't at all what he had expected.

The building looked old and even a little run-down, and, frankly, kind of sketchy.

"I promise they have the best burgers in the world."

Liam glanced at her and made an agreeable sound. There wasn't a lot to say. Still, judging by the number of cars parked around the place, there had to be something halfway decent going on inside.

"It's one of the oldest—if not the oldest—places in Nashville," she explained as they got out. "You're as likely to run into a celebrity as anyone else. The atmosphere is totally laid-back."

He nodded, deciding to reserve judgment for now.

Inside she grabbed his hand and led him through the bar area and to the dining room. She waved at a waitress who literally whooped at seeing her. The waitress hurried over and ushered them to a table—the only free one in the room. Classic Formica and metal tables, like from the fifties or sixties.

"I haven't seen you in forever, girl," the woman gushed before giving Halle a big hug. She turned to Liam then. "Who is this gorgeous human?"

Halle laughed. "Melany, this is Liam Hart. Liam, Melany. She's the best waitress in town."

The woman grinned. "That and a good tip will get you everywhere, honey. Now, sit and tell me how you've been."

Halle took a seat, and Liam did the same. While she brought her friend up to speed, he pulled a menu from between the napkin holder and the ketchup bottle and gave it a look.

"You won't need that, sugar." Melany took the menu from him and stuck it back where he'd gotten it. "You want the cheeseburger, fries and a cold draft brew."

"Trust her," Halle said. "It's the best."

Liam gave the lady a nod. "I'm in."

"Great. I'll be back in a flash."

Melany hurried away, waving and saying hello to other customers as she passed.

"The staff is definitely friendly," he noted.

"Always."

As promised, Melany was back with two frosty mugs of beer. "Enjoy!" And then she was off again.

"So you came here often," Liam said as he picked up the mug.

"At least once a week. I lived on Woodmont in Green Hills. It was like six or seven minutes to get here. My ex wasn't so keen on the place, so I didn't come as often as I might have."

"The ex." Liam nodded. "Tell me about the ex."

She blinked, looked a little reluctant but didn't balk. "He was good at his job. Very good. He's still one of the top television producers in Nashville. I was a mere lowly reporter but I was good at my job, too."

He'd seen her list of awards. She was good then and now, if the article on Andy Clark was any indication. "But something went wrong."

"He was busy. Always. He wasn't home a lot. The longer we were married—which wasn't that long—the less time he had for me." She shook her head. "Putting all the blame on him isn't really fair. When we married, I was exactly like him. Work was everything. We were the perfect fit. We grabbed the moments we could and were perfectly happy to let our careers be the priority. And once in a while we even shared the same bed or a meal. He wasn't the one who changed, it was me."

"You wanted the whole package," Liam suggested.

"The career, the marriage, kids, house with a white picket fence."

It didn't matter if she answered. He knew this about her. Somehow. The idea was at once exhilarating and oddly terrifying. How could he know her feelings unless all that she alleged were true?

"Yes. I wanted it all. Once I passed thirty, something changed inside me. My biological clock started ticking or whatever. But he didn't feel the same way. He was years away from wanting that sort of commitment. So I left him. Moved back into my old place in Green Hills and waited for him to see the error of his ways. But he didn't. He simply moved on. One day there was a knock on my door and a messenger delivered the divorce papers." She shrugged. "He was never one to waste time on a project he didn't feel strongly about."

"Are you still in love with him?" Liam wasn't sure why he felt the need to ask the question. It was none of his business but somehow he needed to know.

"No. Sometimes I think I never really was." She sipped her beer. "I was in love with the idea of him. The idea of us, when what I really loved was my work. But something inside me changed and nothing felt right again."

The food arrived and Melany waited as they checked to see that all was to their liking. Liam took a big bite of his burger and moaned. Halle and Melany were correct. The burger was fantastic. He told Melany as much and she beamed.

When the waitress had moved away, Halle patted her lips with her napkin and then said, "Told you so."

For a few minutes they focused on devouring their food. The burgers were juicy and tasty. Liam was reasonably certain he'd never had better. Even the fries were damned good. The icy cold beer was the icing on the cake.

"Now it's my turn," she announced when she'd finished off her burger.

"You still have fries on your plate," he pointed out. He picked up the last one of his and popped it into his mouth.

"Don't try and change the subject."

He made a confused face. "How could I do that? I don't even know what the subject is." This was not exactly true. She wanted to ask him questions about his social life. Quid pro quo.

"Tell me why you haven't married."

"I guess I was like you. Focused on my work. My dad passed and it felt like I needed to do even more. Claire is always telling me I work too hard. But she's the same way. Penelope—my stepmother—has just been sort of lost since he died. She spends as much time away from home as possible."

"What happened to your birth mother?"

"I asked Dad that once and he said they were hiking in the mountains and she fell. When he reached her, she was dead. She may have died instantly but he had to be sure so he climbed down to her with me in tow. Anyway, there was no way he could carry me and her body off that mountain, so he marked the place on the trail and carried me out. When he and the authorities went back, her body was missing. They searched for days but never found her remains. The local wildlife evidently dragged her off to their cave or den."

"I'm so sorry. That must have been truly horrible for your father and you."

"I really don't remember anything about it but it was tough for him. He never liked talking about her death. He would talk about her life, but not the end."

"Completely understandable." Halle shook her head and traced her finger around her sweating glass for a moment before asking her next question. "No girl-friend back home?"

"No." He downed the last of his beer. "No girl-friend."

"There's never been anyone special? Someone you considered spending the rest of your life with?"

"No. The past year was really the first time I consid-ered the idea of what happens next. I don't know if it was a delayed reaction to my father's death or if it was just that biological clock thing for guys." He grinned. "Whatever happens next, I haven't figured it out yet."

"When we were kids—" she stopped. "When I was a kid," she amended, "Andy and I used to talk about the future. He wanted to be a policeman or a fireman. A hero." She smiled. "He loved the idea of helping other people. If things had been different, I'm certain he would have been class president and received all sorts of awards and scholarships. He was so smart and so passionate about life."

Her words brought up more haunting similarities. Liam had never been able to ignore the underdog or those in need. Even Claire had warned him recently that he couldn't give so generously to every charity under the sun. Didn't matter that he'd been class presi-dent, either. That was more likely because he was nice to everyone. No reason to mention that ancient history. It would only be another detail she would use as evi-dence of her claims.

"After you showed up," she said, drawing his attention back to her, "I did some research on you. You do more than your share of giving back, as well. You've been honored by community leaders on several occasions."

"Just following in my dad's footsteps." Luke Hart was a bigger hero than Liam could ever hope to be, which was all the more reason the idea of him stealing a child was simply not plausible.

"Tell me about your father."

Melany showed up to see if they needed another round. Halle ordered water this time. Liam went with her choice.

When the waitress had walked away, Halle looked at him expectantly.

"His name was Luke, Lucas Alexander Hart. He never went to college but insisted that Claire and I did. He started with nothing and somehow managed to talk the bank into lending him the money to buy the vineyard and winery." Liam shook his head. "Whenever he told that story, he always laughed and said it was a miracle they didn't toss him out. But for whatever reasons they gave him the loan and he turned the place into what it was meant to be all along. If he was here, he would also tell you that Penelope was his anchor. Without her he couldn't have managed."

"Sounds like the two of them had a good marriage."

"They did. He always insisted the key was that you had to be friends, too. They were good friends."

The water appeared on the table, along with the check.

"I think he was right," Halle said when the waitress had moved away. "Friendship was missing from my marriage. We were colleagues and lovers but never friends, not really. My parents didn't like him, either, so that was a definite downer. But I think we would have had a far better chance had we been friends, too."

"He was a fool."

She met his gaze, then smiled. "Thank you. I think so, too."

She reached for her bag but he stopped her with a hand on her arm. "It's my turn," he argued as he grabbed the check.

He stopped at the counter and paid on the way out. As they zigzagged through the still crowded lot to reach her car, Halle abruptly stopped.

Liam glanced around. "What's wrong?"

She shrugged. "Maybe nothing. I just had that hair-raising sensation." She laughed. "You know, when it feels like someone is watching you."

He took a moment to slowly scan the street and the parking lot. "I don't see anyone now."

She exhaled a big breath. "Maybe it was my imagination."

He opened her door for her. She stared at him a moment, then said, "Thanks."

He climbed in and fastened his seat belt. There was another question burning in his brain but he waited until she had backed out of the slot and pulled out onto the street before he asked. He hadn't been able to stop thinking about it since they were at Burke's house. "Were you considering writing a book about his disappearance?"

"I'd thought about it, but the time never seemed to be right." She braked for a traffic light. "Some part of me thought maybe if I put all my thoughts and memories into a book, just maybe if he was still alive and out there somewhere, he would read it and remember. He would know we hadn't forgotten him and that we still love him."

He stared at her profile as she moved her foot from the brake to the accelerator and the car rolled forward. The line of her jaw, the rise of her cheekbones, her lips, her nose, all of it filled him with a sudden sense of longing. How would it feel to have someone love you that much? Not a parent or a sibling, but a friend…a lover? His heart started that confounded pounding.

He understood how it would feel. It would feel exactly like this.

Liam looked away. He desperately needed answers. As hard as he tried to keep fighting the possibility that he was, in fact, Andy, that certainty was quickly draining from him.

THE PI, Frank Austen with an *e*, lived in a seriously low-rent neighborhood. The duplex was a box-style brick with no architectural features or interest. Very plain, very flat, save the shallow peak of the roofline. A chain-link fence separated the two halves of the small front yard. A cracked and discolored concrete driveway rolled right up to the door on each side. Like earlier, there was still no vehicle in the driveway. Halle turned in just the same and parked.

"This time if no one comes to the door," she said, "we'll start calling on the neighbors."

"Burke wasn't sure he lived here anymore." Liam opened his door and got out of the car. Across the top, he said, "If he has moved, maybe one of his neighbors will know where."

"We can hope." Halle draped her bag over her shoulder and made the short journey to the front door.

While she knocked without garnering a response, Liam decided to have a look around. He walked to the side of the house, opened the gate that separated the driveway from the backyard. Around back was the same, plain, neglected property, nothing to draw the eye from the drab reddish orange brick or the mostly dead grass. Like the front, the yard was cut in half by the same style chain-link that bordered it. A small concrete patio, five-by-eight or so, bordered each back door. A six-foot wooden privacy fence about eight feet wide had been put up on either side of the chain-link to provide some visual separation from the two patio areas. The patio on this side had a chair and a table. On the table was an ashtray overrun with cigarette butts. If the PI still lived here, he was a heavy smoker.

Liam walked to the back door. Gave a knock. Nothing. No sound inside whatsoever. He tried the knob but it was locked. From the looks of the knob it wouldn't take much to open it. He moved on to a window and cupped his hands to have a look inside. Yellow-with-age blinds prevented him from seeing much. Fortunately, several of the louvers were broken, so he managed a glimpse here and there.

"Do you see anything?"

Liam jerked away from the glass. "You couldn't warn me that you were behind me?"

"I thought about it." She grinned. "But the opportunity to startle you was too good to pass up."

"You've always liked doing that."

Their gazes locked and held for a moment longer, with him holding his breath at the realization that came out of nowhere, her looking uncertain what to say or do next.

"You can't see much inside," he said, moving on, "but what you can see makes it look as if whoever lives here is planning a trip or maybe moving."

Halle walked around him and peered through the window, moving from broken louver to broken louver just as he had.

There was a suitcase on the bed and it was already half filled with men's clothes. The dresser drawers were pulled out, their remaining contents hanging haphazardly. The closet doors stood open, many of the hangers now empty.

They moved to the next window, which looked into the kitchen. Dishes were stacked in the sink. An abandoned coffee mug sat on the counter.

"Maybe he's taking a vacation." Halle led the way back around to the front of the house. "Let's go door-to-door and see what the neighbors have to say."

Since the other half of the duplex had a For Rent sign in the window, they moved on to the first neighboring house, the one on the left of the driveway, where a woman with four kids lived. The duplex couldn't have had more than two bedrooms. She had no idea who lived in the house next to her. She quickly closed the door before Halle could ask anything else.

Surveying the street as she moved toward the house on the other side of the duplex, Halle said, "If we don't get anywhere with his residential neighbors, maybe we can find someone next door or across the street from his office. No matter that it's Saturday, there might be someone working around there."

When they'd checked out the guy's office, Liam had

spotted one of those check-cashing places that looked open. "It's worth a try."

He wasn't entirely sure what Halle hoped to learn from this PI. But anything he knew might provide insights, he supposed.

Halle knocked on the door of the next house. Dogs barked, shattering the quiet inside. The yaps told him the animals were small ones. Halle knocked again. Someone inside shouted, "Hold your horses." Female, he decided.

A moment passed. Liam suspected the woman inside was having a look through her security peephole. The door opened a crack. "If you're peddling something, I ain't buying."

"Sorry to bother you, ma'am," Halle said. "We're looking for Mr. Frank Austen. He lives next door to you." She gestured to the house next door. "We've been to his office and now here and we can't seem to find him."

The door opened a little wider. The two little dogs she held, one white and one gray, wiggled in her arms. "You probably know he's one of them private investigators," she warned. "They don't like nobody getting in their business."

"Yes, ma'am, I know," Halle agreed. "But it's very important that we find him."

They might be in luck. It sounded as if he still lived here and that this woman knew him.

"He ain't home much," the woman said. "He travels a lot. Does a lot of them stakeouts like on TV. Sometimes we have us a few drinks and talk about it. He's got a lot of stories to tell."

Now Liam got the picture. "Have you and Mr. Austen known each other for a while?" he asked.

"Oh yeah," she said with a wink. "We've been neighbors for thirty years. I watch out for his place when he's out of town and he brings me little gifts from his travels. I like snow globes. I've got a whole room full of them." She narrowed her gaze at Liam. "I know you were back there nosing around behind his house. He won't like that."

"I thought maybe he was out back smoking and didn't hear us. It's really important we find him," Liam urged. "Not to mention I worried he might be ill. It happens. A man without anyone to check on him."

The neighbor shook her head. "Don't nobody ever check on him except me. I don't think he's got no family and he always said if anyone come around it was probably trouble." She looked from Liam to Halle and back. "Are you two trouble?"

"No, ma'am," Halle denied. "We just need to find him. A friend of ours went missing a few years back and I'm hoping he can help us."

"Oh, I hate to hear that. Far as I know, he's in town. I saw him come in yesterday at the butt crack of dawn. I took coffee to him a little later and he looked like hell. He said he'd been up all night on a stakeout. Grumbled about being too old for that stuff anymore. I haven't talked to him since. He left out this morning around eight and he hasn't been back. Since he didn't ask me to get his mail, he's probably coming back tonight or tomorrow. He doesn't like for his mail to sit in the box."

"If I give you my cell number," Halle asked, "will you call me when he comes back home? It really is very important."

"Sure. Let me get a pen and paper." She disappeared into her house.

"He may not be coming back," Liam whispered.

Halle nodded. "That's what I'm worried about."

"Here we go." The lady appeared back at the door with no dogs in tow. She put her pen to the pad she held. "What's your number, hon?"

Halle provided her cell number.

"Do you have his number, by the way? We could try calling him," Halle said.

The woman hesitated, then gave them the number quickly, as if she was unsure whether to share it.

"He don't often answer," she told them. "Just takes the messages and he calls back if wants to."

They thanked her and left. Neither Liam nor Halle spoke again until they were in her car.

As she backed out of the drive, he said, "His packing up could be coincidence?"

Halle looked at him before continuing into the street. "I don't know. He's lived here all these years. His career is here. My article comes out and suddenly this PI who may have done some work for the Clarks twenty-five years ago is packing up to go."

"Wait, wait, wait." Liam held up his hands as she shifted into Drive and started forward. "Are you accusing a man you've never met of some illegal activity more than two decades old? How are you making that leap? You don't even know him."

"It's just…" she said, then shook her head. "I don't know. A feeling. I've had this creepy feeling since we left Burke's house. Something isn't right about him and this Mr. Austen with an *e*."

Liam agreed with her there, for sure.

"Let's try calling him," Halle said, "even if he hardly ever picks up. You remember the number?"

"Etched in my brain." He pulled out his cell, tapped in the digits and waited. Just as the neighbor had predicted, it went to voice mail. He left a message, saying he was a potential client and needed to talk to him about a job.

After he clicked off, he looked at Halle. "Where to now? Do you know anyone in town who might be familiar with this PI? A cop or someone?"

She braked at a stop sign and grinned at him. "You're brilliant."

Liam closed his eyes and leaned his head back. Not brilliant enough, he decided. Or he wouldn't be having all these doubts about who he was. While she drove, he forced his mind to go backward, to dig into his childhood. He focused on his dog, Sparky. He had loved that furry mutt. He relaxed and let the memories flow. For better or worse, he let himself float into the past.

THEN

Twenty-five years, one month ago...

ANDY SAT ON the porch. He felt sick. He wanted to cry but he was too big to cry. He dropped his head into his hands.

Sparky was gone.

He'd looked everywhere.

His dad had driven him all over the neighborhood. They had talked to all the neighbors and no one had seen him.

It was the worst day of his life.

"Come on, Andy, we've got stuff to do."

He raised his head and looked at Halle. He hadn't heard her walk up. "I don't feel like doing anything." He frowned at the big bag hanging around her neck. "What's that?"

"It's the stuff we gotta do." She sat down beside him and opened the bag. "I got Mom's little hammer. I got thumbtacks and I got tape. And these." She pulled out a paper and showed him.

He stared at the photo of Sparky and his stomach hurt. The flyer read, "LOST DOG. His name is Sparky. Please bring him home." Andy's name and address were under the photo. Then in big letters were the words "REWARD $20."

His eyes got big. "Is my dad offering a reward?"

"Uh-oh." Halle made a face. "I didn't think to ask him."

Andy's face puckered with disappointment. "Then what's this?" He pointed to the line about the reward.

"That's how much was in my piggy bank. Mom helped me count. Twenty dollars." She poked herself in the chest with her thumb. "I'm offering the reward."

Andy hugged her tight. "Thank you, Halle. You're the best friend ever."

She wiggled out of his arms. "Come on. We gotta put these up all over town. Mom's gonna take us."

Andy smiled. His eyes, burning again, forced him to blink them fast. "'Kay."

Hand in hand, they skipped over to her yard.

What would he do without Halle?

Chapter Eleven

NOW

Halle's detective friend was following up with a witness on another case but he promised to catch up with her as soon as he was finished. Until then, he suggested she wait at a place called the Pub on Eleventh Avenue South. It was close to his location.

Wasn't a hardship to hang out. The place was a British-style pub with a variety of cocktails, wines and whiskeys from which to choose. The atmosphere was not unlike one of the pubs he haunted back home. Lots of elegant wood details on the walls and around the bar. Upholstered chairs and classy tables. Soft music. People engrossed in conversation at the tables. The waiter had brought elegant stemmed glasses filled with sparkling water. Liam wasn't a big fan of the stuff, but it was something to do while they waited. Halle pretended to look over the menu, but she wasn't likely hungry any more than he was. They were basically killing time. Waiting to connect with yet someone else who might know some tidbit about Andy Clark's disappearance.

The lost boy.

Liam had almost ordered a whiskey neat but he'd talked himself out of it. He needed a clear head. But that trek down memory lane he'd taken while she drove across town had shaken him. The memory was vivid, too vivid. He'd been worried about Sparky and Halle had made posters offering a reward for the missing pup. There were parts of the memory that he could definitely say her words had prompted—had put the idea in his head—but there were others that had come straight from somewhere deep inside him. Straight out of his own past, or what felt like his past.

There had to be a way to unfurl these scattered clues and sensations and emotions so that he could look at them as a whole, rather than only in pieces. The fragments promised something they had not as of yet delivered—the whole story. As much as he wanted to dismiss his growing suspicions about his identity, there was something here. Some part of this was accurate and he needed to understand why.

Unless this PI or the detective had information that would point them in the right direction, he didn't see how he would ever know the whole story. There was, of course, the possibility that if any of this was actually true, his father may have confided in Penelope. But to interrogate her could cause her pain, he was sure. Why should he put her through that until he knew more?

Liam shook himself. What was he thinking?

His father would never have done this and if he was Andy, someone else had stolen him from the Clarks. But why wouldn't his father tell him if he was adopted or had been taken in under less than normal circumstances? Luke Hart had not been a liar or a kidnapper—he was a good man. A loving, compassionate man. That left no other option except his bio mom, but she had died when he was two.

Or had she?

He didn't remember her or her death. What if his father was covering for her?

Enough.

Liam pushed aside the troubling thoughts. He needed to focus on something else for a while. He leveled his attention on Halle and said, "Tell me about this Derrick Carson."

Halle looked up from the menu. "He's a detective with Metro."

Liam toyed with the stem of his glass. "I know that part. I mean, besides that. You laughed a couple of times when you were talking to him. Sighed one of those little breathy whispers. Fiddled with your hair. You two have a thing?"

"Breathy whispers?" She laughed, then clasped her hands atop the menu as if she worried she might reach up and fiddle with her hair again. She did that when she was thinking, he had noticed. What had she been thinking when the detective was chattering away in her ear?

She moistened her lips and looked directly at him. "No. We do not and never have had a *thing*. He has asked me out to lunch or dinner, to a movie once, but I've always declined. He's a friend. Nothing more."

"Ah." Liam nodded. "The detective has a thing for you but you don't feel the same way. Maybe he's still hoping you'll change your mind."

She smiled and shook her head. "The *detective* is a nice man who dates lots of women, but I never wanted to be one of his women."

"A player," Liam suggested.

"A player," she agreed. "But he's a good cop. We can trust him."

As hard as he tried to stay away from the subject of those unsettling memories that had haunted him today, Liam couldn't keep them out of his head. "When the dog went missing," he began, determined not to use the name Sparky, "you mentioned that was a few weeks or a month before Andy disappeared."

"Three weeks," she said. "Andy was devastated. I wanted to do something to help. My family and I had searched with him and his family but Sparky seemed to have vanished. So I took all the money out of my piggy bank and my mom helped me make flyers offering a reward for his return." Her face turned sad. "We really tried but we could never find him, and the next thing I knew, Andy was gone, too."

He nodded, his throat too tight, too dry to respond. His memory was accurate. Real. Too real.

She stared at him for so long he had to look away.

"Can you still pretend I'm wrong? That you aren't Andy?"

"Liam," he reminded her. "Liam Hart. I'm not Andy Clark." The words ripped from his aching throat, tasted bitter on his tongue.

"Is it because you don't want to think that the man you believed to be your father stole you from your real family?"

"That man was my real family." Liam spoke louder than he'd intended. A couple at another table glanced their way. "Sorry," he said to Halle. "I can show you photos of my father when he was a young man and a child. I looked just like him. Same hair, same eyes.

Same dimple in the chin." He tapped his chin. "I don't know how to explain all these other flashes of—" he shrugged "—insight into the childhood you shared with Andy, but I am telling you my father was Luke Hart."

"Andy's dad, Andrew Clark, had blond hair and blue eyes, too. No dimple, not a chin one anyway. I've seen pictures of him as a young man and maybe one as a child. I can't say that he and Andy looked very much alike beyond their coloring. Andy's features were more like his mother's—like Nancy's. Her hair was darker than his when she was very young, her eyes a shade or so lighter. No dimple, either. The similarities were more in facial structure. The jawline, the nose."

"Well, there you go." He relaxed more fully into his chair. "My father and I could have been twins."

She sat quietly for a minute or so, watching him, assessing him.

"Go ahead." He sipped his water. "Say it."

"We have to do the DNA. It's the only way you'll ever know for sure."

He drew in a deep breath. "What about extended family? Did the Clarks have any siblings? Cousins? Any family that you're aware of?"

"None. They were both only children and their parents had passed before Andy was born."

How convenient. His instincts stirred. He was onto something but he couldn't quite put his finger on what that something was. "They moved to Winchester from Nashville when Andy was eighteen or nineteen months old."

"Nineteen," Halle confirmed.

"Were they ever visited by out-of-town company? Maybe old friends from Nashville. Even if their parents had passed, surely they had friends. Colleagues? People from the church they attended?"

Her brow lined as she considered his question. "I can't remember anyone visiting them. Let me call Mom and ask."

She dug into her bag and withdrew her phone. Before she could call her mom, it vibrated in her hand and the screen lit up.

"Hello."

She listened for half a minute, then thanked the caller and disconnected. Her gaze locked with his. "That was Austen's neighbor. He's home."

Liam left a bill on the table for the water and a tip and they were out the door.

Halle drove slightly above the speed limit to arrive at the duplex in the shortest time possible but the driveway was empty. As she and Liam exited her car, the neighbor bounded out her front door, wiggling dogs in her arms.

"He didn't stay long," she explained. "He went in the house, came out with his suitcase and drove away. I tried to wave. Holler at him but he didn't even look back. I got a feeling whatever is on his tail, he don't want to be caught. Something ain't right. I've known him too long. This ain't like him."

Halle had a feeling the lady was more right than she realized. "Thank you. Please, call me if he or someone else shows up."

"I sure will," the lady promised.

Halle hesitated, turned back to her. "What kind of car does he drive?"

"A black four-door Ford Taurus. Had it forever."

"Thanks again!" Halle waved and hurried to the

car and slid behind the wheel. Liam was already in the passenger seat. "Let's check his office again," she said as they snapped their seat belts into place. She tossed her bag onto the back floorboard and placed her cell on the console. "His neighbor is right. Sounds like he's on the run. We should have staked him out instead of going after my detective friend," she said with regret.

"He could be headed to the airport for all we know."

She backed out of the driveway and pointed her car in the direction of Nolensville Pike. No way was she letting this guy get away.

"If he's headed to the airport, there's nothing we can do. Chances are we wouldn't catch him before he got through security. If we get to his office and he's not there—" she glanced at Liam "—I'm going in to see what I can find. If we're really lucky, he left something behind."

"I doubt your detective friend will be too happy about that move."

"Won't be an issue unless he finds out."

They exchanged a look. "In that case," he said with a widening grin, "I'm in."

Halle shook her head. It was very possible they would both be in jail before morning. As long as they had cells next to each other, she could live with that.

The traffic was heavier now. The quickest way across town to their destination was 440 but it would still take time. Halle merged into the traffic, her fingers tight on the steering wheel.

Her cell vibrated. She glanced at the screen. *Derrick*. She ignored it for now. There was no time to slow down. He would only want to know where she was. She would call him after…*this*.

By the time she reached the exit for Nolensville Pike her nerves were frayed. She had barely pulled onto the pike when traffic came to a dead stop. No! She clenched the steering wheel even tighter and leaned forward to see what was causing the bottleneck.

Blue lights…red lights throbbed in the distance. Police cruisers, two ambulances…a firetruck…this was bad.

"Looks like a major pileup," Liam said, taking the words right out of her mouth. "Hold on."

She turned to look at him as he was opening his door and standing up in the open doorway. She started to ask what the hell he was doing but before she could string the words together to rail at him he was getting back into the car.

"Three-or four-car accident. Injuries, from the looks of things. We're going to be here awhile."

Halle leaned her head back against the seat and groaned.

She had to do something. She checked her rearview mirror and then her side mirror. *Clear.* She eased into the right-turning lane and turned onto a side street that would take them away from this logjam.

No sooner than she turned, other cars started doing the same. The short street led around behind a gas station and intersected with Glenrose Avenue. She took a right on Glenrose and zigzagged over to Whitney Avenue. Whitney would take them beyond the accident and then they could take Vivelle back to Nolensville Pike.

Hopefully.

Her pulse was racing by the time she made all the turns and was back on Nolensville Pike heading toward their destination once more.

It would be dark in another hour and she had a feeling Frank Austen would be gone forever, taking whatever secrets he knew with him.

She slowed and made the turn into one of the few parking slots in front of the office. Austen's office was a part of one of those low, squat strip buildings from a long-ago era. There were bars on the plate glass windows as well as the doors. The sign was turned to the "Closed" side. There were only the five parking slots, not an actual parking lot, and all were empty except the one she'd used. On the opposite end was a vacant office. Across the street was a check-cashing place and a smoke shop.

They were out of the car and at the door and peering beyond the bars before either of them spoke. The deserted lobby was all that was visible from the front windows. A desk, a few chairs and a low table with a stack of magazines. From the dog-eared pages, she surmised they had likely been around a while. A single framed piece of artwork hung on the wall behind the desk. The decor looked as if it had been purchased at a budget motel fire sale.

"Come on," Liam said. "Let's see if there's parking or an entrance in the back."

Her heart thumping against her sternum, Halle followed Liam around the corner of the building.

A black Ford Taurus sat close to the building, the trunk lid raised. Halle's pulse jumped. He was here.

Liam was suddenly pulling her behind him. She wanted to ask why but decided if he had a reason, staying quiet was the better idea. They moved together, like the perfectly choreographed steps of a pair of cops entering a crime scene.

The back door was ajar. Halle knocked on it, causing it to push inward, and called out, "Mr. Austen! My name is Halle Lane. It's very important that I speak to you. We tried to call you!"

They waited. No answer. She called out again. Still nothing. Liam pushed the door fully open and eased inside. Halle stayed close behind him. The door led into a narrow corridor. The first door on the left was a bathroom. A few steps beyond on the right was a small lounge with a refrigerator and a microwave, a table and chairs.

The next door on the left led into a fairly large office. No windows. A long row of file cabinets stood against one wall. Shelves loaded with books and framed documents lined another. In the middle of the room was a long metal desk with two chairs flanking it and another behind it but pushed back so that it sat against a cluttered credenza.

Liam held up his hand. "Stay here."

She followed his gaze, noting the pile of folders on the desk that had been overturned.

He moved around the desk and grimaced. "You might want to call that detective friend of yours now."

Halle skirted the desk and considered the dead man on the floor. Definitely Austen. She had pulled up photos of him on the internet. He had one bullet hole in the center of his forehead. His unseeing eyes stared at the ceiling. His crumpled legs were tucked under him in an odd angle.

Liam knelt next to him and touched his carotid artery. "Definitely dead but he hasn't been for long. His skin is still warm."

A chill raced over Halle. The killer could still be

nearby. She pulled out her phone and dialed Derrick's number. "Sorry I missed your call." The statement seemed ridiculous under the circumstances but she needed a moment to frame how to tell him about the dead man on the floor in front of her or how she'd entered the premises without an invitation.

"No problem. I'm at the Pub. I was just about to order another beer, where are you?"

"I'm at Frank Austen's office." She provided the address. "He's been murdered."

Derrick swore softly. "Don't touch anything. I'll call it in and head that way."

Halle put her phone away. "He said not to touch anything."

"We can look," Liam suggested, "as long as we don't touch, right?"

"I believe we can."

Austen had been going through his files. The pile that had fallen over had sent folders and their contents sliding over the floor. He had probably been looking for ones he wanted to take with him or destroy. No PI would want his work files discovered by just anyone who walked in, especially the police.

Halle read as many of the names on tabs as she could see. None were the Clarks. She moved to the file cabinets. She used the tail of her jacket to open first one drawer and then another. Liam glanced her way and she said, "I'm not touching it. My jacket is."

He laughed and started doing the same at the man's desk, except he used a tissue from the box on the credenza to keep his prints off the drawer handles.

When they had finished, they turned back to stare

at the body on the floor. Liam said, "He could have something in his pocket. A thumb drive maybe."

Halle bit her lip. This would be their only chance to check. "That's possible."

The smell of gasoline and then a distinct whoosh resonated from the back of the building. They'd left the door open.

Halle started that way; Liam was close behind her.

The explosion that followed was loud enough to deafen anyone in or near the building. Liam yanked her back into the office. Debris showered down in the corridor. Liam's arms were around her, his body wrapped around hers like a shield.

For a few seconds she couldn't hear anything. Then there was the sound of flames hissing and sizzling. Liam stood, pulled her to her feet.

"Was that his car that exploded?" she asked.

"I can't imagine what else it would've been." He started forward again, moving toward the rear door through which they had entered. Halle stared at the pieces of metal and glass strewn across the floor. Damn. She'd been right. The killer had been hanging around.

Liam stayed in front of her. When they reached the door he looked out first. She poked her head between him and the doorframe. The Taurus was in flames. Sirens were shrieking in the distance.

"We should go around to the front," Halle said, surveying the area in hopes of spotting the culprit—possibly Austen's killer—responsible for that creepy feeling haunting her. Someone was watching them. She could still feel it. "Whoever did this might still be here."

When she would have stepped outside the door,

Liam pulled her back. "Why don't we stay in here until the police arrive?"

Possibly he was right. Before she could say as much, a crash echoed from the lobby. Liam pushed her into the small lounge room.

Someone was still inside.

Breaking glass shattered the silence.

"Whoever it is, is trying to get out," Liam murmured.

Halle looked up at him. "If the police aren't out there by now, he'll get away."

"You're right." Liam opened the door. "I'm going after him."

Some deeply buried instinct surged and Halle grabbed him by the jacket. "Wait," she whispered.

He twisted to look at her. "Do you smell that?"

Was it the burning car?

Gasoline. Raw. Freshly spilled.

The whoosh that erupted next had Liam drawing back from the door he'd opened, ushering her back, as well. "We have to find a different way out of here."

Halle peeked past the still open door and quickly slammed it shut. Flames were rolling down the corridor, devouring anything in their path.

"We need to hurry!"

He rushed to the set of windows on the other side of the small lounge and unlocked first one and then the other. He pushed the sashes upward, the effort monumental since they clearly hadn't been opened in ages. There were no screens.

He turned back to her. "I'm going out first, just in case whoever did this is out there."

She started to argue but one long leg was already

out the window. The other disappeared and he drew his upper body out. Halle glanced at the closed door, hoped no one burst through it or the flames crept under it. The smoke had already done so and invaded her lungs, making her cough.

"Come on!"

Liam reached through the window, grabbing for her.

She swung a leg over and through the opening. His hands were suddenly on her waist, lifting her away from the danger.

He pulled her away from the building until their bodies crashed into the end of the next one. The sun was setting, daylight going with it.

A shadow whizzed past the alley between the two buildings.

"Did you…?"

Halle didn't get to finish the question. Liam was already racing after the blur that had apparently been a person.

She rushed to the front corner of the building, glanced at her car, then in the direction Liam had gone.

She could follow in the car, catch up with him and whoever he was chasing.

Before the thought fully formed in her head, she was in the car and driving in the direction Liam had disappeared.

She caught sight of him.

There was another man. Dark tee. Dark jeans. Running like hell but Liam was gaining on him. Her heart started to pound. She floored the accelerator. The car lunged forward. When she was a good distance in front of the stranger, she whipped right and slammed to a stop on the sidewalk in front of him.

He almost ran into her car but he managed to skid to a near stop and slide past her front end.

Liam was hot on his trail.

She jumped out of the car and joined the chase. The man ducked into an alley. Liam followed. Halle pushed harder, plunged into the alley after them.

The blast of a gunshot had her hitting the ground.

Another shot. She gasped.

Liam!

She scrambled up and rushed forward. Liam had hit the ground, as well. Was he hurt? The other man had gone over the low wall at the end of the alley.

She couldn't chase him any longer. Had to make sure Liam was okay.

He was on his hands and knees now. Halle dropped to her knees beside him. "Are you hurt?"

He got to his feet. Offered his hand to her and pulled her up. "Just my pride. I almost had him when he drew his weapon and started firing. I had no choice but to hit the dirt."

Halle's knees tried to buckle.

Liam pulled her against him. "Steady there. You okay?"

She nodded, the move a little jerky. "Yes. I'm just glad you're not hurt."

The sound of sirens split the air and Halle felt ready to collapse. She leaned against Liam as they retraced their steps. She ignored her car, leaving it where it was for now.

For the first time since she started this investigation, she realized that there was at least one person who didn't want the truth to be found and was willing to take drastic steps to prevent that.

Mrs. Clark's murder could have been a robbery of some amount of cash she had hidden that no one had known about. Maybe a random act of violence.

But this, this was unmistakable.

This murder victim had something to hide.

Chapter Twelve

NOW

Derrick showed up while the firefighters were working to put out the fire. An ambulance had arrived. Four police cruisers. Now the medical examiner's van.

It was dark and the smells of burning wood, charring metal and melting plastic were thick in the air. The paramedics had insisted on checking Halle and Liam for injury.

She wasn't injured. She was angry and frustrated. Not to mention worried sick that yet another murder had been committed because of her article.

What the hell was happening?

It was possible, she supposed, that none of this was about Andy Clark or her investigation into what happened to him…but every instinct she possessed screamed differently.

This was about Andy. Her gaze landed on Liam where he stood near one of the police cruisers, watching the activities going on around them. Someone did not want the truth to come out. Whatever secrets the past held, whatever evil had stolen Andy Clark, she had awakened that evil, and now two people were dead. If the man who died today, the PI Frank Austen, was the person who killed Mrs. Clark or been involved somehow, there remained at least one more someone who wanted to keep the past in the past.

The person who had either killed Austen or hired him killed.

Her gaze sought and found Liam once more. Her story, The Lost Boy, had set off a chain of events: Liam's appearance in Winchester, Mrs. Clark's murder and now the destruction of an office and the murder of the man who operated his business there. At this point, Liam surely understood that he was without doubt Andy Clark. The only person who could possibly want to keep that truth hidden was the person who took him as a child. His father was dead, so, obviously he wasn't the murderer.

But what about his stepmother? She was supposed to be in Paris. Was she capable of violence like this? Even simply hiring it done?

Would a person go that far—killing two people— to hide a twenty-five-year-old kidnapping? Would the statute of limitations have run out on the kidnapping? Why add two murders to the list?

There had to be more to the disappearance of Andy Clark than they knew.

"Let's go over this again, Halle," Derrick said. He settled on the dock bumper of the ambulance next to her.

"I've already told you everything," she reminded him. The truth was, she knew the routine. The police always repeated the same questions just to see if your answers were consistent. No matter that she and Derrick were friends, he had a job to do.

"You know the drill."

She did. She exhaled a weary breath. "As you know from the article I did on The Lost Boy, I'm digging around in the Andy Clark case."

He nodded. "What brought you to Nashville to talk to Austen?"

"My parents were friends, neighbors, with the Clarks. My mother remembered them going to a private detective when the police weren't able to find Andy. To follow up on that theory, I started with the one in Winchester my folks believed the Clarks had visited. He tried to help them but hit a brick wall, so he sent them to another PI in Tullahoma. The one in Tullahoma had recommended them to Austen."

"But you said he couldn't remember Austen's name."

There it was, an inconsistency. The man didn't miss a thing. Halle dipped her head. "Right. But he did remember the attorney who worked with the PI, David Burke."

Derrick shook his head. "Now that guy is a piece of work. I swear, I wouldn't put it past him to run for president in the next election. He's that cocky and has that kind of money."

"Yeah, I kind of got that impression," she agreed.

"You visited Burke and he gave you Austen's name."

"Yes, but the two haven't worked together in years. He said Austen had decided to go out on his own."

"When you were in Austen's office did you see anything I should know about that won't incriminate you or your *friend*?"

It would have been impossible to miss the emphasis

he put on *friend* or the fact that he blatantly sent a look in Liam's direction. Men could certainly be territorial. Even when they didn't have the right.

"The front door was locked. The sign in the window was turned to Closed. But his neighbor had spotted him hauling a suitcase out of his house. She got the impression he was in a hurry, like someone was after him. Considering that information, we ignored the Closed sign."

Derrick quirked an eyebrow but said nothing.

"I suggested we go around back of his office to see if his car was here. It made sense that if he was making a run for it—for whatever reason—he might want to grab things from his office. You know, a file or part of some case that was important to him. Maybe a hidden stash of cash."

"Did you see a hidden stack of cash?"

"No." She smiled, indulging his teasing. "As I said, we came around to the back of the building and there was his car. I had asked the neighbor what kind of car he drove, so I recognized it immediately. The trunk was open, which suggested he was, indeed, in the office."

Derrick made that rolling motion with his hand for her to go on.

"We walked to the rear entrance. The door was ajar, so I knocked loudly and called out his name. I identified myself and said that I needed to speak with him. There was no response, so I waited a few seconds and called out again. It was clear something was wrong, so we went inside to check it out."

"It didn't occur to you to call the police and allow

us to handle it? I was waiting for you at the Pub, you know."

Things could get sticky here. She shook her head. "Metro is busy enough without me calling to say a door is ajar on a business when the owner's car was clearly parked next to it. I figured he had his head in a filing cabinet or closet and just didn't hear me. How foolish would I have looked if I'd called it in and then your guys showed up and—"

"Okay, okay." He waved his hands back and forth. "I get it. But what I don't understand is why you didn't answer my call."

She frowned and decided on a fib. "You must have called when I was out of the car speaking to the neighbor. I told you we went there first."

"Tell me again exactly what you saw inside and what happened from that point."

Halle went through the story again. From finding Austen's body, his car exploding and then the fire. The chase. She repeated all of it without missing an already stated detail.

Derrick made a few more notes and then heaved a sigh. "I guess that's it." He glanced at Liam, who hadn't moved. "You really think this guy is Andy Clark?"

She nodded. "I do. Back home, the chief of police is looking into it, as well." When he still looked skeptical, she went on. "You'd have to see the photos of him as a kid. It's him. I know it's him."

"Is he the reason no one else could hold on to you?"

Her gaze shot to the detective's. "What're you talking about? Remember, I was married."

"*Was* being the keyword." Derrick shook his head. "Really, this answers a lot of questions for me. I've heard you talk about this case dozens of times. But it wasn't until I saw you with him that I understood." He searched her face. "You've been in love with him since you were a kid."

"We were best friends, Derrick. Of course I loved him."

He smirked. "We are not talking about the same thing, Hal."

She pushed to her feet. "Can we go now? I have a long drive ahead of me."

He got up, put his hand on her arm. "Don't be angry with me. I'm just jealous."

She shook her head. "I'm not angry. Just exhausted and frustrated."

"Look." He glanced at Liam again. "Why don't the two of you stay at my place tonight? I'll see what I can dig up on Austen and we can catch up over dinner. How about it?"

"I really need any help you can give me about Austen." She braced for an argument. "But we should get going. The chief back home will be expecting to hear from me. My boss will want to know about my investigation so far. After all, this is work for me." The last part wasn't entirely true, but he didn't need to know that.

"All right. But next time I call, answer."

"I promise."

Before she could anticipate his move, he hugged her.

He drew back, held her arms. "Be careful and keep me up to speed on your investigation. We could work together and figure this out."

"Thanks, Derrick. I really appreciate it."

With a hasty goodbye she walked over to where Liam waited. "We can go."

"Good." He didn't look at her, just turned and started walking toward where they'd left her car angled across the sidewalk.

Halle followed.

She wasn't really surprised that he seemed more than happy to be getting out of here. She doubted this winemaker had ever chased after a bad guy or climbed out of a burning building. In her line of work she was accustomed to those sorts of intense scenes.

She could imagine him in the middle of a sprawling vineyard, working with the plants, testing the grapes. Peace and quiet. Beauty for as far as the eye could see.

This was a completely different world for him.

She'd taken his quiet, peaceful life and turned it into something painful and uncertain. He would probably hate her before this was over.

At the moment, she hated herself just a little bit.

HALLE'S ONLY REQUIREMENT for the hotel they selected was that they had room service and good beds. Fortunately, the hotel she'd always adored for their amazing beds and room service was available but there was only one room.

Great. Just great. As tired as she was, she stepped away from the counter to tell Liam. He'd gotten a call from his sister and had moved away from the registration desk for some privacy.

"Okay, sis. Don't worry." He smiled. "See you soon." He paused, listening. "Love you, too."

When he ended the call, Halle was smiling, too. She

couldn't help it. The sound of his voice, his smile, it made her feel safe and...

She cleared her head. "They have a room, but only one. There are two beds, however. Do you have a problem sharing a room?" She shrugged. "We could always drive home if you'd rather. Or find another hotel."

"No. This is fine. Driving back tonight would be pointless. We need to relax and talk. Anything but be stuck in a car for a couple of hours."

"And shower," she pointed out. Her gaze roved over him. They were both sweaty and smoky and...

She should get the room.

He passed her a credit card. "I don't want you paying for anything else."

She shook her head. "You flew all the way from California. Rented a car. I'd say you've paid more than your share already."

"Hal," he warned, "I'm paying."

She was too startled to argue with him further. Instead she took the credit card and walked back to the counter. This was the first time he'd called her Hal. He'd called her that all the time when they were kids.

Maybe he'd heard Derrick call her Hal.

No, she decided, it had come naturally because more memories were coming back whether he told her about them all or not.

When she'd taken care of the room, they headed for the elevators. To her surprise the hotel boutique was still open.

"Wait. We need clothes."

She grabbed him by the arm and dragged him inside the chic shop.

"How may I help you?" The clerk grimaced before she could school the expression as she asked the question.

"I know," Halle said. "We were in a fire."

"Oh, my, I'm certainly glad you're all right."

"Thanks. We need a change of clothes. Underthings. Something to sleep in." She stared down at her feet. "Shoes if you have them."

The woman smiled widely and waved her arm. "I'm certain I have everything you need."

Halle wandered through the small women's section. She found jeans, a sweatshirt, ridiculously over-priced ankle boots. And, thank God, panties and one of those sports bras. She grabbed a nightshirt and she was good to go.

At the counter, the clerk was already ringing up similar items for Liam. Jeans, a sweatshirt, hiking shoes, tees and boxers. Socks. Oh, she forgot socks. She hurried back to the women's section and grabbed a pair. Back at the counter, the clerk reached for Halle's armload.

"I'll be paying for my own," she argued.

The clerk smiled again. "The gentleman insists on taking care of everything."

Halle glared at him. He grinned.

She was too tired to argue.

Finally, they were headed to the sixth floor. Halle leaned against the back wall of the elevator and closed her eyes. She tried to remember if she had ever been this tired. Maybe it was all the emotional turmoil making her so exhausted. She should call her mother in case their faces showed up on the news. Later, she decided, after a long, hot shower.

On the sixth floor, they walked silently to the proper

door. Halle slid the key into the lock and waited for the green light. Inside, she tossed her bag onto one of the two beds. "You shower first," she said.

"I'm fine. You go first," he argued, dropping his bag onto the other bed.

"I'm serious," she said, "I'm going to take a while and I need to call home."

He held up his hands in surrender. "I'll go first." He grabbed his bag and disappeared into the bathroom. Seconds later she heard the spray of the shower.

The room was larger than the average hotel room. Another thing she liked about this hotel. She walked over to the floor-to-ceiling windows. She stared out over the sweeping views of the Cumberland River and the city's skyline. She had been so excited moving to Nashville after college and starting her first job as a reporter. She'd felt like her whole life was coming together in the picturesque city where anything could happen.

But at night, before she drifted off to sleep, she'd always thought of Andy. Wondered where he was and if he were safe and happy. In high school she'd made up stories about him. She alternated between him being in some foreign country as a spy or climbing mountains somewhere to break records. Sometimes, she decided he was a private investigator, helping lost children find their way back home because he never could.

She smiled, thought of all the ways she had imagined that they might meet again. In Paris at the Louvre. Or in Washington, DC, at the White House, or maybe in New York, atop the Empire State Building.

She'd kept a big notebook about him. Sometimes she would go months without writing in it, then she would think of him and write him a letter. It was silly and fantastical but she'd never been able to throw the letters away, or the notebook.

It was still at home, in the top of her childhood closet. She'd pulled it down for the first time in a while to start writing this anniversary story.

The pictures. She laughed. She'd put a picture in for each year he'd been gone. She'd also written about the big happenings in the world and the latest fashion and music trends as if he'd been kept in a cave or something.

She'd had no idea that he was just on the other side of the country, growing grapes.

The bathroom door opened and the fragrance of lavender soap and steam filled her senses. She turned around and watched as he scrubbed his damp hair with the towel. He wore one of the new cotton tees and boxers. His legs were as well muscled as his arms. She blinked the thought away, grabbed her bag from the bed and hurried across the room.

"My turn."

She hadn't even called her mom.

"Should I order room service?"

She paused at the door. "That would be great. Order me whatever looks good and lots of it."

He gave her a two-fingered salute and she backed into the bathroom, shut the door. She liked his hair when it was tousled like that. There were a lot of things she liked about him, like his hands and his eyes. Goodness, those eyes.

"Get ahold of yourself, girl."

While she sorted through her bag and removed tags

from her purchases, she called her mom and let her know they were staying the night.

"Are you sure you're okay? You sound a little strange."

"I'm just tired." She broke down and told her about the private investigator and the fire. Her mother was, of course, horrified.

When she'd calmed her down over that event, her mom said, "I've been going through more of Nancy's papers. Chief Brannigan said I could go ahead. But I haven't found anything unusual or suspicious."

"Look for anything related to an attorney named Burke. David Burke."

"All right. Let me write down his name."

She waited for her mother to do so.

"Anything else, dear?"

She suddenly remembered Liam's question. "Did the Clarks ever have any old friends visit? Maybe from when they lived in Nashville. Could have been someone from the church they attended or business associates?"

"Funny that you asked. Your father and I talked about that from time to time. You know, before."

Before Andy went missing. All their lives were divided into two parts. Before and after he vanished.

"Did Dad remember anyone?" Halle felt herself holding her breath. The answer could be important. They might find someone else who knew the family from before they moved to Winchester.

"It was the strangest thing. They never had visitors. Not completely surprising since they had no relatives, just each other and Andy. But they were such social people. Always at church and attending community events. It seemed odd that they had no friends from Nashville who ever visited. Your dad said maybe something happened up there and they cut ties with friends and associates. It happens. Feelings get hurt, people refuse to get past the event."

Something like suddenly having a child without ever having been pregnant.

Halle caught her breath at the thought. "Thanks, Mom. You've been very helpful."

"Will you be home tomorrow?"

"I think so. Unless the police need us to stay for some reason related to the fire." She didn't mention the explosion. A fire was sufficient worry fodder.

"Drive safely and give Liam our love."

"I will. Love you."

Halle placed her phone on the marble counter. No matter how this turned out, Liam would be going back to his home. They were going to miss him desperately. Her heart heavy, she peeled off the smoky clothes and turned on the water.

The shower was like heaven on earth. Her body had needed the hot water so badly. Her muscles relaxed and she took her time, smoothing the soap over her skin and then shampooing her hair. She was grateful for the toiletry pack that included not only soap, shampoo and the usual, but disposable razors, as well.

By the time she was finished, her bones felt like rubber. She dried herself, slipped on underwear and the nightshirt and then used the hotel dryer to dry her hair. That part took the longest of all. When she exited the steamy bathroom the delicious aromas of room service had her stomach rumbling.

"Oh my God, that smells good." She rushed to the table where the silver service sat. "Why aren't you eating?"

"I was waiting for you." He joined her at the table. Ever the gentleman.

Halle curled her feet under her in her chair while Liam removed the covers from the dishes. Fish, chicken, vegetables. He had ordered all sorts of dishes and they all looked amazing.

"I thought we'd try a little of everything."

A bottle of white wine as well as a bottle of rosé had her licking her lips.

"I wasn't sure which one you preferred." He gestured to the iced-down bottles. "And I didn't forget dessert." The final lid revealed a heavenly-looking chocolate cake with fudge icing.

"I may die right now." She wanted to taste it all.

"Eat first." He placed a linen napkin over his lap and stuck his fork into a tiny, perfectly roasted potato. She watched him eat and it was the sexiest thing she had ever seen. She didn't fight it. Surrendered to instinct and that was how they ate. No plates, just taking whatever they wanted with a fork or fingers and devouring. They drank the wine and laughed at stories from their respective childhoods. From all the stories he'd told her, she could not wait to meet his sister, Claire.

By the time they were finished, she was feeling a little tipsy. The food was mostly gone and both bottles were drained. She felt more relaxed than she had in decades. They had discussed the day's events and Burke and Austen—and Derrick. The man was still convinced she had a thing for Derrick. No way. She'd also told him what her mom had to say about any friends from Nashville the Clarks might have had, which was

none who ever appeared at their door. She and Liam
agreed that was somewhat unusual considering how
social the Clarks had been in Winchester.

"You know," she said, after polishing off the last of
the wine in her glass, "I wrote you dozens of letters."

"Me?"

She frowned and shook her head. "Andy." Then she
stared at him. "No. *You*. I mean you. Whatever you believe, I know you're him."

"Okay." He laughed, his eyes glittering with the
soft sound.

God, his mouth was sexy when he was relaxed. She
put her hand to her mouth just to make sure she hadn't
said the words out loud.

"Tell me about the letters," he prompted.

"I told you what was going on in Winchester. Who
was doing what at school. I even put pictures with the
letters." She laughed. Placed her glass on the table. "It
was silly, I know. But I wanted to still feel you and that
was the only way I could."

She blinked. He had moved. He was suddenly next
to her, on his knees, staring into her eyes, and her
breath caught.

"I don't know if I'm this Andy you loved so much
when you were a kid," he said softly, so softly she shivered, "but I would really like to be the guy you care
about now."

Her heart swelled into her throat. She started to suggest that it was the wine talking, but it wasn't. The truth
was in his eyes. Those blue eyes she knew as well as
her own. And despite her wine consumption, she was
stone-cold sober as she considered what could happen
between them tonight.

"I'm really glad, because I would hate to think I'm in this alone," she confessed.

He kissed her so sweetly that tears stung her eyes. Then he stood and pulled her into his arms. He carried her to the nearest bed.

No matter what happened tomorrow, she would always cherish this night.

Chapter Thirteen

NOW

Napa, California

Claire Hart had not stopped pacing the floor since she spoke with Liam. From the moment he'd told her he was staying a few more days in Winchester she had gone through every possible hiding place in the house. There were no photos of Liam from the time he was a little baby—and there were only a few of those—to when he was around seven. There were some listed as being of him during that time period but never showing his face pointed at the camera.

She knew deep in her heart that something was wrong with this scenario.

Alone in this big old house, Claire had allowed her imagination to run away with her. She had searched everywhere, even in her parents' private space. She'd felt so guilty. How could she doubt her parents this way? What had possessed her to believe they would do such a thing—whatever the *thing* was? At the beginning, she had refused to label the notion driving her. But then she had been forced to concede that something was not as it should be. There were secrets.

Then she'd found that box.

Not a large box. More like one of the candy boxes with the double layers of candies and the map that told you what kind was in each slot of chocolate-covered goodies.

She stared at the offending box now. After picking through it, falling apart a little more with each new discovery, she had pulled herself together and brought it to the family room. She had placed it on the coffee table while she decided what to do about it. She stared at it now with its faded gold coloring and painted red ribbon. This box was evidence of the most shocking secret she could possibly have imagined.

Several scenarios had gone through her head when she'd been poking around, but nothing like this. She shuddered. This just couldn't be.

She needed to call Liam.

No, no, she couldn't call him. This wasn't something she could tell him over the phone. She had to go to Winchester and *show* him. He needed to see this with his own eyes. She would not be the one to say out loud the words that were his real story.

She couldn't. She loved her brother far too much.

Stop, just stop. If she didn't stop this confounded pacing she was going to wear a path in her mother's favorite Persian rug. She twisted and started back the other way. Not possible. She had to keep moving to prevent exploding.

It might not be a bad idea to call Halle Lane. The way Liam had spoken about her when he'd called earlier, it was obvious he thought she hung the moon.

Claire could put this monkey on her back. She was the one who'd started this after all, with her search for the truth.

Claire's stomach twisted with a thousand tiny knots. The truth was painful and startling and their lives would forever be changed when it was revealed, and she saw no way around it coming out.

She paused to stare at the box. She could not pretend she hadn't found it.

The sound of the front door being unlocked snapped her from the troubling thoughts. Fear seared through her veins. Why hadn't she set the security system? She had locked the door, hadn't she?

Claire grabbed her cell, ready to dial 911 as she eased to the entry hall.

The door opened.

She stalled, unable to move.

Her mother. What was she doing home?

Outrage blasted her before she could temper it. "What're you doing back? I thought you were headed to London next."

She reminded herself that this was her mother and that she loved her. She had always been a good mother to both Claire and Liam.

But she had lied. Fury flashed anew inside Claire. Her mother had hidden the truth all these years.

Penelope gave her a quick smile. "I'll explain later. I'm in a bit of a hurry right now."

She rushed past. Claire frowned. Where were her bags? Still in the car? Wouldn't the driver have brought them in? She walked to the door and peered out the side glass. Taillights faded in the distance.

What on earth?

She pivoted and stormed after her mother. She wasn't in the family room or the kitchen. "Mom?"

No answer. Claire headed toward her bedroom and found her standing on a chair, poking around in the top of her closet.

"Looking for something?" Claire asked, unable to conceal the suspicion in her tone.

"Yes…there's a box." Penelope kept pawing through hat boxes and handbags, her movements frantic.

"It's in the family room," Claire announced. She might as well put her mother out of her misery.

Penelope stilled, turned to stare down at her.

"I'll be waiting there." Claire turned away from her. She strode out of the room, a volatile mixture of emotions fueling her. Anger and disappointment and something like disgust.

A minute or so passed before her mother joined her. Claire didn't have to be in the room to know she would have put the chair back where it belonged, shut off the closet light and closed the door. Her mother was particular like that.

When Penelope paused at the sofa, her gaze fell upon the box.

The box.

The nine-by-fifteen-inch cardboard container that held the incredible lie that was their life.

"Apparently you opened it," she said, her voice brittle, too faint.

Penelope Hart stood there with her matching silk trousers and blouse and perfectly made-up face and hair. She was beautiful. Elegant. Loving. Patient. Kind. Supersmart.

And a liar.

"What does this mean?" Claire demanded.

Her mother's gaze lifted from the box to meet Claire's. "I will tell you everything on the way to the airport."

Did she really believe she could just leave right now? Good God, it was almost ten o'clock. "You are not leaving until you explain this—" she gestured to the damned box "—to me."

"I have to get to Winchester. There's a flight just after midnight that would put me in Nashville around nine in the morning. I cannot miss it. I have to speak to Liam." She shook her head, the move so faint Claire might not have noticed had she not been glaring at her mother. "Please tell me you haven't told him about this."

How dare she make such a plea!

"I haven't told him," Claire snapped. "I didn't want to be the one to shatter him." Tears burned in her eyes. "Tell me how this is possible!"

Her mother walked to her then, grasped Claire's arms in her hands and held her tight. "I need you to trust and believe in me—"

"Are you kidding?" The tears streaked down Claire's face. She could not hold them back. "How will I ever trust you again?"

A single tear slid down her mother's cheek. "I promise I will explain everything. Please, just come with me and I'll tell you on the way to the airport."

Claire pulled free of her grasp and snatched up the box. "You can tell me on the way to the airport, but I'm going with you to Winchester."

"Claire—"

"Someone needs to be there for him," she argued. "Someone who hasn't lied to him."

Chapter Fourteen

NOW

Sunday, March 15
Winchester, Tennessee

Halle had never been so glad to be home.

She turned all the way around in her apartment above the garage. All these months she had felt as if she'd failed in her career and that being back here was evidence of that failure. A smile spread across her lips. But it wasn't a failure. It was meant to be. Liam was going to stay with her a few more days until they sorted things out. Later today he had to call his sister and his stepmom to talk and then…

Well, she didn't know where they went from there, but whatever happened, it would be good. Wonderful. And full of possibility.

A soft sigh seeped out of her. She had never been happier. She was still a little afraid of how things would turn out. There remained a lot of questions. Liam wanted to do the DNA test before confronting his step-mother with any hard questions. Which was totally understandable. There were still so many unknowns…the perpetrator in Mrs. Clark's murder, for one.

Despite the heinousness of the poor woman's murder as well as Austen's, Halle experienced a strange serenity she'd rarely felt before.

Since waking up this morning she had walked around with a goofy grin on her face, but she wasn't the only one. Liam wore the same happy face. They'd had breakfast in the room and then dressed and driven back to Winchester. Bursts of animated conversation had been followed by lapses into satisfied silence.

Her biggest regret was that they had missed all those years between when he vanished and now. She walked over to her desk to start going through her notes. Laundry could wait. She wanted to get as many of her thoughts down as possible while it was all still fresh.

Liam had just left to get his things from the hotel and to check out. A local agency had agreed to take care of his rental car. Her parents had already left for church by the time they arrived back in Winchester this morning. She couldn't wait to tell them that she and Liam were going to start seeing each other seriously.

The whole idea was a little unsettling when she considered that he lived in California and she lived here… but they would work it out. Somehow.

Everything felt right.

A knock on her door startled her. She pressed her hand to her chest and reached for calm. She'd been jumpy this way since Liam left. She had to get a grip. He was just going across town. He would be back soon. Probably within the hour.

She pushed away from her desk and went to the door. Maybe her parents were home from church already. She opened the door wearing that big old smile, ready to tell her mom—

It wasn't her mom.

"Mr. Burke." She frowned. Surprised—no, shocked— to find the big-shot attorney standing on her landing.

"Ms. Lane, I'm so glad I was able to catch you."

Halle composed herself once more. This was odd. Something wasn't right. "What is it?" If he'd come all this way, surely he had an update for her that might prove relevant to their ongoing search. "Tell me."

He hesitated, made a face. "My time is really short, Ms. Lane, but it was vitally important that I speak to you in person. This is not the sort of thing to be done by phone."

"Okay." Her instincts stirred. Some part of this picture wasn't quite right.

"Can you take a ride with me? There's something you need to see."

Now she was straight up worried. "What's going on?"

"Please." He stepped back from the door and gestured to the stairs. "Let me show you. There's really no way to explain this without showing you."

Every instinct she possessed warned that she should be suspicious—maybe even afraid—but this was the one man who might be able to shed light on what really happened twenty-five years ago.

"Just tell me. That will be faster." If his time was so short, then talking to her right here was the quickest way to give her whatever information he was so eager to share.

She wasn't about to go anywhere with him. Particularly since his former investigator had been murdered not so long after she visited this man.

He pulled a gun from his pocket and pointed it at her. "We do this my way. Get your keys. We'll take your car."

Moving slowly, deliberately, as she tried to think of what to do, she crossed the room and grabbed her shoulder bag, tucking her cell into it.

"All right," she said, turning back to him.

"Ladies first," he told her, waving the gun toward the stairs.

They descended the stairs and strode across her backyard. "Where are we going?" The more she knew, the better. Maybe she could stop this before they got too far. Now she was glad her parents were out. She wouldn't want them in danger.

"It's not far," Burke said rather than answer her question.

Once they were in the car, she pulled out her cell. "I should let Liam know. He'll wonder why I'm not home."

"Drive," he suggested. "You'll want to hear me out first. There are things you need to think long and hard about before you speak with him."

What did that mean? She tamped down her fears and focused on getting away, putting distance between herself and her parents' home before they arrived.

She reached way down deep for calm. Struggled to keep her voice steady. "Why don't you tell me what's going on? And why you felt the need to use force to have me go with you?"

He buckled himself into the passenger seat, keeping the gun trained on her. "No questions now. Just drive."

She backed out of the driveway and then remembered to fasten her seat belt. Not easy with one hand.

"Which way are we headed?"

"Keep going the way you are, then turn right at the intersection."

She did as he asked. When he still offered no explanation for where they were going, she said, "You came a long way. I'm assuming this is important. Maybe about your PI friend who was murdered?" She wanted to learn as much as she could, even as her mind raced, trying to figure out what to do.

He nodded, his expression somber. "It's a real shame."

"The two of you worked together for a long time—before he went out on his own, I mean."

"Decades. He was the best investigator I ever employed. Make a left at the light." He shook his head. "But he got sloppy toward the end. I had ignored a mistake here and there over the years, but it became too much."

Halle glanced at him. "That's too bad."

"You can only overlook so much before you realize that the situation is becoming a serious liability."

She nodded as understanding dawned. He'd killed Austen. She needed to stop Burke before he killed her too.

"Turn left here onto 16."

She tensed. Keith Springs Road, Highway 16, would take them out of town. "Where are we going?"

"I had to drive down very early this morning," he said rather than answer her question about where they were going. "I had to find the right spot." He glanced at her. "That was particularly important." Then he surveyed the interior of the car. "Choosing a means of transportation that wouldn't be connected to me was important, too. I learned a few things from Austen over the years. There are all sorts of people you can hire to do these sorts of things. But some aspects I prefer to handle personally. It's better that way. No worries of anyone talking. No potential witness."

Fear bolted through her. She slowed for the turn. Her heart thumped so hard she could hardly breathe.

He pressed the muzzle of the handgun to her temple. "Do exactly as I say. Do not doubt as to whether I'll use this or not."

Halle stared straight ahead and started moving forward again. "Whatever you say," she said tightly. "But I need you to lower the weapon."

He pulled the gun away from her head but kept it in his hand, laying on the console between them. "Then drive until I tell you otherwise. Drive carefully and within the speed limit."

She did as he asked, potential scenarios for escaping swirling through her head.

"When I first started out, I was a little fish swimming in a big pond," he began as she drove farther along a road that went up the mountain and eventually across the wildlife refuge into Alabama. Once they were beyond the Keith Springs area there was basically nothing but woods and the occasional trail hunters used.

She had to find a way to get away from him...to warn Liam. But she couldn't get the gun away from him here. He'd overpower her quickly. He had an iron grip on his weapon.

"But I was determined to make myself indispensable," he went on. "All I had to do was find the right niche. After a few not-so-successful starts, I found the perfect one. All those rich people in Nashville. There had to be a way to tap into those resources in a way that cut right to the heart. You know, people are far more generous when emotions are involved." He laughed. "Luckily for me, there were plenty among them who suffered from one fertility issue or another. Not to mention the ones who just didn't want to put their bodies through the trauma of carrying a child and then giving birth. There are those unsightly stretch marks and such."

Halle set her fear aside and glanced at him. Playing to his ego would work to her benefit. "You became the go-to attorney for private adoptions."

"Oh, did I. I took every opportunity to offer what no one else could or would. You know, it's amazing what people will gladly pay to get exactly what they want. The problem to overcome was availability. There's not always a child with precisely the desired features. Just the right color hair or eyes isn't such a huge obstacle, but a clean bill of health from the bio parents. Maybe taller parents or certain dimples or—" he glanced at her "—freckles. Sometimes they were just looking to replace the child they'd lost with one that resembled him or her as closely as possible."

The reality of what he was saying filtered through the desperation pounding at her skull. "You had to find the perfect child."

"To the letter. The more specific the request, the more expensive the product."

Product? They were talking about children here.

Her stomach turned in disgust. "Not such an easy order to fulfill."

"Tell me about it. There are some self-centered people in this world. You combine that sort of selfishness with money and you have customers desperate to throw that money around. But Frank, he was good. He had the process down to a science. I gave him very specific parameters from the beginning. The children could only be taken from people who were dirt-poor or homeless or just plain bad. The kind with no means to pursue a real search and the type the police wouldn't likely believe. People who shouldn't have had kids in the first place. The only time he was allowed to go outside those parameters was if the requested product could not be found otherwise. Frank would go all over the place. He never shopped in the same town twice or in places too close together. He was very careful. At least, most of the time."

Halle felt sick. The mere idea of all the people whose children had been snatched from them made her soul ache. What kind of monsters did this sort of thing and dared to look at it as simply supply and demand?

Whatever it took, she was going to take this scumbag down.

"I appreciate you sharing your career-building experience," she said, summoning her bravado and going for nonchalance, "but what does this have to do with me? I didn't even get a chance to talk to Mr. Austen. He was dead when we arrived."

Burke glanced at her then. "Take the next right."

Heart in her throat, she slowed and made a right turn onto a narrow dirt road. She drove slowly until she reached a gate.

"Stop right here."

She did as he asked, put the car into Park and shut off the engine. *Think, Halle!* There was the gun. He had the upper hand, for sure. But she was younger and more physically fit. She could outrun him if she got a chance.

Liam was waiting for her. She would not let him down. She would make the opportunity to escape. They were not losing each other again.

Burke nudged her with the barrel of the weapon. "Don't forget I have this. If Frank were here, he could tell you I know how to use it."

She nodded and he motioned with the weapon. "Get out and bring your cell phone with you."

He kept the weapon trained on her as she got out. He did the same, scrambling across the console and out of the car on her side, not once allowing his aim to deviate from her.

"Now, this is what's going to happen, Ms. Lane. You're going to call your friend from Cali and tell him to meet you here. That your car has broken down. Once he arrives—"

"No." She shook her head. "I won't do it." She might not be able to escape this bastard but she was not bringing Liam into it. She had already turned his life upside down; she would not summon him into a trap.

"Do it." He pressed the muzzle to her forehead. "Now."

"Okay." She took a deep breath. "I will on one condition."

"Not that you're in any position to be tossing out conditions, but let's hear it."

"Tell me how Frank got Andy."

He laughed. "Oh, that was his first mistake. Under

no circumstances was he to ever kill anyone to obtain the product."

She shook her head. "There must be some mistake. No one was killed when Andy was taken."

"You see," Burke countered, "that's because he wasn't Andy the first time he was taken."

LIAM WAS SURPRISED to find Halle's car gone when he returned to her apartment. He paid the fare and thanked the driver. The Lanes weren't back from church, either. He glanced around the yard. Maybe she'd run to the store for a few items. She'd mentioned being out of everything.

As he climbed the stairs that same grin that had been tugging at his lips all morning appeared again. It was a little crazy, he was aware. He'd met Halle only three days ago and he felt things for her he had never felt for anyone. But he had known her before. Somehow, however, he wanted to deny the possibility that he was this Andy Clark. As he lay in bed last night with her in his arms so many memories had flooded him. There was no denying that truth.

There was only the question of how it had happened.

When he reached the door, he hesitated. She hadn't given him a key. There hadn't been any need.

What if something had happened to her parents?

Worry gnawed at him. A car accident or something? But why wouldn't she have called him?

He tested the doorknob. To his surprise it was unlocked. He went inside and all looked as it had when he left. He walked around the apartment, didn't spot a note. Okay, so she had likely just run to the store for milk or something.

Maybe he'd call her.

The sound of a car door slamming had him heading back to the door. He was halfway down the steps before he realized the car in the driveway wasn't Halle's. The woman striding toward him wasn't Halle, either... It was Penelope. Moving up beside her was Claire.

What the hell?

"Liam!" Claire shouted as she broke into a run.

He met her at the bottom of the steps. She hugged him hard. He hugged her back, his eyes still on his stepmom. "Hey, sis. What're you guys doing here?"

Had they decided he'd lost his mind and planned an intervention? Surely Penelope wouldn't have returned from Paris just because Liam had taken some time off to pursue a mystery that she couldn't possibly know the full ramifications of...

Unless his sister had called her.

As if she'd sensed his realization, Claire drew back, looked him square in the eyes. "We need to talk."

Penelope hugged him next, smiling warmly. "It's good to see you."

What was going on here?

"Come on in." He gestured for the two to go up the stairs before him. He'd left the door standing wide open in his haste to get outside and meet Halle.

She would be back any minute, he was certain. Turned out, he realized as he walked into the apartment to join Claire and Penelope, that it was probably a good thing Halle wasn't home at the moment. These two had something on their minds and he had a feeling it wasn't going to be good.

"What's going on?" He closed the door and moved

toward the sofa. "Sit. You must be tired after that flight. What'd you do, take a red-eye?"

"Where's the reporter?" Claire glanced around the apartment.

"Halle will be back in a few minutes."

Penelope had already perched on the edge of the sofa. When Claire did the same, Liam sat down facing them. Claire removed her backpack and started to open it.

"Seriously," he said when neither of them spoke, "what's going on?"

Claire pulled out an old candy box. The gold-colored kind with the painted red ribbon. Looked vintage.

Penelope placed her right hand on the box, seemingly stopping Claire from whatever she'd intended next. "Claire told me about the article, Liam, and why you've come to Winchester."

He nodded, but before he could comment, she went on, "There are things I should have told you right after your father died." She exhaled a big breath. "I always felt he should tell you but he didn't want to unsettle your life, so he kept his secret and I stood by his decision."

Claire glared at her. "Just tell him already."

Worry and fear and a number of other emotions he didn't fully comprehend twisted inside him. "What're you trying to tell me?"

"Not long after you were born, Luke and your birth mother, Tara, found themselves in a very bad place financially. They were homeless and living in the woods, camping, surviving on next to nothing. Luke was looking for work. After the vineyard where he'd worked since he was a child was sold, he was let go, no matter that he was the manager. The news was shocking and, worse, he wasn't able to find work. It was a difficult time for everyone in the business, but especially for your parents since they had a baby."

Liam felt as if he were outside his body watching this scene. He wanted to ask questions but he couldn't form the words. Claire stared at him as if he'd just been told he had terminal cancer.

"Tara was having real problems," Penelope said. "She was sick much of the time and your father was very worried. So much so that he broke down and called his sister—"

"Sister?" Claire demanded before Liam managed to find his voice again. "You didn't tell me that part. You were supposed to tell me everything on the plane."

Penelope ignored her and went on. "Your father had a sister but they had been estranged for years. I don't know the reason. He would never speak of it. But because he was so worried about your mother and, obviously, you, he made the call. He asked for her help but she refused."

The hurt his father must have felt was like a sucker punch to his gut. He could only imagine his level of desperation, and Liam feared he already knew where this was going.

"Your father soldiered on, finding odd jobs to feed his family. But one day, when you were only fifteen months old, he came home and the two of you were missing."

"Missing—" Liam suddenly found his voice "—as in my mother ran away and took me with her or missing like someone took us?"

"Your father had no idea. He was terrified that because she had been so sick, primarily with very serious postpartum depression, she had decided to leave. Perhaps go home to her mother who was still alive at the time. But she wasn't at her mother's. He searched and searched and searched. The police helped for a while as did some of his old friends from the vineyard where he'd worked so many years, but the two of you were not found. He never stopped looking, but eventually he had to move on or lose his mind."

She paused for a moment and Liam felt certain he should say something, but he had no idea what to say. A million little things were going through his head but none of them seemed exactly right. He should call Halle. Find out why she wasn't here yet. She would be able to put all this into perspective. His emotions kept him from finding his footing. Judging by Claire's expression, he felt she was in the same boat with him.

"After two years of watching things fall apart, the new owner of the vineyard had decided he wasn't cut out for the business, so he sought out the former manager, your father, and made him an offer he couldn't refuse. Just to get the place off his hands, he would sell him everything—at a steal of a price—if he would promise to make up the difference when and if he ever got things running in the black again. Luke accepted his offer and threw himself into his work. It was the only way he maintained his sanity. We met shortly after he started. It was a couple of years before he shared the agony of losing you and his wife. The vineyard was back in the black and things were going extremely well. I suppose this allowed him to look back at his painful loss. I desperately wanted to help and I had a few contacts from my time in LA. I had worked in an attorney's office and he had had the very best investigators. I asked him to help us find the truth."

Liam braced himself. For days now, he had wanted to know the whole truth. Suddenly he wasn't so sure.

"Another year was required for the investigator to find someone who had seen something the day you and Tara disappeared, but he did. Even more time was required to track down who that person the witness had seen was. This unknown person turned out to be a PI from Nashville, a Frank Austen."

Liam's heart dropped into his stomach. "Austen is dead."

Penelope made a face but then kept going. "On your father's behalf, my friend made a deal with Austen—he wouldn't go to the police as long as Austen told him what happened to you." Penelope took a moment before going on. "You were the target of one of Austen's searches for a child that was wanted by a couple unable to have their own. Austen waited for an opportunity when Luke was not around and he attempted to take you. But your mother was tougher than she looked. She fought him. He swore it was an accident, but, sadly, he killed her. Took her body with him and buried her. Then he took you to his boss, who presented you to his clients, Nancy and Andrew Clark."

Liam closed his eyes. His mother was dead, his father had suffered unspeakable pain because the Clarks wanted a child. He was going to find David Burke and beat the hell out of him. "Why didn't my father see that Austen went to jail for what he'd done? That PI friend of yours had no business making that deal."

"Liam, he did what he had to do to find you. Nothing else mattered to your father at that point. Not revenge, not even justice. Only finding you."

"So the Clarks were destroyed because no one wanted to go to the police and do this right? My God, they wouldn't have wanted to adopt a child who had been taken under those kinds of circumstances. What you did only hurt another family."

And stole his life.

Penelope drew back at his heated words. "Your sympathies are misplaced, Liam."

Liam felt sick. This was wrong. All of it. He wouldn't have believed his father capable of this sort of underhandedness, no matter the motive. Why hadn't he gone to the Clarks and told them the truth? They could all have worked together to resolve the situation. He glared at his stepmother. "What does that even mean?"

"Nancy Clark was your father's sister. She had, it seemed, been trying to have a baby for years and couldn't. When she found out Luke had a child and was in trouble financially, she decided he didn't deserve the child. She and her husband hired David Burke and his investigator to find you and take you."

Another of those sucker punches landed to his gut.

"When your father found out, he started planning how to get you back. Though he hated his sister for what she had done, she was still his sister and he didn't want her to end up in prison. He took you back. I helped him. And then he called Nancy and told her that if she ever came near you again, he would go to the police with all the evidence he had. She agreed, but she asked for only one thing, that she receive an occasional photo so she could see you grow up, so to speak, and know you were all right." She gestured to the candy box Claire held. "All the evidence, the signed agreement they reached, photos, articles, a journal from your mother, is there when you're ready to look at it."

Liam pushed to his feet, couldn't remain seated a moment longer. "I have to call Halle."

"I am so very sorry, Liam," Penelope said. "He never wanted you to know. The both of you had suffered enough. It was difficult at first, yes. But he was always gentle with you, and slowly but surely you forgot about that other life and came back to him. His son. The one stolen from him. There was only ever one frightening incident. You tried to run away and were hit by a car. You had no life-threatening injuries but you had a concussion and a broken arm. Oddly enough, after that you were fine. It was as if you locked away the life with the Clarks and became Liam again."

He wasn't sure he would ever understand how his mind had hidden so much from him. His cell vibrated with an incoming text and he pushed the disturbing thought away. *Halle.* He frowned as he read her message.

Car won't start. Can you come pick me up? Take Highway 16. Go eight miles and take dirt side road on right just past mile marker sign. I feel like an idiot.

His frown deepened. "I have to pick up Halle. I need to borrow your rental. As soon as we get back, we'll figure this out."

"I'm going with you." Claire set the candy box aside and grabbed her backpack.

Liam shook his head. "I need to tell her myself. We'll all talk when we're back."

Claire handed him the keys to the rental outside. "We'll be waiting."

He accepted the keys. "Thanks."

At the door, Penelope's voice stopped him, "Whatever you're feeling right now, please keep in mind that your father and your bio mom loved you more than you can possibly imagine. Even Nancy loved you. She was just a selfish woman who wanted to hurt her brother."

Liam nodded. "I know they loved me." His gaze held hers for a moment longer. "I know you do, too. That means a great deal to me even if I'm not doing a very good job of showing it right now."

Penelope nodded. Her lips trembled as she smiled. "Be careful."

"I'll be back in a few minutes." He winked at Claire. "Love you, too."

Chapter Fifteen

NOW

Halle couldn't be sure how much time had elapsed, but she was certain it was enough for Liam to be close even if he made a wrong turn or two before finding the correct dirt road. This road wasn't very long. Maybe a quarter of a mile before the locked gate prevented going any farther. Burke had marched her far enough into the woods that they wouldn't be spotted immediately when Liam arrived, but they could see her car from where they waited. The woods around them, however, were so dense it would be impossible to see her car from the main road. No one passing by would spot them.

When she had refused to call him, Burke had sent a text. Bastard.

He had made two calls on her cell after that. He'd spoken to someone on one of the calls but not on the other one. Since everyone was aware that cell calls could be traced back to a location, she suspected he was attempting to lay the groundwork for either his alibi or for framing someone else.

What a low-down scumbag.

"I don't get it," she said, breaking the extended silence. She needed him focused on something else rather than watching her. Time was running out. Desperate measures were her only recourse. In order to avoid ending up dead before she drew him away from this location, she had to distract him.

"You don't get what?" he demanded. "Not that it matters." The way he looked at her as he said this was warning enough that he didn't expect her to leave this mountain outside a body bag.

"Why go to all this trouble? Frank Austen is the one who murdered the kid's mother. Not you. Besides, that was a really long time ago. Even if someone remembered he worked for you back then, it likely wouldn't matter."

He laughed. "If only it were that simple." He pointed at her with the gun. "This is your fault, anyway. If you hadn't written that article, maybe none of this would have happened."

She shrugged, pretending she didn't get it. "What does my article have to do with any of this?"

"It was all over the place," he snapped. "Austen got nervous. He had a feeling the old lady was up to something. So he paid her a little visit to remind her about their deal and then he saw the kid all grown up visiting you. He understood then and there what she'd done. He called me whining like a little baby and I told him to clean it up. It was his mess, not mine."

"He killed her." Halle had never wanted to hurt anyone the way she did this man.

"I couldn't have cared less." He shrugged. "But then he decides it's in his best interest to retire, disappear. Apparently, he hadn't kept his 401(k) up to par so he asks me for money to keep his mouth shut about all those other kids. Bad decision. You see, I'm running for the state senate next year. I have big plans, Ms. Lane. I've made all the money I will ever need and now I want something else. Power and the kind of admiration that comes with it. Maybe I'll run for governor one day. Can't have this sort of thing cropping up in the news. You know how they like to dig up past sins on candidates."

The people who were hurt and murdered meant nothing to this man.

Killing her and Liam would be a mere nuisance for him.

The sound of a car door closing jerked her attention toward the dirt road.

Liam was here.

"It's about time," Burke muttered, his gaze focused in the direction of the road.

Halle ran.

She lunged deeper into the woods and darted first one direction and then the next. Burke screamed at her to stop but she kept going.

A shot rang out.

The bullet hit a tree not more than a few inches away from her.

She ducked and ran deeper to her left.

Another shot and then another.

Her heart was racing. Fear burned inside her but she didn't slow down. Ignored the limbs slapping at her face and her body.

She had to keep going.

Another shot.

She thought of the way Liam had looked at her

this morning when he kissed her before heading to his hotel.

She thought of her parents.

A scream and then shouting echoed through the woods.

She skidded to a halt. Hid behind a tree. The voices were louder now.

"Halle!"

Liam.

She started to shout back at him but she was afraid that would only draw him closer to the trouble.

"Halle, it's okay," he shouted. "We've got him. You can come out now!"

"Ms. Lane!"

Was that…?

"This is Chief Brannigan, it's safe now."

Tears streaming down her cheeks and her heart pounding like a drum, she rushed toward the sound of their voices. She'd run so blindly and so fast from Burke she wasn't even sure how to get back to the dirt road.

Then she spotted Liam. She raced to him. His arms went around her.

"God almighty," he murmured against her ear, "I am so glad you're all right."

She drew back and smiled at him. "I am now."

Burke stared at her, his face red with fury. A plug was missing from the right sleeve of his jacket. The rip was soaked with blood.

"How did you know to come?" she asked the chief.

"Liam called me." He hitched his head toward the man holding her.

"I had no idea how to get to the road you mentioned

and I couldn't make the damned navigation system in the rental work, so I called the chief. His was the only number I had. He knew the area and was suspicious. He wanted to come with me." Liam shifted his gaze to the chief. "I am very grateful he did."

"Thank you," Halle agreed.

Brannigan gave her a nod. "Thank *you*. It's always nice to take criminals off the street." He jerked Burke toward the road. "Let's go. I've got a car coming for you, Mr. Burke. Let's talk about your rights."

Liam hugged Halle again. She could feel his heart pounding in his chest.

When he drew back again, he smiled sadly. "Penelope and Claire are at your place. Penelope told me everything."

Halle swiped her eyes. "I'm sorry I caused all this to happen to you and your family."

"No." He touched her cheek. "You gave me the rest of my family. And I never want to lose you again."

He kissed her on the nose. "Now, let's get you home."

Chapter Sixteen

LATER

Saturday, June 20
Winchester

Halle stared at her reflection. The wedding dress fit like a glove. It was perfect.

Her mother appeared next to her. She smiled. "You look so beautiful, sweetheart. Now aren't you glad you didn't damage that dress when you sneaked it out of my keepsake trunk?"

Halle laughed, used the tip of her ring finger to swipe a tear from her eye before it messed up her makeup. "I sure am." She sighed. "I have waited to do this day right for a very long time."

"Twenty-five years."

Halle turned to face her mother. "I am so glad you and Dad want to move to Napa with us."

Her mother's face lit up. "Are you kidding? I've always dreamed of living in a Tuscan-style villa surrounded by vineyards. It's perfect, sweetie. It really is. I can't wait to spoil my grandchildren. And your father is determined to learn the art of winemaking from Liam."

Halle was so grateful there wouldn't be a trial. Burke had confessed to everything. He'd gone for a deal that kept him from getting a death sentence. Not only had he provided the information on all the children he and his minions had stolen, he'd provided the location of Liam's mother's remains, as well. A private service had been held in Napa last month and she had been buried next to his father.

They could all get on with the rest of their lives now.

Halle kissed her mother's cheek. "You're right. It's like a dream come true. A fairy tale that's finally getting its happy ending."

Her mother nodded. "The right ones always do."

The door opened and Claire slipped inside. She looked stunning in her maid-of-honor dress. "It's almost time."

Her dad stepped into the room next. "I'm not sure my heart can take the sheer beauty in this room."

Halle gave him a hug. "Let's do this."

Moments later as the wedding march played, Halle, holding her father's arm, walked up the aisle toward the man she had loved since she was a little girl.

He smiled at her and she knew without doubt that her mother was right. Some fairy tales did come true and this was one of them.

* * * * *

MYSTERIOUS ABDUCTION

RITA HERRON

To the fans who belong to the Addicted to Danger
Loop—hope you enjoy this new series!

Prologue

They say that you forget what labor is like the moment you hold your baby in your arms.

Cora Reeves Westbrook would never forget.

Still, her little girl was worth every painful contraction.

Cora leaned back against the pillow in the hospital bed and gently traced a finger over her daughter's soft cheek. Alice smelled like baby shampoo and all things good and sweet in life.

Her husband, Drew, dropped a kiss on her forehead. It had been a rough eighteen hours, and she hadn't slept in almost two days, but she'd never been happier.

Her little girl was perfect.

She memorized every inch of her small round face, her little pug nose, her ten little fingers and toes, and that dimple in her right cheek.

"She's the most beautiful baby I've ever seen," she whispered.

"She looks like an angel," Drew murmured.

Cora smiled, grateful he seemed happy, too. When she'd first told Drew about the pregnancy, he hadn't been thrilled. He was worried about finances and had his goals set on a partnership at his law firm. She'd assured him they could handle a family, but he'd still obsessed over the possibility of not being financially secure.

His cell phone buzzed, and he gave her an apologetic look. "Sorry, I need to get this."

He hurried from the room, and she pressed a kiss to Alice's cheek and rocked her back and forth, whispering promises of love.

A few minutes later, Lisa, the nurse who'd helped her during delivery, appeared again.

"We need to take her to run some tests." She patted Cora's leg. "I'll bring her back in a bit. You should rest. Those night feedings can wear you out."

Cora hugged Alice one more time, then handed her to the nurse. She was so excited that she didn't think she could sleep, but exhaustion overcame her the minute the nurse left the room, and she drifted off.

She was dreaming of carrying Alice home to the nursery she'd decorated when the scent of smoke woke her. Suddenly the fire alarm sounded, and the door burst open. Lisa raced in.

"Come on, we have to evacuate!"

She raced to the bed to help Cora, but panic sent Cora flying off the bed first. "My baby! I have to get Alice!"

"The neonatal nurses are already moving the infants outside," Lisa said. "We'll find her out there!"

Cora pushed the nurse aside and ran into the hall. Thick smoke fogged her vision, chaos erupting around her. The staff was hurrying to help patients out, pushing wheelchairs and beds, and assisting those who needed help. Someone grabbed her arm.

"Go down the stairs!"

"My baby!" Cora pushed at the hands, stumbled and felt her way to the window of the nursery. Screams and cries echoed around her as firefighters raced into the hall.

She pressed her face to the glass partition and peered inside, searching for her baby.

But the room was empty.

A sob caught in her throat. Her mind raced. *Outside*. The nurse said they were moving the infants outside.

She tore away from the window and stumbled toward the stairs. The hall was full now, patients and staff frantic to reach the exits. Someone pushed her forward, and she was carried into the stairwell. She clawed at the railing to stay on her feet as she raced down the stairs.

When they reached the landing, someone opened the door to the bottom floor, but heat blasted her. Flames were ripping through the hall. A terrified scream echoed in her ears. Another patient's—or her own? She didn't know. Maybe both.

A fireman appeared and pointed toward a back exit. She covered her mouth, coughing as smoke filled her lungs, then followed as everyone crouched low to make it outside.

Lights from the fire truck and police twirled in the sky. Beds, wheelchairs filled with the injured and those too weak to walk, patients, family, visitors and hospital workers poured onto the lawn. Doctors, nurses and medics were circulating to tend to the hurt and sick. Flames shot from the building and firefighters scurried to douse the blaze. First responders rushed inside to save lives.

A coughing fit seized her, but she brushed aside the medic who approached her. "The babies? Where are they?"

He turned and scanned the area, then pointed to a corner near the parking lot. Cora took off running; she was so weak that her legs wobbled unsteadily. She searched faces for Drew but didn't see him, either.

God, please, let him have Alice.

Praying with all her might, she staggered through the mess, the terrified and pain-filled screams of the injured filling the smoky air. Finally she spotted a row of bassinets.

Tears blurred her eyes, but she stumbled forward and frantically began to search the bassinets. Other parents were doing the same, two nurses trying to organize the chaos and failing as frightened mothers dragged their infants into their arms.

Cora finally spotted the bassinet marked "Westbrook—Girl" and gripped the edge of it.

She reached inside, but her baby was gone.

Chapter One

Five years later

Cora's phone beeped as she let herself into her house, but she was juggling a grocery bag and bottle of Chardonnay and couldn't reach it. She and her ex-husband, Drew, had bought the little bungalow nestled in the mountains of North Carolina six years ago when they'd first married—and were happy.

Before Alice was taken.

That day the world stopped for Cora.

Sometimes she wanted to give up. To die and be rid of the pain.

But every time she reached for the razor blade to slit her wrists, she saw her baby's face in her mind. Sweet, precious Alice with the little round face and a cherub nose and a gummy smile.

A tiny six-pound infant who'd trusted her mother to take care of her.

But Cora had failed.

Her baby was out there somewhere. Cora wasn't going to give up until she found her.

Unlike Drew, who'd abandoned Cora a few months after their baby had disappeared.

Cora wanted to hold Alice and assure her that all she'd ever wanted was to be her mommy. She wanted to rock her when she didn't feel good and clean her boo-boos and pick her up when she fell.

Her phone vibrated again, indicating she had a message. Maybe it was the principal of the elementary school where she taught, saying he'd changed his mind and she hadn't been fired.

When the last bell had rung today, he'd summoned her into his office.

"Cora, I understand how painful losing your daughter was, but you frightened Nina Fuller. Her mother called me to complain."

"I heard she was adopted—"

"I'm well aware of the family's situation, and you overstepped."

"But I thought—"

"You thought about your own obsession," he said, cutting her off. "Not about how that woman had three miscarriages and was on a wait list to adopt for three years before they got Nina."

Cora's heart squeezed. She hadn't known about the miscarriages and was sure the woman had suffered.

"I'm sorry," Cora said sincerely. "I'll apologize to Nina and her mother."

He held up a warning hand. "No, you are to leave them alone. Enough is enough. You need to take a break from teaching and get some help."

He meant psychiatric help. She had already done that. It hadn't worked.

The only thing that would make her whole again was to find her daughter. To tell her how much she loved her. That she'd been looking for her every day since that awful fire when someone had stolen her.

At first she'd been terrified that her baby had died in the fire. But after a massive search of the hospital and grounds, the police found Alice's hospital bracelet tossed on the ground near the parking lot.

That bracelet led them all to believe that someone had abducted Alice during the chaos.

"I promise I'll be more careful—"

"You don't understand, Cora," he said firmly. "This is not a suggestion. I'm terminating your employment."

Panic stabbed at Cora. He wasn't renewing her contract for the fall?

Oh, God, what was she going to do? Teaching had been her salvation the last few years. Her connection with children.

Her way to search for her missing daughter. Every year when the new students piled in, she studied the girls' faces for any detail she'd recognize. Some part of her that her offspring had inherited.

She did the same thing on the street, and at the mall and even the market she'd just left.

She dropped the grocery bag on the counter along with the bottle of wine. Summer break was always difficult as it meant endless hours alone, hours of reliving the past and praying that one day she'd find her little girl. Endless hours of the what-ifs that plagued her and threatened to steal her sanity.

She fished her phone from her purse. Sweat beaded on her forehead when she saw the number for Kurt Philips on the caller ID.

Kurt was the private investigator she'd kept on retainer for the last four years. She'd hired him the day after the police had declared that her case had gone cold.

Drew had left a few months after Alice went missing, and within a year, he'd remarried and started another family. His desertion and the fact that he'd had a son with his new wife had almost broken her.

Maybe Kurt had news.

Too afraid to hope, she uncorked the wine, poured a glass and carried it to the deck off the kitchen. Her backyard overlooked the beautiful mountains and Whistling River, the river the small mountain town of Whistler was named after. A summer breeze ruffled the pines as she sat down on the wrought iron glider and checked her voice mail.

"Cora, it's Kurt." His gruff voice was familiar, but he sounded different. Tense. Worried.

Then he was cut off.

She started to call him back, but a text came through.

Sorry, lead didn't pan out. It's time we give it a rest. You should move on.

His words sent pain searing through Cora. Kurt couldn't give up. He was her last hope.

With a shaky finger, she quickly pressed Call Back. But the phone rang and rang and no one answered.

Desperate to talk to him, she carried her glass of wine back to the kitchen, grabbed her keys and purse and jogged outside to her car.

Kurt had not only worked for her. He'd been her friend the last year.

He'd also cautioned her to prepare for the worst. Had he learned that something bad had happened to her baby and he didn't want to tell her?

She jumped in her vehicle, started the engine and peeled down her driveway onto the street. She couldn't go on without answers.

She had to know why he was abandoning her and the search for Alice.

SHERIFF JACOB MAVERICK parked in the strip shopping center on the edge of town, grimacing at the flames shooting into the sky. The fire department was already on the scene, rolling out hoses and spraying water to douse the blaze.

His brother Griff, a firefighter and arson investigator, was suited up and heading into the building.

Déjà vu struck Jacob and he froze, fear gripping him. He'd lost his father, the sheriff at the time of the horrific hospital fire that had nearly destroyed the town five years ago.

He couldn't lose one of his brothers.

But he couldn't stop Griff from doing his job any more than his brothers could have stopped him from taking over as sheriff after their father died. They all wanted to know who set that fire. They suspected arson. So far, though, they didn't have answers.

But one day he would find the truth.

His father's heroic behavior had inspired each of his brothers to become first responders. Griff had joined the fire department. Fletch, FEMA's local Search and Rescue team. And Liam, the FBI.

Lights from the ambulance twirled against the darkening sky. His deputy, Martin Rowan, had cordoned off the area to keep people away from the blaze. Jacob climbed from his vehicle and strode toward Martin.

"What do we have?" he asked.

Martin shrugged. "Not sure yet. The guy in the insurance office two doors down called it in. Said he came back for some paperwork and spotted smoke."

"The building looks old," Jacob said. "Could be faulty electrical wiring."

Wood crackled and popped. Flames were eating the downstairs and climbing through the second floor. Thick gray smoke billowed above, pouring out the windows and obliterating the puffy white clouds. Firefighters aimed the hoses and worked to extinguish the blaze.

A crash sounded, glass exploded. The roof…collapsed.

His pulse hammered and he ran toward the front door. The raging heat hit him in the face. "Come on, Griff," he muttered. "Get the hell out."

A CHILL RIPPLED through Cora as she passed Whistler's graveyard on the way to Kurt's office. Many of the people who'd died in the town fire had been buried in that cemetery. She jerked her eyes away, determined not to allow her mind to travel to the dark place it had so many times before.

Kurt's text made that impossible.

Had he found evidence indicating her daughter was… dead?

No…she wouldn't let herself believe that. A mother would know. *She* would know if that was true.

Night was falling, storm clouds shrouding the remaining sunlight. With Whistler so close to the Appalachian Trail, the area drew tourists during the summer months. People flocked to the cooler mountains to escape the heat, to indulge in hiking, camping, fishing and white water rafting.

When Alice was first taken, Cora had been shocked at how people laughed and went on about life when she could barely breathe for the anguish.

Tonight the breeze blowing off the water sounded shrill and eerie, a reminder that danger also existed in the endless miles of thick forests and the class four rapids. It also brought the scent of smoke.

She glanced to the right in the direction of Kurt's office, and her pulse jumped. Thick plumes of gray smoke were rolling upward.

She pressed the accelerator and swerved around an SUV, then wove past a caravan of church groups in white vans with the sign Jesus Saves emblazoned on the sides. She swung to the right onto a side street and bounced over a rut in the country road. A mile from the main highway, she reached the strip shopping center. Lights from fire trucks and emergency vehicles swirled against the darkness.

She veered into the shopping center, her gaze tracking the chaos. Flames had engulfed one building and lit the sky.

Dear God. It was Kurt's building.

She threw the car into Park on the hill near the tattoo parlor. Fear clawed at her.

Seconds ticked by. Other rubberneckers had gathered to watch the commotion.

Police worked to secure the area and keep onlookers away. A minute later, a firefighter raced out, carrying a man over his shoulder.

She craned her neck to see but couldn't tell if it was Kurt. Then she spotted a pair of boots. Gray and black. Snakeskin. Silver spurs.

Kurt's boots.

Boots she recognized because she'd given them to him.

Chapter Two

Jacob jogged toward Griff as his brother eased the man onto the stretcher by the ambulance. Instant recognition hit Jacob. "This is Kurt Philips, a private investigator. He was working for Cora. He talked to me about her case a few times."

Griff removed his oxygen mask and helmet, then shook his head. "He was dead when I found him." He gestured toward the bloody mess that had been the man's chest. He'd been shot.

The stench of burnt flesh, charred skin and ash swirled around Jacob. Damn. The fire was most likely arson intended to cover up a murder.

Considering the fact that Philips was a PI, he could have been killed because of one of his cases. His files, which might hold the answer to his killer's identity, had probably been destroyed in the blaze. Could have been the killer's intent.

The ME, a doctor named Ryland Hammerhead, bent over the corpse on the stretcher to examine the body.

"Got an ID?" Dr. Hammerhead asked.

Jacob nodded. "Kurt Philips, private investigator." Which opened up a lot of possibilities for who would want him dead.

The ME photographed the corpse, then brushed soot

from his shirt. "COD is probably blood loss from the gunshot wound to the chest, but I'll conduct a thorough autopsy and update you when I finish."

"Once the fire dies down, I'll have a crime team search the debris for evidence," Jacob said.

"I'll dig out the bullet and send it to the lab." The ME lifted Philips's right hand to examine it. Even through the dirt and ash, Jacob spotted blood. Dr. Hammerhead cut open the man's shirt, and Jacob zeroed in on the gunshot wound. The bullet hole had ripped skin and muscle and shattered bone.

He snapped a close-up with his cell phone.

"Must have been shot at close range." Jacob relayed the scene in his head. "Victim raised his hand to stop the bullet."

Dr. Hammerhead nodded grimly. "And was too late."

"Call me when you're ready with your report," Jacob said. "I'll meet you at the morgue."

The doctor gestured to the medics to load the body for transporting. Jacob joined his deputy and filled him in. He scrutinized the curious onlookers who'd gathered. "Canvass the crowd and store owners and find out if anyone saw anything. A car leaving, maybe?"

Martin nodded. "I'll get right on it."

Jacob scanned the parking lot. Sometimes thrill-seeking perps stuck around to watch the chaos and fear created by their crime. A vehicle on the crest of the hill in the parking lot caught his eye. Firelight illuminated the sky, making it easy to see the car. A red Ford SUV.

Cora Reeves's SUV.

Damn. His heart ached for that woman. Everyone in town knew about the baby she'd lost during the fire—the baby she believed had been kidnapped. He'd worked the case afterward and been frustrated as hell when the case went cold.

Was Philips murdered because he'd found out something about her child?

NERVES BUNCHED IN Cora's stomach. If the sheriff learned about the message Kurt had left her, he'd want to talk to her.

She'd seen enough of the press and police in her lifetime. They hadn't done a bit of good when her baby disappeared. Sure, Jacob, who'd been the deputy back then, had tried to find Alice, but he'd also been grief-stricken over his father's death. The entire town had been in shock and suffering from their personal losses, and confusion came from the chaos and terror. The massive extent of the damage from the blaze had also complicated evidence recovery.

Jacob had even questioned her as if she was a suspect. As if she'd paid someone to take her infant off her hands.

Then police focused on Drew. The questions and interrogations had compounded the agony and destroyed their marriage. Or maybe it had been her obsession with finding her daughter…

Emotions welling in her throat, Cora started the engine and drove away from the scene. But as the flames flickered behind her, lighting up the sky, despair overwhelmed her.

If Kurt was dead, she was really, truly alone.

And her chances of learning what happened to her daughter had died with him.

The rest of the drive blurred as a storm threatened. By the time she reached the house, her hands ached from clenching the steering wheel. She pulled into the garage, closed the electric door and rushed inside. The wine she'd poured earlier was still sitting on the kitchen counter, a reminder that she'd lost her job earlier that day. That summer loomed with the threat of her bank account dwindling.

She curled her fingers around the stem of the wineglass

and climbed the stairs to the second floor. To the nursery she'd decorated for Alice.

Tears clogged her throat as she stepped inside. The pale pink color of the walls still remained. But the furniture and baby clothes had all been removed.

Drew had packed them up one day while she was at her therapist's office. He'd said he couldn't stand to see her stare at the baby toys and clothes, so he'd given them away. He wanted them to move on.

Move on as if they'd never had a child? Erase any evidence she'd given birth.

She'd told him to get out. He might be able to forget about their daughter. But she would never forget.

Exhausted, she decided to shower. Maybe the running water would wash away the images of Kurt being carried from that burning building. She scrubbed her hands and body, then her hair, and let the tears fall. Tears for Kurt.

Tears for the loneliness and emptiness she felt.

Tears of fear that Kurt's death meant she'd never find Alice.

The doorbell rang, startling her, and she stepped from the shower and dried off. She pulled on her bathrobe and ran a comb through her damp hair.

The doorbell rang again. Who would be visiting her this time of night? She'd lost most of her friends over the years.

Nerves on edge, she hurried to the window and looked outside. The sheriff's car sat in her drive.

JACOB STOOD ON Cora's front porch, tapping his boot as he waited for her to answer the door. He'd left his deputy to guard the crime scene and would go back once the blaze died down and it was safe for the crime scene team to search for forensics. Griff would look for the origin of the fire and traces of accelerant.

Maybe the killer had been sloppy, hadn't used gloves

and had left a print. Doubtful, although if the perp thought the fire would completely destroy evidence, he might not have been so careful.

He rang the bell again.

Finally footsteps echoed from the inside. He braced himself to see Cora in person again. She'd come to his office at least once a month over the years to see if he had news. The pain in her eyes always tore him inside out. He'd lost a father, but he couldn't imagine losing a child. Living with unanswered questions, wondering if she was dead or alive. Safe or happy. If she had a home...

He'd heard rumors that Cora had become so obsessed with finding her daughter that she'd pushed friends away. Her marriage had fallen apart, too. Her bastard husband had walked out a few months after the baby disappeared, then remarried, and Cora had reclaimed her maiden name.

He'd never trusted her ex. Drew Westbrook had been at the top of his suspect list five years ago. Jacob just hadn't been able to prove that he'd been involved in his baby's disappearance.

Maybe Kurt had found a lead.

He inhaled a deep breath at the sound of the door lock turning. The moment he saw Cora's tear-swollen eyes, though, he knew Kurt Philips hadn't given her good news.

"Hi, Cora. Can I come in?"

Her deep, sad blue eyes pierced him, as if she hadn't forgotten that he'd let her down. Guilt gnawed at him. He had tried. But he'd failed.

She clutched her robe around her and cinched the belt. Jacob's lungs squeezed for air. Even sad and wearing that cotton bathrobe, Cora looked sexy with her damp, long, wavy auburn hair brushing her shoulders.

A wary look darkened her face, but she stepped aside and gestured for him to come in. He wiped his feet on the welcome mat in the entry, noting that she hadn't changed anything since he'd been here before. The decor was still the same—tasteful but simple.

The open concept living/dining kitchen was furnished in what he thought they called farmhouse style. A distressed-looking table and chairs sat to the left in front of the front window while a large island divided the living room and kitchen. A floor-to-ceiling brick fireplace made the room look cozy, although he'd wondered more than once why Cora hadn't moved from town to escape the painful memories.

Maybe she thought whoever took her baby might bring her to Whistler?

Cora led him to the kitchen and offered him coffee. She had one of those new coffee makers that made a cup at a time using pods, and fixed him a cup. He had a feeling she was stalling, because she knew why he was here.

He accepted a mug of coffee, and waited as she made herself one. Then she led him to the den. She sank onto the couch, and he claimed the leather wing chair by the fireplace.

"I saw you at Kurt Philips's office tonight. The place burned down."

She looked down into her mug. "Do you know what started the fire?"

He shook his head. "Not yet. We'll be conducting a thorough investigation."

She lifted her gaze, her blue eyes piercing him again. "Shouldn't you be there now doing that?"

The disapproval in her tone made him grit his teeth. "I'll go back once the fire dies down and the investigators can get in." He took a sip of his coffee. "I know Kurt Philips was a PI, Cora, and that he worked for you." He intentionally let the statement linger. Not a question really, but he wanted to see her reaction.

She shifted and tucked her feet underneath her on the

sofa as if she was relaxed. But tension oozed from her stiff posture and the tight set of her slender jaw.

Cora was an attractive woman, naturally pretty, wholesome and kindhearted. She did volunteer work with the church to pack meals for needy families.

"He did," Cora admitted.

"I'm sorry, Cora. You probably think I gave up, but I haven't. Liam has kept your case high on the FBI's priority list." Griff continued to search for arson cases similar to the hospital fire in hopes of making a connection. Fletch was keeping an eye out on his search and rescue missions in case the arsonist—killer—was holed up in the woods off the grid.

Her eyes widened as if surprised. "Liam really is looking for Alice?"

Jacob nodded. "I swear, Cora. One day we'll find her."

Emotions streaked her face, and she closed her eyes for a brief moment, pinching the bridge of her nose. When she opened her eyes again, she blinked away tears.

"Did Kurt have any leads for you?" Jacob asked.

She dropped her gaze to her coffee again. "No. He hadn't found anything yet."

Jacob heard the disappointment in her tone. "When did you last see or speak to him?"

She shifted again, and Jacob had the impression she was hiding something.

"Come on, Cora, talk to me," Jacob said. "I need to know what happened at his office."

"I don't know," she said. "Maybe it was an accidental fire?"

He shook his head. "Listen to me," he said gruffly. "The fire was set to cover up something else."

"You mean a theft? Did someone rob his office?"

"I don't know yet, but that's possible," he admitted. "But it was more than a robbery."

"What do you mean?"

"Kurt Philips was murdered."

Chapter Three

Cora gripped her coffee mug so hard she thought it would shatter. "What?" she said in a raw whisper.

A muscle ticked in Jacob's jaw. "I'm sorry, Cora, but Kurt was murdered."

"How? Why?"

His gaze locked with hers. Jacob had always been intimidating. Big, muscular, strong, with a wide, chiseled jaw and dark brown eyes that seemed as if they could see into her soul. She felt as if he was looking there now.

Probing. Wondering. Just like the other cops and FBI had. He couldn't possibly think she'd killed Kurt, could he?

"Just tell me when you talked to him or saw him last?"

The fact that he ignored her question raised her defensive instincts. She could not go here again, not be treated like a suspect.

"I don't remember," she said, hedging. "He works cases other than mine. Do you think he was killed because of one of those?"

Silence stretched between them for a tension-filled minute. "It's too early to tell. But I'll examine all his cases. Although the murder could have been personal. Was he married or involved with anyone?"

She fought a reaction. "I don't know, *Sheriff*." She intentionally emphasized his title. "Now, is that all?"

His gaze latched with hers. Again, his look was so probing that she almost squirmed.

"I thought he might have uncovered something about your daughter." He shrugged, but his demeanor didn't quite meet the nonjudgmental attitude he was trying to convey. "If one of his cases got him killed, Cora, it might have been yours."

Her breath caught. Was he right?

Had Kurt discovered who'd taken Alice and been killed so he'd be quiet?

If so, why had he texted that he was giving up?

JACOB SENSED CORA was holding something back. She looked visibly shaken by the news that Philips was dead. Even more so that he might have been killed because he was looking for Alice.

Or perhaps she was just upset that she'd lost her PI. God knew she'd suffered a lot of knocks over the past five years with her daughter's case going cold and then her divorce. Every day it ate at him that they didn't know who'd set that fire at the hospital, because that person had killed his father, taken more lives and possibly kidnapped Cora's daughter.

She lived with that pain every day, as well, wondering where her little girl was and what had happened to her.

He glanced at her hands. She'd obviously just showered before he'd arrived, so if she had shot Kurt, she'd washed away gunshot residue. He had no probable cause at this point to even test her for it.

Besides, he didn't see Cora as a killer. She was soft, vulnerable and compassionate. She taught school at Whistler Elementary.

"You aren't certain that Kurt was killed because he worked for me, though, are you?" Cora asked.

Jacob shook his head. "Not at this point. We need to search his files and records of his other cases, although the fire is going to complicate that. I'm not sure how much we can salvage." He studied her. "Did he talk to you about anything else he was working on?"

She shook her head no.

"What about his personal life? Did he have family? A wife?"

She shifted and sipped her coffee. "He had no family that I know of. And he was divorced."

He'd talk to the ex. "How long ago was that?"

"A few months, I think." She wrinkled her nose in thought. "He didn't share the details."

"Do you know his ex-wife's name or where she lives?"

She stood and ran a hand through her still-damp hair. She was trembling. From the shock of the news or something else? "I think her name was Erica. He mentioned her once when he asked me about Drew. I have no idea where she lives."

"You two never met?"

"No." She folded her arms.

"Was the divorce amicable?"

"Like I said, he didn't share details, although I had the impression she wanted him back."

If that was the case and Kurt had been dating someone else, his ex might have been jealous and killed him because he rejected her.

Definitely an avenue to explore.

"Thanks for seeing me, Cora," Jacob said. "If you think of anything else that might be helpful, please call me."

She nodded but seemed reluctant as she walked him to the door.

"Jacob?"

Her soft voice, so full of need, made his chest clench. He leaned against the door and faced her. Maybe she had been holding back and was ready to come clean. "Yes?"

"Did you mean what you said about your brother looking for Alice?"

The inkling of hope in her tone stirred his protective instincts. "Yes. It's difficult without current photographs to distribute, but he's kept her file active. He also has someone looking at adoptions that occurred around that time."

She sucked in a deep breath. "If it would help, I've drawn sketches projecting what Alice might look like at every age. I based them on photos of me and of Drew when we were young."

He didn't know what to say.

"I guess that sounds crazy," she said in a haunted whisper. "But I like to draw."

Jacob heard the ache in her words and shook his head. "You don't sound crazy. And it might be helpful if you sent me some of those drawings. I'll pass them to Liam, and he can distribute to other law enforcement agencies and NCEMC. We might get lucky and someone will recognize her."

Hope lit her eyes. God help him, he didn't want to let her down again. He understood the disappointment when a clue didn't pan out.

He'd chased dead leads in search of his father's killer since that damn fire.

But at least he knew where his father was. He had closure.

Cora lived with uncertainty every day.

Cora cleared her throat. "I can drop some sketches by your office tomorrow if that's all right."

He nodded. "That works."

"One more question, Cora. Did Kurt question Drew?"

She hesitated. "Yes, along with everyone who was at the hospital at the time."

"How did it go with Drew?"

"Not well," she admitted.

He didn't expect it had. Drew had been furious when Jacob questioned him. He'd set his sights on making partner at his law firm, and had threatened to sue the sheriff's office if they maligned his character with accusations.

Ironically, the publicity had catapulted him into the limelight and earned him sympathy from his coworkers. He'd made partner a few months after the kidnapping.

Then he'd left Cora to deal with the emotional fallout of looking for their child alone.

Drew wouldn't like to be questioned again. But Jacob wouldn't allow Drew's attitude to deter him.

If the bastard had anything to do with the PI's death, Jacob would find out.

JACOB'S WORDS ECHOED in Cora's ears. *We might get lucky and someone will recognize her.*

He'd said *we,* as if she wasn't alone. As if he truly hadn't given up. As if there might be a chance to find her daughter…

Heart hammering, she hurried up the steps to the room that had been meant for her baby. In her mind, she pictured it filled with all the precious things she'd received at her baby shower—the giant teddy bear and sweet little embroidered dresses. The tiny white kids' table and the storybooks. The pink-and-white polka-dotted sheets and the dancing bear mobile she'd hung over the white Jenny Lind crib.

The memory of the day she'd come home from therapy and found the room empty taunted her.

Drew had been standing at the empty nursery, stoic and calm. "The therapist suggested it might help you move on if we cleaned out the baby's room."

Seeing that empty room had nearly brought her to her knees. "I don't want to move on!" she'd screamed. "I want to find my daughter. I thought you did, too."

Pain wrenched his face. "I do, Cora. But… I can't go on like this. Day after day listening to you cry. Watching you touch the baby clothes and sleep with her stuffed animals. You're driving yourself crazy."

"You mean I'm driving you crazy," she shouted.

"Yes. I'm trying to hold it together, but I can't do it anymore. I can't hold us both together."

"What are you saying? That you're giving up on finding Alice?"

"I'm not giving up," he said, "but it's been months. The leads have gone cold. Bills are piling up. My boss is pressuring me to see clients again. I have to resume my practice or I'll never make partner. It might do you good to return to teaching."

"My life *is* my daughter." She'd waved her hand across the room. "Where are her things? I want them back."

"I took them to a shelter," he said in a low, tired voice. "People need them, Cora. We don't."

"Alice will need them when she comes home."

His eyes narrowed to slits, then a tear slid down his cheek. "What if she doesn't come home? We have to face that possibility—"

"No!" She lunged at him. "You can't give up and forget about her!"

He stood ramrod straight while she hit him in the chest with her fists and cried. Finally she spent her emotions and sagged against him. Then he pushed her away and walked out the door.

Cora fought despair. The moment the door slammed, she'd known her marriage was over. That losing Alice had torn them apart.

She crossed the room to the hope chest she'd bought after Drew moved out. Inside it, she'd placed cards, letters and gifts for every birthday and holiday that had passed. Stuffed animals, baby dolls and puzzles. Books and crayons and coloring books. A pumpkin Halloween costume and a red Christmas dress. Soft ballerina shoes and bows for Alice's hair.

The wrapping paper was fading now, ribbons crushed. But she'd kept them so if—no, *when*—she found Alice, she'd prove that she'd never forgotten her.

The only thing Drew hadn't given away was the pink-and-green blanket she'd crocheted before Alice was born.

She removed the blanket from the chest and pressed it to her face, the yarn baby soft.

She'd never gotten to wrap her daughter in that blanket.

The memory of cradling her newborn in her arms was so distant that she felt as if she was clawing at thin air to grasp it, but just as her fingertips reached it, the wind viciously snatched it away.

Tears blurred her eyes, and she moved to the shelf where she kept the journals of her sketches. She'd drawn at least one sketch a week, marking off the days as she tried to imagine the changes in her daughter's face and how she was growing.

She retrieved the latest journal—Alice at five—and studied the sketches. She'd take them all to Jacob tomorrow and let him decide which ones to use.

Although her chest tightened with anxiety. She'd been searching the face of every child she'd seen or met for five years.

Would she even recognize her daughter if she came face-to-face with her?

KNOWING IT WOULD take time for Griff and the crime investigators to comb the scene for forensics, Jacob found the address for Kurt's ex-wife. If Philips had family, she would know. She also needed to be notified of her ex's death.

He wanted to study her reaction when he told her, learn if she had motive for murder.

He phoned his deputy to inform him of his plan. "Make sure Griff and the crime techs recover Philips's cell phone and computer. They could contain information about what he was working on. Any files they can salvage may be valuable."

"On it," Deputy Rowan said.

"I'm headed to Philips's ex-wife's house now. Will keep you posted."

Jacob kept replaying his conversation with Cora in his head as he drove from town. Her anguish was a palpable force.

The last thing he wanted to do was give her false hope.

The clouds darkened in intensity as he veered onto the mountain road leading to Mrs. Philips's house. Trees swayed in the wind as the storm threatened, thunder booming in the distance.

He hoped to hell the rain held off until Griff and the crime team finished. Rain would wash away evidence that was already difficult enough to recover from the ashes and debris of the crumpled building.

His GPS directed him to a side road on the mountain. He maneuvered the turn, slowing as another car barreled around the curve too fast. He let it go by, then steered his SUV up the incline into a small neighborhood built overlooking the mountain.

When he reached the Philipses' house, he turned into the drive and parked. Lights illuminated the inside of the A-frame cabin. He climbed out and strode up to the steps to the front stoop. A black Lab raced over to him, and he paused for a minute to let the dog sniff him. The Lab licked his hand, and Jacob smiled. If Philips's ex had this dog as a watchdog, it was falling down on the job.

He glanced around the property, then knocked. A noise echoed from inside, then footsteps and the door opened.

A woman with short, choppy black hair answered, a cock-tail in her hand.

"Mrs. Philips?"

She took in his shield and frowned. "Yeah."

"I'm Sheriff Maverick." He took a quick sniff to deter-mine if she smelled of smoke from the fire and detected the scent of cigarette smoke. Hmm…a cigarette lighter could have been used to set the fire. "May I come in?"

She tugged at her T-shirt. "What's this about, Sheriff?"

"We need to talk."

She frowned, but stepped aside and allowed him to enter. The ice in her drink clinked as she took a big swallow. He followed her through a small entryway into her den. Laun-dry seemed to be spread everywhere, magazines and dirty dishes scattered around.

She plopped down into a big club chair and looked up at him with questions in her eyes. Although her drinking might be a result of knowing her husband was dead—or that she'd murdered him and feared being caught.

But judging from two other empty bottles in the kitchen, Jacob surmised she might have a habit.

"Mrs. Philips, when did you last speak to or see your husband?" he asked.

She crossed her legs, then snagged a pack of cigarettes from the coffee table, tapped one out and lit it. "Last week, I guess."

"Last week? Can you be specific?"

She shrugged. "Maybe Friday. No, wait, it was Satur-day."

"You two were separated?"

"Divorced," she said in a tone laced with bitterness. "Eight months ago. Why are you asking about Kurt and me?"

Jacob ignored her question. "Were you and your hus-band working toward a reconciliation?"

"I wanted it, but Kurt…he was interested in greener pastures." She leaned forward with her hands on her knees, her expression worried. "You sure are asking a lot of questions. Did something happen to Kurt?"

Jacob forced a neutral expression. "Yes, ma'am. I'm sorry to inform you, but he was killed earlier tonight."

Her face paled, and she collapsed back against the sofa, her hand shaking as she raised the cigarette to her lips.

"That's why you asked about our divorce."

He nodded. "I need to know if Kurt had enemies. Or if he was involved with someone else."

Her mouth tightened. "You want to know about Kurt, go ask his girlfriend."

Jacob narrowed his eyes. "Can you give me a name?"

She tapped ashes into an empty soda can on the table. "That lady whose child was kidnapped. She's crazy if you ask me, but Kurt had a thing for her."

Jacob's pulse jumped. "You mean Cora Reeves?"

"That's right." She grabbed her drink and tossed the rest of it down. "I think she was just using him, but he didn't care. Kurt was a sucker for a sob story and that lady had one."

Of course she was using him. She'd hired him to do a job, find her missing daughter. But this woman was implying that Cora and Kurt had a personal relationship.

Was Cora romantically involved with Kurt Philips? If so, why hadn't she told him about it when he'd asked?

Chapter Four

Jacob couldn't get Cora off his mind as he drove home. Were Cora and Kurt personally involved?

He didn't know why the thought bothered him. Cora certainly had suffered when her baby was stolen and her husband deserted her. She deserved to find love again and happiness.

If she had been with Kurt, his death would be another loss.

His chest clenched. The sorrow in her eyes always wrenched his gut.

He parked in the driveway to his cabin on the side of the mountain overlooking the river. Although summer was starting and the temperature was climbing, the air felt cooler and fresher here on the mountain.

Still, the scent of charred wood and metal clung to his skin, a reminder of the fire that had robbed his father's life.

His father's face taunted him as he let himself inside his cabin.

Jacob had always looked up to his old man. Seth Maverick was honest, had fought for justice and worked hard to protect the people in town. All Jacob ever wanted was to be like him.

Six months before the fire, his dream had come true. While other classmates had left the small town, he'd learned to love it the way his father had. He'd attended the police academy, then come home, and his father had deputized him. They'd been doing routine rounds when the 911 call came in about the fire.

Perspiration broke out on the back of Jacob's neck, and he walked through the cabin to the back door, opened it and stepped outside onto the deck that overlooked the canyon and river. A slight breeze stirred the trees, bringing the scent of wildflowers and rain from the day before, yet he was still sweating as the memories bombarded him.

By the time he and his father arrived at the hospital, flames were shooting from one side of the building. The fire alarm had been tripped, and the hospital staff was busy helping patients outside. One fire engine was on the scene and another careened into the parking lot, tires squealing. Emergency workers and firefighters raced to save lives, and roll out hoses to extinguish the blaze.

His father threw the police car into Park, and they both had jumped out to run toward the building. Two firefighters rushed out carrying patients while doctors and nurses and medics combed the lawn to help.

Screams from inside the building had filled the night, part of the roof had collapsed and a window had burst, spraying glass. Smoke poured upward into the night sky.

More firefighters had rushed inside and the volunteer fire department had arrived and jumped into motion to help.

His father didn't hesitate. He had dashed toward the burning building.

Adrenaline surging through him, Jacob had done the same.

For the next half hour, they'd helped people evacuate. Jacob carried more than one ill patient in his arms and pushed wheelchair patients unable to walk on their own.

Another half hour, and the terrified cries and screams were embedded in his memory forever. Family members wove through the crowd on the lawn, searching for loved ones. A man ran from the building, shouting as flames shot from his clothing.

Jacob had rushed toward him, taken his arm and forced him to drop to the ground and roll to extinguish the flames. A medic had jogged toward them and taken over as Jacob hurried to help a pregnant woman down the steps.

Jacob recalled the ear-piercing scream that had suddenly rent the air. Shooting to the source, his gaze found a young woman in a hospital gown by a row of bassinets.

"My baby, my baby!" she cried.

Jacob had sprinted through the crowd to reach her. She was frantic, yelling at one of the nurses.

Tears of fear poured down the woman's face. "My baby…where is she?"

Jacob's lungs strained for air as he realized the bassinet was empty.

"The babies were all here," the nurse said. "We brought them out in the bassinets."

Jacob gripped the woman's arms as a sob tore from her gut. "We'll find her," he murmured. "We'll find her."

Jacob closed his eyes, trying to banish the images after that. The frantic search of the hospital and property for the missing infant. When Drew had finally joined Cora, he'd looked frightened that his daughter wasn't with his wife.

A few minutes later, a staff member ran toward them holding a hospital bracelet he'd found in the parking lot. A hospital bracelet with the name "Baby Westbrook—Girl" on it.

The bracelet that had belonged to Cora's baby.

"We'll find her," he'd promised.

But he hadn't.

He hadn't given up, though. He never would.

EXHAUSTION TUGGED AT Cora the next morning. She stumbled into the kitchen for coffee, made herself a cup and carried it to her screened porch. Dawn was just breaking, the sun streaking the sky in orange, yellow and red. As a teenager, she used to sleep half the morning, but since Alice had been gone, she struggled with insomnia. When she finally slept, nightmares plagued her, and she often rose with the sun.

She loved the peace and quiet of the mountains. The beauty of nature and the rolling hills and the blossoms on the trees.

But once again that peace had been disturbed.

She'd cried herself to sleep over Kurt the night before. He had been a good man. Had been kind to her. Had tried to help her.

She'd let him get closer to her than anyone had in years. Still, she hadn't totally given him her heart.

That heart had been shattered by the loss of her daughter and her husband and would never be whole again.

Kurt's text still disturbed her.

She heaved a weary breath. Now what?

Jacob…he'd assured her that the FBI hadn't given up on finding her daughter. She'd promised to drop off sketches for his brother to distribute.

She set her coffee aside, rose and went to retrieve the ones she'd pulled the night before. She traced a finger lovingly over each drawing, her heart swelling with love as she imagined finally pulling her daughter into her arms for a hug.

Although her therapist's voice haunted her. *What will you do if you find her and she's in a happy home? Will you upset her world by telling her that you're her mother?*

How could she not tell her if she found her? Her daughter deserved to know that her mother hadn't given her away, didn't she?

She placed the sketches in her tote bag, then checked the clock. Too early to go to the sheriff's office, so she made herself another cup of coffee and took her stationery back to the porch. She settled on the glider and began to write another letter to add to her collection.

Dear Alice,

Today is the first day of summer break. The kids I taught were so excited yesterday. They drew pictures depicting their plans for the break. Some were going swimming. Others are taking vacations to the beach. One little girl is going to Africa with her parents.

I wonder what you're doing this summer. Are you excited that school is out? Or will you miss your friends?

She paused to wipe at a tear, her heart aching. She didn't know one thing about her daughter or her life now. *Did* Alice have friends at school? Did she like music or gymnastics? Was she learning to ride a bicycle? Did she have a pet?

Did she live with two parents who loved her?

Cora swallowed hard and put her pen back to paper again.

I know you're five now and that this year you were in kindergarten. I wonder if you like arts and crafts or sports, and if you're learning to read. One day when I see you again, you can tell me everything.

I still live in the house in the mountains. The flowers are starting to bloom and the wind is whistling off the river this morning. It reminds me of a lullaby I sang to you before you were born. Of all the lullabies I wanted to sing to you when I brought you home.

You're too old for lullabies now. But maybe you like to sing songs you learned at school.

I'm sitting on my back-screened porch thinking about what we would do today if you were here.

There's a park close by with a swing set and jungle gym. That would be a fun way to start the day.

We might even take a picnic lunch. Then we can go and get ice cream. There's a cute little ice cream parlor in town called Sundae Heaven, where you can make your own ice cream sundaes. I like vanilla ice cream with hot fudge sauce or fresh strawberries. And my favorite ice cream flavor they have is peach cobbler. It's so yummy!

I wonder what your favorite flavor is or what toppings you'd choose. Do you like sprinkles or chocolate sauce or chocolate chip cookies?

I'll tell you a secret. I would love to try Reese's Peanut Butter Cup ice cream, but I'm allergic to peanuts! Yikes, I hate those shots!

I'll keep you close to my heart until I see you again.
All my love,
Mommy

The clock struck the hour, and Cora decided it was time to shower and take the sketches to Jacob. The sooner his brother got them into the database, the sooner someone might recognize Alice.

JACOB'S PHONE WAS ringing as soon as he stepped from the shower. He dried off, yanked on his clothes and hurried to answer it.

It was his brother Griff. "I thought you'd want to know what we found last night."

Jacob walked to the kitchen, poured himself some coffee and nuked a frozen sausage biscuit. "Yeah, I do."

"The fire was definitely arson. The accelerant—gasoline. Point of origin, the man's office. I found traces of gasoline there. Once it was lit, the fire spread quickly."

No surprise. "Any cigarette butts, matches or a lighter in the office?"

"No, why?"

"Philips's ex is a smoker." Jacob hesitated. "How about prints or other forensics?"

"Still working on that," Griff said. "But we did recover a cell phone. I sent it to the lab and just talked to the analyst." He cleared his throat. "The man's last phone call was to Cora Reeves. Looks like it didn't go through. Then he sent a text."

Jacob gritted his teeth. Cora hadn't mentioned a phone call or a text. "What did it say?"

"He said the lead didn't pan out. He was giving up her case."

Jacob's hand tightened around his phone. Cora probably hadn't taken that news well. "Anything else?"

"That's it. Do you think it's important?"

"I don't know yet," Jacob said. "But I'll talk to Cora." He didn't tell his brother that he had already questioned her, and she'd omitted details about her relationship with the man. "Keep me posted."

His brother agreed and hung up. Jacob poured his coffee into a to-go mug, snatched his breakfast sandwich and carried it to his car. Ten minutes later, he was in his office reviewing the original files for the missing Westbrook baby case.

He'd been young and green at detective work at the time. And he'd been grieving for his father. Worse, there were so many people traumatized in the fire. Three lives, other than his father's, had been lost. Several more people had been injured.

He'd enlisted county resources to interview all the parties involved, which had been a nightmare. More than one person in that hospital had enemies.

Whether or not they were strong enough enemies to

commit murder had been the question. If targeting a single person, the perp had also endangered hundreds of lives and was now wanted for homicide.

That person had to answer for all the people he'd hurt and the lives he'd destroyed.

He skimmed notes from the deputies who'd assisted in the interviews.

Drew Westbook claimed he'd only stepped out of Cora's hospital room for a few minutes, then the fire alarm had sounded. He'd tried to reach her and the baby, but the firefighters ordered him and everyone else to evacuate via the back stairs.

He'd rushed into the chaos on the lawn. A few minutes later, he'd heard Cora's scream and run to her.

Jacob had to question Westbrook about Kurt Philips.

But first, he'd talk to Cora. She was supposed to drop by with those sketches this morning.

He had to know why she'd lied to him about her relationship with Philips and omitted to tell him about Kurt's text.

CORA WOVE AROUND the curvy mountain road from her house toward town, her nerves on edge.

The phone had rung as she'd dressed, but the caller had hung up. Twice. When she stepped outside, she thought someone had driven by her house and slowed as if looking for her. But when she'd started down her porch steps, the car sped off.

She shivered and maneuvered the switchback, hugging the side of the road as a beige Pontiac car sped toward her. Some people drove way too fast on the mountain road. The narrow switchbacks were the downside to living on the mountain.

Dark storm clouds rolled across the sky, shrouding out the morning sunlight, shadows from the tree limbs dancing across the asphalt. She inhaled and forced her eyes on the road.

Seconds later, the sound of a car engine roared up behind her. She glanced in her rearview mirror as a dark sedan closed in on her tail. Rattled, she steered around the curve hoping he'd slow, but instead the car sped up. She tapped the brakes, urging him to back off. He slowed slightly but sped up again, then rode her rear bumper.

Her heart hammered. Her hands began to sweat. She veered into a driveway leading to some new cabins being built. Finally the car raced by.

God. She must be paranoid. For a moment, she'd thought the car was going to run her off the road.

Breathing out, she dropped her head forward to calm herself. Last night Kurt had been murdered.

Was someone out to kill her, too?

Chapter Five

Worry knotted Jacob's stomach as he finished reading the notes from the original investigation. Over the past five years, he and his deputy had spoken with Cora countless times.

They'd also received at least three complaints from women who claimed Cora was stalking their child. All were newer residents who'd moved to the area and had little girls the same age as Cora's daughter.

He'd heard gossip in town about her being unstable, but he didn't want to believe it. Although if his own child was missing, he'd probably go crazy with rage and fear himself.

His deputy called to confirm that he was canvassing local residents for information on Philips. Jacob was on the phone with ballistics when the front door squeaked open.

Cora stuck her head in the doorway, and he waved her in.

"Gun was a .38," the lab analyst said.

Jacob thanked him and turned his attention toward Cora. She looked shaken and nervous, although that was nothing new. She always looked as if the threads of her faith and sanity were slowly unraveling.

Except when she was teaching. He'd visited the school a few times for safety programs and seen her with the children. She was animated, sweet, funny and loving with her kindergarteners.

A natural with children.

Jacob stood and offered Cora coffee, but she declined. Vera, his receptionist, arrived and Jacob said good morning. "Let's go back to my private office," he told Cora.

Cora followed him down a hallway into his office. "I brought those sketches," she said.

He shuffled some folders on his desk, moving them out of the way, and she sank into the chair facing his desk. Her hand was trembling as she removed an envelope from her purse.

He narrowed his eyes. "Are you okay?"

She nodded, although her forced smile didn't quite meet her eyes.

Maybe she was just upset about Kurt. Or about lying. "Something you want to tell me?" he asked.

She bit her bottom lip, then shook her head. "I labeled the sketches with the age projection."

He accepted the envelope, then removed the pages. His heart squeezed at her detailed depictions.

She'd included at least three sketches per year, starting from her memory of her infant daughter to Alice at six months, then nine, then a year. She'd added wisps of hair and chubby cheeks and a pudgy belly as a toddler, then slowly captured the changes from toddler to kindergarten.

"These are amazing," he said softly. "You're talented."

A blush stained her cheeks. "I figured you'd think I was crazy for doing them."

His gaze locked with hers. "I don't think you're crazy," he said. She was just a mother who missed her child.

He tapped the latest sketches, when Alice would have been four, then five. "I'm sending the more recent ones over. Maybe they'll be of help to the FBI."

Cora didn't know why she cared about Jacob's opinion, but she did. Over the years, he'd always been kind and understanding. And he had tried to find Alice.

The memory of that car on her tail taunted her.

She couldn't shake the feeling that someone had been following her. Watching her.

That she might be in danger.

She considered telling him but didn't want him to think she was paranoid.

"Cora, I spoke with Kurt Philips's ex-wife last night."

Her heart stuttered. "I'm sure she was upset about her husband's death."

"She was." Jacob's eyes narrowed on her. Studying. Probing. "She claims she hadn't talked to him in a few days."

"Did she have any idea who would try to hurt him?"

Jacob shook his head. "It's possible he was working a case besides yours that landed him in trouble, but…maybe not. The firefighters recovered a phone and laptop. They're trying to retrieve data from both, but with the fire damage, it'll take time."

Cora nodded.

His eyes darkened, lingering on her face. "However, the analyst was able to retrieve some information from Philips's phone."

Cora went still, her pulse clamoring.

"Apparently the last person he called before he died was you."

She sucked in a pain-filled breath. "I didn't talk to him," she said. *Because I was upset about losing my job.* But if she admitted that, she'd have to explain the reason. Then Jacob *would* think she was unhinged.

"The IT analyst said the call didn't go through." Jacob leaned forward and looked into her eyes. "He did send you a text, though, saying that he was dropping your case."

She pressed her lips together to stifle a reaction.

"Why didn't you tell me about the text last night?" Jacob asked in a deep voice.

She shrugged. "I...didn't think it was important."

Jacob's dark brows shot upward. "I told you Kurt was murdered, and you didn't think it was important to mention that he'd dropped your case?"

She searched for a plausible explanation. "That's right. How could it matter? If he was dropping my case, it was because he'd exhausted all leads. So he obviously wasn't killed because he'd found something."

She almost wished that were the case. Not that he was killed, but that he'd found something important enough that it meant he was close to finding her daughter. Because if he'd uncovered the truth, someone else could, and her hopes weren't completely dead in the water.

"Cora, I can understand that you'd be upset with him for dropping the search."

His sympathetic tone stirred her emotions, yet the implication of where he was headed with his questions slowly dawned on her. He'd hinted at this the night before, but asking a second time indicated he considered her a person of interest.

Anger shot through her. "Sheriff, you can't possibly think I'd hurt Kurt," she said, her voice rising an octave. "When you and everyone else, including my husband, gave up on finding my daughter, Kurt stepped in to help me. I would never have hurt him."

She clenched the arm of the chair and stood, anxious to escape his scrutiny. "Now I have to go."

"One more question," Jacob said, stopping her before she could turn and leave.

She gritted her teeth. "What?"

"Mrs. Philips mentioned that Kurt wasn't just working for you, that the two of you were involved personally."

Her fingers tightened around the strap of her shoulder bag. "We were friends," she said, unable to keep the emotions from her voice. "I'm sure you're aware that I don't have many of those. Either people think I'm unstable because I won't give up looking for Alice, or like you, they look at me with suspicion." She swallowed, tears threatening. "That hurts more than anything."

"I never treated you like a suspect," Jacob said gruffly.

Her gaze met his, and she lifted her chin. "You just did." Determined not to cry in front of him, she stormed from his office.

JACOB HATED HURTING CORA, but his job required him to ask difficult questions.

He hurried after her and caught her at the door. "Cora, let's go get some coffee and talk."

Tears glistened in her eyes. He wanted to console her, but Vera was watching, so he kept his hands to himself.

"Please, it's about Drew."

Her face paled, and he thought she was going to make a run for her car, but she gave a little nod. Together they walked to the local coffee shop The Brew, and claimed a booth.

God, she looked pale and thin. "Have you eaten anything?" he asked.

She shrugged. "I wasn't hungry this morning."

"How about a pastry?"

"I suppose I could have one."

A small smile tugged at his mouth. He'd learned early on that she liked sweets, so he chose an apple pastry and a chocolate croissant and carried them to the table. She snagged the chocolate, then tore it into three pieces before taking a bite.

He inhaled his just to give her time to settle down, then took a sip of coffee. "I'm sorry I upset you, Cora, but I'm trying to find out who killed your friend. I'd think you'd want that, too."

She squeezed her eyes closed for a minute as if composing herself. "I do."

In spite of all she'd suffered, Cora was a strong woman.

"I have to consider all angles," he continued. "With the timing of his text to you, I'm going to explore the possibility that his murder is related to your case."

"But his message said he was giving up," Cora said, her expression confused.

Jacob twisted his mouth in thought. "True. And I don't want to give you false hope. But you said Kurt wouldn't give up. What if he'd found a lead, and someone killed him to keep him from telling you? The killer could have forced him to send that text or sent it to you after they killed him."

Cora's eyes widened. "I hadn't thought of that."

"Hopefully his computer will yield insight. Let's talk more about Drew."

Cora frowned and traced a finger around the rim of her coffee mug. "I don't know what more I can add. I already told you that Kurt talked to him about Alice's disappearance."

"Did Drew know you and Kurt were involved?"

Her gaze shot to his, irritation sparking in her eyes. "He knew Kurt was working for me, but like I said, we were just friends." She paused. "Besides, Drew wouldn't have cared if I met someone else. All he talked about was that I should move on like he did."

But she hadn't been able to do that.

"I know this is painful," he said gruffly, "but let's review what happened the night Alice disappeared." If someone had witnessed something at the hospital or afterward, time might be on their side. With the passage of time, sometimes witnesses felt guilty for not coming forward or remembered details they hadn't recalled in the aftermath of a trauma.

Cora sighed. "We've been over this a thousand times before."

"True, but bear with me and just focus on Drew this

time. And your marriage." Directly following the kidnapping, she'd still been in love with her husband. She'd been in shock and terrified and had clung to him.

She might look back and see their relationship in a different light now.

CORA FOUGHT TO keep her emotions at bay as she relived that night once again. "I was in labor for eighteen hours, and I'd hardly slept for two days. After I gave birth, I held Alice for a few minutes, then the nurse took her for routine tests."

"And Drew was with you?"

She nodded. "He'd been anxious about work and the money when we first learned I was pregnant. But he was there for the delivery."

"He wanted to make partner?"

"Yes, he was driven and ambitious. That's one thing I admired. At first."

"What do you mean *at first*?"

She bit her lip. She hadn't meant to say that.

"Cora, you can be honest now. It's the only way to get to the truth."

"During the pregnancy, he worked such long hours and answered calls no matter where we were. He'd miss dinners and seemed so preoccupied with his clients that I wondered if he'd spend time with the baby when we brought her home."

Jacob leaned forward, eyes piercing. "During all those late nights when he said he was working, did you ever suspect he was having an affair?"

Cora's breath caught. She tried to mentally replay those months. "I didn't at the time," she admitted. "I just thought he was focused on his career."

"Was he solicitous to other women when you went out?"

Cora shook her head. "Not really," she said. "But I did wonder if I'd be raising Alice alone while he spent all his time with clients." She tapped her nails on her coffee cup. "Then she was gone and that wasn't an issue."

He'd abandoned them both.

"I'm sorry," Jacob said. "Let's get back to that night. Before the nurse took Alice for tests, what happened?"

"Drew's phone rang, and he left the room. I rocked Alice, then the nurse took her. I fell asleep a few minutes later, and when I woke up, the fire alarm was blasting."

"Do you know how long it had been since Drew left the room?"

She shrugged. "Not long. Maybe half an hour."

"That was a long phone call," Jacob commented.

She sipped her coffee. "His business calls often ran long."

Jacob made a low sound in his throat. "I know we questioned the nurse who took Alice for the tests, but was there anything about her that felt off?"

"Not at all. Lisa was a sweetheart," Cora said. "She coached me through delivery, and afterward encouraged me to rest. I remember her saying the night feedings could get rough."

"How about anyone else? Did another staff member act strangely? Maybe you saw someone lurking by the nursery."

"I didn't go out by the nursery until after the fire started," she said. "When I first arrived at the hospital, I was wheeled directly to the labor room. I was so excited about finally getting to meet my baby that all I remember are nurses and doctors bustling around."

"I understand," Jacob said softly.

He could never understand. He hadn't held his newborn in his arms and then felt the emptiness afterward when that baby was suddenly gone.

"Back to Drew," he said. "Did he tell you who phoned him?"

She strained to remember. "He didn't mention a name.

But after the nurse left with Alice, I thought I heard him talking to someone outside the door. A woman. I assumed it was Lisa."

Silence stretched between them, filled with tension and stirring questions in Cora's mind.

Drew had married within months after they'd separated. Was it possible he'd been seeing someone else while they were still married? That the phone call or the woman outside the hospital room was his lover?

Chapter Six

Doubts nagged at Cora as she walked across the street to the bookstore.

She searched her memory banks and recalled little snippets of conversations with Drew during their marriage when he'd been vague about where he was going. Late-night phone calls he answered behind closed doors. Missed dinners and outings where he'd supposedly been caught up in a case.

She'd trusted him implicitly. Had been so deep into her fantasy of a family that it never occurred to her that he'd betray her.

Yet he was a lawyer, and a good one. Lying with a straight face came easy to him on the job. Why not at home?

Nausea filled her at the possibility that he might have been talking to a lover outside the hospital room only minutes after she'd delivered their child. Surely he hadn't been…

Disturbed at her train of thought, she combed through the bookstore in search of some reading material to distract her. Although she enjoyed sketching outside with a view of the river or mountain, she had her sketchpad in her bag and sometimes came here to draw and people-watch.

The bookstore had added a small café two years ago, which was a popular gathering spot for teens, seniors and parents accompanying children. Computer stations also invited clientele to linger and work or do research.

Being surrounded by books and the people in the store helped fill her lonely summer days.

Her stomach twisted. She would have a lot more of those in the future. The uncertainty was daunting. She'd have to find a job...somewhere. Doing what, though? The only thing she'd ever done was teach.

You could move, find a teaching job in a different city.

But the thought of leaving Whistler made her uneasy. The small mountain town had been her sanctuary during her pregnancy, when she wanted to get away from the city, and then after Alice had disappeared.

Voices from the children's corner drifted toward her. Unable to resist, she maneuvered the teen section until she reached the reading nook where two mothers were reading to their little ones. Three preschool children were putting on an impromptu puppet show behind the puppet stage, and a toddler was thumbing through a picture book, pressing the sound link associated with the animal pictures.

She glanced around for an empty table where she wouldn't disturb the families, then spotted Nina Fuller at a small round table, coloring with markers.

Cora's breath caught. Nina Fuller...the little girl who'd caught her eye the first day of school this past year. She and her mother had just moved to town. Nina was in kindergarten. She wore her long brown hair in a French braid today. A slight sprinkling of freckles dotted the bridge of her nose, and her shy, sweet smile was infectious.

She was also the reason Cora had been fired.

Cora ordered herself to walk away. If Nina's mother saw her—

"Ms. Reeves!" Nina jumped up, ran toward her and threw her arms around her waist.

Emotions swirled inside Cora. She stooped down and

hugged the little girl. Nina smelled like peppermint and felt like an angel. Cora squeezed her eyes shut for a moment, savoring the sweetness of the child's hug.

"Let my daughter go."

The sound of Nina's mother's voice made Cora tense. She patted Nina's back, then gave her another squeeze and slowly pulled away. "Hi, Mrs. Fuller—"

The woman's glare cut her off. She clasped her daughter's little arm. "Honey, get your coloring stuff. We have to go."

"But Mommy," Nina cried. "I wanna stay and talk to Ms. Reeves."

Cora gave the mother an imploring look. "I'm sorry if I—"

"Stay away from me and my daughter." Faye quickly gathered their belongings and rushed Nina from the store.

JACOB STUDIED THE drawings Cora had left. Doubt had filled her eyes as she recounted her relationship with Drew. She was second-guessing her husband now.

If Drew had been cheating on Cora, it changed everything. It also meant he'd lied to the police, which launched him to the top of Jacob's suspect list again.

Knowing Cora would be sentimental about the drawings, he made copies on the machine at his office, placed the originals back inside her envelope and stowed them in his desk to return to her.

Then he drove to the FBI's local field office to see Liam. Sympathy softened the hard planes of his brother's face as he examined the drawings.

"She's really talented," Liam said.

"I agree. She created composites of her childhood photographs along with her ex-husband's to project what Alice might look like today."

"This is a long shot," Liam said. "But I'll see what we

can do with them." He stood. "Come on, there's something I want you to see."

Liam was short on words but quick on ideas. Like a dog with a bone when he was investigating a case, he didn't give up until he had answers. And they both wanted to find their father's killer and make him pay.

Jacob followed Liam into a room housing three analysts. "I retrieved some of the original security tapes from the hospital fire," Liam said. "Some were damaged, of course."

"We've been through these before," Jacob said, hoping Liam had something new.

"But technology has improved. Angie recovered some blurred images and cleaned them up." Liam gestured toward a female analyst whose long blond hair was in a twist at the nape of her neck.

Angie angled her monitor to review the images on her screen. "I've searched all the tapes. Frankly, they're difficult to watch," she said with a pained sigh. "So much chaos and so many terrified people. But then—" she held up a finger "—I started focusing on anyone who looked out of place. And this caught my attention." She clicked a key and scrolled through several frames. "Most everyone is running toward the exits and stairwells." She displayed footage of two women running toward the nursery. A dark-haired woman was quickly ushered toward the stairs. Then Cora.

Both were terrified and frantic as they ran to save their newborns.

Emotions clogged Jacob's throat. Watching Cora suffer made him want to pound something.

"This is Cora Reeves," Angie said. "She's obviously trying to find her baby."

"Which confirms her story and puts her in the clear," Jacob said, although he'd never doubted her. A mother's pain was a palpable force.

"Do you see the father anywhere?"

She scrolled through more footage until Jacob pointed out Drew Westbrook. He was on the phone, head bent, heading down the hall toward the cafeteria.

"After this, we lose him," Angie said. "But I thought this was interesting."

Jacob leaned closer as she flipped through several more frames, then zeroed in on a person in scrubs, head and face not visible, carrying a bundle toward the housekeeping area on the bottom floor.

"We thought someone took the baby during the commotion outside the hospital, but this bundle could be Cora's baby."

Jacob narrowed his eyes, hunting for identifying markers. Hairstyle or color. A scar. A limp. But whoever it was had shielded his or her face from the cameras.

"Body size and height indicate it's either a small man or a woman," Liam said.

"And that the baby was kidnapped while still inside the hospital," Jacob added.

Liam folded his arms. "We're looking into people who lost babies around that time. We also have to consider that this kidnapping could have been professional. I've been investigating a case of baby snatchers who're selling the babies."

Jacob's blood ran cold.

If that was the case, Cora's daughter could be anywhere.

CORA WATCHED WITH a heavy heart as Nina and her mother left the bookstore. The last thing she wanted to do was to frighten a child or her mother.

For goodness' sake, her former best friend had once accused her of behaving like a stalker when she'd chased down a woman in the mall pushing a baby stroller. That day, she'd been certain the woman had Alice.

Just like she'd thought Nina was her daughter when she'd seen her at school.

Terrified she was losing her mind and on the verge of another breakdown, she phoned her therapist, Ruby Denton, and requested an emergency session. The woman agreed to see her in an hour, so she forced herself to comb the bookstore for reading material. Meditation tapes had worked well to calm her. So had books of faith and stories of individuals who'd overcome tragedies to turn their lives around or use the trauma as inspiration to help others.

She selected a couple of autobiographies of survivors, one of abuse and the other, of a terrible, crippling accident. Then she chose a book on artistic styles along with a book on police sketch artists.

She paid for her purchases, then drove to Ruby's office. Her mind kept replaying the incident at the bookstore with Nina while she waited for the therapist to see her.

Finally Ruby opened her door and invited her into her office. Today the perky redhead wore a dark green suit that accentuated her eyes. She was slightly younger than Cora, and was compassionate and straightforward. An old soul, Cora thought.

As usual, she set a bottle of water on the coffee table for Cora, and they faced each other. Cora sat on a plush gray velvet love seat and Ruby in a dark red velvet wing chair.

"Tell me what's going on," Ruby said.

Cora twisted the cap off the water bottle and took a sip, then breathed out to steady her nerves. "I think I may be going crazy," she blurted.

Ruby's look softened. "I doubt that, Cora. But you're obviously upset. What happened?"

Cora explained about Nina and Faye Fuller's complaint to the principal.

"Ah, Cora," Ruby said. "I know you love teaching."

"I do," she admitted. "But maybe I overstepped. I frightened the little girl and her mother." She reiterated her encounter at the bookstore. "I didn't mean to upset them, but Nina hugged me and I couldn't help it. She's such a sweetheart that I hugged her back."

"We never know what someone else is going through," Ruby said. "You can't blame the mother for being protective."

Cora shook her head. "No, I can't. I...had no idea she'd had a miscarriage, much less three." Her voice choked. "I... do feel badly for her."

"Then tell her," Ruby said.

"I tried, but she told me to stay away from them."

A heartbeat of silence stretched between them. "Give her some time," Ruby advised. Cora twisted her fingers together, rubbing them in a nervous gesture.

"I sense something else is bothering you, Cora," Ruby said.

Cora heaved a wary breath. "I told you before about Kurt Philips, the private investigator I hired to find Alice."

"Yes. As I recall, the two of you are friends." Ruby offered her a smile. "I hope you're not feeling guilty about finding a little joy in your life."

"We were just friends," Cora said. "But...the problem is... Kurt is dead."

Another heartbeat of silence. Ruby crossed her legs, her expression concerned. "What happened?"

"He left me a message saying he was ending the search for Alice, and I should move on. I was upset and drove to Kurt's to talk to him, but when I arrived, his apartment and office were on fire." She took a breath. "Later, the sheriff told me Kurt was murdered."

Emotions overcame her, and she burst into tears.

Ruby pushed a box of tissues toward her. She waited patiently, giving Cora time to compose herself, and then asked, "Are you crying because you love Kurt and are upset about his death, or because he was dropping the search for Alice?"

Grief and anger knotted Cora's insides. "I don't know. Maybe both."

Ruby gave a small nod. "That's fair. Does the sheriff know who killed him?"

"Not yet," Cora said. "It's possible he was murdered because of me."

Ruby's eyes widened slightly. "You can't blame yourself, Cora."

"I know. But if he was killed because of my case, maybe he'd found something," Cora said, hope fighting through her anguish.

"I'm sure the sheriff will get to the truth." Ruby waited a second, then spoke softly.

"We broached this subject before. But have you thought about what you'd do if you found Alice and she's happy and in a loving home? Would you uproot her world to tell her that you're her mother?"

Chapter Seven

Anger seized Cora at the question. "You think I'm selfish for wanting to find my little girl?"

"I didn't say that," Ruby said in the calming voice that sometimes worked on Cora's last nerve. "I just want you to be prepared for whatever you find. It's been five years. I understand your pain and your need to be honest and connect with Alice if you find her. But she's not a baby anymore. If she is in a happy home and has loving parents, which I'm sure you want to be the case, learning the truth is bound to be upsetting."

Cora clutched the arm of the chair with a white-knuckled grip in an effort to keep from shouting. "And what if she's not happy? What if she's been bounced around from one foster home to another?" Cora's voice rose an octave. "Or what if whoever has her has mistreated her?" The very idea nauseated her.

"Then she'll definitely be better off if you step in." Ruby leaned forward. "I'm not being judgmental, Cora. You're in a very difficult situation, and if I were you, I'd want to know what happened to my child. You've been robbed of precious moments, of five years of her life. I'm simply trying to prepare you for whatever happens, so you can cope."

"I'm tired of coping," Cora admitted. "I've been coping

for years. I need to know where she is. And I…need to hold her. To hug her. To let her know that I love her."

"But you're feeling desperate because Kurt was going to give up, aren't you?" Ruby asked.

"That's just it," Cora said. "Kurt wouldn't give up. He told me once that he never dropped a case without answers."

"But you said he left you a message."

"He did, but Kurt was murdered shortly after he sent the text. The sheriff suggested someone could have forced him to send me that message before they killed him."

Ruby narrowed her eyes. "Does the sheriff have any proof or any idea who killed Kurt?"

Cora's lungs strained for air. "Actually we talked about the day Alice was taken, and I remembered something."

Ruby shifted in her chair, interest flaring across her face. "Go on."

Cora bit her bottom lip. She felt like she was betraying Drew by reiterating her conversation with Jacob. Yet, she wanted answers and that meant probing every detail of that horrible day.

"Cora?"

"Drew received a phone call after Alice was born, and he left the room. Just as I was drifting to sleep, I heard him talking to a woman outside the door." She stood and began to pace. "I assumed it was a nurse, but the sheriff's questions started me thinking that perhaps it wasn't a nurse."

"I don't understand," Ruby said.

"I told you before Drew wasn't thrilled when he first learned about the pregnancy, that he was worried about money and his job." Was it possible that Drew hadn't wanted Alice?

"What are you saying, Cora?"

She halted, her body tight with agitation. "During the

pregnancy, he was inattentive and distracted. He constantly worked late and took late-night calls."

"You think Drew was having an affair?" Ruby asked softly.

Did she? Cora shrugged. "I don't want to believe that he'd betray me. But…if he was seeing someone else, he might have viewed the baby as an obstacle to leaving me. As long as we had her, he would be tied to me."

Having Alice kidnapped would have solved that problem.

AFTER LEAVING LIAM at the FBI's local field office, Jacob drove to Drew Westbrook's house.

Judging from the ritzy neighborhood and half-million-dollar homes set on estate lots, Cora's ex had done very well financially. The house was a two-story brick Georgian home with massive columns and an impressive view of the sprawling lake.

Jacob would never be able to afford a place like this on his salary. Not that he wanted to. He liked his cozy cabin, the mountains, the river, and the peace and quiet nature afforded.

He parked in front of the house in the circular drive, then strode to the front door and rang the bell. While he waited, he scanned the property. Professionally maintained lawn with topiary shrubs, a rose garden to the side and bench seating by the lake.

Voices from inside echoed through the doorway, then the door opened and Drew Westbrook stood on the other side. He was dressed in gray slacks and a button-collared shirt as if he might be on his way to the office.

Surprise flared in his eyes when he spotted Jacob. "Sheriff Maverick?"

"Hello, Mr. Westbrook."

"Who is it, honey?" Drew's wife Hilary appeared as she came down the winding staircase.

"It's the sheriff of Whistler," Drew said.

Hilary's heels clicked on the marble floor as she sauntered toward them. Her emerald green pantsuit looked as if it was made of silk, and diamonds glittered on her fingers and around her neck.

"May I come in?" Jacob asked.

A sliver of hope sparked in Drew's eyes. "Do you have news about Alice?"

Hmm. Maybe he was wrong about Drew and he really had cared about his daughter. "Not exactly."

Drew's jaw tightened with worry. "Then it's about Cora?"

"What has she done now?" Hilary asked.

Jacob swung his gaze toward Drew's wife, surprised by her tone.

"Let me come in and I'll explain." He stepped into the foyer, which was decorated with expensive paintings and vases.

Drew scraped a hand through his hair, upending the neat strands, then led Jacob to a family room with leather furniture and wood accents. A small corner filled with a kid's table and books was the only indication that a child lived here. He'd forgotten Drew Westbrook had a son a year younger than his daughter would have been.

Jacob seated himself on the leather sofa, then Drew claimed a recliner facing him while Hilary sank into a plush club chair beside him. Both looked anxious as if expecting bad news.

"What's this about?" Drew asked.

Jacob folded his hands together. "Mr. Westbrook, do you know a man named Kurt Philips?"

Drew went still, and Hilary lifted a small pillow and hugged it to her.

"We've met," Drew said stiffly. "He was working for Cora."

"Was?" Jacob asked.

Drew's brows rose. "Yeah. He stopped by and questioned me a few times."

"He was not a pleasant man," Hilary interjected.

Jacob tilted his head toward the woman. He supposed some men found her attractive, but her perfect makeup, designer clothes and smile seemed fake. "You didn't like him, Mrs. Westbrook?"

She stiffened as if she realized she might have said the wrong thing. "I didn't like the way he came here asking questions about Drew, treating him like he was a suspect in his daughter's disappearance. He practically accused Drew of hiring someone to have his baby kidnapped." She scoffed and rolled her eyes. "Everyone who knows Drew will testify that he's a caring and loving man and a great father."

Drew raised a hand to silence his wife. "I understand Philips was doing his job," he said. "Cora seemed to trust him and to rely on him, but I didn't appreciate his insinuations. I had enough of that with you."

Jacob supposed Drew's direct approach came with being a defense attorney. It also meant he had a great poker face and could lie without batting an eye.

"Now, why are you asking about Kurt Philips?" Drew asked bluntly.

Jacob cleared his throat. "First, tell me where you were last night, Mr. Westbrook?"

Drew's chin went up defensively. His wife folded her arms. "Drew and I were together last night, weren't we, darling?" Hilary said.

A slight twitch of Drew's mouth was his only reaction. It also hinted of a lie.

"Is that true?" Jacob asked.

Drew gave a slight nod. "Either tell me what's going on or leave."

Rattling the polished lawyer who'd deserted Cora and

broken her heart gave Jacob pleasure. "I'm asking about Kurt Philips because he's dead."

Shock—real or feigned?—darkened the man's face, while Hilary flattened her palm against her cheek in a stunned reaction.

"Dead? How?" Drew asked.

"He was murdered," Jacob said. "Shot to death actually."

"Oh my God," Hilary murmured.

"Mr. Westbrook, the bullet the medical examiner extracted from him came from a handgun. Do you own a .38?"

RUBY'S QUESTION TAUNTED Cora as she left her therapist's office and drove home. Asking her to keep quiet about being Alice's mother wasn't fair. Her heart had been ripped from her chest the day her baby had been kidnapped.

For five long years, she'd missed precious moments of her little girl's life. The only thing that had kept her going was the thought of seeing her again.

Dark clouds rolled across the sky, threatening a summer storm as she turned onto the street leading to her house.

An image of Alice crying and frightened flashed behind her eyes. What if Alice was unhappy? What if whoever had her didn't love her?

Yet on the heels of that image, she saw her daughter laughing as another mother pushed her in a swing. Alice's hair was flying in the wind, her laugh musical and angelic. The other woman was singing a children's song about five little speckled frogs and Alice was singing along.

Tears blurred Cora's eyes. She hoped her daughter was happy. Laughing. Loved. Taken care of.

Could she destroy that happiness if she found her?

Faye and Nina Fuller's house slipped into view, and she clenched her jaw. She'd find Alice first, then decide what to do.

Maybe Jacob would locate her. Liam had those sketches now...

Her pulse jumped when she spotted Nina chasing a kitten across her front yard. She couldn't help but remember Nina lining her carrot sticks up at lunch the way Cora did as a child. There were other small details that had caught her attention and seemed...familiar. Nina also tore the top off her muffin and ate it first, just as Cora always did.

You lost your job because you frightened her and her mother.

She had to make it right.

She veered into the Fullers' driveway and parked, then inhaled a deep breath as she climbed out. Nina's mother was sitting on the front porch, watching Nina play. She stood when she saw Cora.

Cora braced herself. The woman might call the cops and request a restraining order against her. Still, she had to apologize.

Nina dropped to the grassy lawn, playing with the kitty. Cora forced herself to focus on the mother.

"I told you to stay away from my child," Faye said.

Cora nodded. "I'm actually here to see you. Please, Faye, can we talk for a minute?"

Faye crossed her arms, a wariness emanating from her.

"I promise I'm not here to hurt either of you. I want to apologize."

Faye's gaze locked with hers for a moment, tension stretching between them. Finally she gave a small nod. Cora crossed the distance and climbed the steps to the porch. Faye gestured toward the chair and Cora seated herself while Faye settled back on the glider.

"I realize I frightened you," Cora said. "I never meant to do that."

Faye studied her, her silence indicating it was okay for Cora to continue.

"I'm sure you've heard that my baby was kidnapped the night I gave birth to her."

Faye's expression softened. "I heard, and I'm sorry," she said softly. "I...can't imagine how awful it's been for you."

Cora breathed out. Faye had just tossed her an olive branch.

"It has been. Sometimes I forget about other people's problems."

Faye twisted her hands together.

"I'm truly sorry, Faye. I would never intentionally hurt you or Nina. When I heard she was adopted, I couldn't help myself from asking her about it. But that was wrong." She paused and swallowed hard. "I've just been to see my therapist. She's helping me become more aware of others' feelings."

Faye glanced at Nina, then at Cora. "I suppose I can't blame you. If I lost Nina, I'd move heaven and earth to find her."

Tears pricked at Cora's eyes. "You're doing a wonderful job with her," she said sincerely.

Faye pinched the bridge of her nose. "Thank you. Nina is my life."

"I can understand that," Cora said gently.

"It hasn't always been easy. I had three miscarriages before we adopted Nina. That was so painful. Every time I got pregnant I got my hopes up, but within a few weeks, I lost the baby."

Compassion filled Cora. "I'm so sorry, Faye. That must have been devastating."

Faye nodded and wiped at her eyes. "It took a toll on my marriage, too. My husband and I stuck together for a while, but then he started drinking."

A chill swept through Cora.

"He lost his temper when he drank," she admitted. "I tried to convince him to see a counselor or join AA, but he refused. When we got Nina, I hoped things would get better, but instead, he escalated. He drank all day, stopped going to work, and then he…"

"He what?" Cora said gently.

"He hit me," Faye said in a voice so low that it was barely discernible. "Once was all, though. I left him the day after that. There was no way I'd raise a child in an abusive home."

Cora reached out and squeezed Faye's hand. "I admire you for having the courage to walk away," she said honestly. "You've been through so much, Faye. I truly am sorry for putting you through any more pain."

Faye fluttered a hand to her cheek. "I suppose I overreacted," Faye said. "My ex threatened me before I left. He swore I'd be sorry, that he'd never let me go. Since then, I've been moving around constantly so he can't find us."

Cora sucked in a breath. "Do you have a protective order against him?"

Faye nodded. "But twice he sent people looking for me. That's the reason I freaked out when you asked Nina about the adoption. I…"

"You thought I was asking for him?"

"Yes," Faye said. "No, I don't know what I thought. I just panicked. I couldn't take the chance on him finding me or taking Nina to get back at me."

Chapter Eight

Goose bumps skated up Cora's arms. "Don't worry, Faye. You're not alone now. If you need anything, you can call me. And you should let Sheriff Maverick know what's going on. Whistler is a small town. He can keep an eye out in case a stranger comes around asking questions."

Faye wiped at her eyes again. "Thank you, Cora. I'm sorry I was so hard on you. I was just scared. I'd do anything to protect Nina."

"I understand," Cora said softly. "Your secret is safe with me."

"I appreciate that," Faye said. "Nina doesn't even remember him, and I don't want her upset."

"Of course." Nina looked up at them, noticed Cora and gave a small wave. "She's a good student, Faye. You should be proud of her."

Faye angled her head toward Cora. "I didn't mean to get you fired, Cora. I'll call the principal and talk to him."

Cora considered her offer. "Thanks. But I'm not sure it would help. He was pretty adamant that I need a break." She hesitated. "Maybe he's right. Maybe I should take a year off and clear my head, get a job doing something besides teaching." Where she wasn't tortured every day by taking care of other people's children.

Although she had no idea what she would do. She enjoyed working with kids. Their optimism and exuberance for life had brightened her darkest days.

"Well, let me know if you change your mind," Faye offered.

"What about you?" Cora asked. "Are you working this summer?"

Faye fidgeted. "I sell real estate at Whistler Mountain Realty, so I'll work some. But Nina can go with me."

Nina ran up, hugging the kitty to her. "Look, Ms. Reeves, Mama said we can keep her."

"That's wonderful. Kittens are so much fun." Cora smiled at the sight of the little girl hugging the fluffy yellow butterball in her arms.

"I wants a dog, too," Nina said, "but Mama says we move too much to keep a dog." She stroked the kitten's head. "I like it here. I hope we don't move anymore."

Faye hugged Nina. "We'll see, sweetheart. For now, we're staying put."

"Goody!" Nina bounced up and down. "'Cause I wanna wade in the creek out back and swim in the pond, and maybe we could go camping and sleep in a tent!"

Faye laughed. "I don't know about the tent, but we'll definitely go wading and swimming now it's getting warmer."

"Can Ms. Reeves go with us?" Nina asked.

Faye's mouth tightened slightly, and Cora stood. She'd pushed it enough for the day.

"Thank you for asking," she told Nina. "Maybe one day we can all do something together. But I have to go now."

"Okay. See you later." Nina dropped to the ground again with the kitten, sprawled on her back and set the kitten on her belly. Her laughter echoed in Cora's ears and sent a fresh pang of longing through Cora as she said goodbye to Faye and returned to her car.

JACOB STUDIED DREW and Hilary Westbrook, searching for underlying meanings to the looks they exchanged. He'd never liked Drew, and he didn't care for his wife, either.

"No, Sheriff Maverick, I do not own a gun," Drew said. "And as I stated before, I had nothing to do with my daughter's kidnapping. I'd give anything to find her. And if Kurt Philips had a lead, I certainly wouldn't have hurt him." Emotions strained his face. "I love my wife and son," he said. "But Cora is still suffering and can't move on. I want us to find Alice, so she can finally be happy again."

Jacob raised a brow. That statement was the most sincere thing he'd ever heard Drew Westbrook say. Not that he hadn't been upset after the kidnapping. He had.

His emotional pleas on TV and in the newspapers had garnered sympathy from everyone who'd seen his tears.

"When was the last time you spoke to Philips or saw him?" he asked.

"It's been months," Drew said. "He stopped by my office one day and accused me of using my daughter's kidnapping to further my career." He squared his shoulders. "I can assure you I didn't need to do that. I'm good at my job. That's the reason I earned my promotion."

"He is," Hilary spoke up again. "Don't get me wrong," Hilary said. "My heart goes out to Cora. I tried to be her friend after the kidnapping, but she pushed me away. Then she had a breakdown." Hilary toyed with the diamond dangling from a gold chain around her neck. "One time she chased another mother at the mall and nearly snatched her child from her baby stroller."

Jacob gritted his teeth. Unfortunately, he had heard similar rumors.

"One of our friends was with her, and tried to convince her to leave the woman alone. Cora started screaming, and security came and had to escort her out of the mall."

"Hilary," Drew chided in a low voice.

"Well, it's true," Hilary said. "For heaven's sake, she drove all her friends away."

Jacob's protective instincts for Cora rose to the surface. Cora had gotten under his skin five years ago when he'd first met her. The two of them had been in shock and devastated over their individual losses. "Everyone deals with stress and traumatic events in their own way."

"Maybe so," Hilary conceded. "But poor Cora was obsessed. If that PI decided to give up, no telling what Cora would do."

"I've already talked to Cora," Jacob said. "I don't believe she'd hurt him."

Hilary started to speak again, but Drew laid his hand on his wife's arm. "Hilary, that's enough. This has been stressful on all of us."

Hilary offered her husband a sympathetic look. "I'm sorry, Drew. Of course you're right." She turned to Jacob. "I apologize, Sheriff. I didn't mean to speak ill of Cora. I really want her to find some peace. If I lost our little boy, I'd probably break down, too."

"There's something else," Jacob said, knowing the couple wouldn't like his questions, but he had to ask. "Mr. Westbrook, Cora remembers hearing you talking to a woman outside the hospital room before the fire started. Whom were you talking to?"

Confusion marred the man's face. "I…don't remember. Probably the nurse."

Jacob tilted his head toward Hilary. "I understand you worked with Drew prior to his divorce."

Hilary shifted. "I did. I was his administrative assistant."

He turned back to Drew. "Mr. Westbrook, I know you were stressed about the baby and your job, and that you were working late hours."

Drew's eyes narrowed to slits. "I was new at the firm and trying to impress the partners."

"Was that all there was to those nights?" Jacob asked. "Or were you having an affair?"

JACOB'S QUESTIONS ABOUT Drew taunted Cora as she stopped by the arts and crafts store on the way back to her house. Had Drew cheated on her?

The first few days and weeks after the kidnapping were a blur. Drew had seemed sincerely upset about Alice.

He could have had an affair and still been upset over the kidnapping. But if he was seeing another woman and wanted out of their marriage, and had been involved in Alice's disappearance, maybe he'd faked his reaction.

Tormented by the idea that he would betray her, her lungs strained for air. She practiced deep breathing for a few minutes in the car to steady her nerves, then went inside the store.

She needed more art paper, another sketchbook for her drawings, paints and a couple of canvases.

With time on her hands in the summer, she typically enjoyed working on art projects. Anything to distract her from obsessing over Alice.

Anything to help her hold on to her sanity.

There had been a time when she'd considered taking her own life, when living had been so painful that she could barely get out of bed. But the idea of Alice searching for her when she got older, then discovering her mother had killed herself forced Cora to banish that thought from her head.

If—no, *when*—she found her daughter, she wanted Alice to know she was strong and that she'd never given up looking for her.

On the off chance that Faye and Nina actually visited her someday, she picked up a small art set for children she thought Nina would enjoy. The kit included color pencils, crayons, paints, markers and charcoal.

Her heart stuttered at the image of Nina opening the set and pulling out the supplies.

Stop it, she chided herself. Faye had been cordial, but that didn't mean she wanted to be friends.

She paid for the supplies, carried them to her car, then drove through town. In spite of the dark clouds above, mothers and children were at the park, triggering another wave of longing.

She checked for Jacob's SUV as she passed the sheriff's office but didn't see it, so she headed home. A few raindrops began to splatter against her window. She flipped on the windshield wipers and slowed as she rounded a curve.

The sound of a car engine rumbled behind her, and she remembered thinking she was being followed earlier. Instinctively she slowed and turned into the first drive she saw, then waited until the car moved on.

Breathing out in relief, she backed up, then sped toward her house. But just as she rounded another curve near the turnoff for the river park, a popping sound echoed, then the glass window on the passenger side suddenly shattered.

Another pop and Cora screamed as a bullet zoomed by her head.

She quickly ducked, but her car skidded toward the embankment. She swerved to the right and braked, but her tires squealed and she slammed into the guardrail. Metal clanged and screeched, and her car nose-dived into the ditch.

She tried to brace herself for the impact, but her head snapped back, more glass shattered and she was thrown forward. The airbag exploded, slamming into her, and pain ricocheted through her chest.

Then stars swam behind her eyes as darkness swallowed her.

JACOB STUDIED WESTBROOK'S REACTION.

The lawyer fisted his hands on his chair arms. "I most certainly was not having an affair. I never cheated on Cora, and I resent the implication."

"Is that what she told you?" Hilary screeched.

Jacob shook his head. "No, but under the circumstances I had to ask."

"We went through all this when Alice was first kidnapped." Drew stood and gestured toward the door. "I was treated like a suspect then, and I get the distinct feeling the same thing is happening now. If you have more questions, Sheriff, go through my attorney."

Jacob stood and adjusted his holster. "I can do that if necessary. But if you want to find your daughter, you'll cooperate."

"I have cooperated and told you everything I know." Drew headed toward the entry, and Jacob followed. "If that private investigator was killed because he uncovered information about my daughter, I want to know."

Drew was definitely sending out mixed messages. One moment he genuinely seemed to care about Cora and finding Alice.

The next second, he was lawyering up. The timing of his success seemed suspicious, too. Thanks to media coverage, he'd vaulted to the top of his career in record time after the kidnapping. He'd married within a year after he and Cora separated and had another child.

He also had access to any number of criminals who would kill for him for money or in exchange for a better deal in court.

Jacob stood on the steps to the house for a minute after Drew closed the door, listening for the couple's voices in case they argued, but he didn't hear them.

He jogged down the steps, climbed in his SUV and decided to stop by Liam's office before heading back to Whistler. He called Griff on the way.

"Any word on the computer you retrieved from Philips's office?" he asked gruffly.

"The analyst is working on retrieving files. He thinks he might have something by tomorrow."

"Good." Jacob relayed his conversation with the Westbrooks. "If the PI found a lead about the Reeves-Westbrook baby kidnapping, we need to know what it was."

"I'll keep you posted." Griff hesitated. "There's something else. I've been checking arson cases similar to the hospital fire and found a couple that are similar. One was at a school and the other at a mall. I'm going to talk to the officers who investigated those cases."

"Which means the fire wasn't a setup for the kidnapping?"

"Right," Griff admitted. "We have to explore every angle. True arsonists are thrill seekers who enjoy the thrill of the fire and the chaos that follows."

Jacob gritted his teeth as he hung up. He'd never understand how anyone took pleasure in another person's pain. But Griff was right.

If the hospital fire was caused by a thrill seeker, whoever took Cora's baby may have done so on the spur of the moment, a crime of opportunity. That would also explain why there was never a ransom note or they hadn't found anyone lurking by the nursery watching the newborns prior to the fire.

He stewed over that as he drove to the FBI headquarters. He and Liam spent another hour reviewing security tapes again. Liam pointed out two baby kidnappings he suspected were related to a kidnapping ring.

Finally Jacob headed back to Whistler, the miles clicking away. The temptation to stop by Cora's struck him, but he ordered himself to drive home.

He could not get personally involved with Cora. She was vulnerable and needed answers, not for him to get romantically involved with her. Not that she would be interested...

He turned onto Main Street when his phone buzzed. His deputy. He immediately connected.

"Jacob, it's Martin. A 911 call just came in. There was a wreck on Route 9, a red Ford Escape."

Jacob's blood ran cold. Cora drove a red Ford Escape.

Chapter Nine

Jacob pressed the accelerator. Cora had been in an accident.

Dear God, let her be all right.

He swung the police SUV around, flipped his siren on and sped toward Route 9. Thankfully traffic was minimal. Another plus to living in a small town—people actually paid attention when he appeared and pulled over to let him pass. His heart pounded with fear as he rounded a curve and spotted the guardrail dented and skid marks on the pavement where Cora had careened off the road.

Emergency workers hadn't arrived yet, and he willed them to hurry as he pulled to the side of the road and jumped out. The front of Cora's SUV was in the ditch, smoke billowing from the rear.

He jumped over the guardrail, his boots skidding in the dirt, gravel and rocks flying as he rushed down the incline. His heart hammered at the sight of the shattered driver's window.

The acrid smell of smoke hit him as it seeped from the rear of the car.

A reminder he had to hurry.

He peered inside the window. The airbag had deployed. He pulled his knife from his pocket and tried to open the door, but the corner was stuck in the ditch.

Dammit.

"Cora," he shouted. "Honey, can you hear me?"

Nothing.

Fear pulsed through him. He ran back to his SUV, grabbed a shovel from the trunk and flew back down the hill to the car. He dug dirt from the door then pried it open it so he could reach Cora. With a quick jab of his knife, he ripped the airbag.

Cora moaned. Thank God she was alive. "Hang in there, Cora. Rescue workers are on their way."

A siren wailed, and he stroked her shoulder, hoping she could hear him as he murmured reassurances. He didn't dare move her until the medics arrived.

The siren grew louder, then tires screeched. He glanced up the hill. An ambulance and fire engine roared to a stop. Jacob waved the workers down the hill.

"What do we have?" one of the firemen asked.

"Woman, driver, name is Cora Reeves. Airbag deployed. She's unconscious but alive."

Jacob leaned into the car. "Cora, the medics are here."

She moaned softly and started to lift her head. "Stay still, ma'am," one of the medics said. "We'll have you out in a minute."

She murmured "Okay," and Jacob stepped aside while emergency workers cut Cora's seat belt, then braced her neck before easing her from the vehicle and boarding her. He followed them up the hill to the ambulance and stood beside her while the medic called the hospital.

Jacob cradled her hand in his, disturbed at her ice-cold skin. "Cora?"

She blinked and opened her eyes, squinting as if her head hurt. "Jacob—"

"Shh, it's all right. You had a car accident, but you'll be fine." At least he hoped to hell she would.

"Not...accident," she said in a raw whisper.

"Yes, you had an accident and ran off the road," he said softly.

She shook her head. "No...*no* accident."

Jacob froze. "What do you mean, no accident?"

She swallowed as if her voice wouldn't quite work. "Cora?"

"Someone...shot at me."

Jacob's blood turned to ice. "You're sure?"

She nodded. "Hit window..."

He muttered a silent curse.

The medic cleared his throat. "We're ready to transport her."

Jacob squeezed Cora's hand. "Did you see who it was?"

She shook her head.

"We really need to go," the medic said.

Jacob thumbed a strand of hair from Cora's cheek. "I'll see you at the hospital. I'm going to take a look at your car."

Cora's eyes drifted closed as they loaded her into the ambulance.

Jacob hurried to his SUV and retrieved his evidence kit, then raced back down the hill to comb the car and area for forensics.

CORA'S HEAD WAS still swimming as the medics pushed her into the ER. On the drive to the hospital, she'd tested her limbs and was grateful she could move her legs. She didn't think anything was broken, either.

Thank heavens for the airbag. It had probably saved her life.

The attending physician conducted a preliminary exam. "Everything looks clear," Dr. Pattinson told her. "I'm ordering chest X-rays to look for broken ribs and a CAT scan in case you have a concussion."

Cora hated hospitals. The last time she was admitted was when her daughter was stolen.

"Can I go home after that?" Cora asked.

"Let's see how the tests turn out," he said. "We might keep you here for observation overnight."

The image of flames and smoke taunted her. She couldn't stay here tonight. "No, I have to go home," Cora said.

The memory of the bullet whizzing by her head flashed behind her eyes as a technician rolled her to the imaging center.

She was lucky to be alive. But fear tightened every muscle in her body.

Someone had tried to kill her. And she wanted to know the reason why.

DAYLIGHT WAS WANING. The dark clouds robbed any remaining sunlight, casting the area in gray. Jacob tugged on latex gloves and used a flashlight to examine the car, starting with the shattered windows.

Glass littered the interior of the front seat and floor. A bullet hole made him curse. Cora was right. This was no accident.

He snapped photographs with his phone, then opened the passenger door and shined the light inside in search of a bullet casing.

He walked the area, looking at the vehicle from all angles to estimate the trajectory of the bullet and the shooter's origin.

Judging from the evidence, the bullet had come from the passenger side.

He searched the floorboard and found a partial casing amongst the shattered glass. Next he moved to the driver's side and examined that window. Evidence of another bullet skimming the glass indicated it had traveled through the passenger window and across the car, close to Cora's head. He shined the light across the interior of the door, the ceiling and roof and spotted the bullet lodged in the roof where it met the window casing. Cursing, he used his knife to dig it out and bagged it with the other casing.

Anger railed through him. Except for frightening a few nervous mothers over the years, Cora had never hurt anyone in her life.

But she had been relentless in pushing to keep her case on police radar. And then she'd hired that PI.

Which pointed to a motive. Someone was afraid Cora was about to uncover the truth about the kidnapping.

And that person—the kidnapper—was close by.

Maybe even in Whistler.

He or she was watching Cora.

Jacob turned and scanned the area. Thick woods backed up to the ditch where the shooter could have hidden. The shooter could have been in another car, though, waiting until just the right moment to open fire.

Perspiration beaded on the back of his neck as adrenaline kicked in. He grabbed his phone, called his deputy to explain the situation and asked Martin to meet him at the scene.

When he hung up, Jacob combed the ground in case the shooter had snuck up to the car while Cora was unconscious. He shined his flashlight across the ground and embankment looking for footprints, a piece of clothing that might have snagged on a twig, a button, cigarette, anything that might point to the shooter's identity.

But the only footprints he found were his own. No clothing or anything that might have belonged to the shooter.

A few minutes later, Martin drove up and met him by the car. "Search the woods for forensics in case the perp parked and hid behind the trees before or after he ambushed Cora." He handed the bullet casings to his deputy to courier to the lab just as the tow truck arrived. "Before they move the car, see if you find prints on the door. Mine will be there and Cora's, but it's possible the perp slipped up to see if Cora was alive."

"Copy that," his deputy said.

"Who made the 911 call?" Jacob asked.

"I believe Cora did," Martin said.

She must have regained consciousness long enough to phone for help, then lost consciousness again.

"I'm going to the hospital," Jacob said. "Maybe she saw the shooter or his car."

Fear gripped him as he headed to his vehicle. He had to hurry.

If the shooter knew Cora had survived, he or she might come after her again.

CORA HATED THE hospital sounds and smells.
After the CAT scan, she was wheeled back to the ER.

Her clothes were torn and bloody from the glass fragments that had pelted her arm, so the nurses gave her a pair of scrubs to wear home. Her wrist was bruised and swollen; a small butterfly bandage covered the cut on her forehead at her hairline, and her ankle was wrapped.

It seemed like hours before the doctor appeared with her results. "Thankfully nothing appears to be broken, so that's good." He offered her a sympathetic smile. "The CAT scan looks clean, too. I'd say you were a lucky lady today."

She would hardly call being shot at lucky. But she was alive.

A nurse poked his head into the room. "Sheriff Maverick is here."

"Is it all right if he comes in?" Dr. Pattinson asked.

Cora nodded and rubbed her arms with her hands. Jacob stepped inside, his jaw clenched.

"I'm going to release you," Dr. Pattinson said. "But you should take it easy for a day or two. Do you understand, Cora?"

"Yes, thank you." She just wanted to go home and crawl into her own bed.

"I'll drive you home," Jacob offered.

Cora had no other way, so she simply murmured her thanks.

"If you experience dizziness, nausea or severe headaches, please call," Dr. Pattinson said.

"I will." Cora gripped the edge of the bed to stand.

"I'll get a wheelchair," the nurse offered.

"I don't need one," Cora protested.

Dr. Pattinson cleared his throat. "It's hospital policy."

Jacob stepped to the side of the bed to steady her, but she waved off his concern, determined to prove she was well enough to be released. One of the hospital staff members brought discharge papers, and she scribbled her signature.

A minute later, the nurse returned with the wheelchair. In spite of her bravado, her legs were weak and she was grateful for the ride. Jacob pulled his SUV up to the door, and the nurse wheeled her to the passenger side.

Jacob rushed to assist her, and seconds later, they were settled in the car and pulling from the parking lot.

Jacob gave her a look of concern. "How do you feel?"

"Tired," Cora said, struggling not to fall apart.

Jacob raised a brow. "You sure you're ready to go home?"

She blinked away a dizzy spell. "I'm sure. The last time I was in a hospital, it didn't turn out so well."

"God, Cora, I'm sorry. I should have realized."

"It's fine," she said. "But I'll sleep better in my own bed." If she slept at all.

The memory of that shooter coming out of nowhere haunted her, and she scanned the roads and side streets as they drove through town. Jacob seemed extra alert for trouble, too.

"I had your car towed to be processed for evidence,"

Jacob said grimly. "I found two bullet casings and am sending them to the lab."

Images of those last few minutes before she crashed flashed behind her eyes. The fear. The feeling of having lost control. The sound of metal crashing and glass shattering.

The realization that someone was trying to kill her.

"What were you doing earlier today, before the crash?" he asked.

She narrowed her eyes. "What?"

"Let's retrace your day. It's possible that someone you talked to or saw got nervous and shot at you."

She twisted her hands in her lap. His logic made sense. "After I left your office, I went to the bookstore. I ran into a little girl I knew from school and her mother."

He nodded. "Go on."

She explained about Faye getting upset over her questions at school, then warning her to stay away from Nina. "I felt bad for frightening her and Nina, so I decided to see my therapist."

He remained silent, eyes on the road.

"After that, I dropped by Faye's house to apologize."

"How did that go?"

She shrugged, the movement causing her shoulder to ache. "Actually better than I expected. We had a heart-to-heart. She told me about her miscarriages and I assured her I meant her and Nina no harm. Then I left."

A tense heartbeat passed. "Do you think she was scared enough to try to warn you off by shooting at you?"

Cora gave a little chuckle. "Heavens, no. Faye may have been nervous, but she's not dangerous. Besides, she and Nina were together when I left."

She rubbed her temple as they wove around the mountain road to her house. "But now that I think about it, twice lately, I thought someone was following me."

Jacob parked and turned toward her. "Why didn't you tell me?"

"I thought I was just being paranoid." And that he'd think she was crazy.

His expression turned grim, but he climbed from the SUV and darted around the front to her side. She was opening the door by the time he reached her. He clasped her hand as she slid out. As much as she valued her independence, she wasn't foolish enough to try to walk up her graveled drive on unsteady legs.

Thankfully he'd grabbed her purse from her car, and she retrieved her keys. Her hand was shaking, though, and she fumbled with the keys and dropped them.

Jacob picked up the keys and opened the door.

Cora sighed as they entered. "Thanks for driving me home."

He paused in the doorway and gently cradled her arms with his hands, forcing her to look at him. "Someone tried to kill you tonight. There's no way I'm leaving you alone."

A chill swept through her at his words, and the tears she'd tried to keep at bay seeped from her eyes.

Jacob pulled her up against his chest and wrapped his arms around her. It had been so long since anyone had held her or comforted her that she leaned into him and let the tears fall.

Chapter Ten

Jacob ordered himself to release Cora, but his body refused to listen to his brain. When he'd seen Cora inside that car unconscious, he'd realized something.

He cared more about her than he should.

For some odd reason, the hospital fire and the tragedies in their lives had created a bond. He'd been connected to her the moment he'd met her, when she'd looked up at him with those big, baby blue eyes and pleaded with him to find her baby.

She nestled against his chest, her body trembling. He rubbed slow circles over her back, soothing her and rocking her in his arms.

"You're safe now, Cora," he murmured against her hair. "I won't let anyone hurt you."

She nodded against his chest, then ran her hands up his back. Emotions blended with desire, making his body harden. He feathered her hair from her forehead and forced himself to pull away slightly. He had to wrangle his libido under control.

Cora needed tenderness, not a man's lust.

His own needs be damned. He'd give her what she needed.

"I can't believe this is happening," she said in a low whisper.

Jacob eased himself from her. "I'll find out who shot at you, Cora. Don't worry. He won't get away with it."

She sniffed, her body trembling again, and he took her arm and ushered her to the sofa.

"Lie down and rest. I'll fix you something to eat."

"You don't have to do that," Cora said.

"Yes, I do, it's my job to take care of Whistler's residents, and I intend to do that."

She stiffened slightly, and he sensed he'd said something wrong. Then she laid her head back against the sofa pillow and closed her eyes.

While she rested, he made himself at home in her kitchen. She must like to cook, because the pantry was stocked and so was the refrigerator. He found ingredients for a small salad and chopped lettuce, tomatoes and cucumbers. Then he noticed jars of homemade vegetable soup in the pantry, so he opened one of those, poured it into a pan and heated it up.

While it was warming, he checked on Cora. She'd dozed off, so he spread a blanket over her, turned the soup to warm, then decided to check her house for an intruder.

There were no signs of a break-in at the door or windows. He walked the property outside the house, using his flashlight to illuminate the ground, but found no footprints. At least the shooter hadn't been stalking her at home.

Although since he'd failed today, there was no telling what he'd do.

Jacob would have to convince Cora to install a security system.

By the time he went back inside, Cora was stirring from sleep. He crossed the room to her and knelt beside her. "Are you up for a meal?"

She rubbed at her forehead, her finger brushing the bandage with a frown. "That would be good."

He helped her stand, watching her carefully to make certain she wasn't dizzy. "Let me take a quick shower and change out of these scrubs," she said.

"All right. I'll keep the soup warm."

She disappeared into the bedroom, and he set the table, then walked out onto the back deck and looked out at the mountains. Anything to distract him from thinking about Cora in the shower.

Yet images of her trapped in that car taunted him. Dammit, he could use a beer right now.

But he'd stick to water.

He needed to keep a clear head to protect Cora.

CORA SPLASHED COLD water on her face and stared at herself in the mirror. Her bruises and the bandage on her forehead looked stark in the dim light.

She couldn't believe that big, strong, tough Jacob Maverick was in her kitchen cooking her dinner. It had been a long time since anyone had taken care of her. When they were first married, Drew had been attentive and had occasionally cooked. But as time passed, his attention toward work had replaced his time with her.

She stripped the scrubs, frowning at the black-and-purple skin marring her chest and legs, then forced her thoughts away from the accident. She was home now. Safe.

At least for a little while.

But Kurt was dead. And someone wanted her in the ground with him.

Trembling, she climbed in the shower and let the warm water wash away the scent of perspiration and smoke. She scrubbed her body and hair then rinsed and dried off. A quick comb through her hair and she left it damp, the strands curling around her shoulders. She dressed in an oversize T-shirt and yoga pants, then tossed the scrubs into the laundry basket.

She found Jacob standing on her back porch, staring at the mountains. She'd always loved the view and the quiet, but it struck her that she was completely isolated.

A shiver tore through her. Anyone could sneak through the woods and break in through the back door or window.

Jacob turned to look at her, and another shiver rippled through her. This time not from fear. A sensual awareness that she hadn't felt in a long time heated her blood.

Her gaze locked with his, and tension simmered between them.

"You okay?" he asked gruffly.

She nodded, although she wasn't okay. The memory of his arms and solid chest against hers made her crave the safety of his embrace again. But leaning on Jacob could become a habit.

He was only being nice because it was his job. And she needed him to do that and find her daughter more than she needed him to hold her.

He gestured toward the kitchen. "Are you ready to eat?"

Her stomach growled, and she nodded and stepped back inside. Jacob went straight to the stove and dished them up bowls of soup while she set the salad on the table. It seemed odd to be doing something so routine as to share a simple meal with Jacob.

"Thanks for making dinner," she said as she sank into the kitchen chair.

"All I did was heat it up. You made this soup and canned it?"

She shrugged. "I have a lot of time on my hands in the summer," she admitted. "Gardening is therapeutic. And I like to use fresh vegetables and herbs that I grow."

"You garden and cook and draw. Is there anything you can't do, Cora?"

Be a mother. No, she *could* do that if she hadn't lost her child.

"Cora?"

"I just want to find Alice," she said softly.

Jacob covered her hand with his. "We will. But in the

meantime, we have to keep you safe. I'd like to arrange for a security system to be installed ASAP."

Cora agreed readily. It wouldn't do any good if she was dead when her little girl was found.

JACOB ATTEMPTED SMALL TALK with Cora while they ate, but he failed miserably. Asking about her plans for the summer only resurrected that haunted look in her eyes.

"I'll garden and draw and try to fill the days by helping gather donations for the food pantry at the church," she admitted.

Her unspoken words rang in his ears. *But every minute she'd be thinking of her daughter.*

"I know it's difficult, Cora, but hang in there."

Cora finished her soup and took a sip of water, then explained she'd lost her job. "I'm sure you think I'm deranged." She ran her fingers through the damp strands of her hair. Fresh from the shower and with no makeup, she looked young and sexy.

Except for that bandage on her forehead and the bruises that matched.

"I don't think you're deranged," Jacob said in a quiet tone. "I miss my father every day. Sometimes I think I've been so obsessed with finding his killer that I've forgotten to live."

Cora squeezed her eyes closed for a minute, then opened them and blinked as if battling tears. "Thank you for saying that. I see the way people look at me sometimes. I never meant to frighten Nina or her mother." She tapped her fork on the table, an odd look streaking her face.

"What is it? Did you remember something else?" Jacob asked.

Cora swallowed hard. "I promised I wouldn't say anything, Jacob, so this is confidential, but if anything happened to Nina, I'd never forgive myself."

Jacob tilted his head to the side. "What are you talking about?"

Cora sighed, the sound weighted with worry. "Faye said she left her husband, Nina's adopted father, because he was abusive. She's been moving around because he's dangerous, and she's afraid he's looking for them."

"Where is he now?"

Cora shrugged. "She didn't say. But I urged her to talk to you so you could be on the lookout in case a stranger comes to town asking about them."

Jacob gritted his teeth. Domestic violence was something he couldn't tolerate. His father taught him that being a man meant protecting women and children, not taking your anger out on them.

"I won't say anything, but I will keep my eyes and ears open," he said. "If you see her again, encourage her to talk to me."

"Thank you, Jacob."

"Just doing my job," he said. "After you left the Fuller house, what happened? Did you go anywhere else? Talk to someone? Get a phone call?"

She shook her head. "No, I was headed home when I thought someone was following me."

"Did you get a look at the car?"

"The car I saw earlier was a dark sedan. But tonight... I didn't see anything. As I was rounding a curve, the bullet hit the window." She shivered. "I braked, then another bullet flew through the glass near my head. I ducked and ran off the road, then slid into the ditch."

She cleared the table as if she needed to release nervous energy. Knowing she was sore from the accident, he took over at the sink.

"Lie down and get some rest," he murmured. "I'll finish here."

"I can do it," Cora said. "I'm sure you have other things to do."

He cleared his throat, set his salad plate down and faced her. "I'm not going anywhere tonight, Cora. Keeping you safe is my priority."

A wary look fluttered in Cora's eyes. Was she afraid of him?

He softened his tone. "Tomorrow I'll arrange to install a security system. But tonight I'll sack out on your couch to make sure whoever shot at you doesn't show up."

Panic darkened her face, and he could have kicked himself for what he'd said. Instead of soothing her fears, he'd intensified them.

But someone had tried to kill her today.

And he didn't intend to let Cora die.

JACOB'S WORDS ECHOED in Cora's head. He thought the shooter might come to her house. She wanted to bury herself in his arms and hide until he'd found the person who wanted her dead.

But he was only doing his job. He'd made that plain and clear.

That was what she needed, though. Jacob to find the shooter and to find Alice.

She couldn't afford to imagine anything more between them, not when she was so broken.

"I'll get you a pillow and a blanket." She gathered the items from the closet and set them on the couch.

Jacob had cleaned up the dishes and now stood by the back door as if scanning her property for trouble. Nerves clawed at her, and exhaustion tugged at her, so she said good-night before she did something stupid like throw herself into his arms.

Her cell phone buzzed from her purse, and she retrieved it. Drew.

She started not to answer. But what if he'd learned something about their daughter?

She pressed Accept Call and said hello.

"Cora, what the hell are you doing sending the sheriff over to question me about your PI boyfriend?"

The anger in his tone triggered her own. "He was not my boyfriend—"

"I don't give a damn if he was, but I don't appreciate you insinuating to Sheriff Maverick that I was having an affair!" His breath rasped out. "For God's sake, you don't really think that I had something to do with our baby's kidnapping, do you?"

Cora touched the bandage on her forehead. Someone had tried to kill her. And Jacob had questioned Drew. He was certainly angry now.

He wouldn't try to kill her.

Would he?

Chapter Eleven

Anger struck Cora. "I didn't give the sheriff that idea," Cora said. "But since you brought up the subject, were you having an affair, Drew?"

"What?" His tone sounded incredulous. "I can't believe you'd ask me that."

"Why not?" she snapped. "You certainly moved on pretty quickly, both from Alice and me."

A strained silence stretched between them for a minute. When Drew finally responded, frustration thickened his voice. "That's not fair, Cora. I was hurting, too, only you were too mired in your own emotions that you didn't notice."

Cora sucked in a breath. She felt as if she'd been punched in the gut.

But today had been too frightening and upsetting for her to contemplate whether or not she'd been selfish.

Tears threatened. "I have to go." She didn't wait for a response. She ended the call and turned the phone to silent in case Drew called back.

Still, adrenaline was pumping through her, so she retrieved her stationery, then sat down at her desk to write her daughter another letter.

Dear Alice,
Today I saw a little girl named Nina at the bookstore. I met her at the school where I taught. She lays

her carrot sticks out in rows like I did when I was little. She also eats the top of her muffin first.

She has pretty brown hair and a sprinkling of freckles across her nose, and she likes to draw. I'm making friends with her mother, Faye.

Maybe when I find you and you come to live with me, you and Nina can have a playdate and become friends. If you like to paint or draw, I'll buy canvasses, and we'll carry a picnic to the park by the river and the two of you can paint.

I miss you so much, my sweet little girl. I hope that I get to see you soon. Then you can tell me all about what you've been doing the past five years.

I love you always,
Mommy

A pang seized Cora as the therapist's words reverberated in her head. *What will you do if you find her and she's happy?*

She shoved the voice to the far recesses of her mind.

First she'd find Alice. Then she'd decide what to do.

She carefully placed the letter in her keepsake box, then crawled into bed and flipped out the light.

But as she closed her eyes, Drew's angry words screamed in her head. Drew, who might have betrayed their marriage. Drew, who'd abandoned her after they lost Alice.

An image of Jacob stretched out on her couch flashed behind her eyes. Jacob, who was strong, steadfast, a family man. Jacob, who'd never treated her as if she was unstable. Jacob, who'd promised not to give up the search for her daughter. Jacob, who'd suffered a loss the night of the hospital fire.

But he hadn't abandoned his family because of it.

The temptation to ask him to join her in bed seized her. She wanted his warmth. His strength.

She wanted his touch. His kiss. His hands. His mouth. His big warm body giving her pleasure.

She slipped from bed and padded to the door. She cracked it a fraction of an inch, then peeked inside her living room. But his voice echoed to her, and she realized he was on the phone.

"Don't worry, Liam, I'm not getting personally involved with Cora Reeves."

Cora's pulse jumped as disappointment filled her. Obviously her feelings for Jacob were one-sided.

Battling tears again, she closed the door, tiptoed back to bed and crawled beneath the covers, alone.

JACOB BARELY DOZED off for listening to Cora tossing and turning all night. He checked the perimeter of the house several times, but everything seemed quiet.

Perhaps the shooter thought Cora hadn't survived, and he wouldn't return. Although if Cora knew the person who'd tried to kill her, or if he was watching her, he'd know she was alive.

By dawn, he rose, made a cup of coffee and a to-do list.

As soon as he deemed it a reasonable hour, he phoned the local security company. They agreed to meet at the house at ten to install a system.

Then he tracked down the head nurse who'd worked the neonatal unit at the time of the hospital fire.

Cora opened the door, looking sleepy. Her hair was tousled, and the bruises on her face and arms were even more stark in the morning light streaming through the windows.

He dragged his eyes away from her curvy body in those pajama pants and T-shirt. The pale blue color accentuated the vivid hue of her eyes, eyes that looked wary this morning. "Did you finally get some sleep?" he asked.

She nodded. "A little. How about you?"

"A little," he admitted, although he'd been tormented by

the fact that she could have died the night before. If he'd done his job and found Alice years ago, Cora wouldn't be in danger now.

She walked into the kitchen, removed a mug from the cabinet and made herself a cup of coffee.

"I heard your phone ring before bedtime," he said.

She shrugged. "Drew called."

Jacob stiffened. "What did he have to say?"

She sank into the kitchen chair. "He was furious and accused me of telling you that he had an affair."

"Any investigator would ask the same question," Jacob said. "Unfortunately in a child kidnapping, we have to look at the parents, their friends and enemies, and acquaintances."

"I remember you said that years ago when you first interviewed me."

"I'm sorry that I failed you, Cora. I really am."

Cora's big eyes softened. "It's not your fault, Jacob. I know you did everything you could."

Jacob shrugged, but the guilt wouldn't ease up. "Once the security company shows up, I'm going to visit the nurse who was in charge of the neonatal unit when you delivered," Jacob said. "Maybe she remembered something that didn't strike her as important at the time."

"I'll go with you," Cora said.

Jacob hesitated, debating on letting her come along. Then again, he didn't want to leave her alone.

Especially in light of her ex-husband's phone call. Drew could have called last night just because he was angry.

Or...what if he'd called to see if Cora had survived the accident?

The attempt on Cora's life had come while he was questioning the Westbrooks.

But Drew could have hired someone to kill Cora just as he could have Philips.

CORA QUICKLY SHOWERED and dressed before the security company arrived. While they installed the system, Jacob drove home for a shower and clean clothes.

As the technicians worked, Cora stood looking out her window. She usually felt safe here in the mountains, as if it was a sanctuary until she was reunited with her daughter.

Now everything had changed.

The woods looked spooky, a place for predators to hide. The mountains seemed taller, the cliffs steeper, the ridges sharper and more ominous. The river seemed colder, the rapids more intense and dangerous, as if they could carry a dead body downstream and it would be lost forever.

She gripped her hands and fought panic. She could not think like that. She was not a defeatist. She refused to allow fear to hold her hostage.

Jacob would keep her safe. She had to hold on to the hope that they were making progress.

Jacob returned just as the installation was complete, and the security specialist demonstrated how to work the system.

A half hour later, they parked at Wynona Baker's house. Wynona, who had been kind to Cora at the hospital, had worked in the neonatal unit for fifteen years before Alice was taken.

Wynona invited them in, and they settled at her kitchen table. Ceramic puppies lined a shelf in her kitchen and a picture of a chocolate Lab hung above the fireplace in the corner.

Cora wondered if Alice had a dog.

"How are you, Cora?" Wynona asked.

Cora and Jacob exchanged a look, then Cora murmured that she was okay. Jacob explained about Kurt's death and the events of the day before.

"Oh my goodness," Wynona said. "I'm so sorry, Cora. I hoped you were stopping by with good news."

"I wish we were," Cora said.

"Wynona, it's been five years," Jacob said calmly. "Sometimes immediately following a trauma, our memory is foggy because we're in shock. Have you recalled anything about that night since? Some detail about what happened in the hospital nursery?"

Wynona rubbed her fingers together in a nervous gesture. "I just remember how awful it was. The minute the fire alarm rang and we realized it was real, not a drill, everyone sprang into action. I ordered staff to move the babies out."

"There's some question now as to whether Cora's daughter was taken when the babies were outside on the lawn or before," Jacob said.

Cora scrunched her face in thought. Did Jacob know something he hadn't told her?

JACOB HAD QUESTIONED the entire staff who worked on the maternity floor after the fire, but at the time, no one had stuck out as suspicious. Most everyone's story matched—it was pure chaos, everyone was scurrying around trying to help patients evacuate and calm family members. A couple of infants had been snatched from their bassinets by parents who were close by the nursery when the fire alarm sounded.

No one had seen anyone take Cora's child.

Jacob consulted the notes from his interviews with the staff. "I talked to Dale Friedman and Horace Whitman, two of the orderlies you said helped move the infants. Was there anything odd about either one of them? Maybe a family member who'd lost a child?"

Wynona rubbed her forehead. "Not that I recall. Both Dale and Horace were hard workers. Dale went on to medical school and is doing a residency in the ER in Atlanta now. Horace became a med tech."

Cora shifted. "Please think," she said. "Did you notice anyone lurking around the nursery who didn't belong?"

Wynona sighed, the sound filled with frustration. "I'm sorry, Cora, I…just can't remember."

"My husband left my room before the alarm went off," Cora said. "Did you see him in the hall or by the nursery?"

Wynona rubbed her temple. "I saw him by the vending machine getting coffee. He was talking to a young woman. She had flowers and a baby gift with her. A little pink teddy bear, I think it was."

Jacob chewed the inside of his cheek. Wynona hadn't mentioned this before. "Do you know who the woman was?"

The nurse shook her head no. "She gave him a hug and congratulated him on the baby. They started down the hall toward the nursery, and I assumed he was going to show her your daughter, but the woman's phone rang, and she disappeared down the hall."

"What happened after that?" Jacob asked.

"I don't know. The alarm sounded, and everyone went into a panic."

Jacob retrieved a photo of Drew and his wife on his phone and showed it to Wynona. "Was this the woman you saw talking to Drew?"

Wynona studied the picture for a minute, then nodded. "Yes, I believe it was."

"That's Drew's wife," Cora said tightly. "She worked for his law firm at the time."

Jacob considered the information. If Drew had been having an affair, was it with Hilary? That would explain how quickly they'd married after his divorce.

"There's something else I'd like for you to look at," Jacob told Wynona. On his last stop to Liam's office, he'd copied footage of the person in scrubs carrying the bundle toward the laundry area.

He angled the phone for Wynona and Cora to see. A pained silence fell across the room as they watched the footage.

"Do you have any idea who that person could be?" Jacob asked.

Emotions clouded Wynona's face. "No. I can't see his— or her—face."

He had another clip of the activity on the maternity wing. "Look at this and see if anything strikes you as off."

A frown puckered the skin between Wynona's eyes. "Wait," she said, her breath catching. "That woman there, the one in the dark coat."

Cora leaned forward, anxious. Jacob gave Wynona another minute.

"What is it?" he asked.

"Her name is Evie Hanson. I don't know why she was there. She was put on suspension two weeks before the fire."

"Why was she placed on suspension?"

Wynona bit down on her lower lip. "I hate to gossip."

"Please," Cora said again. "What happened?"

"She learned she couldn't have children," Wynona said. "She was really depressed about it. One of the doctors found her sneaking into the nursery to hold the newborns."

Jacob clenched his jaw. Why hadn't this come up before? "Where is she now?"

"I don't know," Wynona said. "I thought she moved away before the fire."

"We have to find her," Cora said. "What if she was so depressed that she kidnapped Alice?"

Chapter Twelve

"Why didn't you tell us about her before?" Cora fought to keep anger from her voice, but it broke through anyway.

Jacob touched Cora's arm, a silent message to remain calm. She knotted her hands, though, and squared her shoulders. She'd been patronized and treated like she was unstable so many times that her defenses rose.

Wynona looked taken back. "I'm sorry, I didn't think about it. I thought she was gone. I hadn't seen her in the hospital in days."

"And looking at the photograph triggered your memory," Jacob said gently.

Wynona nodded, her lip quivering. "If I'd seen her and thought she might be involved, I would have come to you, Sheriff." She turned to Cora. "Not a day has gone by that I haven't regretted what happened that night. I'd been a nurse for fifteen years before that horrible fire. Although we'd lost a baby or two due to health issues, no child had ever been stolen from our nursery. When I first came on board, I instigated stringent security measures to prevent a possible kidnapping and baby mix-up."

A tense second passed.

"Did you know Evie?" Cora asked.

Wynona offered her a small smile. "I did. And it's not what you think, Cora. Evie was sweet and giving, and she loved children. She worked in the pediatric heart unit."

Questions nagged at Cora but compassion also surfaced. "She must have been devastated to learn she couldn't have children."

"She was," Wynona said. "The counselor on staff assured Evie she was a good candidate for adoption. So I don't see any reason she'd do something as drastic as to kidnap your baby."

Cora wanted to believe her. From Wynona's comments, Evie sounded like a wonderful person. If she had taken Alice, at least her little girl was in loving hands.

"That may be true," Jacob said. "But I need to question her. Do you have any idea where she is?"

Wynona shook her head. "I really don't know. So many people left Whistler after the fire that I lost track. You know it took months to rebuild the wings of the hospital that were damaged and employees were transferred to other hospitals."

Cora clung to the hope that Evie might have answers for them. Or that she might actually have Alice.

Her heart pounded with anticipation at the thought.

JACOB'S PHONE BUZZED with a text as he and Cora left Wynona's house. "Liam is going to meet us at the police station."

"Does he have information?"

"He didn't say. But I want him to find Evie Hanson."

"So do I." Hope flashed in Cora's eyes. "I wish Wynona had mentioned Evie five years ago."

Jacob ground his teeth. "That would have been helpful."

He offered Cora a sympathetic smile, then veered onto Main Street toward his office. "Do you want me to drop you at home before I meet with Liam?"

"No, I want to know if he can find Evie."

Jacob felt the sudden need to protect her from false hope. "She might not have Alice," Jacob reminded her.

Her lips curled downward into a frown. "I know. And don't worry about me, I've survived disappointment before."

Cora leaned toward the window, and he realized she was watching a woman and little girl enter the bookstore. The longing on her face twisted at his heartstrings.

He passed the store, then pulled into the space designated for the sheriff. Cora was out of the car before he could go around to open her door. A lot of young men these days didn't bother, but his father had taught him and his brothers to be gentlemen.

A breeze stirred the air, the temperature in the high seventies. The sun had fought through the clouds from the night before. With the summer break, the park across from the sheriff's department was full. The town seemed crowded, with vacationers flocking to the mountains for hiking, white water rafting and camping. The Whistler B & B had three cars in front, a good sign.

The owner, Beula Mayberry, had been struggling lately, but he'd heard she'd renovated, so hopefully business would pick up.

He spoke to his deputy as he entered, but he was talking on the phone, so Jacob escorted Cora to his office. "Do you want coffee?" he asked.

"No, thanks." She paused and looked around the interior, focusing on the bulletin board above his desk, where he'd tacked two fliers for wanted felons along with a missing persons flier for a teenager who'd disappeared from Raleigh three weeks before.

Liam rapped his knuckles on the door and poked his head inside. Jacob waved him in and gestured toward Cora.

Liam offered his hand. "We met before, Cora."

"I remember," Cora said. "Jacob said you were still searching for my daughter. I appreciate it."

"We never gave up," Liam assured her. "Unfortunately leads went cold for a while, but that could change." He paused, then cleared his throat. "As a matter of fact, one of the major news stations is running a special segment to showcase missing persons' and children's cases that have gone cold. They do it every so often. Sometimes people recognize the child from our photographs, or recall details they've forgotten, and we get a lead."

Cora drummed her fingers on her arm. "They're going to include Alice?"

Liam nodded. "I insisted. I've already sent over the information we have on her disappearance along with your sketches."

Cora blinked as if fighting tears, and Jacob wanted to hug his brother.

He shared his conversation with the nurse. "We need to locate Evie Hanson and question her."

Liam gave a quick nod. "I'll text my analyst and have her start searching." He quickly sent a text, then gestured to Jacob's desk. "I have some photographs I'd like you to look at, Cora."

Liam set a folder on the table, then removed a photograph of a thin dark-haired woman wearing a gray suit. Her expression was drawn and sad.

"Her name is Lydia Bainbridge," Liam said. "She and her husband lived in Chapel Hill and lost a baby when it was born. A heart defect."

"That's awful," Cora murmured.

"It was and they didn't take it very well," Liam said.

"When did this happen?" Jacob asked.

"Three weeks before Cora delivered," Liam replied.

"The timing could be significant," Jacob added.

"Yes. The husband sued the doctor for incompetence, and they settled out of court. After that, they moved to Florida. They adopted a little girl two weeks after Alice went missing. One of our agents is investigating the adoption now."

"You think they may have adopted Alice?" Cora asked.

Liam shrugged. "I don't know, but we're exploring every possibility." He angled the photograph toward Cora, then added another picture of the husband, a tall auburn-haired man in a fire fighter's uniform.

Jacob and Liam exchanged a silent message. If the husband wanted to set a fire, he'd know how to do it and get away with it.

Liam tapped the photograph. "Look at this picture, Cora. Do you recall seeing this woman or man at the hospital when you were there?"

Cora scrutinized the picture of the couple.

"I'm sorry, but I don't recall seeing them. They could have been there, but I was already in labor when I was admitted, so I was wheeled to a labor and delivery room. I stayed there for hours until the birth."

"You didn't go into the hall to walk?" Jacob asked.

She pinched the bridge of her nose. "No." Frustration knotted her insides. "I was so exhausted I fell asleep shortly after the birth. When the alarm sounded, all I could think about was saving Alice."

"I know it was mass confusion," Jacob said. He'd been there.

Liam patted Cora's hand. "It's all right. It was a long shot. They may not have been there. But my analyst is reviewing every inch of the security footage." Liam slid another folder beneath the one of the couple. "We're also working another angle." He glanced at Jacob as if uncertain whether he should continue.

"Please tell me," Cora said. "I promise I won't break down and go maniacal on you."

Jacob chuckled, and so did Liam. "I'm not worried about that," Liam said. "And if you did, I'd understand. Missing children bring out emotions in all of us."

Cora swallowed back a sob. Compassion and tenderness triggered tears every time.

"What's in the other file?" Jacob asked.

Liam scrubbed a hand through his hair, then removed a photograph of a middle-aged lady with graying hair. She was seated on a train with a baby boy and a toddler girl. "An agent in Atlanta sent me a picture of this woman. She goes by the name Deidre Coleman." Liam paused. "We believe she's running an illegal adoption ring."

Cora made a pained sound.

"One of our agents is going undercover to verify our suspicions," Liam said. "At this point, we've uncovered reports of three missing children, including that baby boy, who match photographs of recently adopted children on the dark web and linked them back to her. So far, no legal documents have been located. But we traced large sums of money deposited into an offshore account in the name of Deidre Coleman, although we believe that name is an alias. Our agent is gathering intel for a warrant to pick her up for questioning."

He angled his head toward Cora. "Do you ever remember seeing this woman? It could have been at the hospital or around town or even at your ob-gyn's office."

Cora studied every detail of the woman's face. Although she was definitely in the shadows in the picture, she could tell the woman was austere. A blunt nose. Graying, thin eyebrows. Long fingers with nails that needed a manicure. Even though she was seated, she held a firm grip on the toddler's hand and cradled the baby close to her, its face hidden.

Cora closed her eyes, mentally transporting herself back to her ob-gyn's office. So many happy, pregnant women congregating to share stories and the excitement of upcoming births. Talk of nurseries, baby showers, and little girl and boy names. Laughter over arguments between spouses and grandparents over those names. Talk of different parenting styles.

Dreams of finally nestling their baby in their arms.

Occasionally a woman leaving teary-eyed over bad news. But this woman in the picture—*she* would have stood out in the maternity waiting room because she'd passed her childbearing years.

"I don't remember seeing her at my doctor's office," Cora said. "I guess she could have come in the hospital, or maybe she was on the lawn that night." She gave Liam a pointed look. "Have you found a link between her and Alice?"

Regret darkened Liam's face. "Not yet, but we're looking."

Disappointment threatened to steal her budding hope, but she squashed it. With both Jacob and Liam on her side now, at least Alice hadn't been forgotten.

"I'll keep you posted, Cora." Liam gathered the photographs and files and Cora thanked him.

"Let me know if you locate Evie Hanson," Jacob said.

Liam agreed, said goodbye and headed outside.

Jacob stood and adjusted his belt where his gun hung, drawing her gaze to his big, strong body.

Cora jerked her eyes away. How could she possibly think about how handsome Jacob was when they'd just been discussing an illegal adoption ring?

When the woman with the graying hair might be stealing babies and selling them.

When Jacob had told his brother he wasn't interested in her personally.

Chapter Thirteen

The thought of a person selling children nauseated Cora.

"You want me to drive you home now or to pick up a rental car?" Jacob asked.

She shook her head. "I'll take care of it." Waiting alone at home did not appeal to her at the moment. She was afraid she'd get mired in the fact that she had endless days ahead with nothing to do but think about her daughter and her jobless future.

She brushed her hands down her shirt as she stood. "I'm going to the bookstore for a while."

"All right. Call me if you need anything," Jacob offered.

She thanked him and slipped from his office, determined to keep her feelings for him at bay.

A dark cloud had formed, shrouding the sun and adding a chill to the air as Cora walked down the sidewalk and crossed the street to the bookstore. Mothers and children filled the park, their laughter and chatter a reminder that life moved on, that happiness did exist.

Even if it evaded her.

One day she'd push Alice in the swings and fly a kite with her, and they'd skate on the rink the town erected for the winter holidays.

She reached the bookstore and smiled at the array of children's books displayed for the summer reading program. Through the glass window, she saw Nina at one of the tables drawing, with Faye close by. A minute later, Faye opened her laptop and Cora noticed her browsing the real estate website where she worked.

Envy stirred inside Cora. If she found Alice, would they ever be that close?

She desperately wanted to join them, but Faye's shared confidence gave her pause. The poor woman had suffered. She didn't intend to add to her problems.

Clutching her purse, she walked toward the diner. Inside, the place was bustling with the late-afternoon lunch crowd. She slipped up to the bar, ordered a turkey sandwich and sweet tea, then phoned to arrange a rental car as she waited on her meal.

The owner, a cheery lady named Billie Jean, grinned at her. "There you go, sweetie. You doing okay today?"

"Sure." Cora forced a smile. Discussing baby kidnapping rings wasn't her idea of fun, but if it helped find Alice or saved another mother from experiencing the pain she'd suffered, she'd look at any pictures Liam or Jacob showed her.

She paid for the sandwich and drink, carried them across the street to the park and found an empty picnic table beneath a live oak. The shade of the tree offered her privacy, but also allowed her to people-watch.

Signs for a watermelon festival in two weeks had been tacked up around the park along with a sign for Pet Adoption Day the following Saturday. She'd considered adopting a dog over the years to keep her company, but wanted to wait until Alice came home so they could choose the pet together.

She spread out her sketchbook and pencils on the table, and nibbled on her sandwich as she studied the children on the playground. A little curly-haired blond toddler in a purple romper was learning to walk and kept stumbling. The mother clapped and laughed, offering encouragement as she called the child's name.

A group of elementary-aged children played chase while a father tossed the ball to his son in a game of catch.

She was just about to begin a new sketch of Alice when the sound of a woman's voice made her pulse clamor.

"Cora?"

She clenched her pencil as she faced the woman. Julie Batton. At one time, they'd been best friends.

Before Alice had been taken.

Julie's little boy, Brian, looked up at her with the same grass-green eyes as his mother. Cora remembered the day he was born as if it was yesterday.

It had been exactly one week before Alice came into the world.

Cora had cooked Julie and her husband dinner that night and carried the excited couple a bottle of champagne. They'd toasted the occasion and laughed over dreams they shared for their children.

Cora's homecoming had been the opposite. Filled with fear and anguish. Police hovering around, asking questions. People staring at her and Drew with sympathy and suspicion.

Julie had tried to be a friend. She'd sent cookies. Offered Cora a shoulder to cry on.

But the day Cora followed a woman with a stroller in the mall, Julie had told Cora she needed psychiatric help.

Then she'd run to Drew. Made it seem like Cora was losing her mind. Drew had gotten rid of Alice's things later because of the counselor—and Julie.

She'd never forgiven either one of them for that.

FIVE MINUTES AFTER Cora left, Jacob's phone buzzed. Liam.

"My analyst just called. They located Evie Hanson. She's been working at a hospital about twenty miles from Whistler." Liam paused. "I have a conference call with the task force investigating the baby kidnapping/adoption ring. I'm texting you Evie's home address so you can check it out. According to our information, Evie took a leave of absence about three months ago to be a stay-at-home mom."

"Is that timing significant?" Jacob asked.

Liam hissed out a breath. "Could be, could be coincidental."

"What does that mean?"

"Means it warrants further investigation."

Jacob snatched his keys, anxious to leave. "I'm on my way to question her."

"Jacob, listen, man," Liam said in a no-nonsense voice. "It's possible she may not be involved in the Reeves-Westbrook baby kidnapping. Even if she obtained the baby through the ring, she may be unaware that the child was kidnapped, so tread carefully. If you suspect at any point that she bought the baby, play it cool and don't reveal our suspicions. We don't want to spook her into running or into alerting Deidre Coleman that we're on to her."

"You got it."

Jacob met Martin on the way out the door, relayed the latest turn of events and asked him to cover rounds.

His senses were alert for trouble as he drove through town. This afternoon looked like a normal day in Whistler.

So had the day of the fire, when everything had gone horribly wrong. No one in town had seen it coming. No one knew why the fire was set and the town destroyed.

He passed the square, and veered onto the road leading from town, his adrenaline having spiked at the prospect of solving this case. He sped up once he left the city limits, then maneuvered the curvy roads toward Shady Oak.

The nurse lived in a development a mile from the village of Shady Oak, a quaint little town built in the valley between the mountains.

Minutes later, he reached her house. It was a sprawling ranch house with green shutters and a well-maintained lawn. He scanned the yard and property for a car or children's toys, any sign indicating the family was home.

He parked in the drive, then climbed out and walked up to the door. The carport was empty, no cars in sight.

He rang the doorbell, but when no one answered, he peeked into the windows flanking the front door.

He didn't see movement or anyone inside. He gritted his teeth.

Had Evie left town because she knew the feds were on their tail?

"Cora, is it okay if I sit with you for a minute?" Julie asked.

Cora inhaled to calm her voice. The last thing she needed was to make a scene. Besides, maybe Julie had been right five years ago. She had been out of control.

"Of course." Cora gestured toward the bench seat across from her and Julie slid onto it, angling her body to keep an eye on Brian as he played with another boy about his age. They were tossing a football back and forth. Brian dropped it and giggled, then growled like a monster. Cora couldn't contain a smile.

"Brian has really grown," Cora said. "Was he in kindergarten this year?"

"He was," Julie said. "That's his friend Tony. He lives a couple doors down from us."

"Cute boys," she said. "I'm sure he keeps you busy."

Julie smiled as she watched her son. "He's all boy, that's for sure. Loves cars and trucks, sports and superheroes. He dressed as Spider-Man last year for Halloween."

"Superheroes were the theme this year at school," Cora said with a pang of sadness that she'd miss the school activities next year.

An awkward silence fell between them for a minute. Julie took a sip from her water bottle, then offered Cora a tender look that reminded Cora of when they were good friends. Julie had always worn her feelings on her sleeve. She volunteered at the women's shelter, prepared meals for the homeless, and ran the clothing and food drive at her church.

Julie was one of the most selfless people she'd ever known. They'd actually met during one of the food drives one year and bonded as they sorted and packed canned goods for families who'd lost their homes in a tornado.

"I've been thinking about you a lot," Julie said. "I wanted to see you, but I didn't know if you'd want to see me."

"I'm sorry you felt that way," Cora said. "I was rough on you after Alice was taken." Cora breathed out. It felt good—right—to apologize and let go of her anger. "No matter what happened, though, I was happy for you, and glad you had Brian. I never meant to imply that I wasn't."

Tears flooded Julie's eyes. "I know that," she said. "I always did. And it wasn't your fault. My God, Cora, you're stronger than I am. I don't think I could have gone on if I was in your shoes."

Cora made a low sound in her throat. "Truthfully, Julie, I'm still a wreck. But I'm trying not to give up hope."

Julie reached across the table, and Cora linked hands with her the way they used to do. "I'm so sorry I wasn't there for you the way you needed." Julie wiped at a tear with her free hand. "I just didn't know what to do, Cora. I felt so bad for you, and I was terrified at the same time. I was a mess myself over not being able to conceive."

Cora raised her brows. "What? I'm sorry. I didn't know."

"Because I didn't want anyone to know," Julie admitted quietly. "I was…ashamed. I felt like a failure when we kept trying to get pregnant and couldn't."

Cora's heart broke for her friend. "Oh, gosh, Julie, there was nothing to be ashamed of. A lot of women have trouble conceiving."

"I know that up here." She tapped her forehead, then

her chest. "But my heart said something else. I felt like I wasn't a good wife, that I was letting Jimmy down." She swallowed hard. "Anyway, that's the reason I pulled back from you. I kept thinking, what if it was Brian? What if someone took my little boy?" Julie choked on the last word, emotions overcoming her.

Cora squeezed Julie's hand. She'd been so wrapped up in her own pain and terror that she hadn't considered anyone's feelings but her own. "I guess that's the reason you reacted so strongly when I chased down that woman at the mall."

Julie started to say something, but Cora threw up a warning hand. "I'm not making excuses for it. It was wrong. I'm sure I terrified that poor lady. I understand now why you told Drew."

Julie's brows wrinkled. "I didn't tell Drew about that day."

Cora narrowed her eyes. "You didn't?"

Julie shook her head no. "I went home and cried and rocked Brian for hours. I felt so sorry for you. I wanted to make it up to you, but I didn't know how."

"If you didn't tell Drew, how did he find out?" Cora asked.

"I have no idea. The only person I told was Jimmy."

"Do you think he called Drew and told him?"

"No, I made him promise not to," Julie admitted. "Besides, he was too worried about me. I hadn't been sleeping and was falling apart at home. He insisted I talk to a therapist the next day, and I did."

"You went to therapy?"

Julie nodded. "I should have gone when we first couldn't conceive. The counselor helped me understand my feelings and learn to control my anxiety about the possibility of losing Brian."

"Oh, Julie, I'm so sorry," Cora said. "I should have been there for you."

"No, you were looking for your baby," Julie said brokenly. "There's no one to blame, Cora. It was just a horrible situation."

And Drew had made it worse for Cora by giving all of her baby things away.

The question still nagged at her, though. If Julie hadn't told Drew about the incident at the mall, how had he known?

Chapter Fourteen

Jacob moved from window to window, looking inside Evie Hanson's house.

She was gone.

On the off chance she'd left something, *anything* behind, even a scrap of paper with a forwarding address, he walked around to the back of the house and checked the door. Locked. On the far side, he found the laundry room window ajar, so he climbed through it.

A washer and dryer remained. He peeked inside the dryer and found a lone little pink sock.

His heart twisted.

A child's sock, a little girl probably about the same age as Alice.

He stuck it in his pocket and moved from the laundry room into the hallway, then the kitchen. He scanned the room and searched the drawers. Cleaned out, as well.

Dammit.

He searched the living room next, combed through the coat closet and desk. He glanced inside and found it empty, then ran his hand along the top shelf. Nothing but dust.

Frustrated, he strode down the hallway to the first bedroom. A bed and dresser, but nothing inside the chest or closet, either.

The bathroom yielded a couple of bandages with cartoon imprints, a nail file and a little pink toothbrush. His instincts kicked in, and he removed a baggie from inside his pocket and bagged the toothbrush for DNA analysis.

If it matched Alice's, he'd ask the crime scene techs to search for prints. He also needed to research Evie's banking information, find out if she rented or owned, and if she'd left a forwarding address.

He moved to the smaller bedroom. The twin bed suggested it belonged to the child. Marks from where posters and pictures had been removed discolored the lavender walls. Bare shelves in the closet, although some digging unearthed a book caught in a corner. It was a children's book about giving a mouse a cookie. The soft cover was tattered, the pages worn, the book obviously well-loved.

He bagged the book then skimmed his hand along the top of the shelf. His hand brushed something in the back, and he stretched his hand and snagged the item. A small notebook.

He opened it and found pictures the child had drawn.

One picture stood out. It was a Christmas tree with a string of colorful lights.

Cora liked to draw. Could this child be Alice?

JULIE GESTURED TOWARD Cora's sketchbook. "I see you're still drawing," Julie said. "Working on anything in particular?"

Cora closed her journal. If she was going to be friends with Julie again, she had to be honest. Sane but honest.

"It may sound strange, but I've sketched images of what I think Alice would look like over the years."

Worry flashed across Julie's face, then a gentle smile. "You must think about her every day." She reached for the sketchbook. "Can I take a look?"

Cora shrugged. "Actually I'm just starting a new series. I...gave some of the sketches to the sheriff to send to the FBI. They're going to distribute to law enforcement agencies and NCMEC."

"It's great that you can do something to help," Julie said.

"I don't know if it will," Cora admitted. "I wonder how much Alice has changed. If I'd even recognize her."

A sad look passed across Julie's face. "I have a feeling you will."

Cora's gaze met hers, her compassion a reminder of Julie's confession about her own anxiety.

"Well, we'll see. The FBI is coordinating with a special news segment about missing persons' and children's cases. I'm hoping someone will recognize her and come forward."

Julie squeezed her hand again. "I'll pray that happens, Cora."

They held hands for a moment, the anger and bitterness that had driven them apart slipping away. After the last few lonely years, it was comforting to have a female friend. Someone who wasn't a shrink.

Brian ran over, his cheeks red from playing. "Mommy, can we get ice cream now?"

Julie smiled and ruffled her son's hair. "Of course." She turned to Cora. "Would you like to go with us?"

Cora hesitated, but decided it was time she started behaving like a friend. Maybe having Julie back in her life would help ease the loneliness of the summer.

And waylay the feelings she had for Jacob.

She would just have to keep her obsession with staring at every little girl for her daughter's face under control.

She gathered her things and walked beside Julie as they crossed the park to the street, then the ice cream store. The boys' excitement was contagious. As soon as they entered the ice cream parlor, Brian and his friend Tony started counting the different flavors.

It took twenty minutes for them to decide while she and Julie chose their favorite, mint chocolate chip, a common love they'd discovered the first time they met. They sat at a small table outside and the kids licked their cones, the summer breeze stirring the scent of flowers and an impending rain shower.

Down the street at the bookstore, she saw Faye and Nina exiting, Nina chattering and holding hands with her mother. Cora's heart swelled with longing, but she forced herself to turn away.

The boys finished their cones, and Julie handed them napkins to clean their faces. "Guess we'd better go," Julie said. "I have to get Brian's friend home." She paused as she stood. "What are you doing?"

Cora offered a smile, her brows knitting as a few raindrops began to fall. "I need to pick up a rental car."

"I can give you a lift if you want," Julie offered.

Cora tossed her trash into the bin. "I'd appreciate that."

Together they walked to Julie's minivan and climbed in. "Where are you living now?"

"The cottage Drew and I bought. After we split, I moved in permanently."

Julie gave her a sympathetic look. "I'm sorry about your divorce, Cora. That must have been difficult."

Cora lifted her chin. "I'm fine now."

"I can't believe Hilary and Drew ended up together." Julie's voice softened. "I want you to know that I stopped hanging out with her after they got married. It just…didn't seem right."

"I'm sorry you were caught in the middle." Cora meant it, too.

Julie's comment triggered the memory of Jacob's question. She'd been shocked when she'd realized Drew and Hilary were getting close.

Hilary had stopped by personally to tell her about their engagement. She claimed she felt bad, but that Drew was hurting over Alice's disappearance, too. That she'd tried to be there for Cora, but Cora had pushed her away.

While consoling Drew, they'd fallen in love.

Maybe the divorce had been her fault. In her anguish, she'd pushed him right into Hilary's arms.

JACOB FLIPPED THE pages of the drawing pad and discovered other childlike pictures, then one of a baby crib that was empty. Curiosity filled him, but he couldn't make too much out of the drawings. They could mean nothing.

Still, he'd send them to the lab with everything else.

He finished searching the closet, but found nothing else, then walked back through the house. "Where are you, Evie? Do you have Cora's daughter?"

He left through the back door, scanned the property and noted a neighbor's car next door. The houses were situated on small lots with shrubbery in between.

The houses directly across the street looked vacant, but the green sedan in the drive of the ranch next door indicated someone was home. He hurried up the drive, noting the wreath of spring flowers on the door and the bird feeder in the front yard. A swing set sat in the backyard, visible from the front stoop, and a soccer goal occupied the corner by the fence.

Jacob knocked on the door, tapping his foot as he waited. A minute later, the door swung open, and a boy about ten grinned at him with mud on his face. Jacob couldn't help but smile. The boy reminded him of mud fights and makeshift obstacle courses with his brothers in the backyard when he was that age.

"Hey," the boy said with a toothy grin.

Jacob smiled back. "Is your mother or your father here?"

"Ridley, what are you doing?" A woman's voice screeched. "I told you not to open the door to strangers."

A thirtysomething woman appeared in jeans and a T-shirt, wiping her hands on a dish towel, something that looked like chocolate frosting on her face. Maybe it was frosting on the kid's face, too.

"But Mama, he's a cop," Ridley said. "I seen his police car out the window."

"You *saw* it, not seen it," his mother corrected. She turned her attention to Jacob. "Sheriff?"

"Yes, Sheriff Maverick. I'd like to ask you a couple of questions."

She patted her son's shoulder. "Ridley, Inez needs some playtime. Why don't you take her out back and throw the tennis ball with her?"

"But Mama," Ridley said. "He's the *sheriff*." His eyes grew big with interest.

His mother smiled. "I know, and I promise to tell you if something is interesting, but please take Inez out before she has an accident on the carpet."

"All right," Ridley said, glum faced.

Jacob winked at the boy. "If I need you, buddy, I'll find you outside. Okay?"

Ridley bounced up and down on the balls of his feet. "'Kay." Then he ran toward the back room calling the dog's name.

The mother escorted Jacob to the kitchen, where she could keep an eye on her son and the dog. Outside, the scruffy mutt ran in circles as she chased the tennis ball Ridley tossed to her.

"So," the woman said as she seated herself at the pine table. "What can I do for you, Sheriff?"

"Mrs. . . . ?"

"Owens," she said. "Dayna. My husband owns the hardware store up the way."

"Right. Well, I'll get to the point. Did you know the woman who lived next door?"

She nodded, but a frown creased her brows. "I met Evie a few times in passing, but we didn't really visit much. She kept to herself."

"And her daughter? What was her name?"

"Twyla," Dayna said. "She was adorable. Five, and full of energy and creativity. That child loved to draw and sing. Occasionally she and Ridley played outside together, but Evie seemed nervous and protective. Why are you asking about Evie, Sheriff? Did something happen to her?"

Jacob gave a small shrug. "I don't know. I wanted to talk to her about a connection she may have had to the hospital in Whistler five years ago, but it appears she moved out."

Dayna leaned forward and rested her elbows on the table. "That was odd."

"Where was the little girl's father?" Jacob asked.

Dayna shrugged. "It was just Evie. Her husband died in a helicopter crash in Afghanistan three years ago."

"I'm sorry." Jacob swallowed. "Did she appear to be upset about anything lately? Or did Twyla?"

"No, but like I said, they kept to themselves. I did see a delivery truck bringing in a baby crib one day about a month ago. Last week, when I asked Evie about it, she said she'd hoped to get a little boy, but it didn't work out."

Jacob narrowed his eyes. "She hoped to get a little boy?"

"Yes, they adopted Twyla. Evie was going to adopt again. I don't know what happened but she moved the next day."

She stretched to see Ridley in the yard and seemed relieved to see him climbing the jungle gym while the dog plopped down beside him and chewed on a stick.

"What day was that?"

"Saturday. That morning I saw her packing her things in her car. I went over to inquire, but she waved and took off as if she was in a hurry. I thought something was wrong but didn't get to ask."

Jacob chewed the inside of his cheek. Saturday.

Dammit. That was the day after Kurt Philips had been murdered.

CORA THANKED JULIE as she dropped her at the rental car company, and they agreed to get together later in the week.

A few raindrops splattered the ground as she drove home, so she parked quickly and hurried up the steps. She paused as she fished out her keys.

A gift basket with a bright purple bow sat in front of the doorway.

She stooped to pick it up and read the card.

A friendship offering from Whistler Mountain Realty. Faye.

It felt as if a ray of sunshine had splintered through the dark cloud hanging over her. First Julie and now Faye.

Hope sprouted that her world was about to turn around and get brighter. If it wasn't raining, she might start that garden today, but she'd wait till tomorrow for the rain to pass.

She unlocked the door and carried the basket inside. A chill invaded her, and she made a cup of coffee, then laid her sketchpad on the table in front of the window overlooking the mountains.

Then she turned to examine the items in the gift basket. A lavender-scented candle and lavender-scented bath soaps. A box of chocolates. An assortment of brownies and cookies in a tin.

Yum, she was a chocoholic.

Deciding the brownie would be perfect with her coffee, she removed one from the tin and set it on the table with a mug of coffee. She settled down in front of the window and opened her sketchpad, then began another sketch. This one of Alice eating an ice cream cone.

Only she had no idea what her daughter's favorite flavor was.

Stewing over the possibilities, she sketched the ice cream

parlor with the dozens of choices, nibbling on the brownie as she drew.

Suddenly, though, her throat thickened. She coughed, gagging for a breath. She tried to sip the coffee to wash the brownie down but choked, and coffee spewed from her mouth.

She clutched her throat, desperate for air. God. She was having an allergic reaction. There must have been peanut oil in the brownie.

Her head felt light, the room swimming. She pushed away from the table and staggered toward her purse. Her EpiPen was inside.

One shot and she'd be fine.

Only the room twirled. She gasped. Her purse was just out of reach, her fingers clawing for it as darkness swept her into its abyss.

Chapter Fifteen

Cora struggled to keep her eyes open. She had to keep breathing. Reach her EpiPen. But her throat had closed…

Suddenly her door flew open. "Cora?"

Faye?

Had she forgotten to lock the door when she'd come inside? Hadn't she set the alarm…

No…she'd been distracted by the gift basket.

Footsteps clattered. Voices echoed as if far away in a tunnel.

Fear seized Cora. She didn't want to die. Then she might never find her little girl.

"Ms. Reeves?"

A small voice this time. A little girl's. Nina's?

More footsteps, then a hand gently touched her. "Ms. Reeves?"

"Cora, what's wrong?" Faye's voice this time.

Cora blinked back tears, struggling to see through the fuzziness clouding her brain. She wheezed out a breath, cried out, stretched her fingers toward the end table where she'd left her purse. "Pen…" she choked out.

"Pen?" Faye stroked Cora's hair away from her face and turned her head to examine her. "Cora, I'll call 911."

She shook her head, or at least she thought she did, then

clasped her throat with one hand and pointed to her purse with the other. "Help."

Another sound. Footsteps. Smaller this time. "Mama!"

"Get me my phone!" Faye shouted.

"But Mama, look," Nina cried.

Through the fog, Cora saw Nina running toward them, the EpiPen in her small hand. "Look."

Faye's eyes widened, and she grabbed the EpiPen from Nina, then brushed Cora's cheek. "You need this?"

Cora struggled to nod, but the darkness was pulling her under.

Faye jerked the top off the pen, raised it and quickly jabbed it into Cora's thigh.

Nina cradled Cora's hand in hers. "Is she gonna be all right?" Nina whispered.

Faye soothed Cora by rubbing her hand along Cora's back. "Come on, breathe, Cora. You're going to be fine."

Slowly the ache in her chest receded. Her throat felt as if it was contracting, the swelling lessening. Perspiration trickled down her face as she clutched Faye's hand.

"Mama?"

Nina sounded frightened. Cora had to assuage the little girl's fears. She blinked, inhaling and exhaling slowly to steady her breathing. Finally the dizziness faded. The world stopped moving. Slipped back into focus.

She stared into Faye's eyes, then Nina's. Both looked frightened.

"I'll get an ambulance," Faye said.

Cora shook her head. "No… I'm okay…thanks…"

Relief flooded Faye's face, then Nina leaned over and gave her a hug. "You scared me, Ms. Reeves."

"I… I'm sorry, honey," Cora whispered.

"Can you sit up?" Faye asked.

Cora wasn't sure. Her body felt weak. Languid. Her limbs heavy.

But another look at the terror on Nina's face, and she nodded.

"Come on, I'll help you." Faye slid her arm beneath Cora's shoulders and helped her to stand. Nina clutched her arm and leaned on Faye.

They helped her to the sofa and she sank onto it, leaned back and continued to breathe in and out. Footsteps again, then Faye returned with a wet washcloth and dabbed Cora's forehead with it.

The cool cloth helped to lift the fog. "Thank you, Faye. You saved my life."

A blush stained Faye's cheeks. "I'm just relieved you're okay. I didn't know you had an allergy."

"Peanuts," Cora said. "The brownies in the basket you sent must have contained peanut oil."

"I'm allergic to peanuts, too," Nina said. "I gots a pen just like you."

Cora's heart pounded. "You do?"

"Uh-huh," Nina said. "I hate that shot. Mama had to give it to me twice."

A strange sensation engulfed Cora. She and Nina shared the same food sensitivity. A coincidence, or could it mean more?

She silently chided herself. Peanut allergies were on the rise these days. For heaven's sake, the school had issued letters to parents, making the school a peanut-free zone because the allergy was so common.

A contrite expression flashed across Faye's face. "I forgot to tell one of the mothers when Nina was invited for a playdate, and she gave Nina a muffin containing peanut oil."

"It happens to everyone at some time," Cora said sympathetically. Her mind raced. "What are you doing here anyway?"

"Nina begged to stop by." Faye wrinkled her nose. "But what did you mean, about the gift basket from me?"

Cora straightened slightly and gestured toward the table. "The basket," she said. "It had your name on the card."

Faye crossed the room and examined the basket and card. A frown tugged at the corners of her eyes. "I didn't send the basket, Cora."

If Faye hadn't sent it, who had?

Someone who knew about her allergy and wanted her to die?

JACOB HANDED THE items he'd collected from Evie Hanson's house to Liam. He had broken into the house with no warrant, so it might not be admissible, but right now all he wanted was answers and a lead. And he might have just found one.

Besides, maybe he could justify probable cause. "I thought you could run these for DNA through your lab," he said. "I'm sure you can get results faster than I can through the county."

"Sure." Liam examined the bag with the pink toothbrush, the sock and drawing pad. "You think this little girl Twyla might be Alice Reeves Westbrook?"

Jacob lifted his shoulders slightly. "It's worth exploring. She is adopted. The neighbor said Evie was protective of her daughter and they kept to themselves."

"Being protective of your child is not a crime," Liam pointed out. "In this day and age, parents should be cautious."

Agreed. "But the way she suddenly packed up and moved seems suspicious. The neighbor also claimed Evie was on the verge of adopting a baby boy, but something happened. Maybe she obtained Twyla illegally and planned to do the same again, but got frightened and decided to run."

"You could be jumping to conclusions," Liam said. "But we'll follow up."

"I texted Martin to see if he can dig up more info on Evie, who she rented from, how she paid. I'd like a crime team to search for prints in the house. Maybe Evie's job in the pediatric unit is a front for kidnapping babies."

"That's a stretch," Liam said. "But considering I'm investigating an illegal kidnapping/adoption ring, it's worth considering."

A good working theory.

"Let me start a search for her." Liam clicked some keys on his computer. "And I'll handle the prints."

"Thanks." Jacob shifted. "Any more on the kidnapping/adoption ring?"

"Not yet. Hopefully soon."

Jacob's phone buzzed on his hip. He checked the caller ID. Cora.

"Let me take this. Call me if you get a lead on Evie."

He stepped into the hall and answered the phone. "Cora?"

"Jacob, I...need to talk to you."

Her voice sounded strange. Weak. Something had happened...

"What's wrong?"

"I think someone just tried to poison me," she said in a raspy whisper.

Jacob's blood ran cold. "Where are you?"

"Home."

He hurried down the hall to leave the building. "Hang on, I'll be right there."

CORA'S MIND REELED as she studied Faye. She'd settled Nina at the table to color while they talked.

Faye seemed confused, and had adamantly denied sending the basket.

"Could someone from your real estate office have ordered it on your behalf?" Cora asked.

"I don't think so," Faye said. "We typically send gifts to potential clients. You haven't talked to anyone about putting your place on the market, have you?"

Cora shook her head. "No."

Faye rubbed her temple. "I don't understand, then."

"Did you mention me to anyone?" Cora asked. "Maybe your agency is sending out feelers to find out if anyone is interested in selling?"

Faye pursed her lips. "I haven't talked about you to anyone, Cora."

Now her tone sounded defensive.

"I'm sorry for asking so many questions," Cora said, lowering her voice so Nina wouldn't hear. "But I think whoever sent this knew about my allergy and just tried to kill me."

Shock widened Faye's eyes. "What? Oh my God. You don't think I would do that?"

Cora glanced at Nina. How could she doubt Faye with her daughter in Cora's living room? When Faye had saved her life?

If she'd wanted to kill Cora, she wouldn't have brought Nina to her house to witness it.

"No, I don't," Cora said quietly.

Faye paced the room, then found two glasses in Cora's kitchen, filled them with water then brought one to Cora. Her hand shook as she sipped from the other glass and sank into the chair facing Cora.

She leaned forward, angling her face away from Nina. "Why would you think someone wants to hurt you, Cora?"

Cora debated on how much to tell Faye. But Faye had

confided about her ex, so she decided to reciprocate and explained about Kurt's murder and her car crash.

"You think the same person who murdered that private investigator tried to poison you today?" Faye asked. "If he didn't share information with you, why come after you?"

"I don't know," Cora said. "Unless whoever took Alice believes I might be close to finding her."

Faye's lips parted in a surprised expression. "But trying to kill you would only draw suspicion."

"True," Cora said. "But whoever it is must be desperate."

A knock sounded at the door, jarring them both. Cora pushed forward to get up, but Faye threw up a hand. "I'll get it. You should rest."

Cora still felt a little light-headed, so she leaned back against the sofa. Jacob's voice echoed from across the room, and Faye introduced herself, then led him inside.

A muscle ticked in Jacob's jaw as his dark gaze met hers.

Faye paused beside Nina and patted her shoulder. "Come on, sweetie, we need to go."

Nina ran over and threw her arms around Cora. "Are you gonna be okay, Ms. Reeves?"

Cora hugged her tightly, savoring the sweetness of the little girl. "I'm fine, honey." She cupped Nina's face between her hands and gave her a smile. "Thanks to you and your quick thinking."

Nina's big eyes brightened. "You want us to come back and check on you?"

She did. But Faye seemed agitated and ready to go, so she didn't want to push it.

Jacob saved her from having to respond. "Don't worry, I'll make sure Ms. Reeves is okay."

"Good," Nina said with a toothy grin. "'Cause she's the bestest teacher in the world."

"I'm sorry I scared you, honey," Cora said softly. "You were very brave today, Nina."

Nina hugged her again, and Cora fought tears.

Faye set her water glass on the table beside Cora's, then clasped Nina's hand. "Come on, sweetheart. Cora needs rest."

Cora offered Faye a smile of gratitude. "Thank you so much, Faye."

Faye nodded. "I'm just glad we got here when we did."

Cora remembered seeing them in town. "Did you stop by for a reason?"

Faye gave a sheepish shrug. "We saw you leaving the park and just wanted to say hi. Call me if you need anything."

Nina waved, and she and Faye left. Seeing them and Julie today made Cora realize how much she'd shut herself off from others.

Maybe she and Faye could be friends.

But she turned to Jacob and reality intruded. He was here because someone wanted her dead.

And today they'd almost succeeded.

Chapter Sixteen

Jacob crossed the room to Cora, anger mingling with worry. "Do you need a doctor?"

"No, I'm all right," Cora said. "Faye gave me my EpiPen."

Jacob lowered himself beside her. Her complexion looked pale, her eyes slightly glazed, and perspiration dotted her forehead. "What allergy?" he said, all business.

"Peanuts," she said. "I know what foods to avoid, but when I found the gift basket I saw the brownies and didn't think about them having peanut oil in them. But they must have. I was fine until I ate one."

He narrowed his eyes, then he seemed to scan the room for the basket.

Cora pointed toward the table. "That was on the front porch when I arrived home. The card said it was from Faye and her real estate agency, but she denies sending it."

Jacob chewed the inside of his cheek. "Did she know about your allergy?"

Cora took a sip of water. "I don't see how she could have. We only just met."

"Who knew about your allergy?" Jacob asked.

Cora ran her fingers through her hair. "Some of the teachers at school. Of course Drew and all my former friends."

He folded his arms. "Isn't Faye the woman who complained to your principal?"

Cora clenched her jaw. "She is. But we came to an understanding when she told me about her ex."

"What was she doing here?" Jacob asked in a tone full of distrust.

"She and Nina saw me in town and decided to stop by and say hi."

"Has she ever done that before?"

Cora shook her head no. "But like I said, we're just getting to know each other. I think she felt bad about having me fired."

Jacob mulled over that possibility. Faye had seemed perfectly normal. Friendly, although maybe a little wary. "She was in a hurry to leave when I came in."

"I think my reaction frightened her and Nina," Cora admitted.

"Was the child upset?" Jacob asked.

Cora's expression softened. "Actually Nina was a trouper. She grabbed the EpiPen from my purse. Her quick thinking saved my life."

Jacob pulled a hand down his chin. "How did she know about the pen?"

Cora searched her memory. The last hour was blurred. "I tried to tell them. And... Nina is allergic to peanuts, too. Maybe she recognized the signs of my reaction because she's had a similar reaction before."

Jacob retrieved his phone from his belt. He examined the gift basket, read the card, then punched the florist's number.

"This is Sheriff Jacob Maverick. I have a question about an order delivered to Cora Reeves. Can you tell me who placed the order?"

He waited while she searched their records. "Actually the order was placed online."

"The name of the sender?"

"Whistler Mountain Realty."

"Was there an individual's name?" Jacob asked.

"No, sir."

"How was it paid for?"

"Hmm, looks like a PayPal account. Sheriff, is something wrong?"

"I don't know. Maybe." He'd need a warrant to search the accounts. Unless Liam could gain access...

"Let me know if that account orders anything again."

"I sure will."

He ended the call, then phoned the real estate agency, tapping his foot in agitation. Cora was watching him with avid curiosity.

"This is Penny from Whistler Mountain Realty," a cheery young woman answered.

Jacob identified himself and explained the reason he called. "Did someone from your agency order a gift basket for Cora Reeves?"

"Hang on, and I'll check." Jazz music echoed over the line while he was on hold. A second later, she returned. "I'm sorry, sir, but we haven't ordered anything for Ms. Reeves. Were we supposed to?"

"No, but she received a gift basket with a card with your company name on it."

"That's odd," Penny said. "Why would someone use our name to send a gift?"

"Good question." And one he intended to find the answer to.

"Ask around the office and see if anyone else might know and call me back if they do."

She agreed, and Jacob thanked her and hung up.

"Who sent it?" Cora asked.

"I don't know." Jacob snapped a photograph of the basket. "But I'm going to have the lab analyze the food and ask Liam to dig deeper into the order to see who placed it."

CORA STRUGGLED TO understand what was happening as Jacob phoned his deputy to pick up the basket. His concern heightened her own.

Fatigue from her reaction tugged at her muscles, and she yawned into her hand.

Jacob finished the call, then joined her on the sofa again. "How are you feeling?"

"A little tired," she said. "But I'll be fine."

The look that flashed in his eyes mirrored her own fears. She almost hadn't been fine.

"Tell me what happened after you left the station," Jacob said in a quiet but serious tone.

She massaged her forehead, then relayed her movements and explained about her friend Julie.

"When did you last see her?" Jacob asked.

A fresh wave of pain splintered Cora as she recalled the way their friendship had fallen apart. "It's been over four years," she said. "This cabin was our vacation home—mine and Drew's. When Drew and I split, I moved here permanently, and Drew kept the house in Charlotte." She cringed as her accusations against Julie taunted her. "It was my fault that Julie and I haven't spoken."

Jacob stroked her arm. "Cora, none of this was your fault. Any parent who lost a child would have had a difficult time."

"But I wasn't a good friend to her," Cora said. "I thought she called Drew and told him I was crazy, because I followed this woman at the mall one day. I'm sure I seemed like a stalker."

"You're not crazy now, and you weren't then," Jacob said.

Jacob's big blunt fingers gently brushed her arm, calming her. "Fear does strange things to people."

Cora sensed he wasn't just talking about her now. "I know you suffered and miss your father," she said. "My parents died when I was in my twenties. But I lost them in a car accident. Your father was killed because someone set fire to the hospital. You must want to know who's responsible."

Emotions streaked Jacob's face. "Not knowing weighs on my mind," Jacob admitted in a low voice. "My brothers and I made a pact years ago that we'd find the person who set that fire and make him pay."

Compassion for Jacob and his brothers made her want to reach out to him. "You and your brothers are all admirable men."

Jacob gave a wry chuckle. "We're just trying to live up to my father's reputation."

"He died a hero." Cora couldn't help herself. She lifted her hand and pressed it to his cheek. "You're a good man, too, Jacob. In spite of your own tragedy, you tried to help me five years ago, and you're helping me now."

Emotions blurred as heat simmered between them. Shared pain and the need for answers had driven them both for years.

Jacob and his brothers were the most handsome, honorable men to ever come out of the North Carolina mountains.

She'd wondered why Jacob had never married. Never had a family of his own.

Now she understood. He'd devoted himself to protecting others instead of taking care of himself.

Admiration stirred, along with an attraction Cora couldn't deny. In the face of a crisis and when she'd needed him most, Drew had bailed.

But Jacob was here now. Protecting. Serving. As determined to unearth the truth as she was.

Kurt had been kind. Had vowed to help her. Had wanted more than she could give.

Because even in his kindness he hadn't heated her blood.

Not like Jacob.

He was so sexy that for the first time in years, she yearned for closeness with a man. Not just a man. Jacob.

He was kind. Caring. Loving.

His tenderness warmed her heart and made her feel as if she wasn't alone. As if she mattered. It gave her hope.

And his touch was so soothing that she craved his hands everywhere on her body.

Caught up in the feelings, she traced a finger along his strong jaw. His brown eyes darkened to black. His breath quickened. He leaned toward her.

She cupped his face in her hands and closed her lips over his.

JACOB HAD NEVER felt anything so sensual and sweet and tantalizing as Cora's tentative kiss. He should stop it, but reason gave way to passion.

He'd wanted to do this forever.

At first, in a comforting gesture. But the more he got to know Cora, the more he'd come to admire her strength and perseverance. She didn't deserve to beat herself up for not taking care of her friends when she'd been in the most horrible pain a parent could possibly fathom.

His own mother had crumbled after their father's death. She'd had health concerns before, but grief had taken its toll and her heart had given out. He'd always thought she died of heartsickness.

Cora's hand against his cheek urged him to deepen the kiss, and he traced his tongue along the seam of her mouth and probed inside. She parted her lips and accepted his sensual exploration, his chest constricting at her moan of pleasure.

He wanted more. To taste her neck and strip her clothes and touch her all over. To bring her enough pleasure to erase her fear and sadness.

She lifted her hand and threaded her fingers in his hair,

and he gently pushed a strand of hair from her cheek. Her quick intake of breath suggested she liked his touch, so he lowered his head and trailed tender kisses along her throat. She tilted her head backward, allowing him deeper access, and he slid one arm behind her head to pull her closer.

Her chest rose and fell against his as their bodies touched, igniting his desire. She planted kisses on his cheek and drew him closer as he teased her earlobes and the swell of her breasts.

His body hardened. Her breathing turned raspy, and she ran her hands down his back, stroking him, firing his need.

Hunger burst inside him, and he trailed his fingers along her neck to her shoulder, then lower. But just as he started to cover her breast with one hand, a knock sounded at the door.

Jacob froze, reality interceding. Cora leaned her head against his. For a moment they stayed that way, heads touching, breathing erratic, need still simmering between them.

The knock echoed again.

"I'll get it." Jacob slowly pulled away, but tilted Cora's head to face him. "You okay?"

Her face flushed. "I'm sorry."

He bit back a comment, then strode to the door. When he opened it, his deputy stood on the other side. "You wanted me to pick up something to take to the lab?"

Jacob gestured toward the table, then retrieved the gift basket. When he glanced at the sofa, Cora had disappeared into her bedroom.

Dammit, he didn't want her to have regrets. He wanted to kiss her again. Most of all, he wanted her to *want* him to kiss her again.

But that wasn't fair and he knew it.

"What's going on with the basket?" his deputy asked.

Jacob explained about Cora's allergy and the fact that

the card had been misleading. "I need to know who sent this. I'm going to get Liam to follow up on it."

"Do you think someone knew about her allergy?" Martin asked.

Good question. "It's possible. Especially considering someone tried to kill her by shooting at her."

Martin angled his body toward Jacob. "By the way, the lab called about the ballistics."

Jacob raised a brow. "And?"

"The bullet casings from Ms. Reeves's car match the one the ME removed from Kurt Philips's body."

Chapter Seventeen

Jacob's stomach clenched. "That means the same person who killed Kurt shot at Cora."

"They're still working on his computer," Martin said. "But Griff called and said the crime team recovered a key of some sort. They're trying to figure out what it goes to now."

"Did he have an office or home safe?"

"They didn't find one."

"How about his vehicle?" Jacob asked.

"A black SUV. The back window was busted out. Whoever set the fire must have looked through it."

"To get rid of evidence linking him or her to Philips's death."

"Exactly." Martin shifted.

"Find out if Philips had a safety deposit box," Jacob said. "Maybe he hid some documents or files inside."

"On it." Martin carried the basket to the door and left. As he drove away, Jacob heard the shower in Cora's bath.

He forced himself to banish images of Cora naked beneath the spray of water and ordered his libido under control.

Finding Kurt's killer might mean saving Cora's life, so he had to focus on the investigation, not on his personal needs. Maybe there'd be time for that later.

He retrieved his laptop from his car, brought it inside and booted it up, then connected to the police database.

His conversation with Cora echoed in his head. If the gift basket was sent by the same person who'd shot at Cora, that person knew about her allergy.

Her ex-husband certainly had. And he was smart enough to create a fake account for a flower order. He texted Liam and asked him to follow up on the order from the flower shop.

Drew's wife, Hilary, would also have known about the allergy. And Cora's friend, Julie. Although Julie had her own child and hadn't adopted, so she had no motive to take Cora's baby.

The pediatric nurse was a possibility. She could have gained access to Cora's medical records and learned about her allergy through her files.

Liam was investigating Evie, so he decided to check out Faye Fuller.

She'd saved Cora's life with the EpiPen, but she could have sent the basket, then had second thoughts and changed her mind about hurting Cora.

He entered her name and ran a background search. No arrests, outstanding warrants or charges. Not even a speeding ticket.

According to Cora, Faye was frightened of her ex. He did some digging in search of the husband, but didn't find records that she'd ever been married.

He checked records for domestic violence reports and found nothing on anyone related to a Faye Fuller.

Interesting.

He continued searching, hoping to find adoption records, although the adoption could have been closed. Or…what if she hadn't obtained Nina legally?

Curious and determined to explore every avenue, he removed a handkerchief from his pocket, picked up the glass Faye had used and bagged it. He'd send it to the lab to run for prints and find out exactly who Faye Fuller was.

If she was lying to Cora, he wanted to know the reason.

As she showered, Cora silently chided herself for kissing Jacob. She'd never made a move on a man before, but she hadn't been able to stop herself from that kiss.

She'd slowly begun to think of Jacob as more than the sheriff. As a friend. Maybe as a lover?

You don't have time for sex or romance. Your daughter is missing. And the man who was looking for her was murdered.

Yet the two attempts on her life now made her realize she wanted to live. Not just go through the motions. For so long, she'd cut herself off from caring about anyone.

It had hurt too much to lose Alice and then Drew. She didn't think she'd survive if she lost anyone else.

Being alone had been the answer.

She dressed in clean jeans and a T-shirt, ran a brush through her hair, then studied herself in the mirror. Her cheeks were still flushed. Her eyes looked…needy.

It's okay to care, she whispered to herself. *You deserve love.*

But fear hacked at her resolve.

Jacob risked his life every day on the job. His father had died protecting others. While it was admirable, it also meant he might not come home at night. That every time he stepped out the door, he was endangering his life.

She had to keep her distance. They'd find Alice. Then she and her daughter would build a life together.

Jacob would focus on work again. Hopefully he'd even find out who set that fire and killed his father, then he and his brothers would have closure.

The sound of voices drifted to her from the living room. Was Jacob talking to someone?

Determined to refrain from throwing herself at him, she stepped through the doorway.

Jacob gripped his phone in his hand, but he wasn't talking on it. He had turned on the news. "This is a special report featuring missing persons' cases across the Southeast," the reporter said. "First we're beginning with this story which originally aired five years ago from Whistler, North Carolina."

Her heart jumped to her throat at the sight of the reporter displaying her photograph and the caption about Alice's disappearance. Cora's heart ached as she listened to the reporter recount the details of the hospital fire and Alice's abduction.

"We have established a tip line for viewers who have information regarding the cases we're featuring today and throughout this special series," the reporter said. "But first we're asking viewers to look at these projected images of what Alice Reeves Westbrook would look like over the years."

A wave of sadness mingled with hope as Cora watched. What if she had the images wrong?

The sketch faintly resembled Nina although they also resembled a couple of other little girls she'd taught.

When the latest sketch was displayed and the tip line number flashed on the screen, she had to grip the table edge to steady her legs.

She'd been down this road five years ago. This time had to be different.

JACOB WANTED TO alleviate the pain in Cora's eyes, but finding Alice was the only way she'd have peace.

He phoned Liam to request information on Faye and Nina's adoption.

"On it," Liam said. "I have news on Evie Hanson. Her mother lives about thirty miles from Whistler in a retirement community. I'm forwarding you her address."

"Anything on that adoption?"

"Not yet. My forensic account is reviewing Ms. Hanson's financials. Looks like she withdrew about ten thousand dollars from her account around the time she adopted that little girl Twyla."

Ten thousand—to pay for legal fees or to buy a baby illegally?

"Did she get the child at an agency or through a private adoption?"

"Haven't determined that yet, but I'm working on it. Maybe her mother can shed some light on the situation."

"I'll drive out and talk to her now." He didn't want to waste a minute. If Evie had illegally obtained Twyla, she might be on the run.

He hung up and found Cora watching him. "Is there news?" Cora asked.

He explained about Evie's mother, Adelaide Evans. "I'm going to see her."

"I'll go with you."

His gaze was drawn to her pale pink mouth, and memories of that kiss taunted him. He wanted to kiss her again. Promise her that he'd take care of everything. "Maybe you should stay here and rest," Jacob suggested. "And be sure to activate the security system. Faye seems to have just walked in."

"I'm going," Cora said. "If she's reluctant to talk to you, maybe I can connect with her as a mother."

True.

She grabbed her purse and he snagged his keys, then they walked outside to his vehicle. With dusk approaching, the wind whistled off the river and cast shadows from the spiny needles of the pines across her drive and yard, which resembled long bony fingers.

Cora rubbed her arm as if to calm her nerves as he drove around the mountain. He followed his GPS onto the winding road toward the cluster of assisted living homes called Shady Oak. The mayor had spearheaded the development when his father had been diagnosed with Parkinson's. A small café, store, park and activity center added a community feel for the residents.

Silence stretched thick between him and Cora as he drove, and he forced his eyes on the road and his mind on the job so he wouldn't touch her. The SUV bounced over the ruts in the road, and he slowed to avoid a possum as he neared the turnoff to the holler.

He maneuvered the turn into the development, passed a place called The Club, where residents gathered to play games and other communal activities. Three white-haired men sat around an old whiskey barrel, engrossed in a checkers game while several women worked on a quilt on the porch.

A young woman walked beside an elderly man in a garden by the park, and wheelchair residents were gathered by a pond.

"It looks like a nice facility," Cora commented as he parked in front of Evie's mother's cottage.

"It has a good reputation." He and Cora climbed out and walked up to the front porch. A tiny woman with a gray bun sat in a rocking chair on the front porch, her gnarled hands working knitting needles back and forth.

"Ms. Evans?" Jacob asked.

The woman dropped the needles in her lap, then tilted her head to the side. Her eyes looked glazed slightly, as if she couldn't quite focus on him. Then he realized she was blind.

"Who's there?" she called.

"It's Sheriff Maverick from Whistler, and I have a friend with me. A woman named Cora Reeves." Jacob climbed the steps slowly, so as to not startle the elderly woman.

Her rocking chair went still. "What's wrong?" she said in a harsh whisper. "Did something happen to Evie?"

Jacob stooped down in front of the woman, his instincts

alert. "Ms. Evans, why would you think something happened to your daughter?"

The woman lifted a trembling hand to her mouth as if she'd said something she shouldn't have. "I... I don't know, motherly instinct, I suppose." She fidgeted with the knitting needles. "Besides, you've never come to see me before, Sheriff, so something has to be wrong." She angled her head as if staring at Jacob. "Now, where's my daughter?"

Jacob cleared his throat. "That's what I was hoping you could tell me."

Ms. Evan's lower lip quivered. "I don't know," she said in a voice that warbled. "But I'm worried."

"When did you last talk to her?" Jacob asked.

"That's just it," Ms. Evans said. "She was supposed to stop by and visit today. But she never showed up and she didn't call."

"Does she usually let you know if she's not coming?" Jacob asked.

"Yes, Evie is always dependable. She...knows I get lonely here. I live for visits from her and my granddaughter."

Jacob exchanged a look with Cora. "Do you have a number where I can reach her?"

The little woman nodded, then pulled a phone from her pocket. "She programmed it in here for me after I lost my sight."

Jacob took the phone from her while Cora sat down in the rocker beside the woman.

"I'm so worried about her," Ms. Evans said. "Two days ago, she called and was upset."

"What was she upset about?" Cora asked.

She gathered her knitting in one hand. "She was supposed to adopt a little boy, but it didn't work out."

"Did she explain what happened?"

"No, but she was devastated. And she…sounded scared, but she wouldn't say of what."

Was she frightened because the police were asking questions about her daughter's adoption?

Chapter Eighteen

Cora knelt by the woman to comfort her. "I'm sorry, Ms. Evans."

"Honey, call me Adelaide. No one calls me Ms. Evans anymore."

Cora gave her an understanding look. "I know you're worried about your daughter and granddaughter," she said, compassion for the woman filling her. "You can trust Sheriff Maverick. He's a good guy. He's been trying to help me find my missing daughter."

"What did you say your name was, dear?"

"Cora Reeves," Cora said.

Adelaide pressed a hand to her chest. "Oh my goodness. You're that woman they were talking about on the news earlier, aren't you? The one with the baby named Alice?"

Sensing the woman's agitation, Cora patted her hand. "Yes, ma'am. I've been looking for her for a long time."

Adelaide inhaled. "I remember your story from when it first aired," she said in a strained voice. "Your baby disappeared about the same time Evie was told she couldn't conceive." Her voice lowered. "That was an awful time."

"Yes, it was," Cora said, her gaze meeting Jacob's. "I gave birth to my daughter the night of the fire, and she was stolen during the chaos."

Adelaide reached for her hand. "My daughter and I prayed for you back then," she said. "Evie was so upset that she couldn't have kids that she cried and cried for you, and then it was like a miracle. This woman she met in her support group called her and told her about this adoption. At first she was hesitant. She wanted to have a child of her own." Adelaide rubbed her chest. "But I told her that love doesn't come from genetics. It's in your heart."

Cora's throat closed. Evie had cried for her?

She'd received countless messages of support and prayers. Yet she'd also received disturbing messages where people blamed her for her daughter's disappearance. Those vile accusations had nearly destroyed her.

"Finally she opened herself up to the idea of adoption," Adelaide continued. "And she discovered it's true. She loves little Twyla like she carried her for nine months and gave birth to her herself."

Cora pictured a woman devastated because she couldn't bear children, then learning a baby was available. Evie must have jumped on the opportunity.

Had that baby been kidnapped from its mother?

JACOB QUICKLY EXAMINED the older woman's phone. There were only two numbers programmed in it—Evie's and the desk for health services at the assisted living facility.

He pressed Evie's number, but her voice mail kicked in, so he left a message. Then he called the health care office and identified himself to the receptionist.

"I'm talking with Adelaide Evans," he said. "She's concerned about the fact that her daughter hasn't called or visited. Have you heard anything from Evie?"

"Not today. Is something wrong?" the receptionist asked.

"That's what I'm trying to figure out," Jacob said. "Ms. Evans would feel better if we could talk to her daughter. Let me know if she checks in."

She agreed and he hung up, then called Liam with Evie's number and her mother's for a trace. Technically he couldn't declare Evie missing. She was an adult and could have simply moved and not have had time to contact her mother.

But...if she was in trouble, or if she was involved in a kidnapping, she might be on the run.

Jacob stepped back to join Cora and Ms. Evans. "Your daughter didn't answer. I left a message for her to call me."

"I left her one, too," Adelaide said. "That's what worries me most. She's such a good daughter. She always calls me back."

"You mentioned she was on the verge of adopting another child. Did she use an adoption agency, or was it a private adoption?"

The elderly woman ran a finger over the Afghan she'd been knitting. "All I know is that a lawyer was handling the arrangement."

"Do you know the lawyer's name?" Jacob asked.

Adelaide rocked back and forth in the chair, obviously agitated. "She didn't say, only that she'd paid him."

Cora patted the woman's hand. Adelaide and her daughter did seem close. It was strange Evie would have moved without informing her mother of her plans.

"Tell me more about your granddaughter," Cora said softly.

"She's a sweetheart," Adelaide said. "She always brings me fresh flowers when she comes. She likes pink carnations. Lilies used to be my favorite until Twyla. Now I like carnations."

Cora smiled. "If you don't mind me asking, when is her birthday?"

Adelaide's hand fluttered her chest. "That's the funny thing. It's the same day as mine. June 8." A smile brightened the woman's face. "Evie and I thought that was a sign she was meant to be part of our family."

Cora's heart skipped a beat. Alice had been born on June 9.

Could Evie have lied about the little girl's birthday?

"There's a photograph of her on my mantel," Adelaide said. "Of course I can't see it, but Evie took it of us on our birthday, and Twyla insisted on setting it above the fireplace."

Cora exchanged a look with Jacob. "Would you mind if I looked at it?" Cora asked.

"Of course not," Adelaide said. "I love showing off my granddaughter."

A sliver of guilt streaked through Cora. Adelaide hadn't made the connection that Twyla's adoption and Cora's missing baby might be related. She didn't want to upset the woman if there was nothing to their suspicions.

"I'll get it," Jacob offered.

He slipped inside the cottage and returned a moment later with a five-by-seven silver-framed photograph. He studied it for a moment, looking back and forth between Cora and the picture.

Cora's hand trembled as she took it from him. Adelaide was grinning as her granddaughter handed her a bouquet of flowers. Cora narrowed her eyes, scrutinizing every detail of the child's face.

Her wavy blond hair was clasped in a high ponytail. She had hazel eyes and a dimple in her right cheek.

Cora's heart twisted. Could Twyla possibly be Alice?

JACOB SHIFTED AS indecision played on Cora's face. Unless her daughter looked like Cora or her ex, how could she possibly recognize her?

He left her with Evie's mother and ducked back inside the house under the guise of using the restroom. Several pictures took homage on the mantel—first, a photograph of a younger Ms. Evans and a little girl he assumed to be Evie, when Evie was about ten years old.

The second was a photograph of Evie and Twyla with a man he guessed was the husband. Jacob noted the scenery.

Mountains, a creek. A sign for Little Canoe. The couple stood in front of a cabin overlooking the theme park for children.

Did Evie own property at Little Canoe?

He searched the small desk in the living room, then the kitchen drawers for an address or reference indicating where Evie might have gone. Nothing inside but prescriptions for Evie's mother's medications, including insulin, along with bills from the facility.

He quickly searched the dresser in the woman's bedroom, but found nothing helpful. When he returned to the porch, Cora was listening to Ms. Evans relay a story.

Jacob listened politely for her to finish before he spoke. "Ms. Evans, I noticed a picture of your daughter at Little Canoe. Did she and her husband own a place there?"

She paused in her rocking. "Hmm, they bought one a long time ago, but I don't know if Evie kept it after she lost Roy. She hasn't mentioned it in a long time."

"Do you have the address?" Jacob asked.

The woman smiled. "Of course I do. I'm blind, but my memory is still pretty good." She gave him the address along with an intricate set of directions.

His phone buzzed on his hip. A text from Liam.

Got a hit on Evie Hanson. She traded her car at a used car lot for a dark green sedan. Seller said she seemed nervous and in a hurry. She was headed north.

Jacob sent him a return text. Think I know where she's going. Little Canoe. Am leaving now.

He motioned to Cora that he was ready to leave, then stooped in front of Evie's mother. "Ms. Evans," he said. "I understand that you're worried about your daughter. I'll drive up to Little Canoe and see if she's there."

The little woman pressed her hand to her chest again. "I would feel so much better if you'd do that, Sheriff."

Guilt threatened at her sincerity, but he squashed it. Work took precedence. He had to follow every lead to find Cora's baby and Kurt Philips's killer.

If Evie Hanson was involved, or in trouble, he needed to find her ASAP.

CORA COULDN'T STOP thinking about Adelaide Evans as she and Jacob drove toward Little Canoe. Adelaide seemed like such a sweet lady, a caring mother and grandmother.

If Twyla was Alice, Cora would destroy the happiness Evie had found with adoption. That bothered her more than she'd expected it to.

Still, she had to know the truth. If Twyla was her daughter and Evie had innocently adopted her without knowing she was kidnapped, she'd work with her to transition Alice. The last thing she wanted was to hurt her own child by ripping her from people she loved.

The unfairness of the situation nagged at her as Jacob maneuvered the mountain roads to Little Canoe, a resort community with year-round homes as well as rental cabins. Set at the top of the mountain, the rustic cabins offered breathtaking views of the mountain, canyon and river. Swimming, white water rafting and camping drew tourists and locals.

At Christmas, the entire community was lit up with sparkling lights and decorations. The Christmas Cottage bed-and-breakfast catered to families seeking a holiday getaway. The lighting of the fifty-foot tree in the center of Santa's village was talked about year-round.

Cora had dreamed of bringing her family here, of visiting Santa's workshop and taking a sleigh ride through the tree farm with her own children.

Jacob drove through the main village and followed the GPS onto a side street leading to a group of cabins.

"Number six," Jacob said as he pointed to a rustic ranch in the woods.

Cora spotted a green sedan parked beneath a carport. Lights from the dormer windows glowed softly against the darkening sky, making the place look homey and cozy.

Cora's pulse hammered as Jacob eased toward the house. When he reached the end of the drive, he parked and surveyed the area.

"Looks quiet. Hopefully Evie is inside."

"Let's go see." Cora reached for the door handle and climbed out. Her legs felt shaky as they walked up to the cabin. A handmade wreath made of twigs and greenery hung on the door boasting a welcome sign.

Cora glanced toward the window as Jacob raised his fist and knocked. The blinds were closed, though, making it impossible to see inside.

The side door opened, and a woman ran toward the car, pulling a little girl behind her. They jumped in the vehicle, and the woman cranked the engine and sped down the graveled drive toward the highway.

"She's running! Let's go!" Jacob jogged down the porch steps and Cora raced on his heels. A second later, they chased the car onto the highway.

Chapter Nineteen

"Dammit," Jacob muttered as he flipped on his siren.

"That little girl is in the car with her," Cora cried. "She needs to slow down."

If Jacob hadn't been so frustrated, he would have smiled at Cora's protective tone.

"She's spooked about something." Jacob veered around a curve, tires squealing. He sped up, then blew his horn, signaling for Evie to pull over.

She maneuvered a turn, barreled over a rut in the road and nearly careened over the edge. The mountain roads were winding, forcing her to slow, but he stayed on her tail as they broke onto the main highway.

She made a sharp right to leave town, but he pulled up beside her, lights twirling, siren wailing. A mile later, he finally forced her to pull off the road into the parking lot for the Little Canoe Café. A few cars were parked in the lot, indicating some of the dinner crowd customers were lingering.

He parked beside Evie's sedan then gestured toward Cora. "Stay inside the car."

"But I want—"

"Cora, she could be armed."

"With a little girl inside?" Cora gasped.

"I don't know. Stay here for now." He gave her a pointed

look. Cora wrapped her arms around her middle, her eyes sharp with fear.

Jacob climbed from his car and walked toward the sedan. Instinctively, he glanced inside. The little girl was strapped in the seat hugging a teddy bear, her head buried against the bear's head.

His heart squeezed, but he had a job to do. He rapped on the driver's window, and Evie pushed the automatic window release. Her face became visible as the window slid down. Fear streaked her eyes.

"Evie Hanson?" he asked.

She nodded. "I'm sorry I was speeding, I didn't feel well and wanted to get some medicine before the drugstore closed."

He gave her a deadpan look. "License and registration, ma'am."

"Of course." Her hand trembled as she removed her wallet from her purse and handed him her ID. It took her a minute to comb through her glove compartment for her registration, but it all matched.

"Please, if you want to just write me a ticket, I'll pay it. But my little girl—"

"Was in the car as you drove recklessly around the mountain," Jacob said sternly. "You should be more careful with her in the car."

A tear trickled down the woman's pale face. "I know and it won't happen again. Now can we go?"

"I'm afraid not," Jacob said. "Why did you run when you saw me at your house?"

"Like I said, I wasn't feeling well—"

Jacob cut her off. "Your mother is concerned about you."

Evie ran a hand over her face. "Is that what this about? Did my mother report me missing or something?"

Jacob gave a noncommittal shrug. "Actually I needed

to talk to you and contacted her. She said you hadn't come by to see her and that she called and you didn't answer."

"For heaven's sake, she worries a lot now she's older. I'll phone her and reassure her that we're fine," Evie said.

"Good. But I still need to ask you some questions." Jacob gestured toward the little girl in the back. "Your daughter looks frightened, and I don't want that. Let's go inside the café, have some coffee and you can get her a treat?"

Evie nodded, although she gave him a wary look as she opened the door and slid out. He stepped aside for her to help her daughter from the car, and he motioned for Cora to join them.

The longing on Cora's face when she saw the little girl emerge from the car clutching the teddy bear tore at Jacob's heart.

Evie's eyes widened as if she recognized Cora, her fear palpable as they walked toward the café.

CORA'S HEART ACHED at the fear on Twyla's face. Being stopped by a policeman must be frightening for her.

Or was she afraid for another reason?

She wanted to comfort the child but held her distance and walked beside Jacob. Evie clutched the little girl's hand in hers, talking softly to her as they entered the café.

The heavenly scent of barbecue and apple pie filled the air, and vases of sunflowers created centerpieces on the gingham tablecloths.

Evie ruffled her daughter's hair. "You want ice cream, honey?"

Twyla's face brightened. "Strawberry."

"You got it, kiddo," Evie said.

Jacob gestured toward a booth in the back. "There's a small arcade inside. Maybe Twyla would like to play while we talk."

Evie looked at him warily but accepted the change he

offered. Then she patted Twyla's shoulder. "I'll order your ice cream while you play."

Twyla grinned, her fear dissipating as she raced to the arcade corner. Evie slid into the booth nearest the arcade, and Cora and Jacob claimed the bench seat opposite her.

A waitress appeared, and they ordered coffee and Twyla's ice cream. Jacob waited to speak until the waitress disappeared into the kitchen.

Evie fidgeted, obviously nervous. "If you want me to call my mother now, I will," Evie said. "Then can I go?"

Jacob shook his head. "A man is dead, Ms. Hanson. Cora's daughter was kidnapped five years ago. And I think you may be connected to both."

Evie gasped softly. "I don't know what you're talking about."

"Did you know a man named Kurt Philips?" Jacob said.

The waitress delivered their coffee, and Evie picked up a sugar packet, tapping it between her fingers. "No."

The slight flinch of her eyes suggested she was lying. "He was a private investigator who was searching for Cora's daughter. She was kidnapped from the hospital in Whistler the night she was born. A terrible fire broke out, injuring several people and killing some, as well."

Evie ripped the top of the sugar packet, dumped it into her coffee and stirred vigorously. "I remember the fire. That was horrible."

"You worked at the hospital around that time, didn't you?" Jacob said.

Evie twisted her mouth in thought. "Yes, but if you think I had something to do with that fire, you're wrong. I'm a nurse. I help save lives, not hurt people."

"But you were on suspension," Jacob pointed out. "So what were you doing there?"

Evie made a low sound in her throat. "I…wanted to see if I could get my job back."

"I know you're a pediatric nurse," Cora said. "And that you adopted Twyla."

Evie's eyes widened with unease. "Oh my God. You think I took your baby?"

Cora swallowed hard. "I think Kurt was killed because he discovered a lead about my little girl."

Evie leaned forward. "Listen to me, Cora, I didn't kidnap your child. I would never do that to another woman."

Cora glanced at Twyla, who was laughing at a little boy who'd joined her. Evie sounded sincere, but she kept fidgeting.

And she had run.

Was she lying to them now?

JACOB CLEARED HIS THROAT. "Philips contacted you, didn't he?"

Evie sipped her coffee. "He called once about a week ago and left a message."

Jacob studied her. "Did you return his call?"

She gave a small nod. "He asked about Twyla's adoption. I thought he might be working for Twyla's birth mother, that she'd changed her mind about seeing Twyla. I told him her mother signed away all her rights, that I had paperwork to prove it."

Cora bit down on her lower lip. "Her mother?"

"Where did you get Twyla?" Jacob asked.

Evie tensed. "Is that why you're here? *Does* her mother want her?"

Jacob and Cora exchanged looks. "Who is her mother?" Jacob asked firmly.

"Her name is Delaney," Evie said. "She was fifteen, pregnant and scared when I met her at the hospital. Her mother encouraged her to give her baby up for adoption."

"Did you go through an adoption agency?" Jacob asked.

"No. We used a private lawyer. But like I said, Delaney signed away all rights."

Facts could be checked. "What is the name of the lawyer?"

Evie ran a hand through her hair. "His name was Pitts. Arnold Pitts." She bit her lower lip. "Now tell me. Does her mother want her?"

"I don't know anything about this girl named Delaney," Jacob admitted. "So as far as I know, your adoption is not in jeopardy."

Unless Twyla was Alice, which he was beginning to think wasn't the case.

Still, what had Philips learned that had led him to Evie?

"Evie, if your adoption was legitimate, and you had nothing to do with the kidnapping of Cora's baby or Kurt Philips's murder, why did you run?" Jacob pressed.

"I...didn't run," Evie said although she didn't make eye contact with Jacob.

"Then why was your house completely cleaned out?" Jacob asked.

Evie looked down into her coffee again as if she could hide inside it. "I planned to adopt a little boy, but it fell through at the last minute, so I decided to get away. There's no crime in that."

"No, there isn't," Cora interjected. "What happened with the adoption?"

"Another couple got the child," Evie said, her voice cracking. "And don't ask me who, because I don't know."

"Were you working with the same lawyer you used with Twyla?" Jacob asked.

Evie gave him a wary look. "No, it was a lawyer I saw in an ad. He specialized in arranging adoptions for couples and single-parent families, so I contacted him."

"Again, why did you run?" Jacob pressed.

Evie made another low, pained sound in her throat. "Because they pressured me for more money." She stared at the window, a faraway look in her eyes. "Another couple paid twice as much as I'd agreed to, so they got the baby instead of me."

"They were selling the baby to the highest bidder?" Cora asked in an incredulous voice.

"That's what I started to think," she said quietly. "When I asked for more details about the baby's parents, the lawyer became angry. He said if I couldn't have kids of my own, I should be grateful for anyone who'd help me."

Cora sighed softly. "That was a horrible thing to say, Evie."

Evie gulped. "I told him he was unethical. That I planned to report him to the police. And…and…"

"And what?" Jacob asked.

Evie released an agonized sigh. "He said if I reported him, I'd be sorry. That… I would lose Twyla."

Jacob's heart pounded. "What he said, what he did, was very wrong, Evie. My brother is with the FBI and is investigating a baby kidnapping/adoption ring. This man may be part of it."

Evie raised a brow. "You think that baby boy was stolen?"

Jacob shrugged. "It's possible. Even if the baby wasn't kidnapped, this lawyer may be promising the child to multiple people for adoption, then pitting prospective parents against each other to inflate the price."

"I can't believe I got caught up in it," Evie said. "I lost my husband a while back, and I was desperate and…stupid."

"You're not stupid," Cora said. "That man is a vile predator."

"She's right," Jacob said. "He's taking advantage of vulnerable people, and he needs to be stopped."

"But I can't risk losing Twyla," Evie cried.

"If your adoption is legitimate, you won't lose her," Jacob assured her. "But if we don't stop him, he'll do the same thing to someone else." He paused. "Worse, if he's selling kidnapped babies, their mothers and fathers are looking for their children just like Cora is."

CORA COULDN'T IMAGINE selling babies as if they were objects. "He's right," she told Evie. "You can't allow this man to hurt anyone else."

A myriad of emotions played across Evie's face as she glanced at her daughter.

"Just think how you'd feel if someone took Twyla from you and sold her to someone else."

Evie's gaze shot to Cora's. "It would tear my heart out."

"Just like it did mine," Cora said softly. "The only thing that has kept me going is the hope of one day finding my daughter."

"Twyla isn't your child," Evie said emphatically. "I swear, I met her mother. I was there when she gave birth. I can give you her contact information."

"I believe you," Cora said, although doubts still plagued her. But she didn't want Evie to run again.

"I'll take that information," Jacob said. "I'm going to contact my brother Liam—Special Agent Liam Maverick. Then I want you and Twyla to come back to Whistler with us. Liam will find that bastard lawyer you worked with. He'll also want you to look at photographs of suspects in the kidnapping/adoption ring he's investigating." He leaned closer. "I promise, Evie, we'll keep you and Twyla safe."

Twyla raced over. "Mommy, can I have my ice cream now?"

Evie squeezed her daughter's arm. "Of course, honey. Then we're going to take a little trip."

"What is this lawyer's name?" Jacob asked.

"Tate Muldoon," Evie said in a low voice.

Jacob stood. "I'll phone Liam and give him a heads-up."

Cora waved the waitress over to bring Twyla's treat, indecision warring in her head over Evie's innocence as the waitress brought the dish of strawberry ice cream.

She chatted with the little girl about kindergarten and her favorite activities and stories as Twyla ate. Evie relaxed slightly, the love for her little girl obvious.

If Evie was in danger, she needed a friend.

But if she had some part in Alice's kidnapping or this baby ring, she deserved to go to jail.

Cora struggled to remain calm. Was this nefarious ring responsible for her baby's disappearance?

Chapter Twenty

Jacob kept an eye on Evie, Twyla and Cora as he stepped into the hall near the restroom to phone Liam. "She's scared out of her mind this guy will come after her daughter. I don't know if he'd hurt the child or just try to take her. She claims the adoption was legitimate, but we'll have to verify that."

"I'll start looking into it ASAP," Liam said. "If this lawyer is involved in the kidnapping/adoption ring, this could be a big break."

There were a lot of ifs. "Even if he's not, what he's doing sounds illegal and warrants an investigation."

"Agreed." Liam hesitated. "Do you think Evie will testify?"

"If it means protecting her daughter, yes. But we have to assure her that they'll be safe."

"I'll guard them myself," Liam said.

"Do you want me to bring them to Charlotte?"

"No, I have room at my cabin in Whistler. They can stay there."

A smart choice. It was off the beaten path, and Liam had a security system. Someone would also be pretty bold to come after Evie under an FBI agent's own roof.

Liam would make certain the mother and daughter's whereabouts remained confidential.

"All right. I'll escort them there myself."

"Copy that. What's the lawyer's name?" Liam asked.

"Tate Muldoon."

"Good work, Jacob."

"I hope it pans out," Jacob said. "And if he had some-thing to do with Cora's baby's kidnapping—"

"He'll pay," Liam assured him.

Jacob inhaled, and they ended the call. He joined Cora, Evie and Twyla just as Twyla finished her ice cream.

Jacob grinned at the little girl. The innocence of a child's laughter and enthusiasm for simple things like ice cream warmed his heart and made him think about how lonely his house was.

He had been so focused on finding his father's killer and locating Cora's child that he hadn't made time for a personal relationship. Hadn't considered having a family of his own one day.

It had just been him and his brothers. No big holiday celebrations or family dinners. Christmas meant grabbing a beer and a burger in between jobs.

Cora looked up at him with those wide beautiful eyes, and his chest squeezed. Kissing her had been spontane-ous and…nice.

Hell, who was he kidding? It was a lot more than nice. It was passionate.

He wanted to do it again.

"Everything okay?" Evie asked.

Jacob jerked his mind back to the case. "Yes. You're all set. We're meeting Liam at his place."

Wariness flashed in her eyes again, making him won-der if she was still hiding something.

Liam was an excellent interrogator. If Evie was holding back or lying, his brother would get the truth out of her.

TENSION STRAINED THE air between Cora and Evie as they followed Jacob back to Whistler. Thankfully, Twyla's con-stant chatter and giggles eased the ride.

To soothe Cora and Twyla's nerves, Cora shared a story about a stinky skunk she'd written for her class. She'd been working on illustrations lately. Maybe one day she'd publish it.

"I loved Stinky Dinky," Twyla said. "Do you gots another story?"

Cora laughed softly. "I think I might."

For the remainder of the ride, she told stories and the three of them sang children's songs Twyla had learned in kindergarten.

But as they neared Whistler, Evie's hands tightened around the steering wheel, and her body grew rigid.

Cora patted the woman's arm. "It's okay, you can trust Jacob and his brother. They're good guys."

Evie shot her a wary look, then gave a little nod. "I hope so," she said in a raspy whisper. "Twyla means everything to me."

Tears pricked at Cora's eyes. "I understand. I really do."

Evie parked behind Jacob, her hand trembling as she opened the car door. But she lifted her chin in a show of courage as she climbed out and opened Twyla's door.

Cora followed, her emotions boomeranging in her chest. Liam met them outside on the porch, and he and Jacob exchanged a quick brotherly handshake.

Evie squared her shoulders as if she was intimidated by Liam's size.

"You don't have to be afraid of him," Cora whispered as they walked inside. "I can vouch for the Maverick men."

Evie relaxed slightly as they entered Liam's cabin. The house was slightly larger than Jacob's, with a cathedral ceiling boasting a ten-foot stone fireplace and a deck that ran the length of the back of the house. Though it was dark, she'd heard the sound of the river outside when they parked. The back deck probably offered a view of it and the canyon below.

"You and your daughter can stay here tonight," Liam said after greeting Evie and Twyla. "There's a private wing upstairs you'll have all to yourselves."

Evie offered him a tentative smile.

"Do you have suitcases?" Liam asked.

"In the car," Evie said. "We hadn't had a chance to unpack."

"I'll get them." Jacob hurried outside to retrieve their luggage while Liam showed them around.

"The refrigerator is stocked." Liam grinned at Twyla. "I wasn't sure what you liked, but I have my favorites. Pizza and mac and cheese."

Twyla's eyes sparkled. "I love pizza and mac and cheese!"

"Really?" Liam made an exaggerated face, and Cora couldn't help but smile. The Maverick men amazed her with their bravery and kindness.

"It's been a long day," Evie said. "Is it okay if I get Twyla settled before we talk?"

"Of course." Liam gestured toward the stairs. "There are two rooms with a Jack and Jill bathroom in between. But if you're more comfortable sharing a room with her, that's fine."

Evie raised a brow at Liam as if surprised by his sensitive comment. "Thank you."

She ushered Twyla up the stairs, leaving Cora alone with the Maverick men.

Liam gestured toward the laptop on the breakfast bar. "My people have been researching Tate Muldoon."

Cora and Jacob looked over Liam's shoulder as Liam displayed a photo. "This is Muldoon meeting a woman we suspect is involved in the kidnapping ring." He hissed. "It appears the two are connected."

In the photo, the woman was holding an infant to her, the baby wrapped so tightly in a blanket that you couldn't see its face. She'd also angled her head downward to avoid direct contact with the security camera at the airport.

Cora's stomach roiled. Who did that baby belong to?

JACOB INSTINCTIVELY PLACED a hand on Cora's back to comfort her.

"Do you know how long this ring has been active?" Cora asked.

"Not yet," Liam replied. "But now we've identified Muldoon, we can dig into his background and activities."

Jacob gently squeezed Cora's arm. "He may or may not be responsible for Alice's disappearance, Cora."

Liam shifted. "But we won't rest until we have the answers."

Evie walked down the steps with a troubled expression.

"Is Twyla all right?" Cora asked.

"She fell asleep as soon as her head hit the pillow," Evie said.

"I'm sure you're tired, too," Liam said. "But I need you to look at this photograph."

Evie joined them at the computer and studied the picture of the man and woman with the baby.

"Is that the lawyer you worked with?" Liam asked.

A sick expression darkened Evie's eyes, then she murmured that it was Muldoon. "Oh my God. He's really selling children, isn't he?"

Jacob nodded. "You sensed something was wrong?"

She took a minute to answer. "Not at first, but when he started demanding more money, I became suspicious."

"How did you connect with Muldoon?" Liam asked.

Evie explained about the ad. "I realize it was stupid to choose a lawyer from an ad, but he specialized in helping bring families together. When I first spoke with him, he sounded caring, as if he enjoyed matching children who needed parents with mothers and fathers who wanted to open their hearts and homes to them."

"He's a professional. He knows how to play on people's vulnerabilities," Liam said.

"I feel like such a fool." Evie rubbed her temple.

Cora curved her arm around the woman's shoulders. "You aren't a fool. You wanted a child, and obviously have a lot of love to offer."

"You're not the only one he's done this to," Liam said. "But you can stop him from taking advantage of others by testifying against him once we make an arrest."

"I just want Twyla to be safe," Evie said. "I can't lose her."

"You're both safe here," Liam said.

"If he's running a big operation, he could have a number of people working for him," Jacob added.

"You're right." Liam checked his watch. "If my suspicions are correct, the kidnapping ring is international. They're selling babies all over the world. Transporting them across states and countries complicates the situation and makes it harder to identify and trace the children."

Jacob understood the problem. The media did what they could to broadcast nationwide, but if the babies were shipped to another country, they might never be found.

Liam glanced at Evie. "It's late. Why don't you get some rest, and I'll make some phone calls."

"Thanks." She glanced at Jacob. "And I'll call my mother." Evie said good-night and disappeared up the stairs. Liam walked Jacob and Cora to the car. Cora climbed in, but Jacob hung back to confer with Liam.

"I still think Evie is holding out on us," Jacob said.

Liam shrugged slightly. "Maybe. Let's give her some time. She's obviously frightened now and needs time to learn to trust us." He patted Jacob's shoulder. "I won't let her get away, bro. Just take care of Cora."

Liam was right. Cora was still in danger.

And he'd do anything to protect her.

CORA COULDN'T ERASE the image of Evie and Twyla's frightened faces from her mind as Jacob drove her home. Dark storm clouds rumbled above, raindrops splattering the windshield as they unleashed a torrent of rain.

Jacob snagged an umbrella from the back seat and handed it to her. She opened the door and then the umbrella before hopping out. Jacob raced to join her and they ran up the path to her porch, hunched beneath the umbrella together. She almost slipped on the wet steps, but Jacob caught her arm and steadied her.

When they reached the door, she fished out her keys while Jacob scanned the perimeter. She had set the new alarm, so she checked it as she entered. Still, Jacob motioned for her to wait at the door while he combed through the house.

"Don't you trust the system?" she asked as he returned to the foyer.

Jacob shrugged, the dim light from the porch accentuating his strong, square jaw. His eyes looked as dark and stormy as the night outside.

"I just don't want to take any chances. If Philips connected Evie to this kidnapping ring, and they know we're onto them, they may be the ones who came after you."

A shudder rippled through Cora. She dropped her purse on the end table and rubbed her arms to ward off the chill from the rain. "I can't imagine anyone so coldhearted as to steal and sell children."

A muscle ticked in Jacob's jaw. "Me, neither, although people keep surprising me. Unfortunately not always in a good way."

Despair threatened to overcome Cora as Liam's statement about transporting children to different states and countries taunted her. "If these people kidnapped my baby, she could be anywhere."

Jacob stepped closer to her, then cradled her hands between his and pressed them to his chest. "I promise you we'll find her, Cora. Keep the faith."

The conviction in his tone made her believe anything was possible.

That she might have a future filled with love and laughter again and be reunited with Alice.

She looked up into Jacob's eyes and became lost in the sensual brown depths. Jacob was one man who did what he said. Who never gave up.

A man she…was falling in love with.

Emotions glittered in his eyes as he brought her hands to his lips and kissed them. Her heart stuttered. Her breath caught.

She didn't want to be alone tonight. Jacob angled his head, his dark eyes searching hers. Asking permission?

She parted her lips on a sigh, then stood on tiptoe, cradled his face between her hands and pulled him toward her. He met her halfway.

Then their lips melded in a kiss that sent tiny bursts of desire rippling through her.

Chapter Twenty-One

Jacob had wanted to kiss Cora again ever since his lips had first touched hers. Her sweet taste had invaded his senses. But what had moved him the most was the fact that she'd trusted him enough to return his kiss.

He pressed his lips to hers and drew her closer to him, teasing her lips apart until he dove his tongue inside. She made a low sound in her throat as if she wanted more, and he deepened the kiss.

She threaded her fingers through his hair, and he raked his hands down her back to her hips, pulling her against his hardening body. Need and hunger spiked his blood, and he walked them backward toward her sofa.

She ran her foot up his leg, tormenting him further, and tugged at the top button of his shirt. His breath rushed out in a burst of passion, but he forced himself to pull back and look into her eyes.

They had to slow down, or he was going to take her on the floor.

She clung to him with a whimper and gazed back at him, need flashing in her beautiful eyes.

"Cora," he murmured. "We shouldn't do this."

"Why not?" she asked in a raw whisper. "We're adults. I want you. Don't you want me?"

He arched a brow and pushed his thick length against her. "You know I do. But I want to protect you, not take advantage."

"You aren't taking advantage," she said. "I don't want to be alone tonight."

His lungs strained for air. "Are you sure?"

A smile curved her mouth, and she gave a little nod, then took his hand and led him to her bedroom. She lit a candle on her dresser, then turned to him, a vulnerable look on her face.

"It's been a long time for me," she said softly. "I haven't been with anyone since the divorce."

Her admission only fired his emotions and made him want her more. "I'm honored that you'd even consider me."

"Jacob," she said softly. "You're the most amazing man I've ever known."

His heart swelled with longing and…love. No…it was too soon to think about love.

He had to find Alice first.

But she reached for his buttons again, and he forgot about rational thought and the case and anything except holding and touching her. He removed his holster and gun and placed it on the nightstand, then stripped his shirt. The look of pure desire in her eyes nearly sent him to his knees.

No woman had ever looked at him like that.

He cupped her chin between his fingers, angled her face and kissed her again. Deep and hungry, long and sensual. His breathing turned raspy as he slipped her T-shirt over her head. His body hardened at the sight of her black lacy bra. Her breasts were full and voluptuous and overflowed the lacy barriers, her nipples stiff against the lace.

She reached for his belt and slid it off, then lowered his zipper. Just the sound of it rasping made his heart pound with excitement. He reached for hers as well, and within seconds, they'd shed their jeans and tossed them to the floor.

The scrap of black lace covering her sweet femininity elicited a groan from deep in his chest. The smile that she graced him with at the sound of his arousal made him throw her back on the bed.

Inhibitions fled as their tongues mated and danced in a sensual rhythm, and their bodies rubbed together, teasing and tantalizing, skin against bare skin.

He trailed kisses down her throat and neck to the swell of her breasts. She was the sweetest thing he'd ever tasted. He unfastened the front clasp of her bra, inhaling sharply as her breasts spilled out. Her nipples were tight and pink, begging for his mouth.

He closed his lips over the tip, suckling her and drawing one stiff peak between his lips. She moaned and raked her fingers over his back, her nails digging into his skin, urging him to continue.

He teased and tormented her until she clawed at his shoulders and wrapped her legs around his waist. He moved against her, craving her even more, and she pushed at his boxers until he shed them and tugged off her panties.

Heart racing, he climbed above her and kissed her until she begged him to join his body with hers.

CORA RAKED HER hands down Jacob's back, sensations spiraling through her. It had been so long since she'd experienced pleasure that Jacob's kisses almost sent her over the edge.

He paused long enough to roll on a condom, then rubbed his thick length against her thighs. She moaned and parted her legs, urging him to move inside her. He kissed her deeply again, his tongue mimicking their lovemaking, and she gripped his hips and pulled him closer.

He stroked her thighs again, then probed her opening

with the tip of his sex, tormenting her. She closed her hand around his hard length then guided him to her.

One thrust, and she moaned his name as he pushed deeper, pulled out, then thrust inside her again. Her body quivered with excitement, passion igniting between them and urging him deeper and deeper. She wrapped her legs around his waist and clung to him as he pumped faster and harder, stirring her hunger to a fever pitch.

She murmured his name again as erotic sensations spiraled through her, and her orgasm claimed her. He buried his head against her neck as he thrust again, then he groaned her name as he came inside her.

Cora savored the feel of his warm body against hers as they clung to each other, bodies hot and intertwined, breathing ragged. Lost in pleasure, she couldn't bear to release him. She wanted him again. And again.

The thought frightened her. Yet she deserved to have pleasure, didn't she?

Jacob nuzzled her neck, then slowly extricated himself and disposed of the condom. She missed his body next to hers while he was in the bathroom, but she tugged the covers over her, still tingling from his touch.

Seconds later, Jacob crawled in bed under the covers with her and drew her into his arms. "That was wonderful," he whispered against her hair. "Are you okay, Cora?"

She curled into his arms and pressed her hand over his bare chest. She could feel his heart beating. Strong. Caring. Loving.

She felt a strong attraction that was more than physical. She liked the man. She admired him. She...wanted to be with him again.

"I forgot what it was like to be held," she said softly. "To not be alone."

His breath rasped out, and he dropped a kiss into her hair. "You don't have to be alone, not anymore."

She couldn't make promises, and she didn't expect him to. But she appreciated his words and the fact that he was still here in her bed. That he wasn't spooked by all her baggage and her emotions, and the fact that some people in town thought she was unstable.

"What about you?" she asked softly. "Why is a handsome eligible bachelor like you still alone?"

"Work."

"I don't believe that," Cora asked. "You must have women throwing themselves at you."

Jacob chuckled, then looked into her eyes. Tension and passion simmered between them, his eyes darkening with need again. "I guess I haven't met the right person," he murmured.

Their gazes locked. Cora's heart fluttered. She'd thought she'd met the right person when she married Drew. But theirs had been a whirlwind romance, and hadn't lasted. Now she realized the two of them weren't really meant for each other.

What about her and Jacob? Was it possible that Jacob might care about her more than as just a woman who needed his help?

EMOTIONS WARRED INSIDE Jacob. He was getting way too close to Cora.

Hell, they'd gotten naked and sweaty together. And it wasn't just sex, dammit. He'd made love to her.

He wanted to do it again, too. Tonight. And tomorrow.

He'd never thought about being lonely. He'd simply been alone and focused on his job. On finding the person responsible for his father's death.

But the thought of leaving Cora and not holding her again made his stomach knot.

She tilted his head down toward her and kissed him, and he forgot to think. He gave himself in to the moment, and they made love again, this time slow and languid. They took time to explore every inch of each other's bodies with slow kisses and tender touches. Her soft moans of pleasure were so titillating that he teased her with his tongue and mouth and fingers until she crawled on top of him.

He cradled her breasts in his hands, then licked each nipple, tugging one in his mouth to suckle her. She threw her head back in wild abandon, her body swaying as she impaled herself onto his erection.

He groaned and gripped her hips, thrusting into her with his whole being. His heart pounded, need and hunger driving him to increase the tempo until their bodies shook and convulsed with pleasure.

She collapsed on top of him, and he wrapped her in his arms and rolled sideways, tucking her close until she fell asleep in his arms. He hugged her next to him, knowing tomorrow he'd have to resume his role as sheriff instead of Cora's lover.

But tonight, he intended to revel in the pleasure of their bodies nestled together where they blocked out the world.

And the fact that a kidnapper might have sold Cora's baby five years ago.

Hopefully Liam and his team would crack this kidnapping ring, and Evie would divulge what she knew, and they could make an arrest. Someone, the head of the operation, or the person who'd actually stolen Cora's baby from the hospital, had to know where Alice was.

He fell asleep with dreams of bringing Cora's daughter back into her life but woke a few hours later with his mind humming that he needed to get up and get busy.

He slid from bed, then stepped into the shower. He quickly washed and dried off, then wrapped a towel around his waist just as he heard his phone ringing. He hurried to the nightstand, snatched the phone and stepped back into the bathroom to answer it.

"It's Griff," his brother said.

"Yeah?"

"IT just called about Kurt Philips's computer. They found a reference to that woman Faye Fuller."

Jacob tensed. "And?"

"She was never married. And the adoption she claims was legal was never filed. Philips suspected she might have bought the child."

Dammit. "Do you have the name of her lawyer?"

"No, that's just it. He couldn't find anything on the adoption. It was almost as if it never happened."

Maybe it hadn't. Cora had thought Faye's little girl seemed familiar. Had been fired because she'd asked questions about her. She'd been nearly killed, and Faye was close by.

"I'll talk with her," Jacob said.

He looked up and saw Cora watching him. Her hair looked tousled, her cheeks chafed from his lovemaking. She raked her gaze over his near-naked body, and heat flared in her eyes.

He wanted to take her back to bed. Make love to her over and over.

"Jacob?"

Griff's voice jerked him back to the moment. "Yeah. Anything on that key?"

"Not yet."

"Okay, keep me posted." He ended the call, forcing his mind away from images of Cora naked and panting beneath him.

Cora inhaled. "What is it?"

He cleared his throat. "After the incident with your allergic reaction, I decided to run a background on Faye Fuller."

Cora's eyes widened. "And?"

"So far, we haven't found a record of her adoption."

Cora leaned against the doorjamb. "Then she lied to me?"

"She could have an explanation, but I'm going to question her," Jacob said.

"I'll go with you." Cora threw off her robe, turned on the shower water and climbed inside.

Jacob wanted to join her, but now wasn't the time. He had to focus.

While she showered, he dressed and made coffee. By the time she emerged in a clean T-shirt and jeans, he'd retrieved his clean clothes from his vehicle, changed into them and prepared scrambled eggs and toast.

"I'm not hungry," Cora said as she eyed the breakfast.

"Maybe not, but let's eat. It's early. Faye and her daughter may not even be up."

She reluctantly agreed and joined him at the table. A smile softened her face when he served her plate.

"And you cook? What don't you do, Jacob Maverick?"

He blushed. He wasn't accustomed to such intimacy with a woman.

"Thank you," she said as she forked up a bite of eggs.

"You're welcome." He wolfed down his food, anxious to question Faye. Cora ate hers quickly, too, then they cleared the table and headed to the door.

Silence stretched between them as they drove down the street to Faye's. Cora frowned when he pulled into the drive. "I don't see Faye's car."

"Maybe they went on an early outing," he said, although a bad feeling slithered through him.

Cora opened the door and rushed out, and he followed, the two of them hurrying to the front door. He rang the bell while Cora looked through the front window.

"I don't see anyone," she said, a shrill note to her voice.

Jacob twisted the doorknob and the door squeaked open. He motioned for Cora to stay behind him, and he eased inside. The furniture was in place, but he didn't see any toys or personal items in the kitchen or living room.

Cora's breathing rattled out and she raced to the first bedroom. The house seemed deserted. Cora jerked open the dresser drawers and closet and turned to him with a panicked look.

"They're gone, Jacob."

Chapter Twenty-Two

Cora's heart sank. Where had Faye gone? And why had she left so quickly?

Fear for Faye and Nina struck Cora. "I wonder if her ex found her."

"Cora, there's no record that Faye was ever married."

Cora's pulse jumped. "What?"

Jacob turned her to face him. "I think she lied to you about everything. There was no abusive husband. There was no record of an adoption."

Cora's mind raced, the truth dawning on her with a wave of nausea. "No marriage or abusive husband or adoption records because…she hadn't legally obtained Nina?"

A muscle ticked in his jaw. "That's the logical conclusion."

The memory of Nina tearing her muffin like Cora did taunted her. Her drawings. The peanut allergy. Cora had sensed something familiar about the child.

But Faye had sounded so convincing about her abusive ex. Cora had started to think of her as a friend. Anger and hurt mingled with shock. "I felt sorry for her," she said. "I promised to keep her secret and be her friend. But she… lied to me and…you think she took my baby? That Nina is Alice?"

"We can't be certain," Jacob said. "Even if she did obtain her daughter illegally, it doesn't mean Nina is Alice."

Cora had been disappointed so many times that she dared not count on anything.

"What next?"

"I'm going to grab my kit from my SUV and see if I can lift some prints and collect DNA from the house. Then I'll send it to the lab, see if we can find out exactly who Faye is, and what she's running from." He pulled his phone from his pocket. "Meanwhile I'll call Liam to start a search for Faye."

"How can I help?"

"What kind of vehicle did Faye drive?"

"A gray minivan."

"Did you happen to notice the license plate?"

Cora shook her head. "I never even thought about it."

"Don't sweat it. Our tech team will find it. She can't have gone too far."

"But where is she going?" Cora said, her voice cracking.

"I don't know. Maybe she left something somewhere inside the house that will give us a hint." Jacob handed her a pair of gloves. "Put these on and look through the bathrooms and bedrooms. See if you can find a brush or toothbrush we can use for DNA analysis. Even a strand of the child's hair or Faye's can help."

Cora yanked on the gloves while Jacob phoned his brother and then hurried outside for his kit. Cora walked through the kitchen first in search of a used spoon or fork that might hold DNA, but the dishes in the dishwasher were clean. She checked the drawers, but they held cooking utensils, pot holders, dishes and a few staples.

Faye had rented the place furnished, but it also appeared that she'd wiped the counters and table down before she left.

She walked down the hall to the main bathroom and glanced at the kitchen sink. Clean, as well. She opened the medicine drawer, but barring a pack of unopened Q-tips, it was empty. The drawers in the vanity had been emptied, too. The scent of pine cleaner indicated Faye had also scrubbed the bathroom before she left.

Jacob poked his head inside the room. "Find anything?"

She shook her head. "It looks like she cleaned before she left. I'll look in Nina's room."

"Okay. I lifted a couple of prints from the doorknob and doorjamb. People usually forget to wipe those down." He hesitated. "I'll check the mother's room if you want to look through Nina's."

Cora murmured she would, then crossed the hall to the room Nina had slept in. The twin bed looked bare now, the shelves void of toys. She checked inside the dresser and closet, but they were empty.

She examined the small desk in the corner, her heart clenching when she discovered a notepad Nina had left behind. She flipped it open and smiled at the childlike drawings of herself and her mother. There were also sketches of different houses in the book, obviously places where Nina and her mother had lived.

Faye claimed she was running from her ex. If she'd gone to a shelter, she might have gotten help there. Underground groups helped abused women establish new identities across the country.

Or...was she really running from the law?

JACOB STOWED THE prints he'd collected in his evidence recovery kit, then shined his flashlight along the furniture in the room where Faye had slept, searching for a hair strand. The drawers had been cleaned out in the bedroom and master bath. No toothbrush, comb or brush, dammit.

Faye had left nothing behind. That fact made her behavior even more suspicious. Did she have Alice? If so, where had she gone this time?

He stooped down on the floor and shined his light along the edge of the bed. Something red caught his attention. He stretched his arm beneath the bed and his fingers touched a rain hat.

His pulse jumped, and he dragged it out and examined it. A small hair clung to the inside of the cap. He bagged the hat, hopeful it belonged to Faye or Nina, then went to find Cora.

She was sitting in the desk chair looking at something. He approached slowly, struck by her sad expression.

"What is it?" he asked.

She moved slightly to the right to offer him a view. "Nina drew these," she said softly. "There are half a dozen houses here where they lived."

Jacob squeezed Cora's shoulder. "Kids adapt."

"I know, but if Nina is my daughter, I would give her a stable home."

Jacob sucked in a breath. "I know you would, Cora. But let's find Faye. Then we'll go from there."

Cora lifted her chin in a show of bravado. She wasn't going to fall apart.

Dammit, he wanted to make everything right for her. But what if he failed?

"Did she draw or write anything in there about where she and her mother might have gone?"

"I don't see anything about the future, except Nina drew a Christmas tree in this house with a puppy beneath it. She must have hoped Santa would bring her a dog."

"Did Nina or Faye ever talk about some place they'd like to visit? Maybe a city or town or state?" Jacob asked.

Cora rubbed her temple as if her head ached. "Not that I recall."

Jacob drummed his fingers on his thigh. He hated to leave Cora alone, but if they got a lead on Faye, he wanted to pursue it without involving Cora.

"Let me drive you home. I need to take the prints and a hair fiber I found to the lab for analysis."

Cora stood and collected the sketchbook. "Whether she's Alice or not, Nina deserves to have a safe and secure home, not to be on the run."

TEN MINUTES LATER, Jacob dropped Cora at her house.

"Keep the doors locked and the security system activated," Jacob told her as he started to leave.

Nerves fluttered in Cora's stomach. She was growing accustomed to having Jacob around to protect her. But she wanted him to solve this case.

"Keep me posted."

Jacob feathered a strand of hair away from her cheek. "Of course. Hang in there, Cora."

She'd been hanging in there for five years now. But what else could she do? Falling to pieces was not an option.

As Jacob drove away, she considered calling Julie to visit, but she was too antsy to entertain anyone. She carried Nina's sketchbook to her writing desk and flipped through it again.

Her heart in her throat, she pulled out her stationery and began another letter.

Dear Alice,
It's another beautiful summer day. I smell the flowers in the air and imagine you and me walking along the riverbank picking wildflowers to bring back and put in a vase on the kitchen table.

She glanced out the back window and imagined building a tree house for her daughter. As a child, her father had built one for her and it had become her sanctuary. She'd climb the ladder to the inside and sit for hours drawing and daydreaming.

Most of all, she would give her little girl a home where she felt safe and loved.

Her therapist's words taunted her again. *What if you find her and she's happy and loved?*

But what if she wasn't?

She put her pen back to the paper.

> *I feel like I'm so close to finding you. I love you so much that I'll never stop looking.*

A loud knock sounded at the door. Cora startled, then realized it might be Jacob, so she hurried to the door. But she hesitated before opening it. "Who's there?"

"It's me," a woman said in a muffled voice. "Faye."

Cora quickly unlocked the door.

Tears streaked Faye's cheeks, and she stormed in, swinging her hands in agitation. "Cora, I...didn't know where to go."

Cora closed the door, her arms crossed. "What's going on? I was just at your house and you'd packed up and moved out."

"I know, I...was scared," Faye cried. "I didn't know what to do, so I ran again."

"What are you scared of?" Cora asked. "And don't lie to me this time, Faye. I know you weren't married and there's no abusive ex."

Faye staggered back as if she'd been hit. Maybe she was wrong. Maybe Faye had changed her identity to escape her ex.

Faye rubbed her hands over her face, her face milky white.

"Talk to me, Faye. Did you lie to me?"

Faye nodded, her voice choked, "I'm sorry, I never meant to hurt you."

A sense of betrayal welled inside Cora. She wanted to scream at Faye for deceiving her. But she had to remain calm so Faye would confide in her. "Sit down and tell me everything."

Faye followed Cora to the den and sank onto the sofa, but her hands were shaking as she accepted a glass of water.

"Is there an abusive ex or isn't there?" Cora asked bluntly.

Faye shook her head, her expression pained. "Not exactly. I made up that story because I was scared, and you were asking about Nina's adoption."

Cora sucked in a breath. "And that upset you because you didn't legally adopt her?"

Faye went stone-still, her face crumpling. "I...thought I did."

"What does that mean?"

Faye closed her eyes and sighed, then opened them and looked up at Cora. "I was distraught over my latest miscarriage," Faye said. "A couple of nights after that hospital fire, this woman approached me. She said she knew I lost a child, and that she had a baby who needed a good home. She claimed the baby's father paid her to take the child and give her away."

Cora stared at her in shock. Was she talking about Alice? "And you believed her?"

Faye nodded. "She said that the mother died in childbirth, and the father couldn't bear to look at the baby because she reminded him of his wife's death." Her voice broke. "She had adoption papers already drawn up, and I signed them and the little girl was mine."

Cora's heart pounded. Drew had been worried about his career, but he wouldn't have paid someone to take Alice away.

Would he?

Perspiration beaded Cora's neck. "Where is Nina now, Faye?"

Faye released a sob. "That's just it. I don't know where she is."

Panic shot through Cora. "What do you mean?"

Faye's voice cracked. "Last night, I got this threatening phone call warning me that if I talked about the adoption, I'd be sorry. So early this morning, I packed up Nina and told her we were taking a trip."

Cora's blood went cold. "Go on."

Faye swiped at tears. "On the way out of town, someone ran me off the road. I hit a ditch and blacked out. When I came to, Nina was gone."

Chapter Twenty-Three

Jacob met Liam at the sheriff's office to hand over the evidence he'd collected at Faye's house.

"How are Evie and her little girl?" Jacob asked.

Liam shrugged. "Fine. I left her with your deputy looking over mug shots of suspected child kidnappers."

Jacob explained about finding Faye's place empty. "See if Evie recognizes Faye or if there's a connection between the two of them. Faye had miscarriages and Evie couldn't have children. Maybe they met at a support group or a fertility clinic or something." That was a long shot, but Jacob couldn't ignore any possibility, no matter how remote.

"I'll ask her," Liam agreed.

Liam's phone buzzed, and he checked the text, then returned one. A second later, Liam addressed Jacob. "The analyst found a file about Drew Westbrook and his wife. Philips was supposed to meet with him for questioning the morning of the day he died."

Jacob had disliked Cora's ex from the beginning. How could you respect a man who abandoned his wife when she was grieving for their kidnapped child?

Some men wanted a namesake. Perhaps he'd been disappointed Cora had delivered a daughter?

Acid boiled in Jacob's blood as Liam described the man's findings. If Drew Westbrook orchestrated the kidnapping of his own child, he was a cold-blooded monster. He'd nearly crushed Cora.

Jacob would see the damn man behind bars.

"I'm going to question him, and this time he'd better talk," Jacob said.

Jacob rushed outside to his car, then dialed Cora. But she didn't answer.

Dammit. If something had happened to her, he'd never forgive himself.

A minute later, she texted him. Call you in a minute.

Relief spilled through him. At least Cora was safe.

CORA BARELY CONTROLLED her panic. "Who was the woman who gave Nina to you?"

"She said her name was Valerie and that she worked for an attorney who'd already drawn up the adoption papers."

"And you believed her?" Cora asked.

Faye's face wilted. "I know it was stupid, but at the time I was so desperate for a child I didn't question her. She seemed truly afraid that the father would hurt the child if I didn't take her. So I didn't lie about being afraid the father would come after Nina."

"Why did she offer you the baby? Did you know her?"

Faye massaged her temple. "After the last miscarriage, I met her in the waiting room at my counselor's office."

"So she knew you'd lost a child?"

Faye twisted her hands together. "Yes, I told her everything. She seemed so...nice."

Suspicions reared their ugly head in Cora's mind. Valerie had papers from an attorney. Drew was a lawyer. No...she couldn't believe he'd give their child away...

She gritted her teeth. "What was the attorney's name?"

Faye rubbed a hand over her eyes. "I really don't remember. That night is a blur."

"Think, Faye, this is important. He and this woman may have been working together."

"I'm sorry," Faye said, her voice breaking. "I believed her, but I realize now I was wrong. I had no idea she stole Nina."

A chill rippled through Cora. "Is Nina my daughter?"

Tears trickled down Faye's cheeks. "I'm not sure, but I think so."

Cora's breath caught. She had finally found Alice?

Faye cleared her throat. "When you started asking questions and I saw the drawings you did of Alice, and then your allergy… I started putting it together." She released a sigh. "Then the phone calls started."

"What phone calls?"

"From the woman. She warned me to keep my mouth shut or I'd be sorry."

Cora swallowed hard.

Faye's chin quivered. "Cora, I think she tried to kill you and she sent you that basket, and that she killed that private investigator because he found out about her."

Terror clawed at Cora. "Oh my God," Cora whispered. "And this woman has Nina now?"

Faye released a sob. "I'm afraid so."

Cora barely suppressed a scream. "Do you know how to contact this woman?"

"No," Faye said brokenly. "She called from an unlisted number."

Fear seized Cora. "Where do you think she'd take Nina?"

"I have no idea," Faye cried.

"We have to call Jacob. His brother is with the FBI. They can issue an Amber Alert and start looking—"

"No, she might hurt Nina."

Anger rooted itself deep inside Cora. "And if we don't, she may take her someplace where we'll never find her."

Faye looked miserable, but she finally agreed. Cora

punched Jacob's number, pacing as she waited for him to answer. He picked up on the third ring.

"Cora?"

"Jacob… I think Nina Fuller is Alice. Faye is here," she said in a choked voice.

"Whoa, slow down. Did Faye tell you Nina is your daughter?"

Cora relayed Faye's story. "Faye thinks this woman killed Kurt and she tried to kill me, and now she has Nina. You have to find her, Jacob. She sounds crazy."

"Tell me everything you know," Jacob said.

"The woman claims her name was Valerie. Faye can't remember the lawyer's name."

"Does she still have the adoption papers?" Jacob asked. "They would have the lawyer's name on them."

Cora covered the phone with his hand and asked Faye about the papers.

Her face paled. "I…put them in a safety deposit box."

Hope sprouted in Cora's chest. "Then we'll go get them."

"Cora?"

She passed on the information. "Faye and I will get the papers and call you back with a name."

"All right. Meanwhile I'll get an Amber Alert issued."

"Jacob, Faye said the woman told her the baby's mother was dead, and that the father paid her to take the child. What if that lawyer—"

"Was Drew?" Jacob finished. "I'm almost to his place now. Don't worry, if he's involved, he'll talk."

Cora hung up, emotions threatening to overcome her. She couldn't bear to think that the man she'd once loved and married would sell their child.

If he had, she wanted him to pay.

She looked up at Faye and saw the misery on her face. Misery because she loved Nina.

She'd betrayed Cora by lying about being afraid of an abusive ex.

But she was here now. Telling the truth. Asking for her help to find her daughter.

Their daughter.

She had to put her own feelings aside. Once Alice was safe, she and Faye would talk about the future.

But first they had to find Alice…

ANGER RAILED INSIDE Jacob as he drove toward the Westbrook house. He phoned Liam and explained the situation. Liam agreed to issue the Amber Alert and to post Nina's picture on the news.

"That son of a bitch," Jacob said. "If he's behind this, he's going to find out what it feels like to be behind bars."

With every passing mile, Jacob's anxiety rose. He tried not to imagine the worst-case scenarios, but they taunted him, intensifying his fear.

Cora may have overreacted in the past, but this time she'd been right. The girl down the street had been her missing daughter. She'd felt a connection.

He had to bring her home safely to Cora.

But what about Faye? If she truly hadn't known Nina was kidnapped, she was a victim in the situation, too. And what about Nina? She loved Faye and thought of her as her mother…

He maneuvered the last turn down the drive to the Westbrooks, steeling himself against punching the bastard. He had to remain professional. Persuade him to talk.

Confess.

Drew's Mercedes sat in the front circular drive.

His phone buzzed with another text. Liam with news about Philips's computer. He skimmed the information, his pulse hammering.

Jacob parked behind the Mercedes, adjusted his weapon,

clipped his phone to his belt, then climbed out and walked up to the front door. He rang the doorbell, shifting to survey the land. He didn't see Hilary's car, but the garage door was closed, so her vehicle could be tucked inside.

The door opened and Drew stood on the other side, his brows knitted in a frown. He wore dress slacks and a collared shirt suggesting he'd been at the office or was heading there.

"Mr. Westbrook," Jacob said. "We need to talk."

Drew tunneled his fingers through his neatly clipped hair. "What now?"

"Let me come in and I'll explain."

"If you came to accuse me of killing Kurt Philips again, I'll phone my lawyer."

Jacob swore silently, then elbowed his way past the man. Westbrook closed the door and spun toward him. "Listen to me, Sheriff Maverick, I'm fed up with—"

"Shut up," Jacob said, barely holding onto his temper. "Your daughter may be in danger."

Drew's face went stark white. "What the hell are you talking about?"

"We found notations in Philips's files indicating that he'd uncovered evidence implicating you in your daughter's kidnapping."

"That's impossible," Drew shouted. "Because I wasn't involved!"

The man sounded convincing, but he could be adept at lying. "Really? Because we think we know who adopted her, and she claims the baby's father didn't want her."

"What?" His voice rose. "That's insane. I loved my baby. Now, who has her?"

"I don't believe you." Jacob jabbed Drew in the chest. "I think you wanted your career more than you wanted a family and you gave this woman money to get rid of Alice so you could make partner."

Chapter Twenty-Four

Worry nagged at Cora. How could they find Nina when they had no idea who this woman Valerie was? If she was desperate, which she must be to have kidnapped Nina, she could be anywhere.

For God's sake, she could be hopping on a plane to a foreign country.

Panic made her heart pound as she drove Faye to the bank to access her safety deposit box.

She remained in the lobby while Faye met with the bank manager, then Cora followed her to retrieve the papers.

Frustration knotted Cora's insides as Faye read the name on the documents. Tate Muldoon.

She searched her memory banks in case he worked with Drew, but she didn't recall a lawyer named Muldoon. Although hadn't Evie mentioned Muldoon?

"I'm texting Jacob the lawyer's name. If he can find him, maybe he can force him to talk."

Faye nodded and closed the safety deposit box while Cora sent the text.

She and Faye walked outside to the car together, but she was at a loss as to what to do now. They could go back to her house and wait.

She'd been waiting for so long...

"Why don't you try to sketch what this woman Valerie looks like," Cora suggested.

"I'll try but it was a long time ago."

Faye's phone buzzed just as they settled in the car. She snatched it from her purse, her face paling as she read the message. She angled her phone toward Cora.

If you want to see Nina again, do exactly as I say. Meet me and bring Cora Reeves with you. No police or you'll never see the little girl again.

JACOB SCRUTINIZED DREW'S reaction for a tell that the man was lying. But he seemed genuinely upset.

Because he was innocent or because he'd been caught?

"Look, Drew," Jacob said, forcing a calm tone, "if you tell me everything now, tell me where this woman has taken Nina Fuller—Alice—I'll see about cutting you a deal."

"I don't need a damn deal," Drew bellowed. "Because I had nothing to do with my baby's kidnapping. And if I knew where she was now, I'd be in my car on the way to get her." He paced, sweat trickling down the side of his face. "I know you think I was cold and that I should have stayed with Cora, but it was just too damn hard. I loved my baby, and I felt guilty for not protecting her. And not because I paid someone to take her. Because I was her father, and fathers are supposed to protect their children." He sank onto the sofa and dropped his head into his hands. "I would have done anything to have found Alice. It just hurt too much to look at Cora every day, because it reminded me that I'd failed her, too."

Jacob breathed out. "You certainly moved on quickly."

Drew pinched the bridge of his nose. "It may seem that way, but I never stopped loving Cora. We were both such a mess, though, and when I tried to help her by cleaning out the baby room, she accused me of not caring, of forgetting about our baby." He pounded his chest. "But I never forgot. Not for a moment."

"You have another child," Jacob said.

"Yes, and I love him. But he didn't replace my daughter." He scrubbed at his face and the tears tracking his cheeks. "Now please tell me. Do you know who took Alice and where she is?"

Jacob read the lawyer's name that Cora messaged him. "I was hoping you could help with that."

"But I don't know anything," Drew said between clenched teeth.

Jacob released a breath. He didn't like Drew, but he was starting to believe him. "She told the woman who thinks she adopted your daughter that her name was Valerie."

Drew's brows knitted in a frown. "I don't know anyone named Valerie."

"What about a lawyer named Tate Muldoon?"

Drew frowned. "No. I've never worked with anyone by that name."

Jacob glanced around the room. "Is your wife here?"

Drew shook his head. "She dropped our son at the nanny's because she had a luncheon with her friends. Why are you asking about Hilary?"

"She was at the hospital the night Alice was kidnapped. She also worked with you before the kidnapping."

"So? A lot of people worked with me. She was there to congratulate me and Cora."

Jacob shook his head. "We looked back at security cameras and found a woman dressed in scrubs carrying a bundle through the downstairs laundry area. We think that woman may have kidnapped Alice."

For the first time since he'd met Drew, hope brightened the man's eyes. "Did you identify her?"

Silence stretched between them for a long minute. "No, but I have an idea who she is."

Drew stood up and fisted his hands by his sides. "Dammit, Sheriff, stop beating around the bush and tell me everything you know."

Jacob stared into the man's eyes, gauging his reaction. "I think the woman in the scrubs was your wife."

Drew staggered backward as if he'd been punched. "Hilary?"

"Yes," Jacob said.

"That's crazy," Drew said. "Hilary would never do something like that."

"She was at the hospital the night Alice was born, then disappeared when the fire alarm sounded. And according to the private investigator's notes, someone at your office suggested Hilary was interested in you before your baby was taken." The pieces clicked together in Jacob's mind. Now he had to make Drew see the truth. "He also uncovered a police report regarding Hilary when she was in college. Apparently she was obsessive about a guy she met, and began stalking him. He had to take out a restraining order because she became violent."

"My God," Drew said, his voice edged in disbelief. "I had no idea."

Jacob gave him a moment to absorb the revelation. "What if Hilary took your baby and gave her away in order to break up your marriage?"

Drew shook his head in denial, although Jacob saw the wheels of suspicion begin to turn in the man's mind. "But she tried to console Cora…and me."

Jacob raised a brow. "You were both distraught. Her scheme was working. So she comforted you. That was part of the plan, too. You were vulnerable, and she stepped in to hold your hand. It was her way of winning your affection."

Emotions darkened Drew's eyes. "No…she wouldn't…"

"Has your wife been acting strangely lately? Nervous?"

Drew's gaze locked with his, the fear in his eyes palpable, as if he realized the woman he married might be a cold, calculating monster. "Well…after you left the other day, she accused me of still being in love with Cora."

Jacob's gut knotted. Was he?

"Someone tried to kill Cora, Drew. Twice. I believe it was because Kurt Philips was on the verge of revealing who took your baby. If Hilary thinks you still love Cora, that could have been a double blow. She may have feared she was about to get caught and that she was going to lose you. So she panicked."

"My God, I…just can't believe Hilary would do that. She had my son—"

"Not long after you were married," Jacob said. "Another clever ploy. Giving you what you lost cinched the deal for her. Having a child with her meant that you'd never reconcile with Cora."

Drew leaned over, breathing deeply as if he was going to be sick.

"We need to find your wife," Jacob said. "Where is she?"

"I told you, having lunch with her friends," Drew said, his voice strained.

"Then call her." Jacob shifted. "Do it now, Drew."

Drew nodded and reached for his phone.

He pressed his wife's number and put it on speaker-phone. But the phone rang and rang, and no one answered.

CORA BATTLED COMPLETE panic at the idea that this woman would hurt a child. What kind of horrible person was she?

Someone who'd tried to kill her because Kurt had figured out her identity.

"I have to call Jacob," Cora said. "We could be walking into a trap, Faye. This woman might kill us both. Then what would happen to Nina?"

Faye clasped her hand, terror emanating from her. "You heard what she said. Do you want to get Nina hurt?"

Cora barely resisted correcting her and telling her Nina's

real name was Alice. "No, of course not," Cora snapped. "More than anything I want my baby back."

Faye's gaze latched with hers. A mixture of fear, pain, regret, even sympathy rippled between them.

Cora's throat closed. They were two mothers who loved one little girl. Saving Nina—Alice—was all that mattered.

"Please," Faye cried. "I couldn't stand it if anything happened to my—our—daughter."

Tears pricked Cora's eyes. "All right. Let's just go to the location she texted you. Do you know where it is?"

Faye shook her head. Cora entered the address from Faye's phone into her GPS, then started the engine and pulled away from the bank. They headed north, deeper into the mountains.

Cora's phone rang as she veered onto the mountain road. Jacob.

The temptation to answer it seized her full force. She wanted to hear Jacob's voice. Have his expertise on her side. Know he was behind her and with her, and that he would be there to rescue Nina. Alice.

God, they had to find her. Save her.

Faye twisted a tissue in her hands. "I can't imagine what you've been through," Faye said. "I swear to you, Cora, I didn't know Nina was kidnapped."

Tears blurred Cora's vision at the sincerity and anguish in Faye's voice. Cora wanted to be angry with her for having the last five years with Alice, years she'd missed.

But if Faye hadn't adopted Alice, someone else might have. Someone who might not have loved and cared for her and protected her as Faye had. Nina was strong and confident and funny and creative—an amazing kid. She had Faye to thank for that.

Thunderclouds darkened the sky, threatening rain, and they fell into silence as she concentrated on driving. The winding mountain roads were treacherous and dangerous enough without a storm.

She clenched the steering wheel with a white-knuckled grip. She had to get them safely up the mountain.

Although fear consumed her. She and Faye might be walking into an ambush. This woman had killed Kurt and tried to kill her twice.

Who would raise Alice if something happened to her and Faye?

JACOB PHONED CORA to see if she'd heard something from Nina's kidnapper, but she didn't pick up. Dammit, where was she?

He left her a message warning her that he suspected Hilary was behind the kidnapping, then asked her to call him.

"Cora didn't answer," Jacob told Drew. "Any word from your wife?"

"No," Drew looked defeated. "I've called all her friends. She didn't make their luncheon today, and no one has heard from her."

"Drew," Jacob said, struggling to remain calm. "Is there a place where Hilary would go if she wanted to be alone? Do you two own another home or vacation property?"

Drew leaned his head into his hands, shaking his head back and forth as if tormented. When he raised his head and looked at Jacob, tears filled his eyes.

"I can't believe she'd do this. But if she has Alice, I want you to find her."

"A place? An address?" Jacob asked.

Drew rose and walked over to the corner. He opened a desk drawer, rifled through some papers, then turned back to Jacob.

"Hilary's family owned a place in the mountains. She inherited it when they died last year."

"Where is it, exactly?"

Drew swiped a hand over his eyes. "It's up north. It's a little hard to find, but I can take you there. We visited once with her family when we were first married."

Jacob snagged his keys from his pocket. "Let's go. If she has Alice and she's scared we're on to her, Alice might be in danger."

Jacob raced outside to his police car, anxious to get on the road. Every minute that passed meant Hilary was getting farther and farther away with Cora's daughter.

Chapter Twenty-Five

Nerves tightened every muscle in Cora's body as she drove up the mountain. Dark clouds threatened to unleash rain on the winding road and lightning zigzagged across the foggy sky.

She prayed it held off. Rain would make the roads more treacherous. She sped around a curve, struggling to keep the car on the highway around the switchbacks.

The GPS directed her to turn onto a side road that seemed to disappear into the thick woods. Trees shrouded the light, the branches clawing at her as if they were long arms and hands trying to keep her from reaching her daughter.

Faye sat stone-still, her fear palpable.

Finally they reached another turn that wound up a long hill and ended deep in the forest. A rustic cabin was perched on the side of the mountain, and a gray SUV was parked sideways near the front door, as if the driver had been racing to get inside the house.

Cora's heart pounded as she rolled to a stop and threw the gearshift into Park.

"She can't have hurt Nina," Faye said in a raw whisper. "She just can't."

Cora gripped Faye's hand for a minute. She wished Jacob was here, but the woman had said no police and she couldn't take any chances with her daughter's life.

Cora gathered her courage. "Let's go."

Faye climbed from the passenger side, and they walked up to the door together. The shades were drawn, the dark sky adding an eerie feel that sent a chill through Cora.

She knocked on the door, then Faye reached out and pushed it open.

Before they could step inside, the shiny glint of metal flashed, then Drew's wife ordered them to come in.

Dear God. Hilary. She was behind this.

Faye exchanged a terrified look with her, fear clawing at Cora. But she'd do anything to save her little girl.

The composed, well-manicured and polished Hilary had disappeared. In her place stood a crazed, disheveled-looking woman waving a gun in their faces.

"Where's Nina?" Faye asked.

"She's safe in the other room," Hilary said shrilly. "She'll stay that way as long as you do as I say."

"She must be frightened," Cora said. "You have a child of your own, Hilary, don't hurt her."

"I told you that she'll be fine if you cooperate."

"What do you want us to do?" Faye asked in a shaky voice.

Hilary motioned for them to move into the den where she'd drawn all the curtains.

"Tell me," Faye cried.

Hilary spun toward her, the gun raised. "I'll let you go if you take Nina and leave town. Go far, far away and keep your mouth shut."

Faye's eyes darted toward Cora. "But what about Cora?" Faye asked.

A bitter laugh escaped Hilary, cutting into the strained silence in the dreary interior of the cabin.

Hilary barked a sarcastic sound. "She's going away for good."

Cora steeled herself against reacting. If she was going

to die, she wanted answers. "You killed Kurt, didn't you? Then you tried to kill me."

"You wouldn't stop looking for that baby," Hilary cried. "I thought you'd give up eventually, and Drew would see how crazy you were, but no, you were so damn persistent."

The truth dawned on Cora. "You told Drew about that day at the mall, not Julie."

"He had a right to know how unstable you were."

"Because you kidnapped my child," Cora said, rage hardening her tone. "Did you and Drew plan it together?"

Another bitter laugh, almost maniacal. "Ha. Drew had no idea. I fell in love with him the minute we met. I knew I could help him reach his career goals, and that you didn't care. All you talked about was having a kid."

Cora clenched her hands by her sides. Drew hadn't known?

Hilary waved the gun in Cora's face, her eyes wide with rage and hatred. "I knew when you had that baby, he'd never leave you, that you were going to ruin him. He'd never have made partner so quickly if he'd stayed with you and been saddled with a kid."

"But you had a child with him a year after you married," Cora said, anger surfacing through the shock.

Hilary paced in front of the fireplace, her arm jerking as she waved the gun back and forth between Cora and Faye. "Only because he felt so damn guilty over you and that baby of yours. I figured the only way to help him get over it was to give him another child."

Tears burned Cora's eyes. "Does he know what you did?"

Hilary paused in front of Cora, the gun aimed at Cora's head. "No, and he never will!"

"Don't do this," Faye pleaded. "It's not right, Hilary. Think about your little boy."

"I am," Hilary shouted. "He needs for me and his father to stay a family." She turned a hate-filled look at Cora. "That means I have to get rid of you."

JACOB SPED TOWARD the cabin Hilary's parents owned, hoping Drew wasn't leading him astray. If Drew was lying about not knowing what Hilary had done, he could be guiding him into the wilderness to kill him and dispose of his body where no one would ever find him.

But Drew's anguish and shock seemed too real to be faked. The man literally looked physically ill.

Jacob's phone buzzed as he climbed the mountain. Liam. He pressed Connect. "I'm driving. You're on speaker."

"I got your message about Hilary Westbrook. We're closing in on Muldoon. If he faked adoption papers for Alice, he's been at this a lot longer than we thought."

"Good. We're on our way to find Hilary," Jacob said.

Drew made a pained sound in his throat.

"Drew's with me. Hilary's family owns a cabin in the northern part of the mountains. We're on our way there now."

A tense heartbeat passed. "Send me the coordinates and I'll meet you there. This woman sounds dangerous."

Jacob glanced at Drew, who gave a nod as if consenting for Liam to provide backup.

"I don't know the exact address," Jacob told him.

Drew cleared his throat. "The house is owned by Selma and Wilton Jones," Drew said. "It's off Route 5."

"Thanks. I'm on my way."

The line went dead, and Jacob glanced at Drew, his stomach twisting. "She won't hurt Cora or the little girl, will she?"

Drew looked at him blankly. "I have no idea. If she stole Alice, apparently I don't know my wife at all."

"PLEASE, HILARY," CORA PLEADED. "Think of Drew. When he learns what you did, he'll want to know where his daughter is. If you hurt her or Faye, or me, he won't be able to forgive you."

"He won't find out," Hilary screamed. "He won't, because you'll be dead and Faye and her daughter will be gone." She glared at Faye. "And if Faye tells anyone, I'll kill her, too."

"Put the gun down," Faye said. "You don't have to kill anyone, Hilary. Cora can go away just like me, move to another state, and your secret will be safe."

"You're lying," Hilary bellowed. "You and Cora will go to the police!"

She swung the gun toward Cora and aimed. Faye suddenly lunged at Hilary. Cora screamed, "No!"

Faye tried to knock the gun from Hilary's hand, and they struggled. She pushed Hilary against the wall, but the gun went off. Faye cried out and collapsed, one hand clawing at Hilary. Hilary shoved her away, and Faye dropped to the floor, her hand covering her chest where blood gushed.

Hilary staggered from the wall, her face etched in shock, her hand jerking as she still clenched the gun.

Cora ran to Faye, dropped down, then grabbed a pillow from the sofa and pressed it over Faye's chest. She placed Faye's hand on top of the pillow. "Keep pressure on it, Faye. I'll call for help."

"Save Nina," Faye reached for her hand. "Save our daughter, Cora. Please. Save her and love her for me."

Tears burned Cora's eyes. She wanted to help Faye, but she had to rescue Nina from this madwoman. Then she could phone an ambulance.

Hilary was staring at her gun hand and the blood, as if she was dazed and confused. Cora had to hurry.

She jumped up and ran down the hall. "Nina?" she called as she entered the first bedroom.

No answer. Please, dear God, Hilary hadn't hurt her, had she?

Trembling with fear, she tried the closet, but it was empty. Adrenaline pumped through her, and she ran to the last bedroom. "Nina, if you're in here, call out!"

Silence.

Fear drove her to cross the room, and she checked that closet. Nothing. Terror pounded in her heart.

She ran back to the hall and noticed a door, then opened it. An attic. She raced up the steps, the darkness engulfing her and adding to her terror. "Nina?"

A low sound. A cry.

Cora almost burst into a sob. She had to get Nina out of here. She raced across the room and opened the door to another closet. It was so dark inside she could hardly see.

"Nina?"

A whimper.

"Nina, it's Cora Reeves are you in there, honey?"

"Ms. Reeves?"

It was the faintest whisper of her name, but relief surged through Cora. She knelt and reached out her hand. "Come on, sweetie, we have to hurry!"

Nina took her hand. The little girl's fingers were icy, and her legs almost gave way. Tears tracked her cheeks, but Cora gave her a quick hug.

"Where's Mommy?" she cried.

I'm right here, Cora said silently. But Nina was talking about Faye. "We're going to get out of here, then find her."

She clasped Nina's hand, ran down the steps, then veered down the hall toward the rear. But just as she and Nina reached the back door, Hilary pressed a gun to Cora's temple.

"Walk into the woods," Hilary ordered.

"Ms. Reeves," Nina cried.

Cora squeezed Nina's hand and pulled her against her. "Stay close to me, sweetie."

"Walk," Hilary ordered.

Cora scanned the dark woods, debating what to do. If they made it deeper into the trees, she could trip Hilary up, then she and Nina could run back to the car.

She'd just found her daughter. She couldn't lose her.

She wrapped one arm around Nina's small shoulders. Nina's body was shaking, her lower lip quivering. She wanted her mommy, Faye. But Cora had no idea if Faye was still alive.

One step. Two. She trudged deeper into the thicket of trees. Leaves crunched and twigs snapped beneath their feet. A breeze picked up, stirring the brush, and thunder boomed in the sky.

The sound of the water rippling over rocks echoed in the wind. Another few steps, and Hilary halted. Cora's breath lodged in her throat. They'd reached the edge of a cliff.

She inhaled, desperate to save Nina. Alice. They were one and the same. All the letters she'd written to her daughter and the presents waited.

She turned, determined to make one more plea. "You can do anything you want with me, Hilary, but promise me you won't hurt Nina."

"You just couldn't give up, could you?" Hilary said in a rage-filled whisper. "If your little girl dies, it's your fault."

Then Hilary raised the gun and fired.

Chapter Twenty-Six

Jacob eased up the drive to Hilary's cabin, scanning the area for an ambush. Hilary was a desperate woman. It was possible she'd hired someone to help her escape justice.

Her husband was a criminal defense attorney. He knew people who would work for hire. She'd worked at his law firm and knew how to access information. She could have snuck into Drew's files or on his computer at any time.

Cora's car was parked behind a gray SUV.

"That's Hilary's car. She drives it instead of the mini-van when she meets her friends," Drew said in a strained tone. "Do you want me to call her?"

Jacob debated on the effectiveness of a call as compared with a surprise attack.

"I think seeing you in person might be our best bet. If she did all this for you, maybe you can get through to her." Jacob narrowed his eyes. "But it could be dangerous."

"I don't care." Anger sharpened his voice "I'll do anything to save Alice."

Jacob gave a clipped nod. "Her name is Nina now," he said quietly. "That's what the woman who adopted her calls her. Nina."

Pain streaked Drew's face. "Cora knows this now?"

"She suspected. We figured it out. I'm sure she came here to rescue your daughter."

"God, she's the strong one," he said brokenly.

A gunshot blasted the air as Jacob climbed from his SUV, and pure terror seized him. Drew cursed and jumped from the vehicle.

"It came from the woods." Jacob removed his service revolver from his holster and clutched it at the ready. Drew started ahead but Jacob grabbed his arm. "She's armed, Westbrook. Stay behind me."

Drew growled another obscenity, and the two of them scrambled around the side of the house. The wind whistled, and lightning zigzagged above the trees.

The sound of a scream reverberated over the rustle of the branches. "That way." Jacob hooked his finger toward the right and pushed Drew behind him again. He eased forward, ducking from tree to tree until he spotted Hilary, who was waving the gun like a crazy woman.

"You can't hide forever!" she yelled. "I'll find you and it'll all be over."

Drew lurched forward. "Hilary, stop it!" Drew shouted. "Drop the gun!"

Jacob searched the darkness for Cora and Nina but didn't see them.

Hilary whirled toward her husband, eyes crazed. "What are you doing here? You weren't supposed to come!"

Drew held up a warning hand, inching closer. "You kidnapped my baby five years ago, Hilary. How could you do that to me?"

"I loved you," Hilary cried. "I always did. I was the one who was supposed to help you climb to the top, but you married that woman instead."

Drew inched another step closer, his voice low. "So you stole my child to break up my marriage?"

"I had to show you that you were supposed to be with me," Hilary said, her hand bobbing with the gun. "And then you did see…"

"You wrecked my life, and you devastated Cora. That was cruel, Hilary." He fisted his hands by his sides.

Jacob braced his gun to shoot the woman, his gaze still scanning the woods.

Dear God, Cora had to be all right. He was in love with her. He had been for a long time. And he'd never told her how he felt.

They knew who her daughter was now. She had a chance to know her, to love her little girl, to make up for lost time.

"For God's sake, Hilary," Drew said. "Cora and I were crazy with worry and fear. We didn't know if Alice was alive or dead. And you knew all along and stood by and watched us suffer."

"I consoled you, then I helped you make partner. Don't you see? Taking your baby was the best thing for you. It garnered you all kinds of publicity and sympathy."

Rage filled Drew's eyes. "I didn't want to make partner by having people pity me." He stepped closer. "You know I had nightmares about what might have happened to Alice. Terrible, horrible nightmares that she might be hurt or thrown away in a ditch somewhere."

"I gave you a baby!" Hilary screamed, venom in her voice.

A movement to the left caught Jacob's eyes, and he eased toward it. Relief surged through him when he spotted Cora stooped down, hiding behind a boulder. The little girl was tucked beneath Cora's protective embrace. But where was Faye?

Jacob aimed his gun at Hilary, squared his shoulders and crept into the clearing. "It's over, Hilary. Put the gun down and let's end this peacefully. No one has to get hurt."

"No, I can't go to jail," Hilary shouted.

Drew took another step toward her, but Hilary backed toward the cliff. She glanced over her shoulder, a strange look in her eyes. Jacob had seen that look before, the look of a criminal cornered and panicking. She was going to throw herself off the cliff.

"Hilary, please don't," Drew said, a calmness overcoming him. "Just think of our son. You don't want him to remember you like this."

She released a sob, her gun hand lowering, but inched backward.

Jacob raced forward and caught her just before she slipped over the edge.

He jerked the gun from her hand and tossed it into the dirt, then dragged her away from the cliff. She collapsed into a hysterical sobbing fit as Jacob snapped handcuffs around her wrists.

"Cora, it's all right," Jacob called. "You and Nina can come out now."

Hilary rocked herself back and forth, crying while Drew's gaze searched the woods.

A second later, Cora emerged from behind the boulder, carrying the little girl who was crying in her arms.

Brakes squealed, and the sound of an engine cut through the night. Liam. He was going into the house.

Cora looked at him with shock in her eyes.

"It's over," Jacob murmured. He wanted to go to her, but he had to guard Hilary.

Drew walked toward them, anguish, regret and awe on his face as Nina lifted her head.

"You didn't give up, you found her," Drew said in a raw whisper.

Cora nodded, although tears streamed down her face.

"I'm so sorry," Drew said. "I...didn't know. I swear I didn't."

Emotions colored Cora's face, but when Drew held out his arms, she and Nina went into them.

Jacob's heart squeezed. He had fulfilled his promise of reuniting Cora with her daughter.

Drew was the little girl's father, though. He'd also essentially admitted that he still loved Cora. It was obvious he was hurting.

The little girl deserved to have both of her parents together.

If that was what Cora wanted.

He had to give her time. They also had to deal with Faye. Cora didn't need pressure from him.

She needed to be with her little girl and make up for the years they'd missed.

CORA WAS SO happy that Nina was safe she could barely contain her emotions. Yet Faye was Nina's mother. She pulled away from Drew and motioned to Jacob, mouthing that Faye was in the house.

A second later, Liam bolted through the woods. Jacob yelled out their location. Liam's gun was drawn, but he lowered it when he saw Jacob had handcuffed Hilary.

"Faye?" Cora mouthed to Liam.

He shook his head, his expression grave, and fresh tears blurred Cora's vision. She wanted Alice back, but she hadn't wanted Faye to die.

Nina would be brokenhearted. Faye was the only mother she'd ever known.

"I'm so sorry, Cora, so sorry," Drew murmured. He looked at Nina with such longing that Cora couldn't help but find forgiveness in her heart.

Cora choked back a sob. Nina—Alice—was going to need all the love she could get.

The next few minutes passed in a blur. An ambulance arrived, and Liam oversaw a crime scene team as they collected Hilary's gun and went in the house to process it.

The ME arrived and the ambulance loaded Faye's body to transport to the morgue.

Cora rocked her daughter in her arms while she waited. The little girl was so exhausted she fell asleep on Cora's shoulder.

"We'll run DNA to verify that she is Alice," Jacob told her.

"I'll start the paperwork to make sure that Cora is deemed the legal guardian." Drew stroked Cora's arm. "You won't ever be without your daughter again."

Emotions choked Cora as she hugged Nina to her.

Drew looked lost, then he gestured to Cora's car. "Sheriff, I'll drive her home. I know you have to transport Hilary to jail."

Jacob's mouth tightened, but he agreed.

Hilary screamed Drew's name, but he glared at her, then turned his back on her, took Cora's arm and walked her and Nina to the car.

Cora looked back at Jacob, but he was all business. She hugged Nina to her, her heart soaring with happiness that she'd finally found Alice. The transition would be difficult for her baby, but she'd share the cards and presents and her letters, and help her daughter any way she needed.

Only now she had Alice back, did Jacob plan to walk out of her life?

Chapter Twenty-Seven

Six weeks later

Jacob had stayed away from Cora to give her and Alice time to adjust and get acquainted. But he missed Cora so much he hadn't slept in weeks. He dreamed of her. He fantasized about her. Hell, he'd even bought a damn ring.

A ring, for God's sake, when for all he knew, she might be deep in bed with her former husband, building back the family she'd lost.

He drove to her house anyway. He had to see for himself. He'd made up his mind he'd accept whatever she wanted, but his brothers had cornered him the night before during their weekly burger-and-beer night and told him he was a coward if he didn't tell her how he felt.

They were right. He was a coward.

No. Correction. He *had* been a coward. Now he was on his way to her house to confess his feelings like a lovestruck fool.

Unless she opened the door with Drew on her arm.

Then he'd do what?

Fill them in on the case against Hilary. Tell her they'd arrested the man who'd shot at her, an ex-con Hilary had picked from one of Drew's former client lists. Liam had also busted the child kidnapping ring and made several arrests.

Then he'd act like he wasn't brokenhearted if she chose her damn ex over him.

Son of a bitch. Drew didn't deserve her.

He swung his car into her drive, the twinkling stars above glittering like the diamond in his pocket. He stuffed his hand inside and ran his finger over the velvet box. He hoped she liked it.

Hell, he hoped she wanted it. And him.

Cora's red SUV sat in the drive. He'd made sure her car was repaired and had it dropped off to her.

Drew's Mercedes was not in the drive.

A good sign.

He inhaled a deep breath, climbed out and walked up to her house. The door opened before he knocked. Cora stood on the other side, looking beautiful in a T-shirt and denim shorts, her long hair draped over one shoulder.

He ached to run his fingers through the silky strands.

"Jacob?"

"Yeah." *Nice opening, idiot.*

She shifted from foot to foot, her fingers curled around the doorjamb.

"Is Drew here?" he blurted.

Her brows bunched together in a frown. "No, why? Are you looking for him? Did Hilary get out of jail?"

He shook his head. "No, I just thought that Drew might be here. That the two of you, well, now that you have your little girl back, that you might…um…"

She made a low sound in her throat. "That we might what?"

"Reconcile," he said, deciding to confront the issue.

She crossed her arms. "No, Jacob. We didn't get back together just for Nina. But we have agreed that he'll be part of her life. He really didn't know what Hilary did."

"I understand." He started to back away, but she cleared her throat.

"Wait a minute. Why are you leaving?"

He silently called himself all kinds of names. He was acting like a moron. A coward. A cowardly moron.

His brothers had encouraged him to go for it. He had to tell her how he felt.

"I didn't want to interfere," Jacob said, his voice breaking.

"You aren't," she said. "Drew and I don't belong together, Jacob."

His heart skipped a beat. "You don't?"

Her lips curved into a smile. "No. How could I be with him when my heart belongs to someone else?"

Hope fluttered in his belly. He felt like he was an awkward fifteen-year-old.

He gave her a flirtatious look. "And who does it belong to?"

She leaned toward him, then pressed her hand against his cheek. "You."

Pure joy filled his chest. She angled her head to kiss him just as he dropped to one knee. He caught her before she pitched forward, and they both tumbled to the front porch.

Laughter spilled through the air, then he removed the ring from his pocket. "I messed this up, the proposal, but I love you, Cora, and I want to be with you."

Emotions glittered in her eyes. "I want to be with you, too. But you know I'm a package deal. We're still adjusting, but Nina has good days and bad ones. She'll stay in therapy as long as she needs to."

"I'm sure your love will help her heal."

"Like she's helping me. We've been working on my children's story. I'm planning to publish it soon."

"I'm so proud of you." Jacob's heart swelled with love and longing. He opened the ring box and held it out to her. "And I'm a patient man, Cora. I've been in love with you for years. We'll give Nina whatever she needs."

"Just love," Cora whispered. "That's all we both need."

He pulled her to him for a kiss. "I have plenty of that for both of you."

Then he slid the ring on her finger and closed his mouth over hers.

* * * * *

COMING SOON!

We really hope you enjoyed reading this book. If you're looking for more romance, be sure to head to the shops when new books are available on

Thursday 6th March

MILLS & BOON

THE HEART OF ROMANCE

A ROMANCE FOR EVERY KIND OF READER

MODERN
Prepare to be swept off your feet by sophisticated, sexy and seductive heroes, in some of the world's most glamourous and romantic locations, where power and passion collide.
8 stories per month.

HISTORICAL
Escape with historical heroes from time gone by. Whether your passion is for wicked Regency Rakes, muscled Vikings or rugged Highlanders, awaken the romance of the past.
6 stories per month.

MEDICAL
Set your pulse racing with dedicated, delectable doctors in the high-pressure world of medicine, where emotions run high and passion, comfort and love are the best medicine.
6 stories per month.

True Love
Celebrate true love with tender stories of heartfelt romance, fro the rush of falling in love to the joy a new baby can bring, and a focus on the emotional heart of a relationship.
8 stories per month.

Desire
Indulge in secrets and scandal, intense drama and plenty of sizz hot action with powerful and passionate heroes who have it all: wealth, status, good looks…everything but the right woman.
6 stories per month.

HEROES
Experience all the excitement of a gripping thriller, with an inte romance at its heart. Resourceful, true-to-life women and strong fearless men face danger and desire - a killer combination!
8 stories per month.

DARE
Sensual love stories featuring smart, sassy heroines you'd want as best friend, and compelling intense heroes who are worthy of th
4 stories per month.

To see which titles are coming soon, please visit

millsandboon.co.uk/nextmonth

MILLS & BOON
MEDICAL
Pulse-Racing Passion

Set your pulse racing with dedicated,
delectable doctors in the high-pressure
world of medicine, where emotions run
high and passion, comfort and love are the
best medicine.

JOIN US ON SOCIAL MEDIA!

Stay up to date with our latest releases, author
news and gossip, special offers and discounts, and
all the behind-the-scenes action
from Mills & Boon...

 millsandboon

 millsandboonuk

 millsandboon

It might just be true love...

LET'S TALK
Romance

For exclusive extracts, competitions
and special offers, find us online: